Mary Leo

The Spia Family Presses On

This is a work of fiction. Names, characters, places, and incidents are products of the author's imagination or are used fictitiously. Any resemblance to actual persons, living or dead, or to events or locales, is entirely coincidental.

THE SPIA FAMILY PRESSES ON
Copyright © 2012 by Mary Leo
Published by Pryde Multimedia, LLC
ISBN: 978-0-615-68534-2

All rights reserved. No part of this publication may be reproduced, stored in a retrieval system, or transmitted in any form or by any means—electronic, digital, photocopy, recording, or any other—except for brief quotations in printed reviews, without the prior permission of the author and/or publisher.

For Ma, who could cook up a Sunday pasta dinner the likes of which I've yet to see on any cooking show. For all those times we sat together on the back porch sharing warm Italian bread dunked in olive oil, while we watched the rain fall on the lush grapevines in the backyard. And for all those inspiring stories you made up while we cuddled in bed before I fell asleep. Our time together helped shape the woman I became and for that, I will be forever thankful. Miss you, always . . .

Acknowledgments

I could never have done this book without the support and love from my family and friends. They nourish both my creativity and my need for someone to laugh and cry with. I'm blessed to have each and every one of them in my life.

Many thanks to Janet Wellington for her editing expertise, her spot-on suggestions and her unwavering friendship. More thanks to my writing buddies, Chris Green, Sylvia Mendoza, Cheryl Howe, Lorelle Marinello, Ann Collins, Ara Burklund, and Judy Duarte, who encourage me each and every time we meet. To my favorite roomie and cheerleader, Lisa Kessler, for convincing me to join her at the RT convention in Chicago where we made our pact. To Erin Quinn and Calista Fox who helped restore the joy of writing.

A special shout out to Laura Haug who accompanied me to Sonoma and to Italy so I could do all my research. Thanks for all your patience and laughter. To Liz Jennings who is possibly the sweetest, most generous woman I know and who helps run the absolute best conference in the entire world, the Women's Fiction Festival in Matera, Italy. Thanks need to go out to Donna Bagdasarian who helped shape this book into what it is today. To my sweet daughter, Jocelyn Hughes, for her constant encouragement, her unbridled love and for making me a grandma to possibly the most remarkable baby girl on the planet... at least I think so. To her amazing husband and father of that remarkable baby girl, Paul Milton. To my talented and incredible son, Richard Hughes, who is always there whenever I need him.

To the members of RWA-San Diego. Hugs all around!

To my readers who really are the best!

To The Olive Press located in Sonoma, California, where all that golden liquid is made. A special thanks to Carol Firenze for her informative book: *The Passionate Olive: 101 Things To Do with Olive Oil.*

To Erin Kost Gentile and her amazing master-chef husband Giuseppe Gentile who provided some of the recipes in this book. If you're ever in L.A. drop by their restaurant, Pizzeria il Fico, for an unbelievably delicious Italian meal.

And finally to my compassionate, encouraging, and loving husband, Richter Watkins, who helps make all my most seemingly unattainable dreams come true. *Ti amo!*

"Athena . . . posturing with Poseidon for dominion, sprung the first olive tree from the stone of the Acropolis . . . said the flesh of an olive was bitter as hate and scant as love, that it asked work to soften it, to squeeze the golden-green blood from it."—*A Thousand Days in Tuscany,* Marlena De Blasi

ONE

The Freedom Party

I awoke out of my sleepy fog late Wednesday morning thinking now was the perfect time to take a vacation, a long vacation on an island somewhere with palm trees, white sandy beaches and suntanned, absurdly ripped single men all vying for my attention—a perfectly reasonable fantasy considering my pathetic life. I had been working nonstop for almost two years, a habit I'd gotten into after I gave up binge drinking and partying. My thirtieth birthday was fast approaching so it only seemed natural to take some time out to celebrate the momentous occasion.

Besides, I needed a break in a truly bad way. Our family business was finally in the black, and it was time to relax and allow myself some fun . . . sober fun. I was hoping that was still possible.

I considered getting out of bed and searching for island vacations on the Web, but the idea of it seemed taxing. Instead, I rolled over and snuggled in, wanting nothing more than to conjure up that white sandy beach with all those eager-to-please-me men when I heard someone running up my stairs and from the sound of those heavy footsteps, that person was in a hurry.

So much for sandy beaches and adoring men.

Grabbing my white terrycloth robe, I slid out of bed and made my way to the glass front door of my apartment where I saw my mother, Gloria Spia, holding onto the metal railing, looking as if those last few stairs were going to ruin her.

I swung open the door then held open the screen. I never

locked either one at night; there wasn't any need to. Living above Mom's office, a converted two-car garage, on our olive orchard, the only people who had real access to this area of our land were relatives, a handful of trusted employees and close friends.

Mom never was one for strenuous physical exercise, like stairs. Her idea of a good workout was playing poker on Sunday afternoons with my two aunts and Federico, our groundskeeper.

"Mia," she mouthed, but no actual sound came out, just heavy breathing.

My mom thought of herself as a tall, fifty-something—no one knew her precise age—slim woman trapped in a short, plump body. Because of this misconception, her sleeves and pant legs were always rolled up, and her blouses were always too tight. Today was no exception.

I pulled my rocking chair closer to the door, and she plopped down so hard I heard it creak under her weight.

"You are not going to believe who just called me," she said, shaking her head then looking around me in the direction of my tiny kitchen. This was my cue to make the coffee. Mom had bought me my very own espresso machine for my last birthday knowing full well I only drank tea. She liked me to be equipped for her impromptu visits.

"Who?" I asked while preparing her a shot of espresso. I knew instantly whatever had her by the throat would require at least two shots, so I tossed in an extra scoop.

"I don't understand how this could happen, Mia, especially now when this business is finally going to make us a sizable profit. It's as if the son-of-a-bitch knew."

The business she referred to was our olive oil business here in Sonoma, California. My family was into pressing and selling extra virgin olive oil, or EVOO as the now famous Rachel Ray would say.

"Mamma, talk to me." I was leaning up against the faux granite countertop waiting for the machine to give up its last drops. When it finally gurgled, her face lit up like a kid's on Christmas morning and I knew she would relax with the first sip.

"What a sweet girl you are, going to all this fuss to make me a cup of espresso. You always know just what I need."

I rolled my eyes, poured the double shot in a white demitasse and brought it over to her along with a rose-colored sugar bowl and her favorite tiny spoon, all presents from Mom. I then sat across from her on my cushy blue sofa, crossed my legs and leaned forward, eager to hear what she had to say.

She took a sip, made an umm sound and settled in the rocker, a small floral pillow tucked behind her lower back. She gave herself a little push with her foot and said, "It's your cousin Dickey. He's out."

This was not particularly good news. Truth be told, this was bordering on dreadful news. Dickey's "out" was not the gay kind of "out." His "out" could only mean one thing: big trouble.

"Last time I heard, murder was a life sentence," I said, hoping there had been some sort of mistake, that she had gotten the facts wrong.

"They found new DNA evidence that cleared him."

Now don't get me wrong, I was all about springing the innocent because of advanced forensic techniques, but not Dickey. If he wasn't guilty of one crime there were ten more following close behind. "And this is a problem for you because?"

"He's a shit, that's why. He was never any good to anybody, especially to your Aunt Babe, who had the good sense to divorce his sorry ass a long time ago, but now he's coming here."

You know how they say a person can feel the hairs on the back of their neck stand up? Well, I swear I could feel each and every one of those little guys wiggling around.

I uncrossed my legs, rubbed my neck and sat up straight. Cousin Dickey was potentially a huge problem with a capital

C as in Cosa Nostra. Not that my family didn't have its share of Soprano knockoffs, it did. In fact the entire olive ranch was swarming with recovering mobsters and born-again Italians. But Cousin Dickey was different. Way different. For one thing, as far as I knew, he was still a practicing member of the mafia. Family lore said he even had ties to 'Ndrangheta, the single most powerful society of organized crime in Italy, possibly the entire world.

And let us not forget that mobbed-up Cousin Dickey once owned all our land.

"Why would he come here? He knows how much Babe hates him."

Mom sighed. "It has nothing to do with Babe, or so he says. Dickey wants me to throw him a freedom party. He said it was the least I can do."

"A what?"

"A freedom party to celebrate his release."

Normally, whenever someone in my family was sprung from prison they hid out for awhile, kept a low profile just to make sure another goon didn't have an old vendetta to fulfill, but apparently Dickey felt confident enough to forgo the usual precautions. This fact alone was disconcerting, but I figured we still had a few months to plan a festive mobster gala, plenty of time to get used to the idea of him being a free man and coming back to the orchard. I was thinking we could possibly put this carnival off for like, forever.

"Maybe sometime in the spring or summer, if we're not too busy," I said.

"Don't be silly. It's tonight."

My stomach pitched. This was getting completely out of control. "You're not going to do it, are you?"

"What choice do I have? The bastard can cause me a lot of trouble if he wants to."

"I thought that was all settled when he was locked up," I told her, but my words didn't seem to stick. She took a few more sips of espresso as she kept the chair rocking, faster now. I could see the tension building on her face. Her forehead actually moved, a nearly impossible achievement considering all the Botox that had been pumped into it.

"It was, but you know how your cousin can be."

"A shit?"

"And then some."

I sat back on the sofa, grabbed a pillow and contemplated our options. "Mom, he can't come here. Not now. Not when we're on our way to Hawaii."

"Since when?" Her face brightened. I was on to something.

"Since right now," I said, pumping up my enthusiasm. Not that I particularly wanted to go to Hawaii with my mom, but at this point I would do anything to keep her away from Dickey. "I was just about to make the reservations. I'll take you and Aunt Babe with me. We can leave tonight." I figured she'd jump at the chance for a free trip to paradise. Who wouldn't?

She stared at me for a moment then blinked a few dozen times, a habit she indulged in whenever she was contemplating her options and wanted to stall. "I need another espresso," she said, holding out her empty cup.

She was going to take some convincing. "Mom, you can't get involved with him again."

I didn't know all the facts, but Dickey and my mom had owned some sort of business in North Beach in San Francisco when I was a kid. It took her several years to clear her name after the business dissolved, and even now she sometimes had trouble getting a line of credit.

"Don't be silly. You sound like Federico. He said the same thing and I'll tell you what I told him. I'm not getting involved. I'll throw the bastard his party and that's it. He'll be gone in the morning."

"You hope so," I said.

"I know so," she shot back in that voice she used whenever she needed to get her point across. Her intense reaction told me there had to be more to this story than she was willing to spill. Ever since I admitted I had a drinking problem, my mom tried to keep me in the dark when it came to family tensions. I suppose she thought any little crisis could get me going again. I tried to convince her it didn't work that way, but Mom had her own opinions and nothing changed her mind.

I stood and went to the kitchen area to make her another espresso, and myself a cup of badly needed tea. When I returned, she was staring out the window. I handed her the espresso.

"Don't worry about me," she said attempting a bright smile. "I can take care of myself."

Yeah, right. My mother was sharp when it came to running this business, but when it came to family and her emotions she was a bowl of mush.

Sitting on the sofa again while holding onto my mug of green tea, I leaned in closer to her this time, wanting desperately for her to reconsider the freedom party. I thought some kind, indulgent words might encourage her to see the error of her ways. I reached out and gently lay my hand on her knee, knowing how much my mom loved warm physical contact. "I know that, Mamma. You're a strong, intelligent woman. You know how much I admire you. It's everybody else that I'm not too sure about. Dickey is a powerful force. Perhaps you should reconsider this party."

She swept my hand away, and sat back in the rocker. A triumphant look crossed her face. "That's all in the past, Mia. We're so over all that crime business. This family's been through counseling!"

Mom looked at me as if I was completely out of the game. As if I should suddenly see the score and agree with her sound reasoning, but I couldn't. Not where Dickey was concerned. After a moment, when I didn't respond, she said, "I have far too much to do today to talk about this any longer. Could you please be a darling and run to the bank for me? I need some documents out of our box. Your Uncle Benny needs to go over a few things. Plus, I think a family meeting may be in order to discuss a couple details. I really have to start calling everybody as soon as I finish this lovely espresso you made me."

I sat back and sipped my tea. I never could understand my mother's reasoning, but I took comfort in knowing that this was true for most daughters throughout the world. None of us would ever be able to figure these women out. Mothers operated on some other frequency, and, according to one of my many past therapists, until I was a mother, I should stop bashing my head against that wall.

Fine.

But what was clawing at me at the moment was her sudden need for Uncle Benny, who wasn't really an uncle. He was more of a family friend who used to be a lawyer for the Genetti crime family out of Chicago until Benny was forced into giving up incriminating information to the Feds in the late 80s. Most of the Genettis went to prison and Uncle Benny went undercover for awhile, hated it and came back out eight years ago when Mom took over this olive orchard. He'd been instrumental in getting the grove going again, helped plant a couple hundred trees, pruned them in the spring and helped with the harvest and the crush, like we all did.

"Mamma, is there something you're not telling me?" I thought I'd give this thing one more try.

"Just be a good girl and get my papers. Oh, and Dickey's ring. I kept it safe for him. It's a gold and diamond pinky ring in the shape of a horseshoe."

I hated when she shut me out.

"Fine. I have to go to Readers bookstore anyway. Lisa's having a signing." Lisa Lin was my best friend, and a best-selling author. "I'll get the papers and the ring, but whatever this is about can probably be handled by our local law firm." I found myself clutching my tea mug so tight my hands were beginning to hurt.

"All lawyers are crooks."

I had to grin at that one. "Oh, and Benny isn't?"

"He's family, that's different."

Now why didn't that give me any sense of comfort? I needed to tell her how wrong headed she was, how this whole thing sounded dicey, or at the very least, odd. Why would Dickey want her to throw him a party? Why here? And why tonight? She just wasn't thinking clearly. Probably caught up in the excitement of the moment. My mother loved parties. The whole family did, but something about this party stunk, and it was my duty as her daughter to warn her of the endless complications of Dickey's return.

I took a deep breath and said, "But—"

She held out a hand, a warning shot that I shouldn't go any further. She'd been giving me "the hand" ever since I was a little girl, and even though I had grown way past puberty, Mom's hand still had an effect on me.

I caved, resigned to fate.

"Please, just get the papers and bring them home. I already phoned Benny and he'll be here in a couple hours." She took another sip of espresso, a loud one this time, and her hand shook as she held the tiny cup to her melon colored lips.

"Mom, you're shaking. Please tell me what's wrong."

She smiled one of those phony grins she slapped on her face whenever she was reeling on the inside and didn't want anyone to know. "Nothing's wrong, sweetheart. Everything's perfect. I've just had too much espresso is all. Besides, if there is something wrong, and there's not, Benny will take care of it. Just bring me my papers." She gazed out the window for a moment then her entire demeanor turned deadly serious. "I only hope that bastard doesn't try anything funny with this orchard," she said. "Cause there'll be hell to pay if he does." Then she downed the entire cup of espresso and gently placed the cup back on its white saucer, her charm bracelet of diamond studded Elvises, a bracelet I hadn't seen in years, clinked against the china.

I left my mother sitting in my rocking chair sipping her third cup of double espresso, decaf this time, while I took a quick shower, weighed myself like always—one-twenty, almost the ideal weight for my five-foot-four inch frame—got dressed in a comfy, black velour Juicy Couture tracksuit with a cute little sprinkling of silver stones, over a pink Banana Republic tee, and pulled on cozy, chocolate colored Uggs. Just because I lived on an olive ranch didn't mean I didn't do fashion. Granted, Juicy Couture and Banana Republic weren't exactly high end, but at least they were still in the game. I then hurried through a decent amount of makeup—lip gloss, mascara and blush—and pulled my unmanageable dark-brown hair up into a wet pony tail. Thankfully, by the time I was presentable Mom had finished her espresso and disappeared.

Nothing like a morning visit from my stressed-out mother to brighten my day.

But I refused to let my family throw a bomb into my otherwise happy vacation mood. Taking in a few cleansing breaths, I crossed my studio apartment to the kitchen area. I needed my morning tablespoon of extra virgin olive oil in a bad way. Just one tablespoon per day on an empty stomach kept my skin glowing, my digestive system working, and connected me to Sofia Loren who, it was said, had the same morning ritual.

I opened the cupboard and pulled out an unopened bottle of our award winning Sevillano, made mostly from a Spanish olive with a nutty flavor and a medium intensity. At any one time, I kept about five to ten open bottles of various types of Spia's Olive Press oils in my cupboard. We all did. Olive oil was our life.

I uncorked it and took in the fragrant scent, then poured a generous tablespoon into a tiny plastic cup, the same ones we used in our tasting room. In order to get the full effect of an olive oil you needed to pour some on your tongue, then clench your teeth and suck it to the back of your throat. It could have a pleasantly bitter taste, like some Italian oils, or a smooth nutty flavor, like a few of the Spanish oils or even a bright fruity flavor with a subtle peppery finish ideal for salad greens, or grilling seafood.

Whenever I thought about our oils, I mentally practiced the description that went with them. It took me months to get the hang of sounding like I knew what I was talking about as opposed to an olive oil greenhorn, which was one of the nicer things my family said about me.

This one was a perfect blend, with just a hint of bitterness for added flavor. Now olive oils acted as aroma therapy on me, and Sevillano was one of my favorites. It usually made me feel all blissful, and sexy, but no matter how much I inhaled its pungent fragrance or felt the smooth golden liquid on my tongue, I couldn't quite get that feeling going.

Just as well, there was no one around to be blissfully sexual with.

I sighed, poured enough oil in a frying pan to coat the bottom, tossed in a little chopped garlic and let that cook for a bit. Then I added onion and cilantro, tossed that around until the onion became opaque and the garlic was just about to brown. I threw in two handfuls of pre-cooked linguini, broke an egg into a bowl, whisked until it began to foam then added it to the pan. I stirred that around in the hot oil until the egg was almost cooked, tossed in chunks of a buttery avocado, a chopped Roma tomato, a little water, more olive oil, a three-finger pinch of hot pepper flakes, and two cranks of black pepper. When the egg was cooked through, I slipped the steaming pasta mixture into a yellow bowl, drizzled our hot pepper Italian blend olive oil over it, sprinkled on a mixture of chopped fresh Italian parsley, spring onions, pitted Gaeta olives, and finely grated parmesan cheese. Then I sat down to feast. I was desperate for some comfort food.

Cooking always seemed to sooth me. It was one of the few domestic chores that I had mastered during my quest for sobriety. The entire sensory experience somehow gave me just enough of a diversion that while I was cooking I didn't crave booze. I could get through anything as long as I could mix, chop, fry, bake, and boil.

At times I even fantasized about writing a cookbook for recovering alcoholics that praised the therapeutic benefits of meal preparation using olives and olive oil. I would call it: One Olive at a Time. . . a cook's guide to addiction recovery.

Of course, I'd have to add a few side notes. It wouldn't be just recipes. The recovering alcoholic would have to know which meals to prepare during their various levels of alcohol need. Take, for instance, after a mother's visit. Depending on the amount of mother intrusion, the stress factor might only be a level one. Thirty minutes in the kitchen along with a twenty-minute eating fest should be all that was required.

However, I sometimes had a real problem during the actual meal. Swapping out a hearty red wine for sparkling water could be a hardship for some people—especially for a good Italian girl like me who grew up thinking wine was just another fruit juice—but determination would win out. And like me, the recovering cook would sit at his or her table, pour the sparkling water, and prepare themselves to indulge in my all time favorite breakfast.

I breathed in the seductive aroma of onions, olives and cheese. My mouth watered as I twirled the steaming pasta on my fork, which was pressed up against a spoon, the only way to successfully twirl slippery linguini.

"Umm," I moaned aloud right before I took my first bite.

That's when my stomach flipped, cramped and generally turned into a ball of pain.

Dickey!

Just thinking about him ruined my appetite. I got up, slid my plate into the fridge, popped a couple antacids, and started up my laptop to check out flights to Hawaii. I found one on Travelocity that left Sunday night from SFO at ten-thirty. I bought the flight and an extravagant hotel room right on the beach in Maui. I told myself that no matter what happened I was getting on that plane, and nothing or no one was going to stop me.

Pasta a la Gloria - Level One or Two

2 cups of cooked fresh linguini
1 clove garlic, crushed and chopped
1 tbs. finely chopped onion
2 to 4 tbs. chopped cilantro, depending on your palate
1/4 tsp. salt
1/2 chunked avocado
1 Roma tomato (chop half, reserve the rest)
2 tbs. Sevillano EVOO
1 to 2 tbs. Gaeta pitted olives (or olive of choice)
2 tbs. freshly grated Parmesan cheese
1 tbs. chopped spring onions (optional, but more chopping is always good)
1 tsp chopped fresh Italian parsley (optional, but again…)
1/2 tsp. hot pepper flakes (optional, but hot peppers act as a stimulant)
Hot-pepper blend EVOO

You can use cold linguini or linguini that has been cooked for about three minutes. Fresh linguini cooks faster than packaged linguini, and if you want to turn this dish into a level three need, make your own pasta. *Recipe follows. Fry the garlic in a pan with the oil until the aroma of the garlic permeates the air. Do not let it brown. Add the spices and cook for less than a minute, savoring the sights and smells. Add the pasta with about 1/8 cup pasta water or tap water. Flip and mix to get all the flavors to penetrate the pasta. Add the avocado and chopped tomato to the pan to heat through. Give it another flip and serve in a flat green, white or yellow bowl. Garnish with the mixture of cheese, cilantro, and the chopped Gaeta olives, or any mild flavorful olive. Drizzle on the hot pepper oil. Slice up the remaining fresh tomato and place it in the center of the pasta a la Gloria with a sprig of parsley or cilantro or both. Presentation is key. This dish is perfect anytime you're feeling tense, and can also be used as a reward on a Sunday morning to congratulate yourself for having made it through yet another Saturday night, stone sober. There's enough for two, so share the fun.

TWO

Whose Land Is This, Anyway?

I drove my cherry-red pickup down Arnold Drive through Glen Ellen, turned on Madrone Road passing Valley of the Moon winery, then turned right onto Highway 12 toward the city of Sonoma. The grapevines along the highway were in full autumn glow, with more dazzling shades of yellow, bright orange and sienna than most years. Fortunately, the road was nearly free of cars so I could glance at the ribbons of color against the backdrop of deep-green mountains without killing myself or anyone else.

I lowered the windows to let the wind race through the cab. My mind wandered to the beach in Maui as I passed the Russo vineyard. It was home to the man I had a love-hate relationship with. We were in the hate stage at the moment, having broken up four months ago after a weekend that nearly put me back in rehab. Leonardo Russo was the man I lusted over, woke up dreaming about, and wanted so bad it hurt.

Leo and I were like fire and kindling when we were together, hot being the operative word here, both with our sexual encounters and our ability to party on. A real shame considering I truly loved the man, but he was bad news as far as my sobriety was concerned. I was trying to focus in on that negative fact as I slowed to cruise by and fantasize about any future possibilities. It was just then that I saw two men standing toe-to-toe talking out on the front porch of the tasting room, a large two-story clapboard painted gray with white trim.

I pulled over, thinking one of the men was Leo, and already I could feel the tingle in my toes. I hadn't seen him in awhile, but the man still had a powerful effect on me. Perhaps a little wine buying might be in order for Dickey's freedom party. There could never be enough wine at one of our family events.

Leo's Pinot Noir had won a gold medal at Vinitaly. I figured heartfelt congratulations would serve as my opening act, just a bit of friendly conversation between two neighbors.

I knew my limits, sort of. And anyway, it wasn't as if I could start anything up again with him anyway. I'd heard he had a new girlfriend, a Marley or Sharley or something. She lived over in Napa. A wine critic or a food critic. I wasn't sure of all the details, not fully wanting to admit that he had already moved on, but I did know she had a fat ass according to Aunt Babe who was somewhat of an expert on fat asses, having one herself.

The sun was in my eyes as I stared at him. His rich brown hair seemed longer than usual, and there was quite a bit of facial hair going on, most likely due to Marley or Sharley's insistence because the Leo I knew shaved at least twice a day, but it was Leonardo all right. I mean, if it wasn't, he looked enough like him to be his brother, and as far as I knew, Leo didn't have a brother.

I let out a long, slow lustful sigh, completely envious of fat-ass Marley or Sharley or whatever the hell her name was. And what was wrong with my ass anyway?

I sighed again hoping he would notice my pickup. It was obvious this truck belonged to me: I rode around with my olive-picking ladder sticking out of the back. A prerequisite this time of year; one never knew when they would be called on to start picking.

For a moment, he glanced my way, but there was absolutely no sign of recognition.

Fine.

What did I care.

I shifted my gaze. The other man didn't look familiar. He was much smaller than Leo, both in height and weight, had thick, gray hair combed straight back, and wore a shirt the same color as the autumn leaves.

He must be a tourist.

I was just about to back up so I could head for the driveway, thinking my mother would truly appreciate a case of wine, when the man started poking Leo's chest. Leo slapped the man's hand away and I knew from my many years of watching my volatile relatives, these two guys were in the heat of a battle.

I watched for another moment as arms flailed, and tempers elevated to a point where another man came out to try and put a stop to their escalating argument. I was thinking perhaps this was not the optimum time for a visit, so I pulled back on the road, thankful to let the temptation pass.

When I arrived at the bank just off the Plaza in the village of Sonoma fifteen minutes later, the parking lot was almost empty. I figured I could get in and out in no time. I so didn't want to run into anyone I knew because I was lousy at hiding things and I simply had no stomach for spilling my guts about Dickey's release.

I parked the Ford, hurried inside and found forty-something Liz Harrington eager to escort me to Mom's safety deposit box. My name was on all my mom's accounts. "Just in case I get hit by a bus," she'd say. The likelihood of my mom getting struck down by a bus in Sonoma was equal to her getting hit by a meteor. The woman hardly left the orchard, and when she did, someone else would drive her. She wouldn't even cross the street in the village without an escort let alone walk somewhere alone in the presence of crazed bus drivers.

But she insisted, so there I was doing her banking with the help of surly Liz Harrington who, for some inexplicable reason, seemed eager to please.

"I hear your cousin Dickey was released from Soledad yesterday," she surreptitiously inquired as we walked toward the back of the bank, her well-worn cowboy boots clicking on the gray tile floor.

"That was quick," I answered. Sonoma Valley was like any other small town. News traveled through it like wildfire in a dry forest.

"I also heard your family is throwing him a party tonight. Boy, I'd like to be a fly on the wall at that one."

"It should be pretty boring," I muttered with indifference, hoping she would get the message that I didn't like where this conversation was heading. It was bad enough that I came from a family of aging ex-mobsters, but did I have to hear about it even from my banker?

"Not the way I heard it."

I couldn't resist. "And what was that?"

"You have relatives flying in from all over the country to be there," she said as we walked into a small, stuffy room, the walls lined with tiny metal doors, each one with double key holes.

The woman knew more than I did about my mother's plans. "Not likely, but you know how families are," I told her trying to sound as if my family was as normal as the next guy's.

"No. How are they?" Her head bobbed in a curiously disjointed way. I stared at her wondering if that movement was natural or was it some old neck injury that had never quite mended properly. Either way, it seemed like something she should get fixed "I grew up in an orphanage and the only parents I ever knew died from a crack overdose when I was ten. I never married, never had kids and from the looks of it, I won't be getting those things any time soon."

While she spoke I was thinking that perhaps it was her neck injury that had turned her into such a disagreeable woman.

Or not.

I decided to go for a more holistic approach. "Love can come when you least expect it."

"That's a bunch of baloney," she said bitterly.

I smiled, not having a good comeback for that one, so I let the silence of the airless room take over.

We turned our keys in the locks. I slid the box out of the slot, and Liz Harrington stood a little too close-by, key in hand, while I went through Mom's things. I could smell the shot of bourbon she'd mixed in with her coffee that morning, and the sweet cologne she had sprayed on her clothes to cover it up. It made me feel a little sorry for her. I knew all about the need to smooth out the day.

I found the papers Mom had asked for, along with my dad's simple gold wedding band, Mom's matching wedding band, a couple of photos, a picture of me in first grade missing a front tooth, some little girl I'd never seen before who was also missing a front tooth, a small mesh bag filled with gold coins and a larger one containing silver change—Mom's security just in case the economy took a real dump and paper money became worthless—and Dickey's flashy ring. For some reason, I remembered the ring, but not on Dickey's finger. I stared at it for a few seconds, trying to visualize who else could have worn it, but nothing came to me.

I thought about when Mom had put all these things in this box when we first moved here. How sad she was, and how much I still missed my dad. He had left on a business trip while we were still living in North Beach—I was twelve, way before we moved to Sonoma—and had simply disappeared. Mom hired a private detective to find him, someone not connected to our ever-growing family, but we never saw him again.

Not that this was anything new to a mob family, but my dad had always tried to steer clear of "family" matters so I never had the impression he was actually connected, at least that was the innocence of my childhood. Somewhere during my late teens I finally realized the truth, everyone around me was connected.

Still, he was different than Uncle Benny or Uncle Ray who were Made Men since they were in their twenties.

My dad loved to make people happy, and loved to cook. Almost every Sunday afternoon he'd boil up a few pounds of pasta, fry about fifty meatballs, throw them in a rich tomato sauce, then make a mountain of salad and invite everybody he knew over for dinner. Those were some of my best memories, and most likely where I got my love of cooking.

I took out the ring and the papers Mom had asked me to fetch, put everything back into the box, slid the box back into its slot, turned the key, and Liz stepped forward and did the same. I told her thanks and to have a nice day. She threw me a tepid smile, never uttering another word, thank God, and I walked out of the bank.

I still had a little time before I had to be at the bookstore for Lisa's book signing, so I decided a stop at Maya, a Yucatan restaurant off of the Plaza. Maya's was located on the historic Sonoma Plaza on the corner of East Napa and First, a stone's throw from Readers bookstore. I felt actual hunger pangs and thought I'd stop in for one of their prawn enchiladas in a cream sauce with sweet peppers, onions, cilantro and rice. It had to be one of my favorite lunches. That and a Maya Margarita made with agua fresca (whatever juice the bartender squeezed that morning . . . guava was my absolute fave) served in a chilled martini glass. I drank it sans the tequila, a concession I'd made with myself months ago.

When I stepped inside the colorful restaurant with the stone walls and polished cement floor, the hostess greeted me with a friendly smile and asked if I would be sitting at the bar or a table. I opted for a table. The bar, better known as the Temple of Tequila, was far too much of a temptation. I'd spent many a night worshiping at the Temple with tequila flights lined up in front of me. All I wanted now was a quiet spot to read.

"A table would be fine, thanks," I told her. She picked up a menu and I followed her to the table next to the front window. I could see my pickup parked curbside. Someone in a monster black Tundra was busy trying to parallel park in the tiny space behind my pickup and was having one hell of a time getting into the space. I just hoped he didn't hit my bumper. I wasn't in the mood to exchange info.

As soon as I pulled the wooden chair out to sit, my waiter appeared and I ordered. I didn't need to look at a menu. When he left, I began reading the documents. I wanted to see if I could find anything that might indicate a problem for my mom. I didn't understand her urgency to get the documents, and I was curious about what they said.

My food and drink arrived before I finished reading, and the Tundra had apparently given up and moved on when I glanced out the window again. I was grateful no damage was done. My plate of food smelled wonderful and I couldn't wait to dig in.

For the moment, all was right with the world.

I took a big gulp of my margarita, and a bite of a perfect enchilada, the taste a complete delight.

Everything in the document seemed fine, except for the last page. It was signed by my cousin Dickey, my mom, Uncle Benny, and notarized by somebody named Peter Doyle.

I took another sip of margarita. I would have liked it better with a shot of Don Julio tequila or perhaps El Tesoro, but I told myself this was much more refreshing.

Yeah, right.

To summarize what I was reading, and if I was understanding the legalese correctly, it stated that in the event that Dickey Spia was cleared of the murder of Carla DeCarlo, the olive grove, any subsequent buildings and the business itself would revert back to him as the sole owner. I had to read that over several times before it sunk in.

Then as if my body reacted before my mind could take hold of this disturbing information, a tiny ripple of panic swept through me as my stomach roiled, and my chest began to tighten. If ever I needed a drink it was at that moment. I took a deep breath, pulled out some cash, stuck it under my essentially untouched plate of delectable looking fare and left the restaurant. I had to get home. Now! I had to know if this document was legal, and if it was, what did it mean for our company? For the family?

For me?

I raced home as fast as I could without getting a speeding ticket or causing some massive pileup. As I approached our olive orchard from the road, I could see that the family Spia was out in Mom's front yard, apparently holding that meeting she had talked about.

Mom's yard served as our usual meeting and party place. It was about half an acre wide, with a cluster of olive trees for shade that everyone was now standing or sitting under, drinking wine and participating in the animated conversation. Their attention abruptly turned to someone in the group. I couldn't tell who, but arms moved about, hands sliced the air and gyrating body language told me they were in a tizzy. Most of the time everyone got along, but there were occasions when tempers flared and all hell broke loose.

I pulled my pickup in closer to the fence and hoped for calm, but from the looks of what was already going on, I couldn't tell if the gestures were of the friendly variety or the "may you rot in hell" type.

Just about everyone who worked on our land was there, which was unusual for a Wednesday afternoon. Normally they'd be tending to their shops. Seeing them all together in the front yard in the middle of a work day was not particularly a good sign.

The friends and family who worked on the land considered

it their personal small town. We even had our very own mayor, Uncle Ray, my mother's honorary brother. In my naïveté, I used to refer to him as Godfather, until he put me straight one day and told me in no uncertain terms should the word Godfather ever be uttered in the same sentence with his name. Uncle Ray had done his time in a Federal pen for racketeering—he ran a highly profitable plumbing business in New York City with no real plumbers—but rumor had it racketeering was the least of his undertakings.

Mom had built a sort of one-street town on the land when she first took it over, hoping the charm and ambiance would attract more tourists to our olive products. Little did she know some of our more notorious relatives would want to take up residency and call it home.

Mom owned two rows of attached two-story buildings, which consisted of small storefronts on the first floor, and a few one bedroom apartments on the second floor. She collected rent for both, but the revenue from the businesses stayed with the shopkeepers. Each business boasted an Italian motif, and was run by various relatives, honorary relatives, adopted relatives, divorced relatives and a sprinkling of friends. It had been difficult to get all the permits to create an independent small town of sorts, but with Uncle Benny's help she was able to eventually pull it off.

The orchard or farm, as we sometimes referred to it, served as a means for everyone to pursue more legitimate goals, not that anyone's past was ever mentioned. It was a way to stay connected with each other and avoid having to find a new identity in the outside world.

I made sure there was no skimming, money laundering or racketeering. Once a month I went over their books, and if I found anything that didn't quite add up or if somebody began pulling money out of their freezer, the family would band together and kick him or her out, which we've had to do on one or two occasions.

There was a time when the Feds would tap our phones and hide in parked vans and watch the place, but that stopped years ago when Mom walked right out to a parked van and began pitching the benefits of olive oil. The pitch that put it over the top for us was the day she mixed a cup of olive oil with four tablespoons of baking soda and taught them how to polish their guns with the concoction. Not long after that the vans disappeared, along with those pesky clicking sounds on our business phones.

As I pulled into the main driveway with the arching metal "Spia's Olive Press" sign, I saw that we were closed for the day. A heavy chain hung across the entrance. I backed up and made a U-turn and headed for the private service road that led to the back of my mother's Victorian, and would eventually end at the old stone barn.

The last time my family had closed the shops and olive oil tasting room early, my great-grandfather, Bisnonno Luigiano, who was ninety-six at the time and barely able to sit up in a chair, had drifted off to heaven during a Fourth of July celebration. And even then we only closed for a few hours while the paramedics were there. My family did not like to lose revenue, no matter what went on. So for them to close their shops in the afternoon meant that Dickey's freedom party was bigger than death.

THREE

My Cousin Dickey

Making my way up the service road, I knew no one could see my entrance. The road was blocked by trees and a four-foot-high lava stone wall—the same lava stone that had been used to build Jack London's "Wolf House" back in nineteen-eleven.

As I pulled the truck into the private parking lot between Mom's backyard and the stone barn, the usual set of late model cars were lined up along the fence, along with my mom's new white Mercedes C350. There were also several current model cars lined up in a row that I didn't recognize: a black Mercedes E class, a black Tundra, two black Cadillacs, a black BMW SUV and a black BMW Roadster. My family had a thing for black cars.

I didn't recognize any of them, but I assumed they belonged to my relatives from San Francisco. Most everybody tended to get new cars every year, something my father liked to do to keep his enemies guessing, he would say. It seemed that these relatives had no shortage of enemies.

I grabbed Mom's paperwork, slid out of the front seat, slammed the door behind me and just as I walked up the steps to Mom's back porch, Aunt Hetty came charging out from the screen door. As soon as she saw me she pulled in a breath, let out a little "yeow" and grabbed the front of her white cotton blouse, which was half unbuttoned, a strange phenomenon for my overly modest aunt. "Holy buckets! You scared the bejesus out of me. Don't you know better than to sneak up on a person?"

Aunt Hetty had a hearing problem she wouldn't admit to which caused her to be a little edgy. She thought everyone snuck up on her.

"Sorry. Is my mom in there? I've got something for her."

She spun around, buttoned her blouse, pulled her skirt around so that the seams went down her hips, straightened her frazzled hair, smeared on some lipstick from a blue tube she always kept in her pocket, then turned to face me, grinning. That alone told me something was up. Aunt Hetty never grinned.

She and Aunt Babe were half-sisters, and sadly looked nothing alike. Babe had all the good looks in the family, while Hetty had nothing but a talent for baking. Her graying short hair stood out in little tufts around her heavily creased face, and because of her tendency to wear bright red lipstick that extended above her lip line, she always reminded me of an aging clown.

Unfortunately, Hetty took life seriously so the clown part was only in my imagination.

"She might be, but I didn't see her. I'm too busy delivering cookies for the party. But I saw her go into the barn earlier. Or did I see her go into the barn this morning? I can't remember. Don't ask me these questions when I have so much on my mind. I don't have time for them."

Aunt Babe and Aunt Hetty, who weren't actually my aunts—more like married-into-the-family-because-of-Cousin-Dickey—who actually was a cousin, owned and operated the pastry shop on the property: Dolci Piccoli, Little Sweets. They also shared a small California bungalow on the opposite side of the main driveway and were part owners of the orchard along with me and Federico, who also lived on the land in a one-bedroom house. Mom owned the lion's share, or at least I thought she did. Now, after reading that document, there was no telling what would happen.

"Do you want some help?" I knew it was going to take a lot of cookies to satisfy this crowd.

"No thanks," she said, and gently squeezed my arm with

affection. I was momentarily put off. This simple act of warmth was something Aunt Hetty rarely did. Aunt Babe called her a "cold fish" because Hetty never offered a hug to anyone, and whenever she received one, her arms would be glued to her sides. "You're such a sweetheart."

Sweetheart?

I wondered if the woman had been drinking, not that she ever did. Hetty was a dry state all the way. A role model if there ever was one. Then it dawned on me. "You're worried about Babe being around Dickey again, aren't you?"

"Huh?"

I was sure she was playing the dumb card for my benefit. Or she simply couldn't hear me.

I raised my voice and enunciated my words. "I said, YOU ARE WORRIED ABOUT DICKEY AND BABE, RIGHT?"

"Don't shout Mia, it hurts my ears."

"Sorry." She categorically ignored my question, which I let pass thinking perhaps she was preoccupied with her baking.

"I have to get back," she suddenly announced after an awkward moment of silence. "Babe has two more trays of biscotti to take out of the oven and she won't be able to handle them on her own. I'll have to do the slicing before they cool, then get them back into the oven. I don't have time to chat right now. The relatives are restless."

Then she hugged me, and it was so shocking my arms never left my sides. As she pulled away she said, "When someone hugs you, Mia, you should hug them back."

I wanted to say something like, what do you mean? You never hug back. Or, what's going on with you today? Why are you so friendly? But before I could get the words formulated she turned and walked off toward her pastry shop.

You could have knocked me over with a twig.

I walked into Mom's kitchen and called out her name, but didn't get a response. Trays of amaretto, wedding and anisette cookies, cream puffs, torrone—a chewy flavored nougat and hazelnut candy that I absolutely loved—braided egg breads and several varieties of cannoli were piled high on every flat surface. The tiny country kitchen smelled like a bakery, only sweeter. I snitched two slices of orange-flavored torrone, took a delicious bite—Aunt Babe made the best torrone in the world—and made my way into Mom's dining room through the arched open doorway.

I called out for my mom again.

Still no answer.

I could hear my relatives out in the front yard arguing and laughing, normal behavior for that group. Accordion music rose above the din, which meant Cousin Maryann was in good spirits. Maryann and her traveling accordion never missed a family gathering, no matter what the event. She even played at my mother's bedside during my delivery, which could account for my abnormal fondness for accordion music. I even took lessons when I was ten, but then realized that playing an accordion was just about the geekiest thing I could do, so I gave it up, but only after I learned to play and sing e' Gumbad e all the way through, with all the musical instrument sound effects, I might add.

I still harbored a longing to pull out my old accordion whenever Maryann came around. Problem was, if I did, she would never let up and I'd be the one accompanying her at these events instead of Jimmy. I could hear him out there picking on his mandolin. He owned and ran a tavern in North Beach called Labella. If I had our lineage correct (there were so many honorary family members that it was hard to keep up), he was Maryann's younger brother, both somehow related to me on my father's side of the family.

My mom's house was silent except for the ticking of the cuckoo clock she had inherited from Bisnonno Luigiano, which would drive me crazy in my drinking days when I was nursing a particularly bad hangover. Especially when that damn bird popped out to announce the time, boring a hole right through the middle of my skull. My great-grandfather was a masochist and a sadist, I was sure of it.

I checked my mom's bedroom on the first floor, a romantic shabby-chic haven of pastels and excessive lace, but she wasn't there. Her jewelry armoire caught my attention and I decided to leave the paperwork from the bank in the top drawer instead of out in the open on her small desk. I figured she wouldn't want me to hand them to her in front of any of our more notorious guests.

As soon as I slid open the top drawer Torno Sorrento began to play, my mom's favorite Italian song, especially when performed by Pavarotti. I shoved the stack inside on top of mom's antique handgun, and closed the drawer tight, glad to be rid of the responsibility. Dickey's ring was still tucked inside my pocket. With the amount of tension she had going on that morning, she probably would want to hand it over as soon as possible.

I left the room and ran up the polished wooden steps to the second floor, sliding my hand along the white railing as I went. I scoped out each room. All I found were various open suitcases and clothes scattered across the beds, but no Mom. One of the bedrooms had a small balcony, but the French doors were closed so I figured she wouldn't be out there. A black suitcase lay open on the rumpled bed, and I couldn't help noticing the brightly colored clothes inside. All neatly folded with the price tags still attached.

Giving up my house search, I thought it might be time to join my family out on the front lawn, but just as that damn cuckoo chirped its time, a shadow moved on the creamy walls in the hallway. The combination of the two sent a shock wave through my body and I grabbed onto the wooden railing to make a speedy retreat, but then thought better of it. I was teetering on the edge, and if I took even one step forward I would end up on the landing in a heap of splintered bones.

"You gotta be my little cousin Mia," a deep male voice bellowed as the shadow turned into a rather short, slim, fifty-something man wearing a tailored brown suit, a dark gold shirt, and spit-shined brown shoes. He was hand combing his hair back from his face, wiped his face with a white hanky, shoved it into his pants pocket while straightening his suit coat as if he had just put it on, his shoulders adjusting to the confines of the jacket in typical male fashion. "I'd recognize you anywhere. Had your picture up on the wall. Of course, you was younger in the picture, but you still got them pretty almond eyes." He stopped. "Hey, I didn't mean to scare ya. I was out on the balcony admiring all them olive trees. This place is bigger than I remember, and them trees all got taller."

He came in close to give me a kiss. I let him. He kissed both my cheeks and I instantly knew I was face to face with the man of the hour. He smelled clean, with the hint of red wine on his breath.

"Cousin Dickey," I said, throwing him a smile. After all, I didn't want to seem inhospitable. There was no telling what he would do if I was disrespectful. Respect was the linchpin in a family like this. If you crossed that line, things could get ugly real fast.

"In the flesh." He gave me a toothy grin, and I could feel the tension building between my shoulders.

I'd never met someone who seemed so proud to be who they were. He oozed self-confidence, and even though he must have weighed less than my mom, was no more than five-foot-four inches tall, had a ravaged face, gray silky hair combed straight back with the help of some kind of oil—olive oil, no doubt—and sported a classic Roman nose. The man had an infectious smile, and piercing blue eyes.

I now realized that it was Pinot Noir that permeated the air. Releasing my death grip on the railing, I took a step toward him.

"It's been a long time," I said, wishing the time was even longer, like perhaps not in this lifetime.

"Eight years, two months, three days, and seven hours, but hey, who's counting."

Then he laughed, a great big deep laugh, and he tapped my arm like I was supposed to laugh with him.

I knew enough about my family to join in when one of these aging Made Men thought something was funny. "You've got me there," I answered, chuckling, nodding my head, and so wishing I was out on the front lawn with the rest of my family, taking accordion lessons from Maryann. For the first time ever, while I stood a little too close to Dickey, accordion lessons didn't seem like such a bad idea, and even though he seemed genuine enough, I couldn't get murderer out of my head.

Had he gotten away with it, or was he truly innocent? I couldn't decide.

"It's nice to see you again," I said, but it was an absolute lie and I hoped it came out as a genuine statement.

The moment was awkward as I waited for his response. I didn't quite know what to say to someone who'd just been released from a state prison. Usually, when I'd meet up with one of my recovering uncles or cousins, they'd have been out for a while and somewhat acclimated to their freedom. But this guy was fresh from the pen and the scars weren't quite healed. Small talk felt weird. I mean, asking him what he'd been up to or discussing the weather didn't quite seem appropriate.

"Hey, ease up. I didn't come back here to cause no trouble for your mom. I got a couple things to do and after that, I'm outta here. I got no time to be hanging around this place when there's a cute little babe waiting for me in the city. I'm getting married, ya know."

I clenched my teeth. Who in their right mind . . . but then I flashed on the Menendez brothers—Erik got married while he was serving his life sentence to a woman who, by California law, can't even have sex with him. "Congratulations!" I said and shook his hand.

"Yeah, ain't that something? But don't tell nobody. There's a few people around here that don't want to see your cousin happy. One in particular who wanted to see me burn, but hey, I'm a free man. I ain't carryin' no grudge. Grudges don't do nothin' but give you a bad stomach."

A few measures of Turno Sorrento drifted our way, then a thud and a door slammed. The cuckoo announced it was half-past something as our attention immediately focused on the stairway. "Mom? We're up here." I called out, but no one answered and Dickey's whole demeanor changed. I didn't like what I saw. He looked mean.

Angry.

Intense.

Was it our conversation on grudges? Or did he hate cuckoo birds as much as I did?

I coughed. "I have something for you," I said hoping to squash his sudden nasty disposition. "My mom kept this for you."

I pulled the ring out of my pocket and handed it to him. He stared at it for a moment and his demeanor changed back to the charming man.

"Your mom's a good woman." He slipped the ring on his pinky finger on his left hand. It seemed too tight and he had to work at getting it over his large knuckle. I figured arthritis must have changed his fingers since he wore it last. He held up his hand to admire the ring. "Mark my words, baby doll, this ring is gonna give somebody real heartburn."

I couldn't imagine why, unless he was talking about some jealousy thing that continually ran through the family. There were a lot of bright diamonds on the horseshoe. One thing this family never could get over was one-upmanship.

"Maybe we should join everyone in the yard," I said not wanting to be alone with him any longer. I was feeling way too weird.

"Good idea," he said as he stepped in front of me and headed down the stairs. "And I want to apologize for callin' you flat face when you was a kid. I thought it was funny back then, but you was a pretty little thing, and you're a beautiful woman now."

"Thanks," I said, thinking maybe he wasn't such a bad guy after all. Maybe he hadn't killed his mistress, Carla DeCarlo, and he was actually on the road to recovery like the rest of my family. I needed more empathy for my relatives.

More compassion.

More therapy.

"You know," he said. "I woulda thought you'd hate me. I know everybody else around here does."

I followed behind him, thinking my act had worked. It wasn't that I hated him exactly; I didn't know him well enough to feel that emotion. I'd heard plenty about him, so scared silly was more to the point.

As we descended the stairs I noticed his perfectly manicured long nails. He'd been out of the slammer for less than forty-eight hours and he'd already had time for a manicure.

I was jealous.

The steps creaked under his feet. For a little guy, he carried a lot of weight, muscle weight, I supposed. "Hate's a strong word."

"Not necessarily. I think it makes things easier."

"You mean when someone holds a grudge?"

"I already told ya. I don't hold no grudges," he said as he stepped on the landing then headed for the front door, grabbed the glass knob and swung the white door open as far as it would go. Maryann's music slowly faded. Conversation stopped. All I could hear was Bisnonno's clock ticking.

Tick-tock. Tick-tock.

Before he stepped out on the porch, he turned back to me, leaned in closer, smiled, revealing a dimple on his left check and whispered in a low, raspy voice, "I get even."

Trying to get my mother alone during the party was like trying to isolate one snowflake in a blizzard.

FOUR

For a Few Bottles More

She scampered around attracting family as if no one could breathe without first learning how from Mom. Even Uncle Benny couldn't seem to get her alone. I know because I watched him follow her around for about an hour.

It didn't help that Mom glued herself to Dickey's side so tight that I was sure their hips had fused.

And never mind that the only time she spoke to me was to ask if I could bring out another plate of olive focaccia, panini with buffalo mozzarella, tomatoes and chicken or anis cookies or pasta drenched in our Limonato olive oil, browned garlic and fresh parsley, or grilled veggies brushed with our Estate olive oil. But the strangest request was to help open more bottles of wine for the guests—Leo's wine. I couldn't imagine who might have brought it since most of the people in my family didn't like the Russos or their uppity wine.

But that was beside the point.

As if anyone in this group needed help with a wine cork!

Then she fussed over not having enough olives on the tables, but when I looked around, there were mounds of olives on every surface.

Federico had gathered all the varieties we cured and filled up several wooden bowls he'd commandeered from my mom's kitchen. Believe me, we had enough olives. Plus he brought out his famous tapenade made with chopped black Kalamata olives and sweet wine. His was my mom's all-time favorite.

I was thinking that making good tapenade took time, especially if you didn't use a food processor like Federico who insisted on chopping everything by hand. It would be a great addition to my cookbook, especially since you had to refrigerate the mixture for about ten hours. All that chopping and marinating could work for a level two alcohol need, like right before a job interview or a date to meet the parents or having to wait to talk to your mom about a document that could potentially change your entire life.

If I didn't clear this up soon, I would have no choice but to slip away from the festivities and whip up a couple dozen pizzas just to ease the tension.

Taking in a deep breath and looking around, I noticed I wasn't the only tense one in the bunch. Federico appeared to be just as uneasy as I was. He usually enjoyed watching people eat his olives and delight in his tapenade, but not today. He seemed a bit uptight as he leaned against my mom's porch railing, sucking on his pipe, staring at the crowd. Then again, he never was one for family gatherings. They made him uncomfortable.

Federico was not only our groundskeeper, and olive expert, he was also my dad's younger brother. My mom and I never would have made it through my dad's disappearance if it wasn't for Federico's help. He kept a roof over our heads when money was tight, and taught me all those things a dad taught his daughter.

Admittedly, in this family those lessons included how to lock and load a weapon, how to shoot to kill, and the ever popular, never trust anyone, no matter who they are. He must have told me that one a hundred times.

I wasn't too keen on the weapons program, but I learned the trust mantle in spades. Every shrink I've ever been to said the same tired refrain: You have trust issues.

Ya think?

Uncle Federico also taught me the basics that my dad never had time for: how to ride a bike, how to tie my shoe, how to pitch a baseball and how to leave your lover.

I was very good at leaving a lover, it was the taking the lover back when I knew he was bad for me, that I sucked at.

The thought gave me a headache, so I popped a dozen spicy olives hoping they would take away the pain.

Truth be told, as the day wore on and dusk began to engulf our front yard, everyone seemed edgy. Perhaps they were all thinking what I was thinking: What was Dickey planning?

There seemed to be a rumor going around that Dickey was trying to convince everyone to plow under the olive trees and plant grapevines. Another rumor had it that he thought we should sell the land to developers for a resort. Still another rumor had him taking over the business. And from what I had read in those documents earlier that day, any one of those scenarios seemed possible.

I held on to one thought: Dickey said he had a few things to do then he was out of here.

Did he lie?

It wouldn't be the first time. I was sure of that.

I looked around at the familiar faces and thought this party was getting way too weird.

The cousins seemed downright angry. The uncles looked irritated. Even Aunt Babe wore a scowl, or was that her Lauren Bacall look, or could it be Mimi Van Doren? I couldn't be sure. She liked to dress like the blond sirens from the Noir films. Aunt Babe loved to play the starlet, and what better place than at her former husband's freedom party?

Aunt Hetty had reverted back to her "cold fish" self. Maryann and Jimmy's music had taken on a decisively melancholy tone. Uncle Ray no longer spoke to anyone. His wife Valerie was on her fourth or fifth glass of wine, and Zia Yolanda—who was somehow a great-aunt—sat alone under a tree, crying, kind of. In all the years I'd seen her cry, which happened at every family event, never once did she shed one real tear.

Just when I was falling into a pit of believing some of the rumors, I spotted my best friend, Lisa Lin, heading straight for me. The mere sight of her smiling face put me in a better mood. If anyone could lift me out from this gloom and doom disorder, she could.

"Nobody will talk to me," she said, half pouting, a glass of white wine in one hand and a biscotti in the other. Lisa was a dunker, and a biscotti dunked in wine was one of her favorites. She looked fabulous in her skinny black jeans, high black boots and a bright red girly sweater, completely accessorized with big glam jewelry, and a tiny floral shoulder bag that screamed Betsy Johnson. The woman was all about high-end designer. Her silky black hair was pulled back in a long braid, her almond eyes sparkled, and her face lit up when I smiled back at her. Lisa and I were exactly the same height, had the same creamy skin tone and probably weighed in within a pound of each other, and while she outgrew all her training bras in one summer and went on to a sturdy underwire, sadly, I remained in that training-bra stage. Well, maybe that was an exaggeration, but not much of one.

But the one true thing about Lisa that set her apart from everyone else I knew was her genuinely warm smile and that Julia Roberts laugh. It was infectious, and once she got going no one around her was immune.

"They're all jealous of your success. What are you doing here?"

We hugged, kind of. Her hands were otherwise occupied.

"I had a book signing at Readers Books today, remember?"

Instant guilt ripped through me. I had completely forgotten about her signing. "I'm sorry. I'm a lousy friend. Why you put up with me . . . I was actually on my way, but this whole Dickey thing had me spinning. I'm surprised you're here after I didn't show up."

"Not that you even invited me. My mom had made dinner plans for me tonight in Chinatown with yet another of her "he's the perfect boy for you" dates, but when I heard about the big freedom party at Spia's Olive Press, I had to stop by and meet Dickey. Besides, he gave me a great reason to escape another match made in hell."

"I had every intention of showing up for the signing. Honest. And I would have invited you then, but my brain flipped into save the family mode, and you know I'm worthless when that happens."

She shrugged. "I didn't expect you to show up. Sounds as if you're getting way too involved with your family, girl. You need a break."

"That's the plan. Sand, beach, sun and men. No family. Want to come to Maui with me? I leave Sunday night."

"Can't. I'm signing in Chinatown that day. My relatives from San Diego are coming in."

"The flight doesn't leave until ten-thirty. We haven't been on a trip together in a long time."

"Actually," she said, leaning on one foot, pushing out a hip. "I do need to go to Maui for research. I'm doing a guide on how to survive on an island."

"Maui doesn't seem like an island that requires survival techniques."

"Oh? Think spring break, plucky young chicks and eager young studs. Lethal combination. I'm teaching these women how to survive raging hormones, not how to build a fire, although, come to think about it . . . "

She pulled out a tiny digital recorder and made a verbal note to herself on bonfires on the beach.

Lisa seemed to have an idea a minute, and all of them were of the high concept variety that publishers gobbled up.

"I've got some of those raging hormones of my own," I said.

"My mother can hook you up."

"I'd rather take a cold shower."

"Try a vibrator. It's a lot more pleasant."

We laughed and hugged again. This time Lisa put her drink down on a table to get in for a tight one.

She and I grew up in San Francisco together. I lived in North Beach surrounded by my Italian family, and she lived three blocks away in Chinatown surrounded by her Chinese family. We used to do everything together, even drinking. Thing was, Lisa knew when to stop. I didn't. But ever since I started working for my mom, we rarely saw each other. She was busy writing, and I was busy keeping my family honest.

When we pulled apart she said, "I brought you my latest book. It's up on your desk. I know how you never lock your door, so I let myself in."

"Thanks."

"Do you ever read my books?"

"Of course I do," I lied.

She raised an eyebrow, an endearing habit, but one I knew well. Whenever that eyebrow went up, she knew what you were saying was total bullshit.

Truth was I simply never had time to read, not that I was ever a reader. Even in school she would write all my book reports and term papers. Hell, I hardly watched TV, and lately I didn't even date. I didn't do much of anything. Our business and my family sucked up every spare moment.

I was truly pathetic.

Lisa, on the other hand, was on her third best-selling book, The Girly Girl's Guide to Bad Boy Survival. Her first and second books in the Girly Girl Survival series, Country Survival, and City Survival had made her a very wealthy woman, much to the chagrin of most of my family. Anyone who potentially generated more money than they could, posed a threat. I didn't exactly know what kind of threat, but in my family those little details were irrelevant.

"You really should read them. I put a lot of research into those babies and who knows, you might need to use one of my tips someday."

As if...

"Absolutely. I'll read one tonight." In all honesty, I had every intention of reading her books that very night, but, what was that saying about some road being paved with good intentions?

"Liar." She knew me too well. "You hate to read. It's the only reason I don't take it personally."

"Okay, but if you come with me to Maui, I promise I'll read one on the plane."

"Do you even remember how to read?" She took a couple sips of her wine. I watched, remembering the taste on my tongue. I was partial to an Italian red rather than one from Napa. Not that I didn't think there were some fabulous California wines, but wines from the Basilicata region in Italy were my absolute favorite. "I mean, maybe you should take a refresher course first. Reading one-oh-one."

"Don't get snide. Just come with me, and I promise to read an entire Girly Girl book of your choice. If I don't, I'll pay for your trip. Deal?"

Not that I had that kind of money lying around. But certainly I could get through one of her books—I mean, what were friends for if not to support each other's creative endeavors?

She shrugged. "What the hell. Maybe you'll actually buy one of my books next time."

"I always buy your books." Of course, I couldn't truly remember buying any of them, but I owned them all, so I must have.

"I always give you my books."

Probably true. I just sighed. She had me.

"I buy all your books, and read them from cover to cover. But you already know that, babe," Uncle Federico's voice boomed as he moved in closer to us. He had been standing a couple feet away, arranging his olives on the table.

Lisa turned to face him. "Ooh, tell me more," she flirted, moving up closer to him. "I love when you talk books to me."

He grinned and chuckled, flashing a set of perfect white teeth. Uncle Federico had one of those deep, guttural laughs that could charm most any woman, even Lisa who had a crush on him since she was a little girl. He was in his mid-forties, with rich brown hair, graying temples, bedroom eyes and a body that was sculptured from years of working in the grove. He dressed in casual cool, jeans mostly, and either a white fitted shirt or V-necked tees. He always wore a thick silver necklace that his dad, my grandpa, gave him when he turned sixteen.

Uncle Federico had a sexiness to him that attracted all types of women, but he wasn't much interested in a steady relationship. Said he didn't want to be tied down to one woman. My mom said he'd gotten burned once and never recovered from the loss. A short fling was about all any female hopeful was ever going to get out of him.

"Your books aren't just for girls. Men can get a lot out of them, too."

She moved in closer and gave him a hug. "You know I love you."

He kissed her on both cheeks. "Love you too, babe. It's great to see you here. Haven't seen you at the orchard in a long time. Where you been hiding?"

She pulled away from him. "In my apartment in the city. Doing a lot of writing. You should stop by sometime. I could show you my process."

Lisa was a blatant flirt, especially when it came to Federico.

A big smile creased his lips. "Love to, but my olives are waiting to be picked. They're my first love, babe. Sorry. Always pure and they never lie." He winked. "Besides, Gloria won't let me wander too far during picking season. I haven't been off the property in days."

"Damn that woman." Lisa gave him a sly little chuckle as if they were sharing a secret. "Always in our way."

"Matter of fact, I was on my way to talk to her right now."

I said, "When you find her would you please send her my way? I've been trying to get her alone all night."

"Will do," he said. "Great seeing you, Lisa." And he walked off into the crowd.

"You wouldn't seriously have sex with Federico, would you? I mean, the man has a dark past, not to mention that he raised me since I was twelve so he's kind of like a dad, and I don't truly know all he's been into."

Her eyebrow arched.

"Don't answer that," I said.

"By the way," she said, "speaking of dark pasts. You think I could get a moment alone with Dickey? I'd like to ask him a few questions. I'm thinking of doing a follow-up to my bad boys guide . . . Truly Bad Boys."

"If you can pin him down he'll probably answer anything you throw at him. He seems to be in a good mood."

"Thanks for the tip," she said, and went off looking for Dickey.

Tapenade –Level Two

½ cup pitted black olives
1 cup pitted Kalamata olives
2 tbs. Italian capers, rinsed
2 desalted anchovy fillets, salted anchovies will also work
1 lg. clove of garlic
¼ cup Italian parsley, no stems
2 tbs. grated Parmesan-Reggiano cheese
2 tbs. sweet wine
2 tbs. pine nuts, toasted, not chopped
¼ cup EVOO, use an Italian blend for extra flavor

Using a sharp paring knife, finely chop olives, capers, anchovies, garlic, and parsley. Take your time doing this and enjoy the aromas of each of these foods. Breathe deeply, allowing the tension and the need to dissipate. When everything is sufficiently diced and sliced, and you're feeling less stressed, (this may take a double recipe) gather ingredients into a deep, narrow bowl and add the wine, being careful not to drink any of it yourself. Note: you may want to substitute a fruity vinegar depending on your conviction level. Slowly add the oil until the mixture is blended. Cover and refrigerate for at least 10 hours or longer to allow the flavors to meld together.

FIVE

Just Another Futso

The afternoon slipped into evening and I still hadn't cornered my mother. Every time I'd made a serious attempt to catch up with her somebody would stop me for a conversation. Mostly about what I thought Dickey wanted here.

As night gathered up the blue sky, and the party lights automatically turned on in the yard, I realized my mother, along with Dickey, was nowhere to be found. Uncle Benny said he'd seen Dickey go into the house with my mom, and Maryann said she'd seen Dickey strolling out toward the olive grove with Jimmy, but Aunt Hetty said she saw him get into his car and leave. Uncle Ray was positive he'd seen Dickey go into the barn with a woman, while Jimmy said he saw him walk toward the shops, and Aunt Babe said she'd just seen Dickey on the front porch sitting on the bench swing with Lisa a few minutes ago, but Zia Yolanda shook her head, called out his name and wept.

Tearless, of course.

"I've got to go, Mia," Lisa said behind me. "But I'd like to buy a few bottles of oil to bring home to my mom. You know how much she loves your Limonato on her pot stickers."

Lisa's mom was a one woman ad campaign for our olive oils. Because of her, practically all of Chinatown bought our oils.

"I made up a case for you. I was going to bring it to the book signing today but . . . anyway, it's in the barn. A gift to you and your family from me and my family."

"Thanks," Lisa said. "Ya know, your Aunt Babe is a riot. I love the whole Barbara Stanwyck thing she's got going on. Don't you?"

I'd never thought of Barbara Stanwyck. Perhaps because I wasn't that familiar with her work, but Lisa knew all the classic movies. It was from them that her mom learned English. They were the only movies her mom allowed Lisa to watch in the house. Anything else was too risqué and off limits. Just going to a movie theater was a major event when we were kids and Mrs. Lin usually escorted us, so we rarely went.

"That's who she is! I couldn't figure it out," I said as we made our way to the barn, the full moon illuminating our path.

"She had me when she told Dickey, "We're both rotten.""

Aunt Babe had a way of getting right to the point. I wondered if Dickey was referring to her when he said I get even. Everyone knew the two of them had a lot of animosity for the past going on. Could she be the real reason why he was here? "She said that?" I asked.

"It's from Double Indemnity, which I suppose you never read or saw the movie."

"Nope. Not on my list."

"Well, it should be. It's great. The Phyllis character says, we're both rotten, and Walter, her lover, says, only you're a little more rotten."

"Is that what Dickey said?" My stomach clenched at the thought. I loved Aunt Babe. She was my other mother.

"No. He just stood there and gave her the cold shoulder. Apparently, he didn't get Turner Classics in prison. Shame. It might do wonders for those guys."

I had to chuckle at the vision of burly criminal types sitting around a TV watching Easter Parade or Roman Holiday, which I knew were two of Lisa's favorites.

"Maybe there's another meaning to what Aunt Babe said to him."

"What else could she possibly—"

I shot her a look.

"I know your aunt outwardly hates him, but I think she's still in love with the guy. I finally pinned him down and had a chance to talk to him. He's a real charmer."

Like a snake.

"Don't let that charm fool you. I've heard stories about him that would make your heart stop."

I opened the back door of the barn, and as soon as we stepped inside I immediately felt the coolness of the stone walls that surrounded us. No matter what the temperature was outside, inside this stone cave it remained a cool sixty-five degrees. The expansive space was dimly lit from a single row of emergency lights running down the center of the ceiling. They automatically turned on whenever someone walked into the barn. The light switch was on the opposite wall next to the main entrance. We headed in that direction.

The barn was fairly empty of bottling equipment now because we had moved most of it over to the new facility behind our new tasting room. I thought it would be a real attraction if we could demonstrate our crushing process through large glass windows. After a family vote, it was decided to go ahead with my idea. We would be doing our first crush in the new facility in a few weeks, but the family wanted to keep some equipment in this barn to be able to fill small orders and perform the community crush for hobbyists and growers with small harvests. We all agreed it would be easier. Plus it was a great place for storage.

We were even moving our now partially dismantled antique millstone, which was taller than me, out in front of the new tasting room before our first crush. Cousin Dickey had imported the stone from Calabria, a southern region in Italy, when he first bought the place. I couldn't begin to imagine how much that must have cost him.

As Lisa and I walked deeper into the barn I watched our

shadows dance on the tin ceiling. Only there was one too many shadows.

"Mom? Are you in here?" I yelled as Lisa and I dodged stacked boxes, and a row of blue, olive oil drums.

No answer.

We peered around the boxes that surrounded us, and I could hear a kind of squeaking noise plus some labored breathing. The smallest sound reverberated between the stone walls, but I couldn't figure out why no one was responding.

"This is creepy," Lisa said, as she stepped in front of me. "Is there somebody in here?" she said in a loud, demanding voice.

Still no answer. I had to admit, I was beginning to feel a little hesitant, like maybe we should do this another time, like when the sun was pouring in through the windows instead of moonlight. I reached out for Lisa and we locked arms as a shadow ambled toward the main entrance. "Maybe they're looking for the light switch," I whispered.

"I hope so, 'cause I'm getting all weirded out in here."

"Relax," I said, trying to calm my own nerves as much as hers. "It's just my family."

"That's the problem," she said, letting go of my arm.

She had a point.

We stood in a maze of stacked cardboard boxes filled with oils ready to be shipped. Shelves of bottled oils from our last crush closed in on the left while various-sized imported Italian stainless steel storage containers, filled with our more popular oils, sat on our right. We stored some of our oils in a thirty- to fifty-liter fusto so we could fill bulk orders, or specialty orders like five-ounce bottles used for wedding favors. A fusto was equipped with a spigot, which made it easy to fill any kind of order in a hurry, and at the moment, those spigots kept hitting my arm as we walked by.

Light bounced off the polished steel and we both looked

up once again, watching the distorted shadows dance on the tin ceiling whenever we moved. "Bisnonno Luigiano said the dancing shadows were good luck. They belong to the olive goddesses Athena and Minerva watching over our bounty."

"Yeah, well, they don't look like any goddesses to me. More like demons."

I didn't want to go there. I was never a big fan of the dark side.

"You've been reading too many Vamp books," I said.

Stepping around the boxes I caught that extra shadow on the ceiling again along with that squeak, and figured whoever it was must still be looking for the light switch. It was hard to find if you didn't know exactly where it was located.

"The switch is in the middle of the outer wall, on the left, about three feet in from the doorway," I called.

Silence.

No movement.

Even the breathing had stopped.

When I turned around, Lisa was gone. I shivered. This was getting totally out of control. Slasher movies flashed through my mind and I suddenly wished I had spent more time watching Turner Classics with Lisa and her mom while I was growing up instead of suspense and thrillers with my dad.

"Lisa, where are you?" And just as I said it, the sound of breaking glass echoed through the barn. "Over here!" she yelled, her voice cracking.

I rushed toward the sound of her voice, which seemed to be coming from the right side of the barn, over by the antique millstone. It only took a moment to find her and as soon as I did I had to slide a few boxes out of my way to get to her. She was looking down at something. Even in the dim moonlight, I knew that intense look she wore on her face. I'd seen it a thousand times before. It usually came right before she was getting ready to either cry or relay some disturbing news. Like when she had to tell me that Johnny Underwood broke up with her for Erin Martin, our fifth grade class president whom we both hated because she told everybody my father was in the mob. I figured this look was over-exaggerated due to our shadow fear plus the glass I'd heard shatter had been a few bottles of oil, and she was upset about breaking them.

"Don't give it another thought. We have plenty more. I can replace whatever's broken," I said trying to calm her.

She turned toward me just as I slid another box out of the way so I could see the oil disaster. Her right hand was dripping with olive oil and she was holding up some kind of thick black metal screw. "I don't think you can replace him, Mia."

I slid the last box out of the way and saw brown, scuffed shoes pointing straight up from the barn floor, and teetering on top of the body attached to those shoes was the excessively heavy antique millstone, which almost entirely covered the obviously crushed body.

"What happened?" I asked, but I could feel myself slipping into pure hysteria. Those little hairs on the back of my neck were doing their dance again.

"It's Dickey, and I'm almost certain he's not going to be able to tell you."

A sick panic accompanied by a red-hot chill raced through me. "Is he, like, dead?"

She nodded. "Pretty much. I checked. There's no pulse."

"Did you see—"

"Not a thing."

I started shaking. My chest tightened. "We should call an ambulance."

"We should try to figure out how this happened first."

"Are you nuts?" I couldn't understand what the woman was thinking, but all I wanted to do at that precise moment was to get the hell out of there.

"I might be able to write about it in my next book. It could save someone's life."

"You are nuts. We need to call an ambulance, or the police or Uncle Benny." That's when I noticed the dark red blood oozing around Dickey's head, and the open thirty-liter futso on the floor not far from the body. I suddenly felt sick. I also felt guilt. I had been the one to have the millstone dismantled. It was my idea to move the damn thing. If it hadn't been for me, Dickey might still be alive. The thought was too much. My head started to swim. Things around me were spinning.

Lisa took my hand, and calmly bent over to take a closer look at his head. "Oh my God!"

"What," I whined, not wanting to know any of the gory details. At this point, I was barely hanging on.

"His head is bleeding out, and it's not from the millstone. I think he's been shot."

I told myself this couldn't be true. She was probably mistaken. What did Lisa know of gunshot wounds? "That's impossible. The stone fell on him. It's all my fault. I had it dismantled."

"Is that what this is?" She held up the screw she had been holding onto.

I nodded.

"Sweetie, I've researched gunshot wounds. I worked with a forensic lab and a coroner for six months. I know what gun shot wounds look like and this hole in his head is from a gun not from this screw or any part of this millstone. It was probably a small handgun, a .22 maybe, at close range."

"You're sure?"

"I'm not an expert, but I'm pretty sure this is the real deal."

My mind raced with scenarios, especially growing up in this family. I slowly made my way in closer and just as I was about to stoop down to get a look at Dickey's head wound, I stepped on something. I kicked at it. The thing was caught up under Dickey's feet. I reached down to carefully move it out of my way, knowing I shouldn't touch anything, but when I recognized it, instinct made me snatch it up.

"Damn!" I said, almost in a whisper.

"Yeah. I know. This is really bad."

"No. I mean yes, it's even worse than bad. It's catastrophic." I held out the problematic object. "This is my mother's charm bracelet."

Lisa stood. "What?"

I held it out for her to see as tiny silver Elvises gyrated on a silver chain. And just like that, those tiny Elvises crooned Trouble in my ear, "If you're looking for trouble, you came to the right place . . ."

"It can't be your mom's. That means—"

"That means we need to think about this before we call the police."

But Lisa was already saying what I would never believe. "Your mother killed Dickey? Your mother who captures flies in a glass so she can release them to the great outdoors? Your mother the Vegan? The Hippie? This woman shot her cousin?"

My head was churning with suspects and reasons and family history. But mostly I was thinking about the paperwork that was now sitting in my mother's bedroom, the paperwork that turned our business over to Dickey.

My heart fluttered and panic washed over me.

"You know she couldn't do it, and I know she couldn't do it, but the police won't know that."

She shook her head. "Mia, we have to call the police. We can get into a lot of trouble if we don't."

"I know, but somebody obviously tried to set her up. This is way too obvious, don't you think?"

"You can tell that to the police when they get here." She pulled out her iPhone to make the call. I couldn't let her do it. Not yet, anyway.

"A minute ago you wanted us to figure this out. What happened to that idea?"

"A minute ago I hadn't noticed the bullet hole."

She began pressing the numbers.

I had to think fast. Lisa was getting carried away with the law, and if I had learned one thing from this family, the law was not necessarily your friend, so I did the only reasonable thing a daughter of a mobster would do.

I snatched the phone out of her hand and threw it in the open fusto. "I can't let you do that."

SIX

La Famiglia

"Tell me you didn't just throw my phone, with all my contact information, and my notes for my next book into a vat of olive oil." Lisa stood with her arms akimbo, mouth tight, eyes narrowed, head tilted as if her brain had suddenly gotten heavy with thought.

"You gave me no other option," I told her.

"There are always options. You simply chose to ignore them."

"We can't call the police."

"Fine, but did you have to destroy my phone in the process? Do you have any idea what a nightmare that little act of defiance is going to cause me?" Her voice went up an octave.

We heard the soft clunk of the phone hitting bottom. She winced.

"I'm sorry, but my mother is not going to prison for something she didn't do. I already lost one parent to this damn family, I won't lose another."

Her face softened. "Ah, now I get it. Why didn't you tell me this sooner?"

"I wasn't conscious of it until this very moment. I just knew my mom wasn't guilty and you were getting ready to call the police and I simply reacted. It was a gut level thing."

"Next time your gut wants to tell you what to do would you please ask your head if it agrees?"

"That's not always an option, but I'll see what I can do. So, any suggestions?"

She eyed the futso. "You think the three minute rule applies to phones floating in olive oil?" She bent over and peeked into the open thirty-liter futso, then slowly knelt next to it trying to get a good look inside, careful to place the long black screw down next to her.

"That's the three second rule, and it only applies to food you drop on the floor. This is an entirely different animal."

"I'm going in," she said and plunged her hand into the olive oil, our Italian Blend, made from a combination of Frantoio, Leccino, Moraiolo and Pendolino olives. Not for the timid. This oil was pungent and spicy.

Half her arm disappeared inside the futso. She began to cough as the scent of the oil caught in her throat. "There's . . . something . . . else…"

But her coughing stole her voice. She retrieved the phone and held it over the futso so the oil could drip back in from both her arm and the phone. A somewhat startled look spread across her otherwise tranquil face.

"What?"

She tried to speak, but still couldn't. Instead, she pulled a handful of tissues out of her shoulder bag to wipe off the glistening olive oil from her arm and phone, careful not to let any of it drip on the table or on her clothes. Neither one of us wanted to contaminate the crime scene if we could help it, but that was probably a moot point by now.

In the meantime, the little problem of one dead mobster still haunted my thoughts and the more we stood there, the more panicked I became that someone would walk in on us. "Hurry," I told her. "We need to get out of here and lock this place up while I think of what to do next."

Lisa finally gained control of her voice. "There's a handgun in there," she said in even tones as if finding the gun along with her phone was a natural occurrence. "I'd say there's a relatively good chance it's the murder weapon unless this is some new way of storing the family weapons."

I gave her a wry look. She didn't flinch.

"Why would the killer leave the weapon where anybody could find it so easily? It doesn't make sense."

"Does any of this make sense? I don't know. Maybe he or she thought the police would never look inside these things, or at least not right away and that would give them time to remove it. I think we interrupted the killer before he or she could make a clean escape."

"But we never heard a gun shot."

"It could have happened right before we came in and the killer didn't want to take the chance of leaving with a smoking gun, so to speak." She focused on polishing her phone. It looked dead, but I could tell she was hopeful.

She said, "Or the killer wanted it to be found. Tell me your mom doesn't own a handgun."

"Is it one of those automatic things?"

She glanced back in the futso. "No, so that's good, right?" She smiled as if everything would be fine now. "It's a small revolver, with a mother-of pearl handle."

For some reason her teeth looked as if they could glow in the dark, or was that just my imagination playing tricks with the mother-of-pearl image playing inside my head. "Then I can't tell you my mom doesn't own a handgun." It sounded exactly like the one my dad gave her as an anniversary present when I was a little girl. The evidence was beginning to pile up. "Just tell me one more thing. Does it say anything on the handle?"

She moved to get a better look inside while I made excuses for the handgun. After all, a lot of people owned guns with mother-of-pearl handles. It didn't have to be my mother's gun, at least I hoped it wasn't. "I can't tell. There's not enough light." She twisted herself and backed up a bit. I held my breath. "Wait. There's something, L-U . . ."

My heart skipped a beat. " . . . C-I-L-L-E," we said in unison. She looked over at me. "It was my grandmother's name, and her weapon of choice. Some families pass down jewels, my family passes down handguns."

"You want me to fish it out?"

As if on cue, the back door creaked open and a voice echoed through the barn. "Hey, Dickey, you in here?"

It was Uncle Benny. Lisa quickly stood up without retrieving the gun, took a step back, caught her foot on the edge of the overturned olive mill, and nearly tumbled on top of it. I grabbed the back of her sweater and pulled her upright just in time. "No, Uncle Benny. It's just Lisa and me," I yelled. "We'll be right out."

"I'm right here," he said behind me. His baritone voice startled me and I let go of Lisa who instantly lost her balance and fell on top of the stone, which caused it to tilt to one side allowing Dickey to pop out like a golden lupini bean bursting out of its shell.

Uncle Benny yelled, "Marone! What the fuck!" and took a couple steps back losing his balance due to those boxes I had moved earlier. He began to fall backwards as he spun around grabbing at air, then for me. I tried for stability by leaning forward. Big mistake. We landed only inches away from Dickey.

On the up side, we didn't hit our heads on the stone mill. On the down side, between the three of us, we had sufficiently contaminated the crime scene so that the police would now believe we were somehow all involved.

As Uncle Benny and I lay there, holding onto each other, staring into Dickey's blank eyes—he was now facing us—I realized that Dickey smelled a little sweet. I took another whiff. Definitely berries. Or was that Uncle Benny who smelled like a ripe berry?

"Are you wearing cologne?" I asked, my face only inches from his.

"What the hell kind of question is that?" When he spoke I caught the scent of tobacco not berries.

He moved away from me in a flurry of frustration and pushed himself up to stand next to Lisa who had managed to get off the millstone on her own. I remained on the floor, and slid in closer to Dickey and there it was again . . . berries. I eased myself up a bit, the stone mill pressing in on my back. That's when I spotted Dickey's left hand pressing up against the millstone—obviously an attempt at stopping the stone from crushing him—twisted abnormally flat against his chest. His perfect manicure now ruined with broken nails and traces of blood.

I stared at his hand for a moment thinking something else was wrong with it. Then it came to me. The horseshoe pinky ring I'd given him was missing. And not only was the ring missing, but his pinky was covered in glistening olive oil that pooled on his suit coat and stained his golden shirt. I didn't have to get closer to know it was our Italian blend, the same oil my mom's handgun was now floating in.

Dickey had said the ring was going to give somebody heartburn. Could that heartburn have turned into murder?

Uncle Benny leaned over toward me. His graying hair slicked back with olive oil, no doubt, and his black, trendy Italian-framed glasses sliding down his Roman nose. "Get the hell out of there, will you? I do not like you lying with that piece of shit. It ain't right. What are you doing? The man is dead."

I grabbed Benny's arm, slid out from under the millstone and stood. "Sounds as if you didn't like Dickey much."

"Too hungry for power. I have no use for that kind of person. Plus, he killed a woman. Murder is one thing, but killing your own woman, that is something I do not condone."

It was comforting to know Uncle Benny's murder limits, just in case I ever stumbled on a dead girlfriend of his. At least I could cross him off the list of suspects.

"But wasn't he just cleared of that murder?"

He smirked, as if I should know better. "Let us just say he was cleared of being in close proximity when the event took place. That does not mean he did not have anything to do with the event."

I hadn't thought of that, probably a good thing.

"What's going on in here?" Jimmy asked, appearing behind Uncle Benny.

"Dickey's dead," Lisa announced as she brushed herself off and carefully checked her hands and face for injuries.

"No shit. Want I should clean it up?" He looked at me when he said it.

"No. We're calling the police," I told him. He took a couple steps back, as if he was getting ready to bolt.

Jimmy had that innocent, freshly-washed looking face, bright amber eyes, perfectly shaped nose, high cheekbones, and creamy skin that always had a hint of a shine. Not an oily shine, more of a clean glow. Other than my dad, he was by far the best looking man in the family, and he knew it. He went through women like a kid goes through crayons. He even dated Lisa for about a minute a few years ago, but she figured him out before their second kiss and dumped him. Lisa was always better at dating than I was. She could spot a truly bad boy just by the way he stood or laughed.

I, on the other hand, could always pick them out in a crowd, but instead of walking away, I would be dawn to them like a masochistic moth that can't seem to avoid the flame. Case in point: Leonardo Russo.

"Hey everybody, party's outside. Whoa!" Uncle Federico spotted Dickey and his eyes bugged for a moment, then he looked away. I almost detected a slight grin, but it vanished as soon as it appeared. "This looks real bad. Tell me it was some kind of accident." He stopped just inches behind Uncle Benny and Jimmy.

And I had so hoped Lisa and I could keep this to ourselves for awhile.

Who was I kidding?

"Not an accident," Lisa said, shaking her head.

"You mean somebody whacked' em?" Uncle Ray asked. I hadn't even seen him come in. It was as if he just materialized out of the shadows. His large frame dominated the cramped space we were standing in.

"Bullet in the left temple." Lisa delivered the news like a pro, indifferent and to the point. "At close range, I'd guess."

"Poor bastard. Not out more than twenty-four hours and somebody takes him out," Federico groused. "You'd think whoever did this could have waited 'til Dickey left the orchard. This is a problem for the family, especially Gloria."

My thoughts, exactly.

Federico didn't like anything even slightly off-color happening on the land, at least nothing that attracted the police. He was a tightly wound man and except for his weekly poker games with my mom and whoever else was willing to try their luck—Federico always seemed to win—the orchard was his only interest.

Suddenly the sound of sobs echoed through the barn. Zia Yolanda had arrived on the scene. "Somebody get her outta here," Uncle Ray ordered.

Jimmy said, "I'll do it."

"Good, and keep the rest of the women outta here."

Jimmy nodded and took off. Zia Yolanda's sobs drifted off leaving a strange sort of echo inside the barn. Normally, her sobs didn't bother me, but the lingering echo of genuine heartfelt weeping was enough to make me sad for Dickey's demise, a man who probably was responsible for more human misery than I could ever imagine. That right there produced goose bumps, along with a few shivers for added emphasis.

"You girls should go. We'll take care of this." Uncle Ray liked giving orders, and most of the time I would follow them, but not this time.

I shook my head. "No. This family doesn't cover up a murder anymore. Remember? We're honest, law-abiding citizens now."

"Tell that to whoever shot Dickey," Uncle Benny said, chomping on his unlit cigar. Uncle Benny always carried a fat stogy. When it wasn't peeking out of his shirt pocket he held it between his fingers or it dangled from the corner of his mouth. He was trying to cut back on his tobacco addiction, so he only lit up twice a day, but the habit of playing with a cigar was too imbedded in his psyche to abandon.

"Somebody shot Dickey?" Aunt Hetty's voice rang through the barn. She walked up to us with Valerie, an overly fit redhead, mid-fifties, piercing green eyes, and an old scar that ran along her otherwise delicate jawbone. Valerie liked to say she got the scar in an old biker accident, but we all knew her first husband gave it to her one night during a battle over the correct way to prepare shrimp. Now Valerie was married to Uncle Ray, a man who had an unnatural aversion to anything that lived in water.

Aunt Hetty nudged Uncle Ray to the side, giving him one of her hard looks. He moved out of her way. "Is the horny devil dead, or do we have to call an ambulance? The son of a . . . probably doesn't have any insurance and we'll get stuck with the bill. Well, you can bet that I won't be making any contributions. I'm done with this devil."

No one said a word as she walked up to Dickey, crossed her arms in tight under her breasts, leaned in closer and said, "He looks dead to me. Ha! Finally you guys did something right. Dirty bastage should'a been knocked off years ago." She stood up again, turned toward me and I noticed her moist eyes.

What was that all about?

Val said, "Babe can finally be free of the cheating, murdering louse."

"I've been free of the louse for a long time, doll. I don't need nobody to kill him on my account." Babe's husky voice rose from the shadows. "Especially not tonight."

"Where the hell is Jimmy? That kid never could take orders," Uncle Ray groused.

"Give it a rest, Ray. I'm a big girl. I can handle it." She peered down at Dickey. "I was kind of hoping he'd stick around for awhile for old time's sake." She struck a pose—one hip cocked, fluffed the bottom of her golden curls with her hand—then she spoke to Dickey. "Too bad it had to end this way, big guy. I was just gettin' in the mood."

In the mood for what, I wondered.

She turned and strolled away from the group, heels clicking on the tile in a slow rhythm that kept the men silently yearning until the sound of her shoes faded into the still night.

This was getting interesting.

Then Maryann, with her ample body and curly auburn-colored hair, steel-blue eyes and a sardonic outlook on life, showed up and made everyone guilty for our general lack of respect for the dead. She told us the story of how Dickey had paid for her accordion lessons when her own family didn't believe the accordion could do "diddly squat" for a heroin addiction. "The accordion saved my life," she said all teary eyed. "Dickey even wrote me letters of accordion encouragement from prison. He was good to me, and you people should respect that."

Uncle Benny lit up his stogy.

"We should call Angelo Conti over at Conti's funeral parlor," Aunt Hetty said. "They do a nice job on a body, even one with a bullet hole in its head. I bet if we slipped Angelo a couple extra grand he wouldn't say nothing about that bullet hole to the cops. Times are tough these days in the funeral business. People are going eco friendly and cremating their loved ones or burying them in biodegradable coffins they buy at Wal-Mart. Not much of a profit in a biodegradable coffin."

"We're not calling Angelo Conti," Uncle Ray declared. "This is a family matter. The Contis aren't family. Can't trust 'em."

"Let's just call the police," I said, finally ready for this to be over with. Of course, there was one minor thing I had to do before they arrived . . . remove my mom's handgun from the futso. I justified this little act of felony with the absolute certainty that she had nothing to do with his murder and would only put the police on the wrong track.

Uncle Ray said, "The cops'll think it was a community killin' or something equally as stupid and it'll ruin everything we've worked for. Hell, the newspapers and cable news might get wind of this and some of our old enemies could crawl outta the woodwork lookin' for a little revenge. Then where will we be? No, the best thing to do is to bury the bastard and be done with it."

"I agree with Ray," Uncle Benny said. "Cops will just bring trouble to the family, and the one thing we do not need is more trouble. I vote we get a place ready under that big olive tree next to the barn."

"One thing's for sure," Uncle Ray said as he hunched down to get another look at Dickey, "none of us here clipped the bastard. We ain't stupid enough to shit where we eat."

"Not unless one of you wanted to get even and set somebody up," I said.

Federico looked over at me, his face in a bunch. "You don't know what you're talking about. Nobody here would do that. We're family."

Uncle Ray stood. "I'm getting' a bad feeling about this. We need to move him outta here. Now."

"But wouldn't you like to know who killed him?" Lisa asked.

Okay, not the best thing to say, at least not in this crowd. If one of their own clipped him, then let sleeping dogs lie would be their motto. If that person didn't want to come forward and turn themselves in, which was highly doubtful, or disappear on their own, then so be it. The problem was if any of them learned who did it, then they'd have to turn that person in or risk their own freedom. No way did any of these born-again angels want to take another trip on the dark side. They were into the legitimate business of olive oil now, and they intended to keep it that way.

The silence was palpable. No one moved, or breathed for that matter. Lisa was an outsider, and even though she'd been my best friend practically since I took my first step, an outsider didn't interfere in family business.

With those few words, it was as if my family finally realized her presence, as if all this time they hadn't completely focused in on her. But now they did, and from the look on their collective faces, I could tell they wanted her gone and fast.

It was my turn to say something. "Lisa's right. And besides, she's the one who found Dickey first, so her DNA is all over this place. She's a stand-up girl, you all know that, and now she's just as much of a suspect as the rest of us."

I looked around for a nod of acceptance, a wink of hope, something that told me they weren't going to unilaterally shun her for the rest of time, but all I got were blank stares. No expressions. No tells. Not even a twitch, which, for my family, wasn't completely bad news.

She leaned in and whispered, "Thank you for that. Up until now I thought I was merely an eye witness to the aftermath of a crime, but now that I'm a suspect I'll sleep easier."

"Sorry, but I had to defend you," I told her.

"Is that what that was?"

I nodded, shrugged and gave her a little smile.

Uncle Ray said, "I only talked to Dickey once all night when he was lookin' for a wine opener. He told me he couldn't stick around long. He had one thing to do and once that was done he was headin' back to the city in the morning."

"What time was that?" I asked thinking I should get some kind of timeline going.

"I don't know. I gave up watchin' the clock when I retired," he growled. "But I was glad to hear it. I didn't want him hanging around here any longer than necessary."

"Are we talking daylight or night?" I asked.

"Still daylight. That I can say for sure. Those little lights wasn't on yet, 'cause I remember lookin' at 'em thinkin' how we should hang some more."

"I opened his wine bottle. Russo's Pinot Noir," Aunt Babe said, the sound of her heels clicking up behind Uncle Ray. "Poured out two glasses, one for him and one for me. I was figuring on getting him to spill on what he wanted by coming here, but all he could talk about was how sorry he was for two-timing me. Crazy to see him so sappy over the past. Never thought the day would come."

"How long did you two chat?"

"Two glasses worth. Honey, when a goodfella is spilling his guts a dame aughta listen."

"That bastard was playing you, Babe. Men like that ain't never sorry about what they done," Valerie said. "I saw the two of you talking and I knew just by watching the prick that he didn't mean nothing he was saying. He was born mean, and there wasn't nothing that could change that. Don't forget he bit off his own mother's nipple when her milk went dry. He was bad to the bone, Babe, and all that sorry shit he was feeding you was just bullshit, plain and simple."

"You're still carrying your own grudge against him, Val. Won't do you any good now. He's dead," Aunt Babe said.

"About time. I was thinking about burning him myself, but somebody beat me to it. Good thing, too, 'cause I wasn't looking forward to makin' that decision."

"What was the grudge?" I asked Val.

"That's something better left with the dead," she answered,

tossing me a dismissive look.

"Don't tread on the past, Mia," Federico warned in a quiet voice, leaning into me. "It can lead where you don't want to go. Especially in this family."

He gave me a wink and a friendly smile, but I couldn't make out if he was talking about our family or giving me some kind of warning about Valerie.

Then just when I was about to ask Benny about the evening, my mother's voice rang through the barn. "Mia, honey," she yelled sounding phony sweet. "You might want to come out here, like right away. Leonardo is here and he brought that nice young man from the Sheriff's Department, Nick Zeleski."

"Cops!" Uncle Ray spit out, and my family scattered like roaches in a spotlight, each taking their own route to the nearest exit.

My stomach clenched and I actually contemplated running out with them. Lisa grabbed my arm, firmly. Her eyes went wide, the only indication that she might be anxious. "We need to remember to breathe," she said, taking in a deep breath then slowly letting it out. "In times of strife it's best to remain calm."

"Are you quoting yourself?"

"Yes. The introduction to my first book: your survival depends on a clear head, and you can't have one if you don't take in enough oxygen."

We filled our lungs with a combination of cigar smoke and fear. The toxic combination caused a chain reaction and we both coughed at the same time as we quickly headed toward the opposite door from where my family had escaped from, toward my mom, Leo and Nick Zeleski—the mouth of the dragon.

"Mia, did you hear me, dear? Are you coming out soon? Because the boys are coming in if you don't?" I could hear the edge to my mom's voice.

"No!" I squeaked out. "We'll be right out. We're on our way

right now."

Lisa followed close behind me as we hurried to the door. "Wait," she said pulling on my arm. "Mia, we forgot your mom's gun."

Dread raced through me. How could I have been so stupid! "I'll run back and get it. Stall them," I told her.

"How? I don't even like Leo, remember?"

"Just tell him I'm bringing out a few bottles of oil for him, or tell him about your latest book. I don't know. You're the writer. Make something up."

She cocked her head, shrugged and spun around towards the door.

I started to turn back, but it was too late.

"Hey, kitten," Leo said, suddenly appearing in front us, his voice all sexy and low, reminding me of how much I missed him.

And that's when it hit me—when I saw Leo standing next to a tall, curly haired stranger with the sapphire blue eyes. I flashed back on that afternoon, seeing Leo standing out on his veranda with another man, an older man, a man in a golden shirt, the man who had slapped Leo's hand away. That man had been my cousin Dickey.

The stranger said, "You hiding something from us in here or what?"

Fainting is a curious thing. It comes upon you in a rush of darkness and in that instant before you lose consciousness you're absolutely sure somebody has turned out all the lights.

"Don't! Stop! Don't! Stop! Don't stop! Don't stop!"
—Olive Oyl, Gym Jam

SEVEN

Enter the Dragon

The good news was I didn't actually faint, at least not flat out on the floor. I merely lost my balance for an instant, slumped, and fell into Leo's eager arms. If I had planned this moment of feminine weakness, the game couldn't have gone better. My "episode," as it would later be referred to, caused one of those turn of events that truly amazed me.

"Let's get her outside for some air," Nick Zeleski said.

And with that, my entire outlook brightened, plus it gave me a strong lesson in feminine wiles. A trait Aunt Babe had always professed as our strongest defense against male dominance.

I played the part well, allowing Leo to slowly walk me out of the barn while I leaned into his fabulously muscled body. I felt safe and warm walking next to him surrounded by his familiar scent—a mixture of red wine, sweet grapes and a whole lotta trouble. The grape scent was even sweeter as I pressed my body up against his. I wanted to be swept up and taken off to his bed and made love to until my bones ached and I could no longer breathe.

The truth was that whenever I saw Leo all I ever wanted was to be in his bed, part of my irrational Leonardo obsession, my therapists had said. Right now, separate from the desire to be naked with him, I wanted to tell him about dead cousin Dickey, and I wanted to ask him what went on during his conversation with Dickey that morning.

But mostly, as I leaned into him and felt his arm around my waist, and his playful fingers pressing against my body, I wanted the two of us to be back together again.

Lisa must have sensed what was swirling around inside my head because when I gazed over at her once we were out of the barn she threw me one of those "you can't be serious" looks and it was then that reality hit me right between the eyes.

"Thanks," I mumbled, moving away from Leo and my momentary delusions. "I feel better. Must have been something I ate."

"Or drank," he joked, but I didn't react. My drinking problem wasn't up for ridicule, especially not with him.

"Always the wise guy," Lisa quipped.

"Hardly, I believe that title better suits some of the characters who just bugged out of the barn. I'm just a lowly wine maker who sometimes oversteps his bounds." He turned to me. "Sorry, Mia, but you had me worried for a minute. I guess a bad joke is my way of breaking the tension. I can be a real ass, but then you already know that."

I gave him a guarded nod and let out the breath I'd been holding. That's when I finally realized he was clean shaven. No beard or unkempt hair like I'd seen that morning. He was back to his usual, neat self.

We were now standing in my mom's front yard. Everyone had gone except for my mom, Uncle Benny and Aunt Babe who sat in white rocking chairs on my mom's porch talking, laughing as if they were oblivious to the fact there was a murdered cousin in our barn and a cop standing not more than ten feet from the murder scene.

Nick said, "I think the entire valley knows what an ass you are, but they tolerate you because your wine is so good. If you didn't have that they'd have shunned you years ago." He turned to Lisa and stuck out his hand. "Hi, I'm Nick. Don't hold it against me that he's my friend. It's a childhood phenomenon. I'm an only child, and he's the closest thing to a brother I'm ever going to have."

Lisa took his hand in hers and in that instant I could see the attraction in her eyes. They were always her one tell, at least for me. I didn't think anyone else noticed, but I always could, especially when she was fascinated by a guy. It was as if an inner glow radiated from her eyes. Those almond eyes of hers actually sparkled and the smile she threw Nick was genuine.

Problem was the man oozed law enforcement—from his clean-shaven face to his spit-shined black shoes. Not that he wasn't easy to look at with those baby blues, and that dark blond hair flecked with golden highlights, a sharp nose and dark lashes that if, they were on a girl, they'd have to be fake. He wore a charcoal-gray knit shirt, black slacks and a smile that could melt even Lisa's cynical heart.

Still, his timing couldn't be worse, and I had no idea why he and Leo would show up when Leo was never invited. But the real question of the moment was why the hell didn't I ever hear about Nick before?

"But Leo grew up here in the valley," I said, then turned to Leo. "You never mentioned Nick before."

"Didn't I?" He shrugged. "I must have mentioned the summers I spent with my aunt Sophia?"

That I remembered. "Wasn't she the one who forced you to learn Italian, and to cook, do your own laundry and essentially how to survive without the hired help?"

"None other. She also never spoke English in her house. It drove me crazy. Half the time I didn't know what the hell she was saying. Nick saved my ass. He and I would get lost every afternoon, after my endless chores were done and I'd memorized my daily allowance of Italian."

Lisa said, "My mother did that to me with Chinese. I hated it back then, but now I appreciate knowing the language."

But that didn't explain Nick. This man was a dyed-in-the-wool cop. I could feel it. "So how did you two meet? I thought Sophia never let you out of her sight."

"She knew his dad from church, so I had an in. The good thing about Nick's dad—he wasn't anything like Sophia. The bad thing—he was the local Sheriff. We didn't get away with anything. Probably what kept me out of real trouble and probably why my mom sent me to Wisconsin every summer, especially when I was a teenager. But that's enough about us. We came here to see the man of the hour, Dickey. Where is he? I brought over a case of wine. A couple bottles of our Pinot included. But what's up with the Spia clan? I've never seen them move so fast."

"Yeah," Nick said. "I'd like to meet Dickey. Didn't see him leave with the rest of the folks."

"Why?" I asked, desperately trying to remain calm. "Somehow I'd gotten the impression this was a social call."

Nick smiled, but it was more of a smirk than a smile. "No reason. Just wanted to ask him a few questions. Get to know the locals, that sort of thing. I've only been in the valley for a couple weeks and haven't had a chance to get to meet many people. When Leo mentioned this party, I thought it would be a great opportunity."

"I bet you did," I mumbled more to myself than to Nick.

"Come again?"

Fortunately, he didn't hear me and I decided not to repeat myself. One absolute fact this family had taught me: never trust a cop when he/she gives an innocuous answer. Sure sign the cop was hiding something.

"So, where's Dickey?" Leo asked. He was all smiles, as if seeing Dickey—again—was some big deal.

"He's around here somewhere, I'm sure," Lisa stated with all the coolness of a trained liar. I wondered where that trait had come from, but perhaps I didn't really want to know.

"Great," Leo said. "I was thinking he might have slipped out with the rest of your family, but if you say he's still around then we'll wait. I'd like to finally meet the guy."

"I'm confused. You already met him. I'm sure that was you and Dickey out on the front porch of your tasting room this morning."

"You already know the guy?" Nick asked.

"Me? No. I've heard stories about him for years, but never met him. Besides I was in a meeting for most of the morning. That couldn't have been me you saw. He was there, all right. Bought a case of our wine, but I never saw the guy." He said this with a straight face, a face I'd seen many times before, but could never read. That was before our last breakup. I'd learned some things about him since then. I was sure this was his big-fat-lie face: calm, no expression other than a hint of surprise that a stranger could never pick up, but I was certain I saw it in his eyes now. That flicker of guilt. It was only there for a moment, but this time I'd caught it.

That explained the Russo wine at the party. Dickey had brought it, proof positive that he'd been the man on the porch. But why would Leo lie about it? What was he hiding, and was he hiding it from me or from Nick? I had to know, but apparently I wasn't going to get at the truth any time soon.

At that point the only thing I could do was smile and lead them to the chairs on the front lawn, away from the barn. I'd have to think of how to sneak back into it later to retrieve the gun.

Nick seemed like one of those cops who never went off duty, always carried a weapon and would turn in his own father at the hint of a crime. I wondered if he saw the lie in Leo's eyes or was it just something I could see.

And, did he suspect Lisa and I were hiding something?

We'd have to be extra careful.

Just as we reached the chairs Lisa gazed down at her diamond studded watch. "I better get going. I have to get up early for . . .

something important."

"But—" I stammered.

"Yeah," she let out a phony little yawn. "Too bad. I really would like to stay and chat, but it's getting late." She looked at the guys. "Nice to meet you, Nick. I'm sure we'll run into each other again." She tossed Leo a cool nod. He returned the nod and added a sheepish grin. I could tell she wasn't receptive to his affable gesture.

"It's not even nine o'clock. Since when is that late?" I asked.

"Since I have to get up early and do that . . . thing."

"What thing?"

"That thing we talked about in the barn. I have to go," she said and walked toward her car.

I left the guys and followed close behind her. When we were out of earshot I said, "Oh, no you don't. You can't just walk away from this and leave me here. Alone. With a dead cousin, a meddlesome cop and my human addiction. I need you. You're my best friend and best friends stick together in sickness and in health, for better or worse, till death—" I stopped myself.

She turned. "You have it right, sweetie. Till death and since there's been a death that gives me an out, so I'm taking it."

She secured her bag over her shoulder and continued walking toward her car.

"But you can't go," I demanded while trying to think of a compelling reason other than I didn't want to go through this without her. Then just as she was about to open the wooden gate to the private parking area next to the barn a chilling thought flew into my head. "It might be dangerous for you go off on your own."

That did it. She swung back around, and walked back toward me, a look of concern on her face. "Define dangerous."

"Isn't that rather obvious?"

"Not really. I've known your family my whole life. They

wouldn't hurt me."

"Collectively, no they probably wouldn't, but one of them killed Dickey and since you were first on the scene that person doesn't know what you saw. You may have spotted just the clue that could finger the killer."

"The killer wouldn't even consider this if you hadn't blabbed my finding Dickey to everyone." She planted a hand on her hip, a sure sign she was angry.

"The killer would've found out anyway once the police got involved."

Her eyes narrowed. "This is getting way too deep for my comfort zone."

"Oh, and it's not too deep for me?"

"You grew up with this kind of madness."

"Not up close and personal. I was always sheltered from the realities."

Which was basically a true statement. I always knew most of my family was mobbed up, but I never knew the exact extent of it. Still don't, and from the looks of things, that fact might be changing rather quickly.

"Well, you're all grown up now and the family wants to bring you into its bosom. In case you haven't noticed, I'm Chinese. I fit the job description. Your family and mine don't quite mesh."

"You and I do. Always have, and I'm hoping always will. And besides, this will make the perfect survival book." I thought I'd try to appeal to her artistic nature, or at the very least, her desire to remain on the best seller list. Her head twisted slightly, dark eyes peered out at me as if I'd hit a nerve. I knew I had. She was a sucker for good copy.

"Surviving the Mob, that just might work if I can come up with the right angle," she said, dreamily, as if she could already see the book on a shelf.

"Anything you want. Just name it. I have secrets."

Her right eyebrow arched. "No you don't. Not from me. I can get anything I want out of you."

Okay, so she knew me better than I knew myself. "I can't do this on my own. At least help me get the gun out of the futso and come up with a plan. You're in this now. You're part of this murder."

"No I'm not. I can claim—" She stopped and looked at me. I guess I must have seemed exceptionally desperate because all at once her entire demeanor changed. "My mother always said you were a bad influence."

"You should have listened to her."

"I couldn't. We were already best friends."

"And we still are . . . aren't we?"

She hesitated, dropped her hand from her hip and said, "What do you want me to do?"

Those few words made me so happy, I hugged her and while we were hugging I said, "First off, Leo was lying about this morning. I know that was him talking to Dickey on his veranda."

"Why does that not surprise me? But why would he lie? What does it mean?"

"It means he has some kind of connection with Dickey that he doesn't want to admit to."

"But you couldn't have been the only person who saw them this morning. It's a busy winery."

"Exactly, and Leo had a full beard this morning, along with long hair. At first I didn't even recognize him."

"Are you sure it was him?"

I refused to second guess myself. For once I was going to stand by my Leo convictions.

"I know his body and his gestures all too well. It was Leo all right."

"Then the man is hiding something, but what?"

"I don't know, and I hope it doesn't have anything to do with the murder. We'll have to figure that out later, right now we need to get rid of him and Nick, retrieve the gun, call the police and tell them everything we know, except for the bracelet and gun part."

"What about the weird-Leo part?"

I considered that for a moment. "I'd like to talk to him about it first."

"This is so wrong."

I pulled away from her. "I know, but it's only wrong for a little while. Just until we can find out who did this."

"And just how do you intend to do that in this family? These people go to the grave defending their secrets."

"Yeah, I know, but most of this group either turned state's evidence or went straight after their time behind bars. They're more likely to come clean."

"So is that why Dickey took a bullet in his head? Because of his willingness to come clean?"

"Hadn't thought of that one, but I'm sure we can figure it out as we go along. There's one more thing I need to tell you, but it shouldn't matter. Not really."

"Out with it."

"There's a ring that my mom had been keeping for Dickey. I gave it to him right before the party and he told me it was going to give someone heartburn. It was the way he said it . . . as if someone in the group was really going to respond to seeing it. Well, when I was under that stone, I checked out Dickey's pinky, and it was gone."

"Maybe it flew off or something, or it was in his pocket for safe keeping."

I shook my head. "I don't think so. His finger was covered in oil and there was an oil stain on his shirt and jacket. I remember he had a hard time getting it over his knuckle. I'm thinking whoever took it couldn't get it off right away, so they slathered on the oil after he was under that stone."

She stared at me for what seemed like a long time. Then she said, "This is good. We have a real clue and a trail to follow. Somebody went to a lot of trouble for that ring."

"The killer?"

"More than likely."

I had another idea. "Or somebody else could have grabbed the ring before we found him."

"Either way it gives us a starting point."

Finally, an opening in her closed mind.

"You said us. Does that mean you're in the game?"

She hesitated for a moment, playing with the strap on her purse. "I know I'm going to regret this, but okay. I'll help, but if I get knocked off in the process, I'll come back and haunt you. I'll make you read all my books, even the ones that were never published."

"How many do you have?" I was thinking this might not be an even deal, not that there was any possibility that Lisa would get knocked off, but still . . .

She snickered. "A lot. Not everything I write gets published. It should, but the editors don't always love what I give them. I personally don't get it, but such is publishing. Deal?" She stuck out her hand.

"Deal," I said, giving her our girly-girl handshake. Then we hugged again. Such was our ritual ever since we saw Sister Mary Benedict, our second grade teacher, give Miss Carson, the music teacher, a limp girly-girl handshake when she agreed to allow Miss Carson to teach the students how to read music. Sister Mary Benedict had sealed our fate for the next four years with the limpest of handshakes. Lisa and I assumed that was the correct female handshake. It wasn't until we were well into our teens that we learned otherwise, but she and I never changed that handshake. It was our way of making a sacred pact.

For the next couple of hours, Lisa and I tried to get Nick and Leo to leave. Nothing seemed to work, and at some point Lisa began to show real interest in Nick, in that I-could-date-you sort of way. I just sat there stressing.

At one point, I played the sleepy hostess trying to get them to leave, yawning, stretching, even stating that I needed sleep. Everyone ignored me.

We still had the minor problem of Dickey's body to contend with, and Lisa was acting as if it didn't exist. Either she was the best actress I'd ever seen, or she simply forgot about it. Neither of which satisfied my burning desire to come clean or run, I couldn't decide which would be more effective under the circumstances.

I thought about disappearing into the barn, grabbing the gun, hiding it somewhere then screaming as if I'd just found the body. A simple, straightforward plan. One that seemed to fit the evening, considering that both Nick and Leo were determined to wait for a dead man, but every time I stood, Leo took the opportunity to try to get me alone. Any other time I would be thrilled to have all his attention, something he rarely gave, but not now. Not when I was trying to save my mother from a life sentence in Soledad.

When Leo opened the bottles of his prize winning Pinot Noir, my mom and Aunt Babe stepped off the porch to join us. Mom wore one of her expressionless grins, which had me wondering what she knew—had Aunt Babe told her everything?—but no matter how hard I tried, I couldn't get her attention, so getting a read on her was impossible.

Botox had its advantages.

Uncle Benny didn't join us. He hadn't really moved from his perch in the rocking chair, except once when he and my mom disappeared inside the house for about a half-hour. Uncle Federico went in the house with them for awhile, but then he came out and walked off toward his house, wishing us a good night. Other than that, Uncle Benny sat in his chair watching, puffing and rocking. About the only body part of his body that moved was his hand to remove his cigar from his mouth so he could take a swig of wine, then he'd replace the cigar and stared at us once again. It would have been creepy if I didn't know there was a body in the barn, which in the scheme of things was far creepier.

Then my mom got into the forties thing along with Aunt Babe, who began reciting whole scenes from noir films. Nick admitted to being a huge fan, which only fueled the Barbara Stanwyck fire. Of course, Lisa played right into it with her own extensive background in classic films.

I sat in silence wondering if Lisa and I would be sharing the same jail cell since it was obvious we were all doomed to a life of judicial confinement.

Aunt Babe said, "I've got one: Yes I love him. I love those hick shirts he wears with the boiled cuffs and the way he always has his vest buttoned wrong. He looks like a giraffe, and I love him."

Nick jumped up from his chair. "Wait, I know that one!"

Lisa nudged his arm. "Too slow. I've got it. Ball of Fire, nineteen-forty-one, Stanwyck and Cooper, and she's a showgirl with the regal name of—"

"Sugarpuss O'Shea," Nick bellowed.

"You know that?" Lisa asked, obviously impressed by Nick's knowledge of movie facts.

He nodded. "Named a stray cat Sugarpuss right after I first saw the film."

Leo said, "So that's where that name came from. I thought it was because . . . when you're ten everything is sexual innuendo."

"And when you're thirty-two?" I asked.

"Everything still has sexual innuendo, honey. It's what spins the globe," Aunt Babe chided, while sipping her wine.

I couldn't take the tension anymore and decided to slip away while everyone was playing the "name that movie" game. The night had succeeded in giving me a royal headache, and unless I got rid of that handgun soon my head was going to explode.

I walked to the barn via my mom's house. I figured everyone would think I was simply making a bathroom run. I walked across the lawn, up the front steps, past Uncle Benny who gave me a slight nod, through the living room, past my mom's room, made a quick pit stop in the bathroom and downed a couple aspirin, continued through the kitchen, which still housed an abundance of food and baked goods, and walked directly out the back door. This time the lure of the cookies couldn't deter my mission. In truth, their sweet smell sickened me, the complete opposite of my normal response to anything baked with sugar and fat.

I made a beeline straight for the barn, jogging across the small gravel parking area, which was now eerily devoid of my relatives' cars. Of course, Lisa's red BMW was still there, and Leo's Mercedes XL was tucked in close to the barn alongside a black BMW SUV, which had to belong to Cousin Dickey, the now deceased Cousin Dickey.

My head throbbed with a vengeance. Apparently, it was going to take more than two aspirin to quell what was going on in my overtaxed head.

When I opened the barn door, it suddenly occurred to me that I had made no plan for the handgun once I retrieved it. Where would I hide the damn thing? I didn't have a pocket deep enough that wouldn't announce hand-gun, and if I moved it somewhere else in the barn, the police would eventually find it.

This deception game was getting entirely too complicated. The bracelet was one thing—I still had it tucked away in my pocket—but that handgun required some creative thinking. Besides it would be dripping with olive oil.

Just as I reached for the light switch, I heard a car door slam, and the distinct sound of footsteps crunching up behind me across the gravel. I hoped it was Uncle Benny coming to assist with my handgun dilemma, but when I turned and saw Leo only a few feet away carrying a case of his wine, the Russo name prominent on the deep red logo, my heat skipped a beat.

Now what?

"Hey," he called out. "Your mom insisted that I couldn't just leave this wine without taking some oil in return. I tried to talk her out of it, but you know how she can be. Once she makes up her mind, there's no room for debate." He balanced the box up on his right shoulder as he walked in closer. "I hear you've got a couple new oils I haven't tried so I decided not to fight her. She said they're stored in the middle of the barn on the right, if that makes any sense. Maybe you could show me."

My mouth went dry. My mom had sent Leo to the exact murder spot.

I froze for a moment trying to think of what to say, what to do. Then, without hesitation, I did the only thing I could think of to keep him from taking another step into the barn.

I leaned in and kissed him.

EIGHT

And Then There Was None

Leo's mouth tasted sweet and familiar, and when his tongue touched mine, those old feelings flooded my body with intense desire. I wanted him so much it hurt; funny how something so bad for you could feel so damn good. I pressed my body up against his as tight as I could, going for all the sensations I could stand and still not lose my cool, although if it went on much longer I'd be pleading with him to take me on the floor. The kiss lasted until I was on the brink of complete surrender, with enough heat between us to power half the county. My only holdout in all of this was the simple fact that he couldn't combine his kiss with an embrace, because if he could it would have been all over.

Leo still held onto the case of wine, thank you very much.

When he pulled away, there was a look of both uncertainty and lust on his beautiful face.

The good news was my headache had vanished.

The bad news was I wanted more of him.

Much more. I took a few steps backward.

"Where are you going with this, Mia? I thought we were through, forever, this time. I'm quoting," he said, looking all flushed putting the box down and walking toward me looking totally hot and sexy, a look I could never resist.

I held up both hands and gently pushed on his chest, stopping him from getting any closer. "We are through. We both know that. So why did you stop by tonight?" I asked, knees weak, the taste of him still caressing my lips.

He was so close I could feel the heat coming off his body.

I wanted him more than I had ever wanted him before. My body ached for his touch.

"You invited me," he said in his raspy bedroom voice while gently running two fingers down my cheek then over my swollen lips. I stopped breathing and walked in closer, nodding, longing to be wrapped tight in his arms, kissing him, loving him . . . "Wait, what did you say?"

"You invited me," he repeated.

That broke the spell. I moved to the other side of the doorway. "Where did you get that idea?"

He looked genuinely confused.

"My assistant left a message that a woman called inviting me to the party. I naturally assumed it was you. Wasn't it?"

I didn't reply.

He went on despite my silence. "Plus she said that you wanted to buy two cases of red wine, and could I please bring them? You know I would never take your money for my wine. Whatever you want, kitten, it's yours."

He moved in closer, but this time when I took a step back I was thinking someone had gone to a lot of trouble to get Leo to come to the party. But why?

"I'm sorry I was so late, but I had a dinner party that I couldn't blow off. Two wine critics from Italy. I know how the Spia parties usually go well into the night, so I didn't think my timing would be that far off. Obviously, I was wrong. I left you a message that I'd be late. Didn't you get it?"

"No. Sorry, it was a busy day." How could I have missed his call? This wasn't making any sense, unless he was lying again.

I had to find out the truth in all of this. I didn't want to believe that Leo could somehow be mixed up in Dickey's murder.

Leo flung the box off his shoulder. "I need to put this down. I have one more case out in the car. It's our Muscato and Chardonnay blend. I brought it especially for your mom. I know how much she likes a sweeter wine."

"You can leave the wine here," I said, standing directly in front of him. "I'll take care of it later."

He peered around me. I knew there wasn't one empty shelf. They were all filled with rows of our bottled extra virgin oils, and our flavored vinegars. If he left the wine on the floor it would be in the way of the doorway. This was becoming a problem. He readjusted the box in his hands. "That's not looking like a good idea. I'll just put this down where—"

"No!" I said with a little too much force. He ducked, as if he was bracing for some kind of attack. I took in a breath and let it out, trying for what Lisa had said about a clear head and breathing. "Tell you what, I'll take this inside while you run out for the other case." I reached over for the case of wine, hoping to have just enough time to retrieve the handgun while he was busy getting the other case out of his car.

But he pulled back just as I heard my mom's laughter closing in on us. "That's okay. I've got it," he protested.

I tried to rip the case out of Leo's hands, but he held tight. My mother was getting closer, which was bad enough until I heard Nick Zeleski say, "I'd like that, Mrs. Spia, thanks."

And just like that, my mom and Nick walked right in the barn, past Leo and me and headed straight for Cousin Dickey. It happened so fast I didn't have time to react. Once my mother had someone interested in our oil, there was no stopping her. She was like a one woman campaign for the benefits of olive oil, and heaven help anyone who got in her way . . . me included.

"It's also great for dry skin and dandruff, and—" But I wasn't hearing her anymore. Lisa had entered the barn, shaking her head and mouthing that she was sorry.

I wanted to yell for my mom to come back. Surely she had to know about Dickey, but she was acting as if it didn't matter. Yet another reason to believe the shooter was trying to set her up for the fall. After all, no killer would purposely lead an officer to the crime scene knowing the evidence could potentially give her a death sentence. At least that's what I was thinking as my mom cavalierly walked toward the crime scene.

Then as if it wasn't bad enough that Nick was headed right for bumped-off Dickey, Leo had also slipped away and gone off toward the crime scene. Was there no justice in this world? Was I completely powerless over these people?

I reached out for Lisa's hand and waited for my mom's scream. Fake or not, I figured Mom would do a good job of reacting to the grizzly sight.

"You realize that as of this moment, my life is over," I told Lisa.

"No worries, sweetie. I'll bring you reading material in prison," she quipped.

"How can you joke when my whole life has come down to this moment? When everything my mom and I have worked so hard to achieve is about to come crashing down on our heads?"

"Who said I was joking? I read somewhere that boredom was the toughest thing for Paris Hilton to endure while she was behind bars. That, and her inability to get a pedicure. I figure reading is so out of your realm that it might be the one thing that keeps you sane."

"Is that all you think about, books and reading?"

"Pretty much."

She squeezed my hand tighter and threw me a smile. I knew she was just as scared as I was, but Lisa never liked to display fear. She thought it was a sign of true feminine weakness.

We stood waiting for my mom's scream for what seemed like hours or at the very least five minutes.

Nothing.

We waited some more, and then we heard a familiar sound rippling through the barn like a sonic boom . . . laughter. My mom's high-pitched, crazy laugh bounced off the walls and pierced my ears.

"I've known your mom for a long time, and this is so not what I expected from her," Lisa said.

"Maybe this is how she reacts to a gruesome scene. I mean, I've never been around my mother in this kind of situation."

The laughter grew louder and suddenly Leo's deep belly laugh joined in along with Nick's chortle.

"What the hell?" I said.

But Lisa had already released my hand and was headed toward the happy group. I had no choice but to follow.

When we reached the threesome, they were standing exactly where only a few hours ago a very dead Cousin Dickey had been lying on the floor bleeding from his head, gazing up at the wrong end of a millstone. Now, the antique millstone was upright and reassembled, the floor was spotless, and all the futsi were lined up in a row. Was my mom's weapon still at the bottom of a futso or had that been removed as well? It was as if nothing had ever happened.

The site was so startling that I half expected to see Dickey standing next to my mom wearing a wide toothy grin.

I was dumbstruck.

Cool-headed Lisa spoke for me. "Can we get in on the joke or is this a private matter?"

"Oh honey, you had to be here," my mom said, and they all started laughing again, my mom really getting into it with tears in her eyes to prove it.

I, in the meantime, was busy checking out the floor, the table, under the table for any trace of a murder, but the place looked cleaner than it normally did. Everything was spotless, too spotless, as if an entire crew of janitors swept through for some kind of cleanliness inspection.

My mind drifted to the old olive tree just outside the barn. Had Dickey been moved out there? Was he now one with nature?

The visual made me a bit claustrophobic, not to mention angry that my family had taken matters into their own hands despite my adamant opposition to the entire affair.

"Wow," Nick said after the laughter finally subsided. He was staring directly in front of the antique millstone, the now totally reassembled antique millstone.

The same mill that had crushed Dickey under its incredible weight, and the same mill that Dickey himself had imported from Italy. "Is this what you use to crush the olives?" Nick walked in to get a closer look.

"We'd never have gone commercial if we used that old thing," Mom said. "No, that's just for show." She turned to me. "Mia, sweetheart, I thought we agreed to move it out front? Wasn't somebody out here just yesterday tearing it down? Did you change your mind?"

I wasn't sure how to answer that. "No, yes, I mean, hmmm. I don't know exactly what happened with that. Maybe the guys couldn't figure it out. It's kind of complicated."

Nick studied the mechanism. "It seems like it's just a couple long screws. The trick is handling the weight once the stone is free. You'll need four strong men to lift this wheel. No one guy could move this alone."

"A forklift with a large bed could handle it. I've got one. You want me to send somebody over tomorrow to move it?"

"That would be so nice of you, Leonardo. Mia's been wanting this thing moved for months now." She turned to me. "Isn't he a dear?"

I smiled. "A dear, but thanks. We have a forklift of our own."

In the meantime, Nick busied himself studying the granite millstone, running his hand over the edge of the wheel, getting up close and personal. As if he sensed something wasn't quite right about it. The whole thing was making me nuts. The guy was like a bloodhound, sniffing for a scent to run with. He walked around the backside of wheel, which was almost as tall as he was. In the meantime, Mom kept talking to Leo about her latest olive oil, and the fact that our Sevillano had won the Los Angeles International Extra Virgin Olive Oil competition three years running. "Take a couple bottles. It's fabulous on toast instead of that artery clogging butter. Plus, you can drizzle it on a fresh baby spinach salad, add some candied pecans, a few slices of ripe pear, sprinkle on a good pungent gorgonzola, maybe a few dried cranberries or pomegranate seeds for color, then pour on our white balsamic vinegar and you'll have a salad to die for."

"Sounds incredible, especially with a glass of our Shiraz." He bunched his fingers together and kissed them looking oh-so-Italian. "Perfecto!"

I tracked Nick who was still busy studying the stone. "Huh," he said.

I could feel the sudden tightness crawling up the left side of my neck.

"Find something interesting?" Lisa asked.

I threw her a "what the hell are you doing" look. She ignored me and moved toward him.

"When did you say that guy was trying to dismantle this thing?" Nick peeked around the wheel, apparently asking me.

My mouth suddenly felt thick. "I believe it was yesterday. Why?"

He fingered the stone, but didn't answer my question.

"Two men stopped by today, honey," my mother said. "Late this afternoon. I completely forgot about that. Two darling men, before you came home, wanting to take another look. I don't know what they did in here. I was too busy with last minute party details, but they were in here for at least fifteen or twenty minutes. Right before they left, the shorter one, with the thick Italian accent, told me he needed more equipment and one more man to move it, even with our forklift. He said he would return tomorrow, or was it the day after tomorrow? Whatever. All I remember is him saying he couldn't do it today."

"That might explain it then," Nick said, stepping out from behind the stone.

"Explains what?" I needed to know.

"There's some blood on the mill, not a lot, but it looks fresh. One of the men must have cut himself on one of those screws trying to take this thing apart. Those screws look nasty."

"I'll have to call the company tomorrow and see if they're all right," I said, relieved that Nick had come to his own innocuous conclusion. "I wouldn't want anyone suing us."

"So that's what happened," my mother mused.

Nick jumped on that little statement. "What's that, Mrs. Spia?"

"Oh, call me Gloria, dear. I saw them right before they left, and one of them had a piece of cloth wrapped around his index finger. I didn't even think to ask what had happened. I suppose that doesn't say much about me. At any rate, I bet that poor man cut himself on those nasty screws and didn't want to tell me."

"Maybe that's it," I alleged, then changed the subject. "Nick, you can't leave without a few bottles of our oil."

He gave me a tepid smile as he walked out from behind the millstone. "Actually, I've been eyeing those steel containers. Can I buy one of those? I do a lot of cooking."

He might as well have stuck a knife into my neck for all the pain that little statement caused. "The smallest we have is three liters." I grabbed one of the empty futso that sat on a shelf next to me, but he kept eyeing the larger ones, the one that contained my mom's handgun in particular. I knew which one it was by the oil smear along the side. Whoever put everything back missed the smear.

I walked over to him, carrying the empty futso, ready to put the thing in his hand and lead the entire group out of the barn. I'd had enough fun for one night. It was way past my bedtime.

"We can fill this up on the way out," I told him while angling toward the door.

But he wanted no part of me or my tiny futso. Instead he glommed onto the very futso that could potentially hold my mom's handgun. Like I said, the man was all cop.

"This should work," he said, grinning.

My mother's eyes lit up. The combination of that thirty-liter futso, plus the oil it contained, was worth several hundred dollars. "Because you're a friend of Leo's I can give you a good deal on that," she cooed.

"No!" I said, tripping over Leo to get to Nick, arms flailing, feet stumbling over feet. "You can't."

But Lisa was next to him holding onto it before I could get there.

"What Mia is trying to say is that I already bought this particular one for my family. We own a restaurant in Chinatown, and we're always running out of oil. This will be great. Really great." She tapped the spigot on the futso.

"But honey, maybe you should stick to our Mission Blend, the Italian Blend might be too peppery for Chinese food," my mother said. She pointed to the Mission-filled futso with both hands, as if posing for an ad. That's when I noticed the missing bracelet. She always wore a charm bracelet. Always. No matter what she wore or what event she was dressing for, one of her many charm bracelets dangled from her right wrist.

Except tonight.

I was so hoping the Elvis bracelet in my pocket had been stolen and purposely placed under Dickey. Now I didn't know what to believe.

I instantly pushed that un-daughterly thought out of my mind and focused on heaving the thirty-liter futso out of the barn, the futso that held my mom's future inside.

"Too late, Nick," I chimed in. "This one is already sold."

Lisa and I hoisted the futso by the two handles and walked it straight out of the barn, hoping everyone would follow right behind us.

We didn't stop until we got to her car where she beeped open the trunk. We hoisted it inside, tucking the stainless steel container into the mesh sling that ran across the width of the trunk, but no way would the trunk close, so we lifted it back out and stuck it on the front passenger seat. There was something on the seat that caused the futso to tip in my direction.

This was not good.

"Hold onto it," Lisa said. "I'll go around to the other side."

I held it on the seat, pushing at it slightly, but that just caused it to tip more in my direction. I moved my upper body inside the car, and held onto the teetering futso until Lisa could get to the other side.

As soon as she opened the driver's door I pulled off the top of the futso, not waiting for her to get the thing upright, and peered inside for the tiny gun.

The overhead light wasn't bright enough so I couldn't see anything but the golden liquid. The initial smell saturated my senses, tickling my throat and caused me to cough.

The futso slipped a bit when Lisa tried to dislodge whatever was under it and I angled it more toward me, managing to steady it and gain control over my annoying cough. There was no time for me to move the now heavy container, so I plunged my hand deep inside groping for the gun. Oil splashed out and felt all warm and silky against my skin. The peppery scent filled the air with its earthy fragrance. Unfortunately, I couldn't feel anything but the oil and the cool metal walls of the heavy container.

"They're coming. Hurry," Lisa warned in a loud whisper. "I can't hold onto this thing much longer. You've made it all slippery."

"I can't find it," I whispered back, now swishing both hands and arms inside the deep container. "I think it's gone."

I heard footsteps on the gravel. "That looks exceptionally kinky," Nick said now standing behind me.

His voice startled me and being completely uptight at that moment, I jumped, turned and somehow managed to swing out my hands so fast that excess oil slapped him right in the face and chest. What didn't land on him somehow landed on my pants and shirt. And as if that wasn't messy enough, Lisa must have lost her precarious hold on the futso because it tipped just enough in my direction so the oil splashed out onto his polished shoes, my suede Uggs, and down the front of Nick's pants. Then, almost in some sort of slow motion kind of weird time warp thing, the futso flipped completely on its side, and my mother's handgun slid out bounced off of Lisa's shiny red foot rail and landed at Nick's feet along with the remainder of the EVOO.

For a moment, no one said a word. I think I stopped breathing, and I'm sure my heart must have stopped pumping or why else would I have just stood there like a deer in the headlights?

I couldn't react or wouldn't react depending on how I wanted to look at this.

A brilliant thought raced through my mind as we stood there, motionless. Perhaps Nick hadn't seen or heard the little nickel-plated aggravation. Maybe it was just too dark for him to truly see anything.

And perhaps penguins could fly.

Nick squatted. The car's overhead dome light was more than ample to make the handgun stand out on the gravel. Hell, I could even read Lucille written on the handle.

"Interesting," he finally said. "A .32 from the looks of it. Nineteen-thirties, maybe. Nice touch on the handle. Seems like it's in great condition. Don't know if keeping it in that much oil is a wise choice for its future, but hey, you're the expert when it comes to olive oil."

I didn't move, but somehow managed a feeble smile.

"You know who owns this weapon?" he asked looking up at me.

I had several options to this question. I could tell him the truth. Tell him I didn't know, or tell him what had to be the dumbest, most ridiculous . . . "It's mine," both Lisa and I said at the same time.

Her eyes went wide. "We, um, share it."

"You share a handgun that you keep in a thirty liter tub of expensive olive oil?" he asked. I knew we were sounding lame, but what choice did we have?

"I'm doing research for my next book," Lisa argued.

"What kind of research?"

"The kind that has to do with guns and olive oil."

"Huh," Nick said.

That's when Leo walked over.

"Wow," he quipped, gazing around at the mess, then down at Nick. "What's your mom's gun doing lying on the ground?"

There are things you should reveal to your lover, and other things that are best kept hidden. This was one of those times when I so wished I had kept my revelation of my grandmother's passed-down handgun, and how someday my mother would pass it on to me, to myself.

Nick picked up the weapon with a pen through the trigger housing, tipped it to drain the excess oil and walked over to take a better look at it next to the light above the barn door.

"Huh," he said, again.

His "huhs" were getting annoying.

"What?" Leo asked.

"It's loaded except for one empty chamber. Now why would you keep a loaded revolver in a futsi?"

"A futso, futsi is plural. Like panino verses panini," I corrected, not knowing what else to say.

"Thanks. I'll remember that." The gun continued to drip oil. "And the fired round—did either of you shoot this recently?"

"No," I said, just as Lisa said, "Yes."

This was not going well.

He took a step back and stared at both of us. "Now, if I went on my instincts here, I'd say you ladies are hiding something. Could that be true?"

"You won't get anything out of them, Nick," Leo teased. "They've been keeping secrets from the rest of the world since they were kids. You'd have to waterboard them in order to make either one talk, and we've got the wrong president if you want to try that one."

"Oh, I don't think we have to go that far. Tell you what, I'll just take this little number with me, run a few checks on it and return it tomorrow, if you ladies don't mind."

He pulled out a plastic bag from his pants pocket, dropped the gun in it and walked off to Leo's car. No doubt about it, the man was one hundred percent cop.

I took a step forward to try to stop him, but Lisa grabbed my arm, kind of. It was too slippery for her to physically take hold of it, but I could tell she wanted me to let him go.

Leo beeped open the door from a distance and went after Nick.

"Let me handle this," Lisa said leaving me there, dripping olive oil.

I was out of options so I let her go. Besides, I really needed a shower.

Spinach and Fresh Pear Salad – Level One or Two

1 bunch of spinach and/or romaine lettuce
1 whole ripe pear, cored and peeled
3 fresh figs, green or purple (optional)
½ cup pomegranate seeds or dried cranberries
1/8 tsp. salt, depending on taste
3 cranks of cracked peppercorns
¾ cup Gorgonzola cheese (crumbled or cubed)
½ cup Koroneiki EVOO
1/8 cup white or any fruit vinegar
¾ cup candied pecans *recipe follows for level two

Clean and wash your greens then pat them dry in paper towels. This is soothing and should take you at least eight to ten minutes. Tear them in bite-sized pieces and drop them in a glass bowl. Slice the pear lengthwise into eight slices. Cut the figs into halves. Break open the pomegranate and pop out the seeds, enjoying a bite or two as you gather up your half cup. Make a mess with the sweet red seeds. The clean up will focus you. Assemble the fruit in the bowl on top of the spinach. Chill for at least a half-hour.

To turn this into a level two meal, buy pecans in the shell and take your time to carefully crack open each one and remove the shells without damaging the nutmeats.

1 pound shelled pecans halves
1 egg white
1 tbs. vanilla
½ cup white sugar
½ cup brown sugar
¾ tsp salt
½ to 1 tsp grnd cinnamon

Rub a delicate extra virgin olive oil on a baking sheet. Heat oven to 250 degrees. Slowly whip egg white with vanilla until it froths. Enjoy the vanilla bouquet. Set aside and mix the sugar, salt and cinnamon in a deep bowl, or large plastic bag. Set aside. First coat some of the pecans in the egg white mixture, remove and toss them in the sugar mixture. Spread pecans evenly on the baking sheet and roast for one hour, stirring every ten to 15 minutes.

Remove from oven and place on large platter.

Remove salad from fridge. Add oil, vinegar, salt, pepper and cheese and toss. Sprinkle five or six or ten warm pecans on top and serve with crusty warm bread, and a flavored sparkling water. This is enough for two. Eat slowly, and enjoy the flavors on your tongue, the snap of each pomegranate seed, and the crunch of sweet pecans. Take your time. Breathe. Stay focused on the food.

NINE

Oh, But It Feels So Good

I was halfway up my stairs when I heard, "Any chance we can continue where we left off?" Leo's voice came from behind and stopped me cold.

I turned to see him standing on my bottom step looking as gorgeous as ever. The motion lights over the garage door cast a sultry glow on his face and hair, making him appear even more male than he normally did. There was always something hypnotic about his face in low lights.

"Don't you have a girlfriend? A Sharley or Marley or something like that. I can't always keep up," I said.

"I did—Marlina—up until about a month ago. She went back to her fiancé. Besides, we were more friends than lovers."

"Smart girl," I said.

"Ouch," he grunted, rubbing his jaw. "But I guess I deserve that."

I shrugged. "I need a shower." Oil oozed from my Uggs with each step. I wondered if they were salvageable.

He walked up a couple steps. "I can help with that."

No doubt he could, more than I wanted to admit. We'd had some of our best sex under running water. "Not tonight. It's too soon, besides it's been a really bad day."

I turned and walked up a few more steps. He followed right behind me. "You know I can make you relax."

I stepped up on my tiny porch knowing that if he came much closer we would be sharing soap suds. "I can't do this right now," I told him, heading for my door, hoping he would get the message and back off.

I was already coming up with excuses to invite him inside my apartment, like I needed to ask him what Dickey was doing on his porch, and why had he lied about it. And more importantly, what had they been arguing about?

"Then why did you kiss me in the barn?" he asked all soft and sultry-like. I could almost taste his kiss.

I turned to face him, oil dripping down my left cheek. "I had a brain freeze. A lapse in sanity. A moment of complete confusion. I don't know. It just happened. You're reading too much into it."

He stepped up on the landing. "I'm reading what you want me to read, that there's hope for us. I can't stop thinking about you, Mia."

"Me, and half the other women who live in this valley."

He gazed down for a moment then looked into my eyes. That's when I felt the crack in my resolve, a big fat crack that ran right up the center of my soul.

"You're right. I was a shit, but I haven't been serious about another woman since we broke up. The day you walked out, I finally realized what you meant to me, what you mean to me now. I was a fool, Mia. If there's any chance, any hope . . ."

I kissed him hard on the lips, completely denying all my apprehensions and months of counseling. I wanted him like I'd never wanted him before. As if I'd been swimming under water holding my breath way too long and surfaced, taking in big gulps of life-sustaining oxygen. As if I would die if I was denied another second.

I opened my door and we tumbled in still clinging onto each other, stopping long enough for me to set the lock. The room was dark, illuminated only by the moonlight streaming in through the windows, which gave everything an ethereal glow.

He helped me out of my sweater and bra, and I helped him out of his shirt. He pulled me in tight against his chest. The sensation of his body on my skin only added to the fire that was already burning through me.

Our shoes came off next as we made our way to the bathroom. When I slipped out of my jeans and panties he was busy getting the water temperature just right. I hit the light switch for the shower and a red glow filled the room. I kept a red light bulb in the sconce in the ceiling over the shower because I liked the way it made skin look, all smooth and satiny.

Steam began to fill the room adding to the intensity of the moment. I unfastened the button on his pants and pulled down the zipper. He'd already gone hard, and I held my breath as I waited for him to step out of his pants and underwear.

Now, fully naked we stepped under the hot water and for a moment we stood apart, taking in each other's bodies. Leo had always liked to get a good, long, delicious look at me before we made love. It heightened his arousal, and drove me wild with anticipation.

We took it slow then, carefully washing each other. I soaped his chest and arms, but he stopped me from going any further.

He spun me around and began my wash by lathering my hair first, and rinsing it, then he slowly moved down my body while standing close behind me using his hands to gently spread the soap, lingering on my breasts and between my legs. The sensations were impossible. I'd forgotten just how amazing his touch could be. Little shivers racked my body and it took all the willpower I had to allow him to continue. God, how I missed this man inside me. How I missed his lovemaking.

I turned to continue my wash of him, but again he stopped me. "Next time," he said and moved in closer. He pressed me against the wall, and lifted me into position while holding onto my butt. I wrapped a leg around him and he entered me as the warm water ran down both our bodies. I shivered, nearing climax before he even began his rhythm. When he shuddered with his own pleasure I joined him, only this time I came so hard that I collapsed onto him, completely and delightfully exhausted.

Ten minutes later we luxuriated on opposite sides of my extra deep whirlpool tub. I had added olive oil and essence of lavender to the water, lit a few candles, while the jazz group Four Play softly entertained us in the background.

Then right when I should have been feeling perfectly content, reality snuck in to change the mood.

I hated when that happened.

"You know this can't work between us," I said. "We're two different people. Besides, I don't drink anymore, and don't want to start up again. Having a winemaker for a boyfriend doesn't exactly help my cause."

His legs brushed mine. "Can't we just take this one date at a time? No commitment."

"See, that's where I get all messed up. No commitment means other people, and other people means I'll get jealous, and when I get jealous because I've fallen for you again, I'll start drinking and if I start drinking again, well, it's enough to give me a headache, especially with everything else going on."

"Mia, I'm telling you I'm not like that anymore. You have to trust me on this."

The real problem was I couldn't trust myself, but at the moment, I felt too content to argue. I simply wanted to go to bed.

Alone.

But before I sent him on his contented way with the possibility of us coupling up again, I needed to ask him about what I saw that afternoon out on his porch. Our future rested on his answer. "So, what's up with you and Dickey?"

His forehead creased. "What do you mean?"

"I mean, what was the argument about?"

"Excuse me?"

His eyes darted to the candle. The man was giving off lie

signals right and left. Didn't he realize what he was doing?

"Come on. Come clean about this. I was passing the vineyard today and I saw you and Dickey out on your porch, arguing."

He stared at me for a moment, as if he had to think about his answer. A stalling tactic he'd used before.

"I don't know who you saw out there, but it wasn't me. I've been in meetings all day and as far as Dickey being at my place, I never saw the man."

"You're lying," I told him.

He smiled, and gazed down at the bubbly water. I expected our usual argument, but instead he said, "As pleasant as this has been, I need to go now."

He stood and I watched the water infused with oil glide down his perfect body. He grabbed a towel, dried off, picked up his clothes and left the room.

This was a new tactic on his part: lying combined with complete avoidance. I wondered how long he would keep this new game up.

I stood and stepped out of the tub, drying off with a plush white towel, my body all smooth from the oil. I pulled on my flannel jammies with the giant red flowers and padded out to the living room.

"Tell you what," he said, now dressed except for a shirt. Just the sight of that chest made me want to start all over again, despite his illusive behavior, but instead I bravely walked past him to the door and unlocked it. "I'll see you at the Martini Madness ball and you can either talk to me or not. Either way, I won't regret what just happened, but if you want a relationship, you'll have to start believing me. We'll take it slow. You can build up your trust. This is your game now, kitten. You can play it however you want to. If you want to. 'Cause it's not looking too promising at the moment."

He gave my pajamas the once over, grinned, slipped on his

shirt and opened the door. He leaned over and brushed my lips with a gentle kiss. It was just enough to make me crave him even more.

I watched Leo amble down the stairs before I slipped into my marshmallow-soft bed, covered my head with my white down blanket and told myself not to think of the man or I'd never fall asleep. The man was a continual menace to my otherwise comfortable life. And what made it even worse, he was hiding something from me about Dickey.

What was that all about?

Normally, I had no problem coping with my temporary celibacy and lack of alcohol. I'd come to look at it as a phase I was going through. That one day I would be enjoying men and wine again only in a sane way. At least that's what my last shrink said. For some reason, I wasn't seeing the vision in my future.

Especially after tonight.

The man's lack of an answer to my question just proved that I was incapable of getting the truth out of him. The very fact that I didn't push him on it was due to my complete lack of courage when it came to Leo. But why would he not answer me? What was he hiding? In the past, he would toss me some elaborate lie, but this time he said nothing. That was clearly more disturbing considering I was asking about a missing murder victim.

I turned on my side, fluffed my pillow, shifted my legs to a more comfortable fetal position, stared through my curtainless window at the night sky filled with stars, and forced myself to think of my favorite sleep inducer—uses for olive oil:

It preserves and cleans cutting boards. It's great to push back cuticles, and it softens the rough spots on your feet. It's a great suntan oil. It can sooth my chapped lips. A few drops will suffocate a tick. It works as a mosquito repellant, not to mention the great effect it has on dry skin in general. Olive oil has been known to lower blood pressure. It decreases blood sugar levels, helps prevent calcium loss and promotes cellular growth. Olive oil sooths sunburn pain, or is that vinegar? Anyway, it will help with a bee sting, and it will relieve my sore throat when I warm it and . . .

I was asleep before I could think of cleaning solutions.

I kept hearing a bird chirping off in the distance. Wait, not a bird exactly, more like a cat with laryngitis. No, it was definitely a bird. A sick bird. I opened my eyes a little and realized morning had erupted, and for the first time in months, I had slept right through the night.

Slowly the bird sound became stronger, along with a faint scent of blackberries. I tilted my head to get a better whiff, but the scent had been so faint that I couldn't really smell it anymore.

As my mind began to clear out of the night's fog, making love to Leo in the shower flashed up on my memory screen. I smiled and snuggled down under the covers while facing the window, realizing my lover was in bed with me. I rolled over to give him a luscious wake-up kiss when Lisa jumped up and dashed out of my bed. I moved away, suddenly remembering that Leo never crawled in bed with me, Lisa had, and thank God I was wearing my best flannel pajamas. I didn't remember exactly how I ended up in my pajamas, but that was beside the point.

The bird I'd heard was Lisa's now-working miracle phone.

"Hello," she cooed into the phone, sensual excitement skipping off of each syllable. I figured whoever was on the other end of the call must be thinking that Lisa was thrilled to hear from them. Little did they know she was simply thrilled that her phone seemed to be working, despite its oil bath.

She giggled, a high-pitched girly giggle. What was that all about? Was a working phone that exciting to her?

She whispered something I didn't catch, giggled a bit more, ended the call and fell back on the bed next to me, grinning up at the ceiling. And not just any old grin, this was more in the category of gleeful grinning, the kind that eventually causes cheek aches.

"At least your phone is working," I said, looking over at her, watching for any tells that she might know about Leo coming up to my apartment last night. I couldn't see any. If she did know, it was only a matter of time before she'd let me have it, with both barrels.

"I bet you're happy about that," I offered, wanting her to volunteer who was on the other end of that call.

She nodded then turned toward me, scrunching her pillow under her head, tugging on the covers, grinning. Apparently, Lisa was in a good mood.

"What? Tell me," I begged. "Did your publisher call with a million dollar deal? Are you going to be on Oprah? Are they making a movie out of one of your books? Tell me."

She giggled again. I scrunched my pillow under my head and faced her, joining in on her contagious laughter.

It had been a long time since Lisa and I shared a bed. When we were little we'd have sleepovers all summer long. We'd never get any sleep, way too much to talk and laugh about in those days. We had endless conversations, and when we weren't talking about someone or something, Lisa would make up stories, long lavish stories about kids living on other planets or kids with special powers. I couldn't count how many times I fell asleep listening to her lulling voice telling me about Zoey the goddess warrior, or Princess Omni, the last female demon slayer on Ozark, a planet on the other side of the universe.

"It was Nick," she said. "But you're not going to like what he said."

My chest instantly tightened as reality came rushing in.

"Oh God! What did he say? No. Don't tell me. I can't take any bad news. I mean, what if Dickey pops up somewhere and Nick still has that gun. I bet you anything he already ran a ballistic check on it. This could get really ugly."

I sat up, turned slightly and looked at her. Her expression hadn't changed. Something was up, and it couldn't be bad. "Why are you still smiling? This has to be good. Right? Okay. You can tell me. We don't have any secrets."

Lie. No way could I tell her about Leo and me. Her expression changed. She stopped giggling, but the smile still clung to her lips. "Okay. So it's not good news. Those were nervous giggles, right? Like when we were caught smoking in the locker-room and Sister Marian Joseph made us stay after school and wait for our mothers to come and fetch us so she could personally tell them of our evil deeds. You kept laughing that day, too. Did Nick find Dickey? He ran ballistics and the bullet matches the gun and he's on his way over to pick up my mom or me or all three of us. I knew this was going to happen. I should have never let him take that weapon. We're in for it now. We could spend the rest of our lives in jail. You won't care. You'll just write more books: Surviving Prison or Surviving Bad Girls. Mom will adjust, she adjusts to anything. But me? I'll die in jail, all that tasteless food, and confinement, not to mention those bad-ass biker chicks. I never could get along with biker women. You may as well just shoot me right now, because I'll die if I go to jail."

I flopped down on the bed, exhausted by my own outburst.

"Are you done ranting?" she asked.

I nodded and braced for the worst.

She stared at me for a moment longer, the smile never leaving her face.

"This isn't funny. Jail time is serious business. Just ask my family."

"You're overreacting. Take a deep breath. Relax. Close your eyes for a minute. Wait to hear what I have to say before you decide we're jail bait."

I did as I was told, but there was still a little part of my mind that saw us in bright orange jumpsuits lifting weights out in a cement courtyard alongside buffed, mean-looking women with tattoos that said Eat Me!

When I opened my eyes, she was still smiling.

I thought I'd go with it and take a different approach. "You're smiling so I'm going to assume it's good news. Nick's coming over with the gun. He believes your ridiculous story about research and wants to drive you to a firing range for target practice."

She shook her head.

"Whaaa-aat?" I whined. "Tell me before my head explodes."

"Okay. But I know you'll hate it, especially after all that's happened. I just can't help myself. I tried, honest, but this is bigger than my willpower, and you know how strong my willpower is."

This was true. I was the binge drinker. Lisa was the designated driver.

"Just tell me!"

She let out a breath. "Nick asked me to the Martini Madness Ball tomorrow tonight."

"Get out. You wouldn't go with him, right? Or would you?"

I didn't quite know how to react to this news.

"Last night, while you were taking a shower to get rid of all that oil, Nick helped me clean up my car, and I helped him clean off his shoes. Anyway, one thing led to another and, well, he's a total babe, so I gave him my phone number."

"But your phone was oil bound at the time."

"I know, but in the heat of the moment I forgot."

This was serious. Lisa never forgot anything.

"He's a detective with the Sheriff's Department and we're witnesses in a murder case. Not only did we tamper with the evidence, the body is missing, and the killer tried to frame my mom, and Nick more than likely has the murder weapon that we provided. I don't care how much of a babe he is, until we can figure all this out, he's trouble . . . several-years-in-the-slammer type of trouble. Bad-ass biker chick kind of trouble."

She sat up, and folded her legs under her butt. "That's not entirely true. I mean let's review the facts. Your cousin Dickey has been murdered, but the body has gone missing, and as long as it's missing there's no murder, at least not according to the law."

"You and I know there's been a murder, not to mention my entire family. And we also know that somebody in my family probably knocked him off, and tried to pin it on my mom."

"But do we actually know this as a fact or are we simply speculating because we found her gun near the body. Who knows how long that gun could have been there?"

"Not long enough. I'd just seen it in her jewelry armoire a few hours before Dickey was killed. That has to be the murder weapon. And what about her bracelet?"

"As long as the police don't get it, it's a non issue."

"But I can't get it out of my head that she wasn't wearing a bracelet later in the evening when we all went back into the barn. For all I know, she really is the killer. Wait. Did I just say that?"

"Don't be ridiculous. You're mom isn't the killer. Maybe she took it off for some reason and gave it to someone and that someone was the killer. Who knows, but that's beside the point."

I shook my head. "Please. She would never do that. When do you ever remember my mom without a bracelet?"

She thought for a moment. "All right, so maybe she did it. And if she did do it, she probably had a damn good reason. And if she had a damn good reason, then it's all taken care of. Obviously, most of the men in the family had to help her. How else would that millstone have gotten moved?"

I flashed on those papers I retrieved from the bank and a curious negative thought pried open my determination to clear my mom. Could my mom have pulled the trigger on Dickey because of that document, with the entire Spia clan standing by her side? The vision was a little over the top, especially if I focused on Hetty with her ruby-red lips and clown hair, but perfectly reasonable considering my family's values.

The family that kills together . . .

Lisa continued. "Your family did whatever mobsters do to get rid of a body, which I don't want to think about, but it was necessary in this situation. It clearly means that Nick isn't a threat. Not as long as Dickey's wearing cement boots floating on the bottom of some lake or river. Nick is simply a sweet guy who I'd like to get to know better."

"Who just happens to be a detective."

"Not a problem, at least not for me. I'm not part of your family, remember? I'm the friend. I can date a judge and it won't make any difference. Besides, I've got nothing to hide."

"Oh?"

She rolled out of bed and stood there, staring down at me, looking rather put together for just having woken up. "Okay, so maybe we didn't call the police the moment we found Dickey. We were just doing what we thought was right at the time. He was a bad dude anyway. A mob boss. You don't seriously believe he didn't kill Carla DeCarlo, do you? Or had something to do with it? Besides, nobody cares if there's one less mobster in this world."

She turned on her naked heels, padded off to the kitchen area, filled a kettle with tap water and placed it on a burner. I rolled out of bed and trudged off to the bathroom, eager to take yet another shower. A shower was always a place for me to think, and brother did I ever need time to think.

I grabbed a change of clothes from my closet and went into the bathroom. As soon as I stepped inside the scent of berries was almost overpowering. I figured it had to be coming from the clothes-hamper where I'd thrown my oily clothes.

When I placed my clothes on the counter, I nearly jumped

out of my flannels. A bloody white handkerchief rolled up in a cylinder sat on the edge of the sink.

I took a step back, then slowly crept in closer, afraid the thing was going to jump up and bite me . . . I figured nothing was impossible after the previous night.

As I moved in closer to the bloody intruder, I picked up a toothbrush lying on the sink and poked at it a couple times. The hankie unraveled a bit and something that resembled a finger fell out of it and rolled around in the sink, leaving a streak of dark red blood.

"That's disgusting," I said out loud.

I leaned over the sink to get a better look and realized that it was, in fact, a pinky finger, a pinky finger with a long, perfectly manicured nail. Undoubtedly, this was Dickey's pinky finger rolling around in my sink. My already tormented tummy reminded me just how disturbing this moment of severed madness was.

"Oh-my-god! Lisa, come'ere-come'ere-come'ere!"

Lisa ran in before I finished getting all my yells out. She spotted the severed digit as soon as she walked in the room and cautiously peered inside the basin.

"Wow," she calmly said. "I hope this finger belongs to Dickey or your family is getting completely out of control."

"It's his. It has to be his. I remember the manicure."

She poked around at the bloody hankie. "There's a note." She picked it up, carefully unfolded it and read the printed words: "If you give me what was on this finger, Dickey will disappear forever. If you don't, you'll regret it. This is my final offer." She looked at me. "This is so Godfather. Couldn't the killer have thought of something more original? I mean, come on. A finger? A threatening note? Whoever this guy is, needs to update his bag of mob tricks."

The teapot whistled. She dropped the note in the sink and

walked out of the bathroom, leaving me standing there still clutching my pile of clean clothes, completely put off by her flippant attitude. We were talking murder here and she was talking Hollywood.

I padded out of the bathroom. "Doesn't this scare you? Aren't you worried, or at the very least, nauseous? Someone just threatened us, not to mention that he or she, although I'm thinking it was a he because the women in this family are pretty squeamish when it comes to blood. Anyway he was in here last night while we slept. The killer was in my apartment planting Dickey's finger. That alone is disturbing."

"I keep telling you to lock your door." She pulled a white six-cup teapot from the cupboard. "It's more corny than anything else. Okay, and disgusting. But nauseous? Umm, not so much. From all I've read about the mob, and from hanging around with you, this seems like some kind of vendetta that we shouldn't be involved in. I mean, we don't have the ring, so obviously the killer is completely misguided. We just need to let him know the facts and stay out of the way. Without a body, the murder isn't our problem."

She busied herself with filling a tea ball with loose tea, placing it inside the teapot then pouring in the hot water.

I sighed and sat down hard on the bed. It was all getting to be too much. "And just how do we let the killer know we don't have the ring? Stand on my front porch and yell it out?" Hello, Mr. Killer, we don't have the ring!"

"I hadn't thought of that one, but we could leave a note on the front door: Dear Killer, Somebody else stole your ring. Sincerely, Mia and Lisa."

"You're not serious."

She found dishes and flatware in the cupboards and placed them on my counter. "Kind of, yes. What else are we supposed to do?"

"Here's the thing. The killer is not going to believe that we don't have it. Not in this group. Too many trust issues. Besides, you said the ring was a lead."

"Yeah, to the killer, not a thief. This is an entirely different game now. We're suddenly in the crosshairs and I'm not sure I'm too comfortable with that. Can't we just forget about the whole thing and leave for Maui early?"

I tossed my clothes on the bed, got up and walked over to the small wooden table in front of a side window. Lisa busied herself setting up a tea party for two complete with anise biscotti, and warm, olive focaccia bread courtesy of Aunt Hetty who routinely brought me a tray of early morning goodies, a couple of ripe pears, deep purple grapes, several thick slices of goat cheese, honey, and a cow shaped creamer filled with warmed milk. I pulled out a chair and made myself comfortable.

"We could do that, but there are a few things that I can't seem to let go of," I said as she poured me a cup of steaming Palm Court tea, our favorite ever since our last trip to New York City and our visit to the Plaza Hotel where we shared high tea. Of course, I had added a couple shots of bourbon to my cup, but that was in another life.

"What's that?" she asked as she placed the tea pot back on the table.

"Why did the killer try to set up my mom? And what makes you think Nick will give up his search for Dickey when he found fresh blood on the millstone, my mom's handgun floating in olive oil and the two of us acting so weird? And what does it say to the family if I don't ferret out the killer? I've been working hard to keep them honest for the past two years. This murder blows that right into orbit. And besides all of that, what the hell do we do with Dickey's pinky finger?"

Lisa stirred milk and honey into her tea and looked at me as if all my worries were totally insignificant. "About the killer setting up your mom, maybe he or she didn't actually try to set her up. Maybe the killer threw the gun in the futso because the killer didn't know what else to do with it when we walked in. Granted, the killer used your mom's handgun, but that's the only gun on the land, right?"

"As far as I know, yes, but these are ex-Mafiosi. Do you really think they gave up all of their hardware? Not likely. And what about my mom's bracelet?"

"I think that's legitimate. Meaning that somehow it came off while she was talking to him in the barn, and it simply ended up under his feet. Total accident."

I was skeptical, but for the sake of argument, willing to go along. For now. "Okay. I'll accept that, but what about Nick? He's like a bloodhound. I don't think he's going to stop looking for Dickey."

She drank down some tea and smirked. "Don't worry about Nick. He's all mine and after one night with me he won't even remember Dickey's name."

"You're that good, huh?"

Lisa leaned back in her chair and smirked. "Better."

I smiled as I poured milk into my tea then drank down half the cup. "One last thing, Ms Vixen, we have a bloody finger sitting in the sink, and a killer who thinks we have Dickey's ring. What exactly do you propose we do next?"

She shrugged. "Bury the finger, and let it be known that we do not have the ring and that we'll forget about finding Dickey's killer. You'll simply let this whole thing slide as long as they don't ever kill anybody else."

"Simple," I said. "I slap their hands and tell them they were bad and I'm done with it."

"Something like that, yes," she said, in between sips of hot tea.

My stomach wasn't buying any of this. It cramped up so tight I thought I was going to hurl my tea.

"You're doing it," I told her.

"Doing what?"

"Falling for the lure of the mob. This is how they suck you in. Their way seems so easy, so simple, but believe me, something always goes wrong. It may not happen right away, but eventually you end up like Dickey."

She sipped her tea for a moment, put the cup down and stared at me, all serious. "You know everything I said was complete bullshit. We have a fucking severed finger in your bathroom sink, a missing dead body, a murderer who thinks we have something he was willing to kill for, and a cop who smells trouble. I'm scared out of my friggin' mind, Mia. Could it get any worse?"

That's when we heard heavy footsteps on my stairs.

Focaccia with Olives and Salt – Level Two or Three

3 ½ to 4 cups unbleached flour
2 ¼ tsp. active dry yeast
¾ cup warm water (not hot to touch)
1/3 cup Italian Blend EVOO
1/3 cup dry white wine (or water depending on your resolve)
¼ tsp. sugar
¾ tsp. salt
2 tbs. fresh rosemary leaves, chopped
3/4 cup chunked Kalamata olives
¼ cup chunked Toscano olives or for a more intense flavor, use Sicilian
12 halved, pitted olives (a blend of the above)

Kneading bread dough is always soothing and distracting, so take your time with this one. It's great to make bread whenever you're feeling especially hostile, tense or jittery. Try to focus on the dough rather than anything else.

Drop 3 ½ cups of flour into a large bowl, add sugar, salt and half of the rosemary. Give it a quick mix with a fork. Then make a hole in the middle, building up the flour all around the sides, like the top of a volcano. Pour in ½ cup of the warm water into that hole, add the yeast, and stir briefly with your fork. Let stand for about 8 minutes or until it gets creamy and bubbly. Take this time to relax, breathe in the scent of the yeast, and chop the olives. When the yeast is ready add the wine, oil, and remaining water. Make sure all the liquids are warm or at room temperature or you will kill the yeast. Mix ingredients with your hands. Here comes the level three part. When you have a nice big ball, and you've gotten all of the mixture to come away from the sides of the bowl (this can be accomplished by adding a bit more olive oil), move the dough to a lightly floured surface and work the hell out of it until the stickiness is gone, about five or six minutes or until it turns smooth and elastic. Add the chunked olives and knead for a few more minutes. All this kneading will take about ten full, glorious minutes to accomplish. Keep adding flour as needed.

Place this beautiful ball of dough in a clean, oiled large bowl, then flip so there's now a soft sheen of EVOO on the top of the dough. Cover with a pretty dish towel, place in a warm spot for 1 ½ hours or until it has doubled in bulk.

During your wait, you can clean up the kitchen, make an accompanying dish, like a beautiful salad, or take a long walk. Getting physical exercise gets those positive endorphins working, which only helps with sobriety resolve.

Set oven to 450 degrees. Gently punch down the now beautifully swollen dough. Let it sit for about five more minutes. Place it on a lightly floured surface and shape into either a ¾ inch thick rectangle or round and transfer to an oiled baking sheet. With your fingers, press down on the dough making several indentations on the surface. Brush lightly with olive oil. Press the 24 halved olives into the depressions, sprinkle on a little coarse sea salt and the remaining rosemary. Bake for 25 to 30 minutes or until golden browned. Remove from oven, and allow to cool for about ten minutes. Cut into squares or triangles and serve. Can be eaten warm or cold.

TEN

Looking for Honey Bear

Jade Batista, a twenty-something tour guide on Alcatraz Island—a coincidence, I'm sure—was dressed in black skinny jeans, four-inch black heels, a black thigh-length sweater, accessorized in dangly silver, sat on my sofa sipping tea after she had added two packets of that pink stuff, which she pulled out of her super-sized, black, hobo bag complete with Woodstock fringe.

According to my mom, who'd brought her to my apartment—thank you very much—Jade had arrived about an hour ago looking for her fiancée, Dickey Spia.

"Naturally, when my honey-bear didn't return my calls I got worried," Jade told us as she carefully placed the white mug down on the coaster on my coffee table.

"Naturally," I said feeling a bit woozy from all the excitement.

Lisa also sat on sofa still wearing my oversized baby-blue flannel pajamas with the golden stars and quarter moons, sipping tea like it meant something. My mother sat in the rocker dressed in a deep red granny skirt she kept rolled at her waist and a floral peasant blouse with sleeves that covered her hands, also sipping on a cup of Palm Court tea. Go figure. I was perched on the arm of my sofa, next to Lisa, unable to commit to either sitting or standing, staring at our guest, who looked vaguely familiar in that extended-honorary-family sort of way.

And Dickey's pinky finger was stashed in the back of my freezer, tucked inside a snack-sized Ziplock.

"What time did you last talk to him?" I asked, still working on that timeline for Dickey's murder.

"I guess it was about seven-ish because that's when the hybrid ferry docks to take some of us back to the city. I work for National Parks and Recreation and my shift ends at six-thirty, but the ferry doesn't arrive until about seven. Anyway, that's when I make all my phone calls or Twitter or text my friends. While I'm waiting for the ferry. One of my friends, Monica, wouldn't stop talking, ya know? She's like that, always talking even when she doesn't have anything to say, ya know? Don't you hate that?"

I nodded.

She continued without prompting. "That's why I didn't call Dickey until I got on the ferry. But we talked all the way in."

"And how long did that take?"

"The usual time, fifteen minutes. I didn't want to get off the phone with him, but he said he had to go because somebody wanted to talk to him. Then the phone cut out. I tried to call him back 'cause I thought it was my phone, sometimes it does that, ya know? But when I called him he didn't answer."

"Did he ever pick up again?"

But I already knew the answer to that one.

She shook her head. "No. Isn't that weird? I mean, I had no choice but to come looking for him. Right? He coulda been dead on the road or something, ya know? But when I pulled in by that barn building, like Benny told me to, and saw Dickey's black SUV was still here, I was relieved that he wasn't dead, ya know? Or lying in some hospital hurt and lonely for his baby-girl. That's what he calls me, his baby girl 'cause I'm so much younger than him. Not that it matters when you're in love. Age doesn't mean a damn thing when you're in love, ya know?"

We nodded in unison.

"Anyway, where is he? I mean, I know how much my honey-bear has looked forward to sleeping in. They don't get to do that in prison, what with all the noise. Plus, the guards wake 'em early for breakfast." She glanced at her watch. "It's getting close to lunchtime. He likes that meal and probably won't want to miss it. You think he's still sleeping?"

We nodded again, like bobbing heads on a spring.

"Well, I don't want to wake him, but—" she paused, placing her bent index finger up to her glossy pink lips, tapping, as if she was thinking of something. It was the first time I noticed the rather large pink rock on her ring finger, no doubt an engagement ring from Dickey. An engagement ring that was worth more money than an ex-con should be able to put together in the short time he'd been a free man, but I was digressing.

Jade's blond hair was pulled up in a tight ponytail. Large silver hoops hung from her earlobes. "Maybe if you guys don't mind, you can tell me where he is and I can surprise him. He might like that."

"Sure," my mother agreed, and before I could stop her, she was standing. "I put all his things in one of my upstairs bedrooms."

Mom had me completely stymied. I couldn't figure out what the woman was thinking. Either she had no clue that Dickey was actually dead, or she was simply playing some sort of elaborate game with Jade. Either way, from the look on Jade's innocent face, Mom had her wrapped around her finger.

Jade smiled and stood to follow my mom's lead to the door.

"He told me not to wake him, no matter what," I blurted out for no other reason than to stall my mom's departure.

"Yeah," Lisa said. "I heard him. He looked exhausted when he said it."

"Dead tired," I added.

Okay, I knew that was over the top, macabre even, but I was desperate to stall her. Not that stalling her had much benefit in the long run, but I was hoping something might pop into my head that could somehow resolve this situation.

"That's all right. I'm sure he won't mind if I wake him," Jade said, looking all vampy, running a hand down her full, round body. "He likes when I wake him up. I have my own special way of doing it, if you know what I mean," she cooed as her voice trailed off.

"I bet you do, but Mia's right," Lisa said. "He was really tired last night, what with all the family stuff going on. Plus, he drank a lot of wine."

"Yeah, a lot of wine. He's probably going to have a mean hangover. It won't be pleasant," I added.

But Jade couldn't be stopped. She had reached my front door, had the door open and was on her way to find her "honey-bear."

"I've got just the thing for that," she announced, all smiley faced. "Oral sex. It works every time. Something about their blood rushing down there that does it. It works for girls, too, but not as well. I never could figure that one out, but it sure does start your morning with a bang, ya know?"

She snickered.

That stopped me cold. In all my years of hangovers, and I'd had more than my share, I never thought about sex, much less oral sex as a cure. It was difficult enough just to open my eyes in the morning. If ever I drank again, which was looking more like a possibility, I'd have to try the oral sex cure.

Leo had that category covered.

My mother's eyes fluttered about a hundred times. She turned a bright crimson, a sure sign she was desperately trying to gain composure and appear somewhat cool. Whenever someone other than Aunt Babe said anything even remotely sexual, Mom went into some kind of temporary meltdown. I didn't exactly know why it never seemed to bother her when Aunt Babe started a sexual innuendo kick, but whenever anyone else did, she fell into an immediate tailspin.

Happily, it only lasted a couple minutes, if that.

"By the way, darling," my mom said, speaking directly to me.

"The clasp must have broken on my charm bracelet last night because I can't find the darn thing anywhere. I really shouldn't have worn it, but Dickey gave it to me for my birthday right before all the trouble started, and I knew he'd be tickled if he saw I was still wearing it. Which he was, but sometime during the night it must have fallen off. I've looked everywhere, but I can't seem to find it. Do you think you might try? I feel awful about losing it."

I walked over to my closet, and slipped it out of the pocket I'd shoved it into the previous night. "Is this it?" I asked holding the incriminating bracelet in the palm of my hand.

"You found it!" Her face lit up. "But where, sweetheart?"

"In the barn, under . . . something."

I saw the flash of recognition in her eyes. But as quickly as it appeared it vanished and a cool smile shadowed her eyes. I knew that smile. It was forever present whenever we both knew there was avoidance circling around us.

"Thank you, dear. You have no idea what this means to me."

"Actually, I think I do."

We hugged briefly and she slipped out the door with Jade in tow. I suddenly had the sick feeling that my mom wasn't completely innocent, but how much she knew, and how involved she may or may not be was now the burning question.

I could hear her chatting up a storm with Jade about Dickey, the orchard and the benefits of olive oil. I wondered if like Goldilocks, Jade would have a rude awakening when she crawled in Dickey's bed, or if my mom had already figured out an exit strategy. Either way, Jade was not going away until she found her "honey-bear."

I closed the door and Lisa said, "You realize you just handed over vital evidence? And don't tell me your mom's totally innocent of this. I saw that look she gave you. That woman knows something."

"Yeah, but what?"

"If you weren't my best friend, I'd start walking and never look back. Are you sure we can't leave for Maui tonight?"

"Not a good idea, especially since the killer thinks we have his precious ring. We may never make it to the airport."

"Scare me more, why don't you," Lisa said.

"I think my family hid the body and the quest for the ring is something only one of them wants. A body has to be easier to find than a ring. If we find the body then the killer can't blackmail us."

"Okay, we concentrate on finding the body."

But I still wasn't sure. "But what do we do with it once we find it? How do we explain everything to Nick and not send everybody to prison, us included?"

I poured myself another cup of tea.

"I told you, I can take care of Nick."

"I wouldn't be so sure. He's all cop, and even you can't change that."

"But it'll be a lot of fun trying."

She beamed confidence.

"Okay, so we're back on the trail of a missing body."

"For now, that's the plan," she said.

"Good, 'cause that part about how nobody will miss one less mobster, I think Jade Batista just became Ms Nobody."

Thirty minutes later, dressed in hiking boots, jeans, and a long-sleeved, cream sweater, I was standing in my mother's kitchen grilling Uncle Benny about the missing body. I hadn't thrown in the part about the finger yet, or the missing ring bit. I guess I was saving that morsel of information for later when I was completely desperate. At the moment I was trying for somewhat optimistic, even with Jade's appearance.

Benny sat at the table, drinking coffee out of an oversized pink mug with red hearts. He wore his threadbare picking clothes, complete with a Panama straw hat that had seen better days. Lisa was in my shower, and Jade was off somewhere with Aunt Babe who was probably trying to convince her to help pick olives. Everyone was recruited when it came time to harvest: relatives, friends, several day laborers who were familiar with hand-harvesting olives, and of course, a neighbor or two who had their own personal harvest to tend to and would be in need of help in the coming weeks.

We were currently picking our koroneiki olives in their young, deep green stage. This usually took a couple weeks of harvesting. Federico would oversee the first crush. We didn't like our fruit to sit more than twenty-four to forty-eight hours, mold could set in. We'd store the oil for blending later with other more mature olives, like the mission or pendolino, depending on the label he and Mom wanted. The high content of polyphenols not only produced a higher level of antioxidants, but it also made for a longer shelf life, not to mention that distinctive grassy flavor with a peppery finish.

"Just tell me what you did with the body and I'll take care of the rest," I said, trying to sound as if I knew what "the rest" was going to be, because in truth, I didn't have a clue.

"I am telling you, I am just as puzzled as you are," he said while chewing on his cigar.

As it turned out, when Jade and my mom discovered that Dickey wasn't in his room, and his SUV had gone missing Jade decided to wait for Dickey's return.

How long could this family keep up the hoax?

"Oh, give it up. You expect me to believe you didn't bury him somewhere? Like under the old olive tree next to the barn? That Jimmy and Ray didn't help you?"

"I swear on my father's grave, I have no idea what happened to that body. I am glad it is gone, but I did not move it."

"Swearing on your father's grave doesn't work. The man tried to have your mother killed. You hate your father."

"That is beside the point, Mia. I do not denigrate the dead."

"I'd feel better if you swore on your mother's grave."

His face went hard. "That, I cannot do. She was a saint, may she rest in peace." He softened, made the sign of the cross and looked toward the ceiling or heaven in his case. "I make it a point never to use my dear mother when I am swearing. Swearing in front of my mother is not something I would ever have done."

"You're not swearing, like in saying a dirty word, you're taking an oath that you're telling the truth. You, of all people know the difference."

He smirked. "You can take it or leave it. It does not matter a lick to me. I have olives to pick, and so do you." He drank down more coffee.

Mom's kitchen still smelled sweet from all the cookies. Some of my favorites were piled on plates on her counter, covered in plastic wrap. A few of them were calling to me, but I didn't want the distraction at the moment.

"I don't have time to pick today. There's a killer loose on the ranch and I have to round him up."

I was suddenly feeling as though I were in a Clint Eastwood movie.

"Do not joke about this. It can be dangerous for you."

"Is that a threat?"

He shook his head. "It is a warning."

"I'll take that under advisement, but in the meantime, what about that document I fetched for Mom yesterday? The one that turned all this land back over to Dickey if he was ever proven innocent of the murder of Carla DeCarlo? That document alone is motive enough to send the whole lot of you to prison for Dickey's murder. I can't believe you let her sign that."

He pulled out a fancy gold lighter and lit his cigar; puffing several times to get it going.

"I do not know what you are talking about," he said as smoke swirled around his head, the fragrance sweet and musky at the same time. My dad used to smoke that same cigar. I loved the smell, and it usually worked like a salve on me.

But not today.

"Oh please. Your name is on that document as one of the witnesses." I thought I'd remind him just in case he overlooked that minor detail.

He slid the long fat stogy out of his mouth, blew out a plume of smoke and said, "I think you are mistaken. I would have never agreed to anything like that."

I stared at him for a moment then decided to get the paperwork. I went to my mom's room, walked in past her bed to the jewelry armoire and opened the drawer, which triggered the music as I grabbed the paperwork, then I shut the drawer, the music thankfully stopped and I turned to walk back out, but stopped at the sight of black men's pants dangling from the hook behind Mom's door. Pants that had tobacco stuck to the pocket.

Benny's pants.

When I caught the brown men's slippers sticking out from under the bed I cringed.

Mom was sleeping with Uncle Benny? How long had that been going on that he was comfortable enough to bring over his own slippers?

I didn't want to think about it. This was all getting way too weird. How could I have not noticed the two of them had a thing for each other? I mean, I knew Mom had an unusual fascination with Benny, but this was more than just a fascination. Slippers bordered on commitment. Even Leo had never kept his slippers under my bed. Hell, I didn't actually know if Leo owned a pair of slippers, probably one of our many commitment issues.

I walked back into the kitchen, just as Uncle Benny was up pouring himself another cup of coffee from the glass decanter on the counter. A large round crystal ashtray sitting on the table held his burning cigar. He slowly added cream and sugar to his pink cup.

"Here," I tossed the papers on the table. "The last page might refresh your memory."

He walked back to the table, sat down on his chair, flipped through the document, read the last page and slid the document toward me. "Like I said, I do not know what you are talking about."

He blew on his coffee and slurped up a drink.

I picked up the papers going directly for the incriminating page, but it wasn't there. I flipped through the rest of the pages, nothing.

It simply disappeared.

Of course it did.

"I should have known better. You took it, didn't you?" He merely stared at me. "There will be copies of it, you know. The courthouse will have one."

"You can check, but if it never existed, then it will not be there, will it?"

"What about the notary, Peter Doyle? He'll have a copy."

He turned to me. His black hair greased straight back, face smooth from a recent shave, but heavily lined from years of criminal stress. These older Made Men had the same set of lined foreheads, and deep creases cutting along the sides of their nose to their mouths. Their notorious lives showed on their faces, just as my years of binge drinking and smoking still lingered around my eyes and mouth. Those tell-tale lines, always visible, like stigmata, and there was absolutely nothing any of us could do about it.

I took in a deep breath and realized he smelled of my mother's cherry-blossom shower gel.

"This is a matter of little importance, Mia," he said with a forced smile while peering over the top of his glasses. "You were mistaken. The document never existed."

There comes a time when a person has to take a step back from the notes to hear the melody. Poetic, but you get the picture.

I couldn't get anywhere with Uncle Benny, but then Uncle Benny was a lawyer. If anyone knew how to make documents and bodies disappear, he did. It was like questioning a priest about something that was said in a confessional.

Impossible.

Benny knew the importance of keeping secrets, and I sure wasn't the person who could penetrate that code of silence therefore I decided to take on a new course of action.

I left my mom's house and headed back to my apartment to report to Lisa, but found her dressed in my clothes cleaning out her car for any leftover oil residue. I gave her a quick rundown of what happened with Benny and the missing document, then I headed off to do some investigative work.

Not that I knew the first thing about investigative work, but I'd seen enough TV shows to be able to fake it. Of course, my family was more into the Jack Bauer method of interrogation, but I didn't think I had the stomach for it, so I'd stick to the more direct tactics of some of the CSI heroes. One of my interrogations had to be with Aunt Hetty. I wanted to know what she meant when she said "she was done with the devil." And why were her eyes moist when she turned away from Dickey? I could only hope she would be more forthcoming than Uncle Benny.

But first I needed to check out the soil near the old olive tree next to the barn. I mean, after all, this family might very well have buried Dickey under that tree just like Ray suggested. At this point, I wouldn't put anything past them.

I came upon the old gnarled tree with mixed feelings. On the one hand, if I found evidence that Dickey was buried there, what would I do? Would I actually call the police? What if someone had set up my mom again? Would I have to unearth the body to check it out first and then bury him again?

Way too much effort.

Fortunately, on closer inspection the earth around the tree was packed solid. Tall grass and weeds lined the ground, providing absolutely no evidence of any activity near this hundred-year-old specimen. I was glad for that. It would have been almost sacrilegious to bury a murdered mob boss under this tree.

This olive tree, with its ripening mission olives, dated back to the time the Mission San Francisco Solano was built on First and Spain Streets in the village of Sonoma in the eighteen twenties. The Mission was the last one in the chain of California Missions. The first one was down in San Diego. Every time I passed this old olive tree I thought of its history. Father Jose Altimira was responsible for the construction of the final mission, which had a sordid past. If I had my history straight, at one point the buildings were sold to a man named Schocken, who built a saloon in front of the chapel. Eventually, the place was restored with the help of the Women's Club and became a state park in nineteen twenty-seven.

I had no idea how this tree ended up here, so far away from the Mission, or why, but for me it was as if the tree stood as a symbol for more than a hundred years, just waiting for somebody to get a clue and cultivate the land around it into an olive grove.

Unfortunately for this magnificent tree, with its twisted limbs and silvery leaves, it was my family.

On the way over to Dolci Piccoli, I walked through our new store, a long room painted a soothing green. Two of the walls were lined with dark wooden shelves that held our various oils in smoky glass bottles with gold embossed labels, our balsamic vinegars, a few imported labels that we knew to be pure, imported

Italian olive oil candles of all sizes and shapes, soaps, lotions and some hand-painted ceramics Mom found in Spain.

Three round tables held displays of various sized wooden spoons and spatulas, vibrant table linens, books, and more pottery. We also sold various posters with an olive theme and a few novels that featured olives in their plot. We were everything olive, and it seemed to be working well for us.

The room was crowded with customers and my mom was busy handing out samples of our oils in tiny white plastic cups, demonstrating the correct way to taste oil. She stood at the wooden bar, which we kept stocked with our best sellers. If sipping oil out of a cup wasn't to your liking, we provided small chunks of bread for dipping.

Valerie, Uncle Ray's wife, was also handing out samples, as Audrey, their nineteen-year-old daughter who helped out two days a week to earn extra spending money while she attended culinary school, busied herself with a tall male customer at the register.

The new tasting room was my baby, and soon we'd combine it with a small restaurant on the north side of the building. We would attract more tourists and locals if we also offered food. Of course, if I didn't resolve Dickey's murder soon, the whole place could come tumbling down around us.

I wanted to ask Valerie a few questions before I went on to talk to Aunt Hetty. I waited for her to finish demonstrating how to taste oil. Val was particularly loud when she sucked back the oil through her clenched teeth, and always drew curious stares from the customers around her. Mom loved her for it.

"Our beautiful oils take on many different characteristics as they travel down your throat. They can be a little grassy, fruity or peppery. Sometimes they even taste like chocolate or green apples," Val said. She had several people captivated.

She poured a bit of the oil into her mouth. A few of the

customers did the same. Then she sucked it back through clenched teeth, making her distinctive loud sucking noise. Everyone followed her lead. Two of the people, a man and a short stocky woman, instantly began coughing, while the rest seemed to enjoy the experience.

"I'm tasting our Artisan Blend, a smooth front body, with grassy, green apple tones, and a slightly bitter finish. There's a hint of a peppery undertone, but not like the Seviano that our two coughing friends experienced."

She smiled.

They smiled.

"I love it," the coughing man said once he had control of his burning throat. "I'll take a case!"

That got a burst of laughter out of the group.

The peppery fire they were experiencing was a result of the oil hitting the mucous membranes near the esophagus, and if you weren't used to that feeling it could be a bit daunting.

Apparently, the coughing man delighted in it.

When Val finished her demo, and everyone was doing their own tasting, she turned to me, grinning. Val had one of those toothy grins that showed her gums, and made her slightly hooked nose prominent. Despite her gums and nose, Valerie was a handsome woman who loved hats. Today was no exception. She wore a black, wide-rimmed straw number with a lime green strip of cloth encircling it that matched her dress and heels.

"What'cha want, kid? I'm busy here," she said low enough so only I could hear.

"This will only take a few minutes. Can we step outside for a few minutes?"

She leaned in closer, and whispered. "If this is about last night, I got nothin' to say, and either do you. You should be happy the louse disappeared. He can't bring nothin' but trouble to this family."

And with that she went back to her customers.

So far this was not going like any TV show where the witnesses voluntarily offered up information without much coercion. I thought I might have to get a little tougher.

I caught up with her and tapped her on the shoulder. She whirled around and flashed me the evil eye. I instinctively flashed one back, admittedly, not a true evil eye, but one that got her attention.

Again, she excused herself. This time I walked with her behind the counter, for a bit of privacy.

"You get one question, kid, so make it a good one," she hissed through a phony smile.

I thought about this for a moment. If I knew Val, she hated violence against women more than anything. "Who would have the most to gain if my mother went to jail for Dickey's murder?"

She blanched. Was it a sign she had nothing to do with the frame-up or did she blanch because she knew something? My gut told me this was news, and now she would be a more willing snitch.

"Is that what this is all about, kid? Somebody tried to frame your mom? Again?"

"What do you mean, again?"

"Don't you remember? You're mom was a suspect when your dad disappeared. Them cops sniffed around her for a long time, even tapped her phone."

"But I always thought the phone tap had to do with everybody else."

"You was young, probably why you don't remember the facts so good. And now somebody set her up for wastin' Dickey? Sporco Diavolo."

I didn't want to tell her any of the details just yet, so I didn't answer, but I knew she could read me. Val could always read me. It was as if she had a window into my head.

She shook her head, and let out a couple sarcastic little guffaws. "Ain't nothin' changed? Ain't nobody sacred in this family?" She paused for a moment, her eyes scanning the room. Then, satisfied with what she saw, she whispered, "Look for the person who maybe's got a fucked up past with your mom, might have the most to gain or was scared of Dickey's return 'cause Dickey knew that person set him up for Carla's murder. If that's the case, then your mom, unfortunately, was the easy scapegoat. That's all I'm gonna say on the subject, kid. But, my advice? Like Paul McCartney says, Let it be. Dickey screwed me over with my first husband and he's the reason why I got this here scar to remind me of them two every day. Dickey got what he had comin'." She started to turn away, but something else was on her mind. "Oh, and one more thing. Get that Jade girl outta here. Never know what could happen if she hangs around too long. She's trouble. Past trouble, if you know what I mean. But you didn't hear any of this from me."

With that she sashayed back to her customers.

My head raced with information. What did she mean that Jade was "past trouble?" This was the first time I'd heard about her, and I thought the first time for everyone. But once again, the family was hiding something from me.

And what was she talking about that my mom had been a suspect for my missing father? How could that possibly have happened? Did my mom know what happened to my dad but neglected to tell me?

The possibility was too disturbing to dwell on, so I told myself I'd deal with it later. One disappearance at a time, and right now, Dickey's was on the top of my list.

I hadn't really focused in on the fact that Jade could be a threat to the killer, but Val knew what this family was capable of better than I did. She was privy to the monthly secret meetings, and I wasn't. Not that I couldn't attend, I simply never thought they were something I needed to hear, until now.

The next meeting started at nine, and this time I intended to be there.

ELEVEN

The Kill Zone

Dolci Picolli sat at the end of a row of storefronts down the red brick path. Wine-colored mums bloomed from clay pots along the path and in front of most of the shops. Young olive trees lined the pavement with their slender leaves gently dancing in the wind, showing off their soft white underbellies. A few of the clay pots were filled with more traditional autumn colors of burnt orange or yellow mums, giving everything that wonderful fall glow.

My mom had said Aunt Babe was showing Jade around. She'd be safe with Aunt Babe . . . at least I hoped so.

The narrow path was dotted with shoppers meandering in and out of the stores, carrying bags announcing Spia's Olive Press and the individual store name or logo. As I walked, thinking that not only was I suddenly desperate for a dozen Amaretto cookies (baked goods made with alcohol were my one allowable indulgence), but I hadn't really eaten in over twenty-four hours. Murder was a great hunger suppresser.

When I walked into the Dolci Piccoli, Aunt Hetty was behind the large glass baker's case helping a couple customers, an older man and an attractive woman with shiny gray shoulder length hair. They were speaking Italian with Hetty, who lapped it up. She loved to revert back to Italian whenever she had the chance. When she and Babe were growing up, their immigrant parents only spoke Italian to their children. Both she and Babe were fluent in the language. Me? I was third generation, and knew a few sentences, a mixture of good swear words and gestures, and could, if pressed, pick out a few words in a conversation.

From what I could make out, which wasn't much, they were either talking about blow fish in the mountains, or Jordan almonds at a wedding. I was going with the Jordan almonds. They were a safer bet under the circumstances.

The top of the counter held several glass displays of cookies and biscotti. A large slate board hanging on the wall behind the counter announced today's special: Two dozen cookies for the price of one.

Apparently, Aunt Hetty was trying to get rid of all the excess cookies from Dickey's party. Usually, the relatives scooped up the excess food after one of these events, but when my mom yelled cop, leftovers was not something that took high priority, even for Zia Yolanda.

The bright yellow walls of the bakery gave the place a happy, light ambiance, and white floor tile with little yellow squares at the corners reflected that happy tone. A padded, red-checkered bench ran across the far wall, with square tables and chairs in front of it. Artwork hung on the walls depicting Italian baked goods and older Italian women pulling bread or trays of cookies out of rustic ovens.

Jade sat at one of only four small round tables in front of the floor to ceiling windows. Aunt Babe was nowhere in sight, but it didn't matter because Nick Zeleski seemed to be a pretty good replacement. I didn't know if I was happy to see him, or scared to death.

"Mia," he yelled out. "Come join us." And he pulled up a white chair from the empty table next to them.

I needed those cookies, bad.

Before I could get up to the counter to place my order, Aunt Hetty already had a dozen Amaretto cookies sitting on a plate waiting for me. "You want tea or coffee with these?" she asked, stone faced.

"A shot of brandy would be perfect, but short of that, Irish Breakfast tea, please," I told her.

"I'll bring it over."

I nodded, took my plate of cookies, inhaled three of them before I arrived at the table, smiled at both Jade and Nick and sat across from Jade, right next to Nick.

Then I ate another cookie, this time I totally could taste the sweet Amaretto and a satisfied sensation momentarily washed over me.

Then Nick spoke. "Well, this is a nice coincidence."

Satisfaction was replaced with apprehension.

I nodded, too busy eating cookies to actually speak.

"Isn't this great?" Jade announced. "Nick's been looking for Dickey, too. I told him about our phone call last night, and about your mom and me just missing him this morning. Nick thinks Dickey went off to town or something. We're waiting for him to get back. In the meantime, I've been telling Nick all about my honey-bear." She turned to Nick. "I didn't ask how you know Dickey." She leaned in closer. "Were you an inmate with him in prison? 'Cause he told me he made a lot of friends while he was in there." She turned to me. "He was a cook, ya know? For the inmates. Wrote a cookbook with all his recipes. I'm going to help him get it published. My brother-in-law is a literary agent in New York." She turned back to Nick. "Were you his cellmate or something?"

I bit into another cookie and gazed over at Nick, waiting for his answer.

"Not exactly," he mumbled.

"Oh, now I get it. She leaned in closer and whispered. I leaned in closer and listened. "You're a friend from his Mafia days, aren't you?"

I sat back, smirked and watched Nick's face get all serious. "I'm with the Sheriff's Department," he told her. "I'd simply like to talk to Dickey." He turned to me. "But that seems to be a bit of a problem."

I swallowed, not wanting to say anything that might incriminate me later when and if the body ever did turn up. "I need more cookies. Can I get either of you anything?"

I stood.

Jade seemed to be in shock. She stopped talking. Nick was all smiles. "Yes, I'll take an éclair, they look great."

When I arrived at the counter with my empty plate, Aunt Babe was standing down at the other end, alone. I walked over to her. "Honey, you need to lose the cop and the dame." She still had that Barbara Stanwyck thing going on.

"Want to give me a clue how I should do that? Where's Dickey's SUV?"

"Don't fret, doll. Uncle Ray moved it."

"Oh, well, that makes sense. Wouldn't want the SUV sitting around attracting attention." I sucked in a deep breath and let it out in a rush of frustration. "This is getting completely out of control. We're diving in deeper and deeper. This is how to end up in jail, you know. I don't think I'll like jail. The jumpsuits are really unattractive."

"I baked an Amaretto cake this morning. How about I cut you a big chunk?"

I narrowed my eyes at her, sort of an evil eye kind of thing.

"You getting a headache, doll?" she asked.

Apparently, I wasn't very good at the evil eye thing.

"I'm thinking I should just tell Nick about the murder."

"And what are you going to tell him happened to the body?"

"I don't know. He's the detective, maybe he can tell me what happened to it."

"It won't be pretty. This whole place'll get locked down for days. We'll all be suspects, and who knows what they'll dig up. Don't forget he's got your mom's gun."

"How did you know about that?"

"Nothing escapes your Aunt Babe."

She pulled out six more Amaretto cookies, added a rather large slice of Amaretto cake and placed everything on a large white plate. "Is this enough, or should I bring over the whole cake?"

"I'll let you know." I grabbed the goodie plate. "Nick would like an éclair."

She slid open the glass door on the counter, pulled out an éclair, placed it on a larger dish, and added a cream puff and a cream filled horn. "These are for Jade. The dame already ate two puffs, but from the look on the doll's puss, she's gonna want more."

"When was the last time you saw Dickey, alive?" I whispered.

"Now's not the time to be asking questions. I might have something to tell ya, but lose the heat first."

She patted the bottom waves on her hair, turned slightly and asked the middle-aged woman who had walked up next to me if she could help her. I thought about asking Aunt Hetty a few questions, but with Nick and Jade in the same room, I knew she would be even more uncooperative than Aunt Babe.

I turned and headed back to the table carrying the plates of goodies. My pot of tea had arrived along with a white mug. As I walked toward them I knew I had to figure out a way to get rid of them, if only for a little while.

"Is that for me?" Jade asked when I returned to the table.

"Yes," I told her, and she grabbed the cream puff before I could put the plate down. I placed the éclair in front of Nick.

"Thanks," he said. "What do I owe you?"

"On the house," I answered.

He took a bite, custard oozed out the bottom and splattered on his plate. I thought it was too bad it didn't land on his pants. He'd have to leave to change if it fell on his pants. Nothing stains like lemon custard, well, except maybe thirty liters of olive oil, but that was last night's fiasco. I'd have to think of something else for today.

Nick calmly finished off his éclair while I finished off the Amaretto cake in three bites and washed it down with the entire pot of hot tea. This was getting scary. I didn't know who in my family had killed Dickey nor did I know who wanted that ring, but the entire incident was enough to make me crave a good solid binge.

I had to get more aggressive with my interrogations if I was going to remain sober and figure out this murder game, or I was destined, at the very least, to become an Amaretto addict.

Jade's phone made a growl. "It's my honey-bear!" she trilled. "He's calling me. That's his ring."

I tried to remain calm as I threw Nick a "see, everything's okay," kind of look, but I could tell he was skeptical, while I was curious about the caller.

At first, Jade couldn't find her phone in her oversized Coach tote. Then by some miracle of female determination, she came up with a pink Blackberry. She put the phone up to her ear and cooed, "Hi honey-bear, where are you?"

Both Nick and I were intent on the call. He pretended to be interested in the cream-filled horn still on his plate, while I pretended to be fascinated in the pot of mums on the other side of the window.

"Ah-huh. Yes. Sure. But are you okay? You don't—"

She listened, head down, staring at the table. "Right away, sweetie. Okay. Love you."

She disconnected.

"I've got to go," she told us, grabbing her bag and standing, a concerned, rushed look on her face.

"Is something wrong?" I asked her.

"No. I don't think so. I just need to go."

"Go where?" Nick asked.

"Someplace," she said. "I, I can't tell you. Just someplace."

Nick's phone rang.

"Excuse me," Nick said, pulling out his cell and greeting the person on the line with a, "Nick Zeleski."

Jade turned to me, whispering, "What's the fastest way to Glen Ellen? I have a GPS in my car, but sometimes it doesn't tell me the best route."

"Is that where you're going to meet Dickey?"

She leaned in closer. "Yes, but I'm not supposed to tell Nick. Somehow Dickey found out he was hanging around here and he told me not to say anything to him about where I was going."

A little warning flag sprung up in my head as she gathered her things, placed a five spot on the table and stood.

"Where in Glen Ellen?" I stood with her.

"Jack London Saloon. He gave me the street it's on, London Ranch Road, but no actual address. Do you know where it is?"

I couldn't let her go alone. "I'll take you."

She looked hesitant. "I don't know if I should. He specifically told me to come alone. That he had a big surprise waiting for me. I couldn't hear him too well. Our connection was bad. He said he was coming down with laryngitis, so he could only whisper."

"I bet," I said.

"Why? Was my honey-bear sick last night?"

"Deadly. I better take you just in case he needs to see a doctor. I know exactly where to find the closest Urgent Care."

At least this part was true. I'd been to the one in Rohnert Park on several occasions. Mostly brought there by other people who thought I was going to die from all the alcohol I'd consumed.

"Okay, but if he gets mad at me you'll have to tell him this was your idea, not mine, ya know?"

"Got it covered," I said.

Nick joined us at the door. "I have something I have to do. I'll catch up with you later." And he hurried out.

Ten minutes later, Jade, Lisa and I were in Lisa's now somewhat oil-free BMW driving up Highway 12 on our way to Glen Ellen. The black leather seats gleamed, and even with the open windows the car still had that lovely musky olive oil scent.

Yet another use for our oils.

Regrettably, not everyone in the car was enjoying the musky moment. Lisa seemed content enough, but Jade still wore a scowl. She had tried to argue away Lisa's joining us, but there was no way to win an argument with Lisa once she set her mind to something. Besides, her car was much more comfortable than my pickup.

The drive from Spia's Olive Press to London Ranch Road usually took about twenty minutes in light traffic. I knew this because Jack London Saloon had been my bar of choice since I turned twenty-one. They made a mean Sex with an Alligator. No skimping on the ingredients. The bartenders poured a generous shot of Midori into a shaker along with sweet and sour and ice. They shook that up and poured the chilled mixture into a cold martini glass, and added a float each of Chambord and Jagermeister. I could usually do three or four of these along with several shots of tequila in one night. That was on a good night when I didn't want to get too drunk.

The taste and sensation of it swirled around in my memory as we drove closer to Glen Ellen. I didn't like going anywhere near the saloon and usually stayed as far away from it as possible, but there was no way I could let Jade go alone. Way too dangerous for her. I was going for the safety-in-numbers routine.

Besides, I needed to see for myself who had made the phone call. I figured it had to be either the killer, or an accomplice. After all, it took a lot of muscle power to move that millstone, even if the killer used our forklift; it still took a lot of effort.

Of course, I didn't know exactly what I would do once I cornered the killer, but I figured Lisa would know what to do when the time came for physical action.

Lisa and Jade sat in the front chatting about Alcatraz Island and the Al Capone years, while I sat in the back alone with my thoughts. I wasn't paying attention to their conversation, too busy going over the list of possible suspects, Uncle Benny taking slot number one because of that codicil. He especially had motive now that he was sleeping with my mom, a vision I didn't want to dwell on. The one problem to that scenario was her setup. Why would Benny set up the woman he was sleeping with? That made no sense. Still, did anything ever make sense with these Wise Guys?

Cousin Jimmy stood at number two because he still followed orders, and would have no problem with slicing and dicing Dickey then spreading him around. I'd heard stories about Jimmy, and although he was never indicted for murder, I suspected he was a good little enforcer to the rest of his crew. It wouldn't surprise me if he had been the Dickey impersonator on the other end of Jade's call.

Uncle Ray came to mind next because of Val's hatred for Dickey; Ray could easily shoot Dickey to avenge his wife. Valerie was a powerful force and for all of Ray's bravado, Val was the master of that household.

Then there was always Hetty and Babe, two women who truly had motive and opportunity.

And I couldn't rule out Maryann just because of her peculiar accordion connection with Dickey. Who knew what secrets that woman could be hiding?

My head was spinning with various compare scenarios when I felt a slight smack on our back bumper.

"What the hell?" I said as Lisa swerved toward the ditch on the passenger side of the road.

"I got it," she croaked then sped up. She pressed a button on the car door and her seat automatically adjusted, along with the steering wheel, and side mirrors. I wondered if this feature came standard.

Lisa sat up straight, locked each hand on either side of the wheel then gazed in the rearview mirror. "Prepare for evasive action," she ordered, voice laden with authority.

"Evasive action?" I didn't know if she was kidding or completely serious.

"Yes. When you're being pursued while in a car do not allow the pursuer to gain the upper hand. Be prepared to take evasive defensive action. This is a contest of both wills and skills."

I tightened my seat belt.

Apparently, she'd already written this section of her book.

I really needed to catch up.

"Shouldn't we just, like, stop?" Jade spluttered, leaning forward in her seat. "Share information? Ya know, call the police? Do all those accident things?"

"Not a chance. That guy's been tailing us ever since we left the orchard. I think we've got something personal going on."

I turned to grab a better look. "This is so not good." A black Tundra was gaining on us.

"But who . . . are you sure?" Jade asked.

"Positive. My radar's been up for the last ten minutes, but I didn't want to alarm you guys. He fits all the criteria for a road warrior: no plates, smoky windows, aggressive driving and I can't shake him. This bad dude is nothing I can't handle." Lisa focused on the street and cars ahead of her. "I've been through the Bob Bondurant Tac Mob course. I know exactly what to do to avoid the kill zone. This fool is messing with the wrong chick."

"The kill zone?" I asked.

"Any place your attacker tries to trap you," Lisa calmly said.

"Anyone you know?" I asked Jade, not wanting to think it

might be the killer giving us yet another warning. Or was this warning meant specifically for Jade? After all, Lisa and I had already gotten the finger . . . so to speak.

Jade twisted around and stared at the Tundra, then shook her head. "No. Like, I don't think so, but I can't see his face too well. And nobody I know would hit our car like that, or wear those awful shades. Those are, like, so last year."

I turned and caught the double-C logo for Chanel on the sides of his shades. What guy would wear big Chanel glasses with a cowboy hat? And didn't he have a mustache?

Something very odd was up with this bumper dude, but I didn't have time to think about it because Jade was still talking. "This is so not cool. I mean some of my friends are crazy, but not this crazy, ya know? Besides, I didn't tell anybody I was coming to Sonoma. It was a spur of the moment kind of decision. I'm supposed to be at work today."

"Can't this thing go any faster? He's going to hit us again." I said, bracing for the next impact. The Tundra couldn't have been more than two feet from our back bumper. I glanced back trying to make out the face, but the window was too dark and the sunglasses too big.

It suddenly occurred to me that maybe I'd been seeing a lot of this Tundra lately. Who the hell owned it and why were they following me?

"Traffic's too heavy. Prepare for impact," Lisa yelled.

The second bump was harder and threw us into oncoming traffic. Lisa swung the wheel to the left and managed to somehow avoid the other cars. My blood thrummed through my veins as I braced my hands on the back of the front seat. Probably not the best idea, but what did I know of car chases and evasive defensive action.

Suddenly we were driving on the opposite shoulder, which wasn't wide enough. Dirt and gravel flew up alongside of us.

Horns blared, Jade screamed, I held on while Lisa remained totally focused on her driving.

"Everybody hang on," Lisa warned as she maneuvered the car over ditches and gravel. We were fast approaching the end of said shoulder, and a deep drop-off loomed before us. Jade's eyes went wide. I put my head down, closed my eyes, and held my breath, hoping for the best. All I could think of in those few seconds of terror was how I couldn't die yet. I needed to have sex with Leo one more time.

Adrenalin rushed through my veins. The car lurched back onto the tarmac, and lost traction for a moment. My stomach spun and I had that sick falling feeling. When I looked up we were headed straight for a tour bus.

I couldn't help myself. The yell just seemed to happen without my being conscious of actually making a sound. Jade's frantic voice mixed with mine and we were a chorus of panic.

"You son of a bitch," Lisa roared as she swung the car out of harm's way. The bus driver laid on his horn, but kept right on going.

I swear we missed the bus by inches.

Once we crossed back over to our own lane, we were directly behind the black Tundra. The driver immediately hit the brakes causing his backend to fishtail. Lisa veered onto the shoulder to avoid hitting him, drove down the embankment onto a dirt service road passing rows of grapevines and the Tundra.

Luckily, the service road forked and she made a sharp right onto a dirt feeder road that led into the orchard. We were going so fast we took out some vines along the way, but the good news was the Tundra was no longer following us, and the airbags didn't deploy. By the time we came to a complete stop we had managed to take out almost an entire row of vines.

Then there was silence—street silence—but our car still made little pinging and ticking noises as if it had been just as scared as we were and needed a moment to calm down.

One by one we slowly exited the car and sat down in a row, next to the fallen vines. The car was cloaked in a thick layer of dirt, leaves and scattered vine limbs. We were no different. Dirt caked in the corners of my mouth, my eyes and I could feel it tickling my nose. I spit out torn leaves and pulled a twig out of my ear. Lisa was in worse shape. The leaves had managed to cling to her hair in such a way that she no longer had actual hair, giving her that coveted mythical goddess look.

Jade was totally covered in dirt and twigs.

We looked like children of the grapevines.

That's when I started laughing, really laughing. That kind of nervous laughter that makes your eyes water, your cheeks ache and your belly hurt. Soon Lisa stepped back, took a look at me and let it rip. We were hysterical.

Jade didn't get it. Didn't get the fact that we had almost died, but because of Lisa's determination we were still taking in air.

After a few minutes, Jade said, "Holy shit! And I thought driving in the city was bad. Does this happen, like, all the time? I mean, I'm glad you were driving, 'cause I would have been dead a long time ago, ya know? Look at me." She held out her hands. "I'm shaking."

"Believe me, you're not the only one," I told her, rubbing my arms. Then the three of us held onto each other for a long time.

"Is everybody all right?" Lisa asked when she finally pulled away.

Jade nodded.

"I think so," I said. That's when I noticed the blood on Lisa's shirt, actually it was my white shirt, but that was beside the point. "You're bleeding."

I visually checked her over, while she quickly ran her hands down her body.

"Nothing's broken. I seem fine," she said. "Except for this."

Blood oozed from a nasty gash on her thumb. I instantly knew where this was headed from all those scraped knees she had as a kid. Lisa had a stomach like a rock when it came to other people's blood. It was her own blood she could never handle.

I ran over and caught her just as she passed out in my arms.

"The big lesson of life, baby, is never be scared of anyone or anything. Fear is the enemy of logic."
—Frank Sinatra

TWELVE

Where Everybody Knows Your Name

Two hours later we were still in the ER of Sonoma Valley Hospital on Andrieux Avenue, a few blocks from Highway 12. When Lisa collapsed, Jade called 911, which, along with the quick response of the Sonoma PD, eventually alerted Nick who then phoned Leo, who phoned my mom. Once that happened it was like a dam broke and the news of our accident traveled so fast that by the time the ambulance arrived at the hospital, most of my family stood waiting outside along with Leo and Nick.

Nick ignored us and went right to our driver. I couldn't hear what they were saying because my mother trumped all other sounds.

"Oh my God, are you girls all right?" she yelled when the back door of the ambulance swung open. Both Jade and I had sat on a side bench during the short ride, while Lisa was prone on a gurney. "This is crazy," Lisa said. "I feel great. I can walk."

But the paramedics would have no part of it. None of us was allowed to walk into the hospital.

"We're fine, Mom," I said, as a male nurse ushered me into a wheelchair.

"Did they catch the bastard who tried to run you off the road?"

"Not yet," I told her.

"Damn bastage. They should cut off his balls," Val said.

"Drastic," the nurse said behind me.

"Not enough," Val countered. "If it was up to me, his dick would come off in the process."

The nurse fell silent.

"Glad to see you girls are all right," Federico said. "Good thing Lisa was driving."

"Yeah," I agreed. "Good thing."

Leo came up alongside me, and took my hand in his. I held on tight, happy to see him despite his lying, although his concern was truly touching. "I'm here if you need anything."

"I'm okay. Really," I told him.

I wasn't used to Leo caring about me. This was a new feature to his otherwise closed personality.

"You girls don't look so fine," Aunt Hetty said, her hair standing straight up in fuzzy tufts, lipstick smeared in the usual manner. Why the woman even wore lipstick remained a mystery. "You look like hell."

"Thanks," I said, wanting to say so much more.

"Wow! I've never been in a wheelchair before," Jade announced as another nurse secured the foot rests. "Interesting."

Aunt Babe came up on the other side, and walked with me as my nurse pushed me toward the glass ER doors. "You can tell me the truth, doll. How ya feeling?"

"I feel all right. A little unsteady, and uncomfortably dirty, but okay, considering." It was the truth. I guess what was really bugging me at the moment was the whole idea of someone trying to run us off the road. I wanted to tell Leo all the details about the Tundra dogging me, but I couldn't take the chance it would get back to Nick.

"That's good to hear, doll."

"That don't mean nothing," Uncle Ray said. "You could have internal injuries. All that bumping can move things around on the inside."

"I can assure you, nothing moved," I told him, still clinging to Leo's warm hand. The nurse ignored everyone and kept moving me closer to the doors.

Uncle Benny chewed on his stogy. "You are going to be fine,

Mia. These doctors are the best. Do not worry about a thing. I will see to it that they take good care of you girls."

A tall female nurse waiting at the door rolled her eyes.

My mother leaned over to Jade who was coming up alongside of me. "Do you want me to phone anyone, dear?"

Jade shook her head then gave it a second thought. "You might call Dickey for me."

All family members within earshot of that little statement backed off, except my mom. She leaned in closer to Jade and said, "Now's probably not a good time."

Jade's forehead furrowed. "I tried to get him a couple times on his cell, but the call went straight to voice mail. Would you please call the Jack London Tavern in Glen Ellen and see if he's there? It would be nice if he could come and get me, ya know?"

Mom patted her hand. "I'll see what I can do."

After that little reality reminder my family did their thing and let the ER staff do their thing. Even Leo let go of my hand and I wondered if someone had told him about Dickey.

But I immediately thought better of it. He wasn't family. Murder would never go beyond family.

As it turned out Jade had a nasty looking bump on her forehead, which required an MRI, and I had somehow managed to wrench my left shoulder, which required a CT scan. Fortunately, for us both there was no major internal damage, just some superficial bruising that would heal in a week or so. A shot of something took care of my shoulder pain, and Jade was told that her bump would probably turn a bit yellow and blue, but wouldn't leave any kind of scar.

Jade and I were released with a "To Do" list, and pain medication prescriptions from the doctor, but Lisa remained behind a curtain somewhere. Most of my family, except for my mom and Aunt Babe, left when they learned all was well. Leo offered to blow off the rest of his day and spend it with me, which was something he would never have done in the past, but I didn't want him around. Way too much to discuss with Lisa.

After much discussion, and his mini-conference with the doctors on top of the millionth assurance that I was fine, he agreed to let me go home and rest. We would catch up at the Martini Madness Ball the following night, my first Martini Madness Ball in over two years. I was hoping to come out of it in one sober piece.

Once he was gone, and my mom and Aunt Babe went off to scope out the recently upgraded gift shop, and to fill my prescription for pain meds, my focus went to Lisa. I hadn't seen her since we were all wheeled in and I needed to talk to her, alone, before we headed back to the orchard with my family.

Nurse Carol, an overly cheery woman with red hair pointed the way. Lisa apparently had not been released with Jade and me. "She's still with the doctor," Nurse Carol said. She had those round buggy eyes that made you think it hurt just to blink, hair that looked as if it wouldn't move in a tornado, and the sweetest disposition I'd ever encountered in someone who worked the ER.

"Just follow me, girls," Nurse Carol instructed. "These kinds of things can be scary and your friend probably needs all the reassurance she can get."

Jade and I followed her along a row of drawn curtains. Voices rose up all around us: a child wailed, a man yelled about his injured foot, and an elderly voice asked, "How much time do I have left?"

My heart was racing the entire time as my mind conjured up horrible scenarios, not the least of which was that Lisa had lapsed into a coma or worse. Perhaps she had internal injuries like Uncle Ray had said and I had foolishly thought she'd passed out from seeing her own blood.

By the time the curtain was pulled back, I expected to see Lisa lying on the bed, completely comatose. The doctor would tell me that my best friend didn't merely faint, she had actually suffered a head trauma and needed immediate surgery. I'd have to call her nearest relative to sign the paperwork. The thought of having to deal with Lisa's mother was more frightening than having to deal with a comatose friend.

I shuddered at the very idea of it.

Luckily, Lisa was sitting up on the edge of the bed, looking all fresh and clean in her little blue gown, watching as an Indian male doctor pulled stitches through her right thumb. She could handle the stitches as long as there wasn't any of her own blood involved.

"But you don't understand. I'm on a deadline. I have to be able to type."

"But I never said you could not type, Miss. I simply said you should not use your thumb for five days. It is badly bruised and combined with these stitches it will need time to heal. I will put your arm in a sling to remind you."

"I don't want a sling, thank you."

He finished stitching, cut the threads and began bandaging her thumb. "I will give you a sling anyway. It is what I recommend."

She started to disagree but I interrupted. "I'll make sure she wears it."

He looked over at me. "It is for her own good, Miss. I will give her a prescription for pain medication as well. This is going to be one heck of a thumb-ache."

"I can handle it," Lisa said.

"Ah, you are like your books then?"

Her face lit up. "You're familiar with my work?"

"I have five daughters, a wife, a mother and a mother-in-law. How could I not know? They have memorized parts of your books and discuss them over dinner. My mother-in-law used your foul-smell method to make my nephew vomit when he ate her pet goldfish, Stan. It was too late for Stan, but my mother-in-law was impressed that your technique worked so effectively. She used her husband's jar of pickled herring. I have to say, that smell would make anyone toss their cookies."

Lisa chuckled. "I'll have to remember that."

"These women practice your survival skills religiously just in case they might need them. My middle daughter has jumped out of a second story window into a garbage container with her hands tied loosely behind her back. I did not approve of this, of course, but she worked up to it, and by the time she jumped, she knew what to do. She was able to find something sharp to cut the rope on her wrists and get out of the container on her own.

Regrettably, she also managed to cut her baby toe when she jumped . . . she wore flip flops, not the best. I cleaned up the cut and gave her three stitches. She refused the pain medication as well. She said she needed to have all her pistons running on full speed just in case she needed to survive something else."

"I'll send you a few autographed copies of my latest book," Lisa told him.

"My family will be so pleased, Miss. Thank you."

"It's the least I can do."

"Ah, the least you can do is to wear the sling for five days," he said. "This will make my family very happy because you will assure them that your thumb will heal properly so you can write more books."

She laughed. "Okay, I agree. Bring it on."

He patted her shoulder. "You are a very intelligent woman. My family will be happy to learn this."

As soon as he left the room, Jade said. "Wow! You're that Lisa Lin? I'm a total fan. I've read all your books. You have to be the coolest chick ever. This is, like, way cool, ya know? To actually meet you and you're so normal. And short. I mean, not that you're short, short, but you're tiny and yet you're a real kick-ass, ya know?"

Lisa smiled. "Thanks. I don't think I've ever gotten such a cool compliment."

"I passed a coffee stand on the way in here. I, like, so need a latte," Jade said. "Can I get you guys anything?"

Both Lisa and I jumped on the opportunity to be alone. We gave her complicated drink orders that would keep her and the barista busy for at least fifteen minutes.

As soon as she left, Lisa turned to me. "I think one of the goombahs tried to kill us, or at the very least give us a warning."

"If that was a warning, I'd hate to think what it would be like if one of them really came after us."

"We wouldn't be having this conversation, that's for damn sure. That guy knew his shit."

"I wouldn't be so quick to assume it was one of the ex-cons." I was thinking about that disappearing mustache. "You were pretty incredible out there."

"Of course I was. I just wrote about it, Chapter Six, How to Survive a Car Chase. I did extensive research with an adorable wannabe NASCAR driver who taught me all about driving defensively, and how to keep control of your car after a rear or side bump, along with some other, more personal moves that still give me a rush."

She threw me a sly smirk.

"Spare me the details."

"I'll put them in a book someday, an erotica. I could make a killing in that field."

"But where would you get the time for the research?"

She gave me a wry look. "You're kidding, right?"

"Of course I am," I said, but I really wasn't. Okay, so up until last night sex had been put on a high shelf in my life. So high it had required a ladder to retrieve it, but her life seemed to be so full I couldn't imagine when she possibly had the time for anything, much less an active sex life.

But then Lisa never did have a problem juggling several things at once. Sobriety does that.

"Did you see who it was?" Lisa asked.

"Kind of, but I couldn't get a good look at the idiot's face under that cowboy hat, and Chanel shades. Although, I think I saw a mustache, but when I looked again, it was gone."

"Okay, so whoever the idiot is uses cheap glue, but buys expensive sunglasses, and has the whole Western monster truck thing going on. I'm betting it's your cousin Jimmy or a friend from his bar in North Beach. Lot's of testosterone coming from that truck."

"Wearing Chanel sunglasses?"

"You have a point, but the women in your family don't drive. How about Maryann?"

I shook my head. "She's into saving the planet and only drives eco-friendly."

"Any other little clue?"

"Well, the idiot didn't have a double chin or any gray hair that I could see, but the windows were heavily tinted, so I can't be sure of anything."

She sighed.

"Here's the thing," Lisa said. "I don't get why anyone would come after me. I was all for the family burying Dickey in the grove."

I sat down on a gray plastic chair, my head spinning with possibilities. "Nobody knows that but me."

"Shouldn't you tell someone? I've got a life to live, deadlines to keep, a mother who looks forward to retiring in my guesthouse."

"You live in a condo in the city. You don't own a guesthouse."

"And I won't ever own a guesthouse if your family keeps trying to run me off the road. The odds aren't in my favor with this group. Eventually they'll succeed. Dickey being the prime example."

"Does this mean you're completely over the idea of allowing my family to cover up Dickey's death?"

"No offense sweetie, I love your family but we need to figure out who this idiot is and turn his sorry ass over to the police before he gets any more ideas about sending us body parts or running us off the road. I have no intention of becoming his second victim. Maybe we need to find that ring first and give it back. That way we can smoke this killer out in the open."

I leaned back on the plastic chair. "Now you're talking like the Lisa Lin I know and love, but first we need to get rid of the doll, as Aunt Babe would say. And quick."

"What doll?" Nick asked as he slid back the curtain.

Somehow, in the family and doctor frenzy, I had completely forgotten about relentless Nick.

"A doll I had when I was a kid," I said.

He grinned. "You don't really expect me to believe that's what you were talking about, do you? The officers at the scene told me about the black Tundra that tried to run you ladies off the road. According to Jade, if it wasn't for Lisa's defensive driving abilities, you girls might be lying in intensive care right now instead of getting a thumb stitched up. Want to tell me who might want to harm you?"

"I have no idea what you're talking about," I said about as convincingly as a five-year-old caught with her hand in the cookie jar.

"Let's see, Dickey seems to be missing, there's a blood stain on your antique olive press, I have a handgun in my possession that has recently been fired, and now someone's tried to kill the three of you on the highway. I'd say there's a reasonable chance you both know exactly what this is all about, but for some reason you're choosing not to tell me or anyone else for that matter. You do know that I can get a warrant and haul both of you into the station for questioning, or you can make all this easy on me and come clean right now."

"Jade is overreacting to a pushy tourist. Okay, so maybe we were bumped a little. Nothing I couldn't handle," Lisa told him.

"Your car is totaled, and your rear bumper was completely torn off. I'd say that's a little worse than a little bump."

"My car is totaled?" Lisa whined. "I loved that car. It was my baby, my friend. I swear it had a personality. I'll never get another one like it. Never." She lay back on the bed, crestfallen.

I liked the effect.

Nick reacted.

"I know what you mean," he said, walking closer to her. "I had a sixty-five Camaro like that. A drunk driver plowed into it while it was parked in front of Bectal's ice cream parlor. I was sixteen. My first car. I cried for two solid days."

As if on cue, Lisa began to cry.

"Now don't go doing that. I'm not good at crying women, especially one I like." He turned to me. "Do something."

"When she gets like this, I've found it's best to just to sit with her until it passes." I glanced at my watch. "Oh, look at the time. I have to run." And I rushed out of the room, hoping that Nick wouldn't follow me, which he didn't.

As I walked out of the ER I ran into Jade carrying the two cups of coffee.

"Guess what?" I said. "I got in touch with Dickey and told him all about the accident. He was relieved to know you're all right."

"Is he on his way?" she asked all doe eyed, handing me a concoction of coffee that must have been five hundred calories. I took a sip. It was like drinking straight syrup.

"That's awful," I said and dumped it in a trash can. Then I took Lisa's and did the same thing.

"Why would you do that? I don't get you guys. There's something strange going on here, ya know? I may not always come across like I'm smart, but I'm a member of Mensa and I know when someone's trying to put one over on me."

"There's nothing strange. Everything's fine. Just fine."

"No it's not and I'm not leaving this hospital until you tell me what's going on."

She sat down hard in a chair in the ER waiting room, folded her arms and planted her feet, a look of determination on her smudged face.

I sat down next to her. "Here's the thing," I began, trying to figure out how to tell her that Dickey was dead. She stared at me and I could tell she wouldn't take the news well. "Do you have a friend you can stay with for a few days?"

"Yeah," she said. "But what does that have to do with anything? I feel fine."

"I think whoever was driving that truck was actually after you."

Okay, so I couldn't tell her about Dickey, but I was telling her the truth. I really did think the guy in the Tundra was after her.

"Me? Why would anyone want to hurt me?"

"Jealousy," I whispered. All right, it was a big fat lie, something I was getting quite good at.

"You mean somebody's jealous because I'm engaged to Dickey?"

Not where I was going, but it worked. "Shh. I wouldn't say that too loud around here. There's no telling who could be listening."

"I never thought of that."

"Oh yeah. Dickey was a babe magnet. Somebody might want you out of the way."

"Out of the way, like in dead?"

I gave her a look, nodded and pretended to check out the room like there might be someone listening to us. Of course, there were only two other people in the room, a man with a gash on his forehead, and a middle-aged woman who looked as if she was about to pass out in her chair.

"My advice would be to get as far away from here as possible and to stay with a friend for a few days."

"But what about my honey-bear? He loves me and I love him."

"If he loved you, he would have been here at the hospital. Last I looked he hasn't shown up. Not a good sign."

Big tears rolled down her cheeks. "Maybe we were moving too fast. My friends said I should think about it a little more before I commit."

"I'd have to agree with your friends. Especially after today. Don't you think?"

She nodded, pulled out a tissue from her pocket wiped her tears and blew her nose with a great big high-pitched honk. It made me want to laugh, but I controlled myself.

"But now I'm scared to drive back to the city."

"Don't worry about it. I have a plan."

Which I did. Suddenly I knew exactly what I had to do with Jade Batista.

The big white tour bus idled in our parking lot in front of our tasting room like it did most days. My mom had made friends with most of the tour guides, and knew several of the drivers on a first name basis. I didn't have a problem talking the guide into taking Jade after I offered everyone on the bus a free three-once bottle of our oil. Luckily, there were only thirty people on the bus and the tiny bottles were a great promotional device. It was one of those win-win moments.

Jade and I stood in front of the bus handing out the oil as everyone boarded. They smiled, thanked us and went away with both the oil and a brochure detailing Spia's olive oil club. For about forty dollars every quarter, the participant received two bottles of extra virgin olive oil of our choice, along with a few recipes, and a fifteen percent discount on any online purchase. A great deal for the EVOO connoisseur.

"You have someone to pick you up at the bus drop-off and someone to stay with for a few days, right?" I asked her. I had to make sure she would be safe.

She nodded. "My ex-boyfriend."

I could tell she was scared, and I felt sorry for her. I knew that feeling well. Plus she kept running her hand over the welt on her head, which was already turning a deep purple.

My shoulder was sore and stiff. Whatever drug they had given me in the hospital was wearing off and it was time for another dose from that filled prescription my mom had picked up.

"Here," she said pulling off her engagement ring. "Tell Dickey I don't want to be engaged anymore. I don't like car chases and sneaking around. That's for movies and books, not for real life."

I closed her hand around the ring. "You keep it. Believe me, he doesn't need it. Sell it and use the money for something you want."

"I can't do that. It's not right."

"Consider it payment for all you went through today."

"No, I—"

"Trust me on this."

She smiled and slipped it back on her finger.

"Tell me about your ex."

"He's just a guy I met when I first moved to the city. We were going to get married, but he didn't like me writing to Dickey or working on the island. I only wrote to Dickey because of research for my thesis, ya know? Same reason I worked on the island. When Dickey was released, part of me got engaged to him just to show my ex I'm my own person, ya know? But it was all a game."

She piqued my curiosity. "A game?"

"Yeah. Confidentially, all that stuff about sex with Dickey, I made that up. I only ever slept with one other boy in my entire life before Jay-Jay, that's his name. And really, all we did was sleep together, and maybe fool around a little, but nothing serious happened. I was a virgin when I first made it with Jay-Jay. I don't like to admit that. Makes me sound like a real nerd or something, which I kinda' was before I moved to San Francisco. Ruins the mystique, ya know? I don't even know if I would have gone through with it with Dickey. I mean, the guy was old enough to be my grandfather, ya know?"

I smiled. "I know. We all like to play games with our sexual prowess."

"Yeah, that's for sure. Even Dickey."

"What do you mean?"

"Well, for all his bravado, he told me he never slept with that Carla woman. That she told him she really was a virgin, and meant to keep it that way until she was married."

"But I thought they were having an affair?"

"That's what she wanted everyone to think, just like our affair. He said he thought she was playing him and all she really wanted was for some other guy to get jealous and marry her."

"Some other guy?"

"Yeah. Dickey said he really loved Carla, but she didn't love him. He said it was sort of like Sophia Loren, Cary Grant and Carlo Ponti. I mean, I know who Sophia Loren is, and everybody knows Cary Grant, but I have no idea who this Carlo Ponti dude is or was, but anyway, he said that somebody killed Carla before she could marry her Carlo Ponti. Does this make any sense to you?"

I nodded. I knew all the details because of Aunt Babe. It was one of her classic Hollywood love triangles. "So Carla was seeing someone else besides Dickey?"

"That's what Dickey said, but he didn't know who. She never told him."

"As far as I can remember, this never came up in the trial."

"Dickey said he told his lawyer, but without concrete evidence, it was inadmissible."

"Then Dickey came back here with the same sort of situation going on. You're still in love with this Jay-Jay dude, aren't you?"

Her eyes watered. "I guess so, only honey-bear, I mean Dickey, and I were supposed to announce our engagement last night. He said he had some kind of plan to ferret out Carla's killer, but then he got a phone call yesterday morning and suddenly he had to meet somebody at Russo's winery. You know where that is?"

"I do," I said, my heart in my throat.

I now had verification that Dickey was on that porch with Leo. I wanted to cry, but first I needed to eat. Food seemed like the only thing that might keep me from passing out from all her disturbing information.

"He told me to wait until I heard from him before I drove over, but when I never did, well, you know the rest."

The driver interrupted our conversation. "Time to go, Miss."

Jade and I hugged. "Call me when you get to Jay-Jay's."

She nodded. I gave her my phone number and she quickly punched it into her keypad, fingers moving at warp speed. I never could do that. Then she turned and boarded the bus.

I gave her a little wave as the bus drove away.

Jade turned out to be a sweet girl. She was going to be sad when she heard about Dickey's demise. Jade was one of the few people I knew who cared about Dickey, Jade and Maryann and perhaps Aunt Babe.

"What was that all about?" Lisa asked, walking up behind me, right arm in a blue sling.

"I'll tell you about it over dinner. I'm starving. I'll cook. Afterward, we have to sneak into a private meeting and try to pick out Carlo Ponti."

Scallops with Myer Lemon and Fennel Dressing – Level One

3 tbs. Liquirizia from Calabria or any other licorice flavored liquor
3 tbs. Mission EVOO or any mild tasting EVOO
1 large clove of fresh garlic, crushed
Salt and cracked pepper to taste
Hot-pepper EVOO
10 to 16 Scallops
four skewers

Dressing
2 tbs. Myer lemon juice (Myer lemons are sweeter and yield much more juice)
1/4 tsp. grated lemon zest
2 tbs. Champagne Balsamic vinegar or cherry vinegar
1 tsp. Dijon mustard
1/3 cup Mission EVOO (or forgo the lemons and use lemon infused EVOO)
2 tbs. chopped fresh fennel tops
Salt and cracked pepper to taste

To make dressing: Blend the vinegar, lemon juice, zest, and mustard in a bowl. Gradually add the Mission oil until well blended. Add the chopped fennel and salt and pepper to taste, mix again. Breathe in the aroma, relax, breathe, feel the tension leaving your body. Set the mixture aside to allow the flavors to meld.

Blend the Liquirizia, Mission EVOO, garlic, salt, pepper and a drizzle of hot-pepper EVOO in a large bowl. Add the scallops, and work them around so each one is sufficiently coated in the mixture. Refrigerate, covered for thirty minutes.

While that's marinating, get the grill going and if it's outdoors, enjoy your surroundings while you wait for the grill to come to life. Take your time. Enjoy the moment. Note: You can also cut the fennel meat in four chunks, coat it in olive oil, (add a little hot-pepper olive oil if you're feeling daring) cracked pepper and salt to taste, wrap the chunks in foil and bake on the grill until the fennel is tender and almost soft.

30 minutes later: Skewer four scallops so they are lying flat and grill for about one to two minutes on a side making sure they are cooked through, but not dry. Remove them from the grill, de-skewer, and place them on a brightly colored serving plate. Generously drizzle the aromatic beauties with the dressing and serve.

THIRTEEN

Will the Real Mobster Please Stand Up?

Jade phoned a little over an hour later saying she arrived home safe and Jay-Jay had picked her up at the bus drop off. She told me that she and Jay-Jay would stop by to pick up her car in a few days, when she was feeling better. She sounded tired, but happy to be back with her old boyfriend.

I had taken my pain meds so I was feeling a little woozy, and in need of a couple hours of sleep, but sleep would have to wait until after dinner.

Lisa filled me in on what Nick had to say about Dickey, which wasn't much more than he'd already told us at the hospital.

"But," she cautioned, "we won't be able to hold him off much longer. That blood stain is making him nuts. He already contacted that worker your mom told him about who disassembled the millstone, but good thing for us, they've been playing phone tag. He may have caught up with him by now, and if he has, we could be royally screwed."

"Not necessarily. My mom doesn't lie, she sometimes leaves out important details, but she never flat out lies, at least I don't think she does. The guy probably did cut himself so that'll buy us a little more time."

I filled Lisa in on everything Jade had told me over broccoli sautéed in our Artisan Blend along with a clove of garlic, and sprinkled with pine nuts. Broccoli sautéed in our Mission extra virgin olive oil was just what we needed after the day we had. The combination is rich in phenols, vitamin C and minerals. For our entrée I served grilled marinated scallops drizzled with a lemony-fennel dressing. I might not be able to drive us out of danger, but I could cook us out of an adrenalin overload anytime.

Lisa sipped a glass of Moscato Bianco from Jacuzzi winery, one of my favorites, a wine with floral aromas and a tropical note. I drank sparkling water with a lemon slice. I whole-heartedly craved a glass of Moscato, but I didn't think I was quite ready to partake. More therapy was required before those fine fermented grapes touched these wanton lips. It was bad enough that I'd made love to Leo—I knew a glass of wine would clearly throw me into the danger zone. A place I'd seen many times before and intended never to see again.

"So, what you're saying is that you think whoever killed Carla De Carlo, set up Dickey to take the fall. And now that same person killed Dickey and tried to set up your mom?"

I dunked a piece of crusty bread in a mixture of Mission EVOO, our white balsamic vinegar and fresh chopped herbs that grew in pots on my deck. "It makes perfect sense."

I took a big luscious bite of bread. A burst of flavors reminded me why I loved our oils so much. There was simply nothing that compared to the mild grassy taste with a hint of pepper, basil, garlic and rosemary.

"But why?"

"Because I think Dickey figured out who that person was and he was going to do something about it. Remember, he told me he didn't hold a grudge, he got even. I think he was here to get even, not to take the orchard back like the rest of my family thought, and the killer figured that out."

"Okay, and did you figure out who?"

"No. we're going to have to do some digging for that answer, and I know just where to get the shovels."

The secret meeting took place exactly at nine p.m., which had given both Lisa and me enough time to catch a couple hours of much needed sleep.

By the time we were headed down the path looking for the out-building somewhere in the middle of our property, we were both ready to get back in the murder game. There were no designated roads that led to it, only a maze through the olive orchard, and if you didn't know the correct turns it was virtually impossible to find, especially in the dark. I knew the roof was camouflaged with fake olive branches and leaves so no one could pick it out from the air. My mom had told me at least that much about it, but even she wasn't privy to its location, nor did she want to be. Of course, that little conversation took place about a year ago. There was no telling what she knew now.

Lisa, wearing my best white sweater with a Donna Karen gray suede vest lined with a trendy lighter gray faux fur, and my barely worn Diesel jeans—which fit her ass much better than mine—along with her Dolce and Gabbana boots, had brought along a night scope that allowed us to find our way without too much tripping. She told me she never went anywhere without her night scope, a stun gun, a Swiss Army knife, three feet of heavy string, two feet of rope, a pack of gum, and candy red lipstick. She said I'd be surprised all she could do with gum, string and lipstick. The woman was nothing if not prepared.

I thought I could find my way to the meeting because I had secretly followed my cousin Jimmy a couple times. The first time we were both drunk, and he had trouble finding the location, and I had trouble concentrating. That blind-leading-the-blind episode turned into a big fat bust. The second time he led me right to it. I was stone sober. Of course, he never knew I was following him. Even a savvy Young Turk wasn't on his game after four shots of scotch.

"Are you sure about this?" Lisa asked as we rounded what seemed like the same olive tree for the third time.

"Yes. It should be only a few more feet."

"That's what you said a half-hour ago. It's been a long day and I'm overdue for a bed."

"I thought you were a survivor. Isn't this all part of it?"

"I tell all my survivors to get their rest after an adventure. Eight hours of sleep is your most important weapon. Without the right amount of sleep you cannot function at top speed. No matter what the danger, you must find a safe and secure environment and get your eight."

"You'll just have to add an addendum in your next book. If the adventure continues and you can't get your eight, buck up and try for a second wind."

She didn't say a word for several minutes. She merely followed. I could hear her doing a deep-breathing routine behind me.

I was tired as well, but I wasn't about to give up now. This meeting could be key. I knew that if Dickey didn't show up in the next twenty four hours, he would automatically turn into a missing person. Once that happened, Nick would be on our asses like wool on sheep. We had to name the killer by then or we'd all be in a whole lot of trouble.

We came around yet another row of trees and right ahead of us I saw a light coming from the small wooden building. I'd found it, which surprised even me. I stopped walking, frozen in my tracks. This was their inner sanctum, so to speak, and we were outsiders. I could only imagine what they would do if they caught us.

Lisa grabbed my arm. "Well, don't just stand there. Let's sneak in. Isn't that what we came here for?"

"I thought you were tired."

"I was, but now I'm not, so let's go."

"Admit it, my second wind theory worked."

"Yes. Okay. You were right. I'll give you credit in my next book. Now let's go before we miss something juicy."

We snuck up on the building like two cats stalking a bird.

"Now what?" Lisa whispered as we plastered ourselves up against the tan wood and stucco building.

"I don't know. You're the one who knows all about these things, I figured you'd know what to do."

"Okay. Okay. Let me think. I wrote a chapter on breaking and entering, but I wrote it for an empty house, not for a room filled with ex-mobsters. This is an entirely different situation. Anyway, I wrote it in my first book. That was three years ago. I can't remember all the details, but I think what we need to do is . . ."

Just then the tiny window right over our heads opened and Uncle Ray's head popped out. "You girls want to step inside or do we have to come out there and get ya?"

And just like that, everything I had imagined about their secret meetings was turned on its head.

"My name is Mia Spia, and I'm a binge drinker," I said in a clear voice while sitting on a black folding chair on the side of the crowded little room. From where Lisa and I sat, along with Jimmy and Maryann, we could see almost everyone.

"Welcome, Mia," everyone chanted.

It seemed the "secret bi-monthly meetings" were actually Anonimo Cosa Nostra meetings, as in Mobsters Anonymous.

Who knew?

There were six rows of chairs with five chairs in each row. Most of them were occupied. I knew nearly everyone there, but a few men were complete strangers. However, they had that "extended family" look to them, and I was positive that in the next few months they would be working for my mom in some capacity like everyone else.

Coffee and hot water carafes sat on the far end of the room on a long folding table covered with a white tablecloth. Italian cookies, including cream filled horns, and Neapolitans were piled high on paper-doily-clad platters. Various types of domestic and imported cheese, cured olives, and Federico's tapenade sat next to the desserts. There were several bottles of our award winning oils waiting to be poured. A tray of sliced Italian cold meats and several loaves of crusty Italian bread along with a large Caprese salad would tempt even the strictest of dieters, not that you could find one such person in this group. Good food was our life, and we had the bodies to prove it. Not that any of us was obese, but anorexia was not a disease anyone in this family would ever have to battle.

And of course, what Italian feast would be complete without several bottles of red wine? I counted fifteen, but I felt certain that was just for starters.

I sighed at the thought.

"I think I have my drinking under control, but lately I've been craving alcohol more than usual. No wonder, considering what's been going on around me." I decided to spill my guts a little, just to see if I could catch a tell from one of these rehab cases who might lead me in the right direction. "I just want to let the person who whacked Dickey and tried to run us off the road today know that I'm closer to finding you than you think."

This was a total lie, but I figured it might make somebody a little nervous and that somebody might give me a clue to his or her identity.

Of course, I was taking a risk that the relatives who were visiting didn't know about Dickey's demise, and that my mom was somehow still in the dark, which was doubtful, but I figured my confession served as a future warning that murder was no longer an acceptable form of self expression.

Then I gave the entire room my best evil eye, a sort of squint mixed with tight lips and a slight furrow on my forehead. My dad had taught me this technique when I was a kid. Some of the women in my family could no longer do it because of all the Botox they'd had injected. That stuff should come with a warning label for Italians: After use of this product, the evil eye is no longer possible.

I waited and watched, but no one moved or coughed or even blinked for that matter.

And just as I was about to give up, I saw a guy on the far end of the third row shuffle his feet and rake his fingers through his long dark-chocolate hair. Then, as if someone had given the all clear signal, everyone moved or coughed or twitched. My plan had completely failed except for the guy I couldn't quite make out. Could he have been the killer? I tried to get a better look, but Uncle Benny was blocking my view.

Suddenly Lisa spoke. "My name is Lisa Lin and I'm a lingerie junkie."

"Welcome, Lisa," the group echoed. I turned and stared at her. This was total news to me.

"I have drawers and drawers filled with expensive underwear and I can't stop buying it."

She shrugged. I continued to stare at her, fascinated by this revelation.

The only way Uncle Ray and Uncle Benny had agreed to let us in was if we participated. Apparently, Lisa took them seriously. The one rule Uncle Ray insisted we follow was the rule that all AA meeting attendees abide by: what's said in the AA meeting stays in the AA meeting, or in this case the MA meeting.

All my relatives listened as Lisa spoke, especially the men, who seemed to be especially focused on her every word.

"It's like every time I pass a Victoria's Secret or the lingerie department in Bloomingdale's I have to check it out. And once I step inside I turn into another person. I lose all control. I now own an abundance of fancy underwear, from lacy thongs with real pearls embroidered on the tiny bit of fabric on the backside, to silky bras with crystals stitched across the tops of the cups. I have so much of the stuff that most of it still bears the price tags.

I simply don't know how to stop myself." Big tears rolled down her cheeks, and Uncle Ray reached across the aisle and handed her his white hankie.

It was sweet to see such chivalry. These ex-Made Men were hiding a murderer, and one of them had probably tried to run us off the road today, but they were quick to show sympathy to a woman with underwear issues.

I glanced around at the group. I could tell that most of the men had fantasies going on. Satisfied smirks grew on their faces. If Lisa was making this up, she was a better storyteller than I gave her credit for. If she wasn't, the girl clearly had some intense shopping issues.

The room fell silent after her revelation and stayed that way for what seemed like forever. Probably due to the intricate fantasies . . . which gave me a slightly creepy feeling.

Then, just when I was about to give up on anyone in this tight-lipped group of ever saying anything that I might use as a clue, the chocolate-brown-haired guy spoke.

"My name is Giuseppe," he said in the Italian dialect I could understand. His long hair was styled in that slicked back mob fashion the Sopranos made popular. Up until that program, most of my family never slicked back their hair. After the first season, most of them followed the Soprano style. Even Uncle Ray enhanced the gray on his temples so he could look like Paulie. I wondered if mobsters throughout the country took on the Soprano style, or was that just my slightly demented family.

"Welcome, Giuseppe," we said in unison.

Giuseppe leaned forward, tugged on his tie like he had a deep aversion to it, glanced over at me for a moment and, I swear, all the air went out of my lungs. Not only did he look familiar, but the man was disturbingly handsome, especially with that scruffy beard. More like he stepped out of a daydream of what a thirty-something Italian man should look like. Thoughts of Adonis and

Apollo swept through my mind—even though they were clearly Greek, I couldn't help thinking of a Greek God while staring at Giuseppe.

"Breathe," Lisa said. "You're turning blue."

I turned to her and mouthed, ohmygod!

"Yeah, but he's obviously mobbed up, girl, so get control," she cautioned.

But I couldn't. It was as if I was hit by cupid's arrow and I saw only Giuseppe.

What the hell was wrong with me?

Just last night I had sex with my ex-boyfriend who continued to lie to me, and now I was attracted to a gangster, an imported gangster, at that.

I needed serious therapy.

"I came here to do a job, but I found out today that my job was already done for me. So now I come here tonight to make peace with the family." He switched to English. "But I no can make peace with the family in Calabria until I show that the man I came to, shall we say, erase, is," he shrugged, "erased."

His Italian was what my relatives referred to as old Italian. Different regions of Italy had slightly different dialects, thus the reason why I couldn't always understand book-learned Italian-Americans or Northern Italians. To my family, anyone who lived in a town even slightly north of Calabria was considered a Northern Italian.

Calabria, where this latest import was obviously from, was known for heavy mob activity, and for the 'Ndrangheta, the most notorious, secretive, and ruthless of all Italian Mafia type organizations. Unfortunately for me, most of my family and honorary family could trace their criminal roots to this region of Southern Italy. My dad was born in a little town called Cariati Marina. He lived there until he was sixteen and told me stories about how he helped his dad pick olives in the local groves and how his mom would clear land for the rich mob boss. Of course, he never actually said the owner was a mob boss, but even as a little girl, I knew how to read between the shrugs and story omissions. My grandfather eventually hooked up with the owner and my dad didn't have to pick any more olives and my grandma didn't have to haul rocks.

I guessed that being born a girl I broke the venerated mob chain.

A short silence, feet shuffled, chairs creaked.

"My name is Hetty, and I'm an alcoholic." My aunt's voice was deep and loud, and what she said was a complete revelation to me. It explained a lot of her reclusive and nasty behavior.

"Welcome, Hetty," we chanted.

"I just want to say, I'm glad the bastard Dickey is dead. I know I shouldn't feel that way, but I can't help myself. I've hated him for a lotta years, and that devil finally got what he had coming. I think now I can let some of my pent-up anger go. I'm working on it by meditating for fifteen minutes in the mornings. I heard about it on Oprah, and I gotta say, after a couple days of the stuff—and the fact that the louse is finally dead—I'm feeling a lot less like I should hit something."

Silence.

I so needed to get Hetty alone after the meeting. The woman reeked of information.

"My name is Maryann, and I'm a user."

This I knew.

"Welcome, Maryann."

She continued. "I'm very sad that Dickey's dead and that his body has gone missing. At least if I knew where he was buried I could pay my last respects with a proper accordion sendoff. I have friends who also play, and we have an entire concerto planned for just this occasion. But, this way, I can't get closure and it's making me cry all the time, play sad songs and even, God forbid, think about drugs. If somebody knows where he is, and I have a strong feeling somebody in this room does, please let me know so I can send him off, proper like. You have my solemn promise I won't rat you out if you tell me." She held up her right hand, oath style.

No one moved. Everyone seemed to be staring at the floor.

"Oh, and I want to say that I'm sorry if I caused the family any grief when I phoned that nice Leonardo Russo to invite him to Dickey's party. I thought I was doing a good thing for our Mia. He's been really working hard at becoming a better person. Even sees a shrink every week, at least that's what I heard. I had no idea he would bring that nosey cop, Nick Zeleski. I had nothing to do with the cop joining him. And that's all I'm gonna say on the subject."

Zia Yolanda filled the room with a forlorn, sniffly sob and I felt as though I should join her.

Leo was actually trying to be a better person. Great news. But the man was still a liar. I wondered if there were Liars Anonymous meetings because those might actually do him some good.

"My name is Jimmy, and I gotta get something off my chest." Uncle Benny cleared his throat. Jimmy shuffled his feet and his face went pale. "I mean, I'm an alcoholic, but I'm doin' good. Thanks."

"Welcome, Jimmy."

He slouched in his chair next to me. Something was definitely up.

"What the—" Lisa quietly mouthed.

"We need to talk to that man," I whispered.

"And fast," she said.

Giuseppe coughed and stood up this time, his right side facing me, making hand gestures as he spoke. "I think I got one more thing I need to say," he said in English. "The family in Calabria, they send me to America to reclaim something from Dickey, but he would not part with this something, which I am very sad about. But now, because things they have changed, I need this something as the proof that Dickey—he's not gonna show up somewhere still making the trouble. If I can have this proof I would be always grateful. Please, I mean no disrespect, but it is very bad for me if I can not have the proof. Mili grazie."

He sat down.

That's when I suddenly recognized him. Giuseppe was Leo, not the real Leo, but he looked enough like the real Leo that I'd mistaken my Leo for the Giuseppe-Leo. It was the beard that threw me. This was the guy on my Leo's porch arguing with Dickey. This was the guy who probably phoned Dickey for a meeting, a meeting that Dickey arranged someplace public. That explained Leo's wine on the table at my mom's party. It all made sense now.

How could I have been so stupid? I could see now that he wasn't as tall as my Leo, his hair was a little lighter, and his body . . . well, I didn't want to dwell on his body . . . but what was even worse, I had accused my Leo of lying when it had been this faux Leo all along.

I truly had to do some major sucking up to my Leo tomorrow night at the Martini Madness Ball, which I was suddenly truly looking forward to.

Giuseppe reverted to Italian. His face flushed and he went deadly serious, his voice going up an octave. "If I cannot get this something I was sent to retrieve, let me make myself perfectly clear, the family in Calabria will not take this news well. It will be bad for me, but it will be worse for your family. This I can promise."

My mom let out a small groan.

Uncle Ray, Uncle Benny, Uncle Federico and Jimmy stood, a couple of their chairs falling to the floor behind them. Giuseppe spread his legs apart, and clasped his hands in front of his body.

The mobster stance.

Two shady looking associates, both dressed in fitted business suits, stood on either side of him. Young buffed Turks. All three of them poised for action.

Lisa grabbed my hand. I shut my eyes knowing this could get really ugly. I waited. She waited. We all waited. I could hear their heavy breathing, like bulls trapped in a ring apprising the matador, getting ready to charge.

Just as the tension was about to ignite, Maryann began singing a Louie Prima tune, That Old Black Magic, accompanying herself on her accordion.

I was never so grateful for Maryann and her accordion as I was at that very moment. And just like that, the men smiled at each other, albeit somewhat tepid smiles, but smiles nonetheless. The young Turks backed off, and I could see the fight leave their bodies.

One good thing we had on our side was that Made Men didn't like to show their aggression in front of their women. Some kind of unwritten law of the streets, and at the moment I was tremendously appreciative of that unwritten rule.

Within moments the entire group was up on their feet, reciting the daily AA prayer, "God grant me the serenity to accept the things I cannot change, the courage to change the things I can, and the wisdom to know the difference."

"Amen," Uncle Ray said.

Soon the men were patting each other's backs and looking as if they all loved one another. Uncle Ray and Giuseppe were hunched over whispering to each other, smiling as if everything that Giuseppe had said had already been forgotten.

But I knew better.

Coffee was poured, wine bottles were opened, cookies, cheese, and sliced meats were served. The Spia clan was a model of all that was good, but everyone knew Giuseppe was serious about his threat and I, for one, had that sick scared feeling in the pit of my stomach. Someone here, other than the killer, had the ring, obviously the ring that Giuseppe was sent here to fetch.

What was up with that ring? It hadn't looked that special to me, at least not special enough that someone would kill for it, and that a family would send one of their own from Italy to fetch it.

Was I missing something here?

Suddenly I was feeling completely inadequate.

Who was I to think I could resolve this murder? Could help keep this family honest? Could keep my mom out of danger? I was kidding myself. These Wise Guys were serious about their vendettas. My own father was probably a victim of one of those vendettas.

My shoulder began to throb, and my knees went weak. A glass of wine would go down so easily, and would help with the sick feeling in the pit of my stomach.

I walked to the end of the table toward the now open bottles of wine telling myself that one glass wouldn't make me a binge drinker. That I was ready to drink again. That I needed it. That I could handle it. That . . .

"Let's get out of here," Lisa said, standing between me and my quest. "Jimmy just left. We should try and catch up with him."

"Not yet," I said as I tried to get around her. "I need a glass of wine."

"No you don't."

She placed herself in front of me, cutting my view of the bottles of wine. I wanted to shove her out of the way, tell her that she was intruding in my life, but when I looked at her I could see the concern on her face. Lisa was on my side. She believed I could shake my temptation. That alone was worth giving myself another chance.

If I drank a glass of wine, I would be giving up on Lisa's

friendship, on my mom's innocence, on finding the killer, but most of all I would be giving up on me.

But the bottles of wine were so close I could reach out and touch them. A glass was waiting to be filled. Almost everyone around me was drinking, enjoying themselves, imbibing in the my forbidden fruit. Why couldn't I?

"Is it really worth it?" Lisa asked.

"You bet it is," I said, then tried to reach around her for a glass. She stood her ground. Never moving. Never flinching.

I hesitated and slowly pulled my hand back from the fire. "I'll have some later."

Lisa's head bobbed. "Good idea."

Having some later was my way of telling that crazed partier inside me that I wasn't going to totally deprive her of getting completely shitfaced. I was simply putting it off until some future time, which I thoroughly believed and planned for . . . someday.

"How long ago did you say Jimmy left?" I asked.

"A couple minutes at most. If we hurry, we can probably catch him."

We left through the side door just as Uncle Benny straightened his gray tie, and lifted his shoulders in pure gangster fashion. A sure sign the room was getting too small for both he and Giuseppe to occupy at the same time.

FOURTEEN

Ring-a-ding-ding

We caught up to Jimmy in the parking lot next to my mom's house. He was just about to take off in his black BMW Roadster. The man always had great taste in cars.

I grabbed his attention through the windshield, and he rolled down the window.

"Yeah?" he asked, looking all pissy. "What's up?"

"What's up with you?" I said, trying to sound concerned.

Lisa and I walked up to his window and for a moment I caught the sent of sweet berries. The same berry scent that I'd smelled on Dickey. I took a step closer to the open window and inhaled, but the scent was gone, overpowered by the stale scent of cigarettes. Jimmy was a pack-a-day smoker.

Light poured into the car from the fixture above the barn door. He seemed more agitated up close. His hands rested on the steering wheel while his thumbs tapped out the rhythm of some imaginary tune.

"Nothin'. Just in a hurry to get the hell outta here."

"This will only take a few minutes."

"If it's about Dickey, you can forget it. I got nothin' to say."

His thumbs tapped harder.

"Actually, it's about that new dude, Giuseppe," Lisa said. "You know anything about him?"

Jimmy gave her the once over, as if he was trying to get a make on her. The way I saw it, he never quite got over her. I could see it all over his face, or maybe he was simply having some sort of sexual fantasy about her underwear. I couldn't tell which.

"Not much. Just that he's still hot. Still connected. Gotta be careful what a person says in front of somebody like that. He could cause us a lotta trouble. Hey," he leaned out of the window to get closer to Lisa. "You want to come over to my place and sign some of your books? I'm your biggest fan, sweet cheeks."

She ignored him. "What kind of trouble?"

"Your loss, sweetheart." He moved back inside the car. "The kind that ain't too good for seeing your next birthday. He's not somebody you girls should be asking questions about. Just watch your own backyard and everything will be okay. You get what I'm saying?"

His face went all serious, complete with nostrils flaring and forehead wrinkling.

"Yeah, we get what you're saying," I said, "but we also know that sometime tomorrow the cops are going to start hunting for one missing Dickey Spia. Got any ideas what they might find?"

"No. Do you?"

I thought I'd take a chance. "Did you know his killer tried to set up my mom?"

The color drained from his face, and he stared out the front window for a moment. Then he turned back to me.

"No, and that's low, way low, but this matter ain't your concern. You got no business sticking your nose where it don't belong. You too, Lisa. This won't end good if you two keep digging around. Like the saying goes, forget about it. Now I gotta book on outta here. I got somebody waiting for me in the city."

He turned the key in the ignition and his car roared to life.

"One more question," Lisa said, leaning in closer. "Got any idea who might have hired Giuseppe to burn Dickey?"

He smiled. "A guy like that? A lotta people. Dickey's got a long history of double-crossin' people. And don't forget the guy grew up in Calabria. Probably made some important enemies who want their own piece of him. Probably somebody in Italy put

Giuseppe up to it, like he said, or maybe somebody here. I don't know, but I can't talk about this no more. You girls need to stay clear of this one or you'll get more than just a little car chase that Lisa here can handle with her eyes closed. The person behind this thing is serious, so keep out of it."

He looked directly at me for a moment then he jammed the gas pedal and backed up his car on the gravel, his wide tires scattering the new gravel my mom had just put down a few weeks ago. "Wait a minute," I yelled.

He stopped.

"What now?"

I jogged up to his window, not wanting any lurking family members to hear me. "Any idea who might want the ring that was on Dickey's finger—other than Giuseppe?"

"You mean the one you girls are hiding?"

Anger welled up inside me. "Where'd you get that idea?"

"Stands to reason. You two found the body, so you must have the ring. Take my advice. Get rid of it. That damn thing'll just get one or both of you killed. Look, I may not be Lisa's wet dream or your idea of a good time, but I don't want to see either one of you burned. Just get the word out that you want to dump the ring and everything will go back to normal."

"But we don't have it."

He stared at me for a moment, rolled his eyes, pursed his lips and said, "Then whatever happens ain't my fault. I warned you." And he took off.

"What was that?" Lisa asked, walking up behind me and sounding as upset as I felt.

"I'm thinking it was either a warning or a threat depending on how you want to take it." I folded my arms across my chest, suddenly feeling a deep chill.

She spun me around to face her. "Wait a minute. Let's not jump to conclusions. He may not be the warmest guy in the group, but

I don't think he was really threatening us."

"What the hell else could he have meant?" I shouted, flailing my arms.

"I don't know, but we need to calm down."

I wasn't in the mood to calm down. Being Italian gave me that right. We rarely calmed down under stress. It wasn't in our DNA. "I'll try, but before we do anything else, or think anything else, we should talk to Hetty. Clearly that woman knows something. I've never seen her so upset. And you know how Hetty likes to talk, especially if I tell her someone tried to set up my mom. That should be enough to put her over the edge. She's like a mamma bear to my mom."

"That gives Hetty motive, you know," Lisa said.

"Motive for what?"

"Motive for Dickey's murder. If she thought Dickey was going to try to take the orchard back, she may have made a preemptive strike to stop him."

She was talking nonsense. "It's not that I don't think she isn't capable of whacking Dickey, I just don't buy that she would whack him and set up my mom."

Lisa shrugged. "People try to save their own skin when they get pushed against the wall. I've researched this, believe me, you'd be amazed what some people will do when their world is threatened."

I felt sure Lisa was totally wrong about this. "Not Hetty. She may be nutty, but she would never kill anyone. Not even Dickey."

"Who else owns this place?"

"Aunt Babe, my mom, of course, Uncle Federico and me. I guess that gives all of us motive. But anyone on this rehab farm could have fallen off the Mafioso wagon and done it. Let's not forget that we've had to kick several of these Wise Guys off the property for thug behavior."

"Could one of them have done it?"

I shook my head. "Not likely. Two of them are dead. One disappeared and the other one is doing life in Soledad."

"But the five who actually own this place have the strongest motive. Good thing you have an alibi. Me."

She had a point. It looked really bad for all of us, even me. "Let's talk to Hetty, and if we're lucky Babe will be there too."

"The girls didn't look any too tired. I'd say there's a good chance they're still awake," Lisa said.

"Then let's hustle up. I've got a few questions that need answers before I can sleep tonight."

"And speaking of sleep, what did you do with Dickey's pinky?"

I'd almost forgotten about his pinky. I wondered what that said about me. "It's still in the freezer, why?"

"And you have no problem sleeping with a severed body part in your fridge?"

I thought about that for a moment. "No. I guess I truly am my father's daughter."

"There's a whole new side to you that I'm going to have to think about and reevaluate."

"Don't think too long. Until we find Dickey's killer, who knows what'll end up in my freezer?" I meant it to be a joke, but from the glum look on Lisa's face, I guessed she wasn't taking it that way.

"You're into this whole mob world more than I thought."

A quote from my past flew into my head. "When you lie with dogs you're going to get fleas."

"Where'd that come from?"

"My dad. He was good at smart little quips."

"Wait, Mia. This is much more than I bargained for."

She stopped walking. I turned to her. "It's too late to back out now. The killer already knows you're in the game."

"I need a drink," she said, and stopped walking.

The mere thought of a drink—a shot of tequila preferably,

with a wedge of lime and a lick of salt—made me want to give up this insane quest and take off for the nearest bar. But instead I continued on the path.

Lisa followed close behind.

"What I wouldn't give," I said when she caught up to me.

"Maybe when we're to Maui, a big fat Mai Thai in one of those bucket glasses with a pink paper umbrella stuck in a slice of cold pineapple hanging off the side," she suggested, but I knew she was merely playing my put-it-off-until-later game. So far, the game was working. My resolve was still in check, but there was no telling how long that would last.

It only took us a few minutes to walk to the bungalow where my two aunts lived.

"Is it always this dark around here?" Lisa whispered as she climbed the porch stairs behind me.

"No. Usually their porch light is like a beacon. This can't be good." Aunt Babe didn't like the dark and their house reflected her fears. Every room usually glowed with light, even when they were sleeping.

But not tonight.

When I stepped up on the porch, I could see their front door was slightly open. "Okay, this is making me scared."

I slowly pushed the door open.

"Upon entering a situation that could potentially be dangerous, always be aware of your immediate surroundings and never let your guard down for an instant," Lisa said, obviously quoting herself while stiffening her body and walking with her arms in some kind of martial arts readiness position.

I tried to take on the same stance, but somehow I just wasn't feeling it.

The living room was dark except for the light coming from their thirty-gallon fish tank gurgling on a shelf to our left. Across the room, a sliver of light glowed from under the kitchen door. My aunts liked to do some of their special orders and try out new recipes in their own industrial strength kitchen where they could bake in their jammies.

"I don't like this," I complained to Lisa.

"That makes two of us. Maybe we're being too stupid to live. The killer could be in there. Or maybe he's already been here and gone. Finding one dead body is enough excitement, I don't need to find another one."

"Don't even think that. I love these ladies."

"Then we need to get some help."

"Don't you have a black belt or something?"

"Yeah, a lovely Prada silk number. It's hanging in my closet. No. I don't have a black belt. I took beginner classes last summer for research."

"Well, pretend you have one 'cause I'm going in."

"Hello!" I yelled. "Anybody home? Aunt Babe, Aunt Hetty, are you here?"

A loud pop then a crash blasted through the house. It came from the kitchen. Immediately, my mind latched onto the gunshot explanation, and my heart raced like a bunny rabbit's.

Then, a loud bang.

"If this kind of stuff keeps up, we're going to have to start packing a weapon," Lisa said. "I've got a nice little Glock at home that would give me a lot more courage."

Without thinking, I took off for the kitchen moving on pure adrenalin. No way could I let anything bad happen to my aunts.

I was fearless.

Or extremely dumb, depending on the outcome.

"Wait for me," Lisa yelled as she raced up behind me.

As soon as I swung open the door, something gooey hit me right smack in my face and clung on. It smelled and tasted a lot like Amaretto.

I licked my lips.

Definitely Amaretto.

Startled, I attempted to open my eyes, but they were gooed shut. As I began to wipe off my face, I heard Lisa yell, "Incoming."

Another glob of something hit me on the left side of my head, and I felt it slowly ooze down my cheek. This one had chunks. I took a taste. Cannoli filling, the perfect blend of chocolate chunks, powdered sugar, a touch of vanilla extract and rich ricotta cheese.

Yummy, but somehow it might taste better if it was served on a plate, stuffed inside a crispy cannoli wrapper rather than dripping down my face.

I cleared off the excess goo around my eyes and opened them.

The large, normally spotless kitchen was littered with flour, cake batter, and an assortment of cookies, smashed cakes and berry pies. It looked as if a pastry bomb went off. Aunt Babe and Aunt Hetty were hunkered down on either side of their huge wooden island flinging Italian baked goods at each other. Clearly, whatever this was about had escalated out of control, and it was up to me to stop it from going any further.

"What the hell is going on?" I demanded as sight finally returned and a seemingly perfect meringue pie sped right for me.

This time I ducked and it flew through the open doorway and landed splat on Lisa's boots, her lovely expensive, high-end boots. She gazed down at the lemony mess then back up at me, a look of utter shock on her face. The woman could take almost anything, but you better not mess with her wardrobe. Her whole body tensed and I could tell there were some evil revenge thoughts going on.

I had to take charge of the situation.

"Wait a minute," I yelled, but the words were stifled when a piece of rum cake landed directly in my mouth. There was so much rum rolling around in my mouth, it was as though the cake was simply a catalyst for the booze.

I had no choice but to chew.

It was then that a luscious thought occurred to me, perhaps if I stood there long enough, with my mouth open, I could get an actual alcohol buzz.

"This is all your fault, you miserable old grouch," Aunt Babe yelled as she hurled a ball of dough at Aunt Hetty, missing her shoulder by an inch. The dough struck Lisa right in the stomach. She doubled over for a moment, straightened, grabbed the ball off the floor and hurled it back at her. It landed on the island in front of Babe with a thud.

"Is this any way for women your age to act?" Lisa shouted.

Aunt Hetty turned toward her, eyes wild, face and body covered with way too much yellow and chocolate cake. Pink icing and some kind of brown goo dripped off her hair every time she moved. "Who invited you two?" she demanded, sticking a fist to her hip. "This is our war, not yours." And she hurled a chocolate frosted bunt cake.

The perfectly formed cake hit Lisa right between the eyes. Her nose poked out of the center for a moment, but only for a moment because the impact knocked her right off her feet onto her ass. She went down hard on the non-skid cork floor. My aunts stopped throwing things long enough to make sure Lisa was still breathing.

There was a moment of truce, a sigh of relief, a collective intake of air while we all waited for Lisa to say something.

Then, knowing Hetty was partially deaf, Lisa yelled, "Are you people all nuts?"

"You're darn tootin' we're nuts," Aunt Hetty roared, while pitching another glob of cannoli filling at Aunt Babe. "Nuts because Babe killed Dickey. I have proof. She has that damn ring, and now we're all going to lose everything we've worked for because she had to whack the bastard."

Then she began pitching and entire tray of cranberry-pistachio biscotti at Babe, and before I could think about it, I was pitching biscotti right alongside of her.

Olive Oil Biscotti with Pistachio and Dried Cranberries – Level Two or Three

¼ cup Koroneiki EVOO, or any delicate extra virgin olive oil
2 tsp. vanilla extract
½ tsp. almond extract
½ to ¾ cup white sugar depending on your sweetness level
¼ tsp. salt
1 tsp. baking powder
2 medium eggs
1 ¾ cup unbleached flour
½ cup raisins, or dried cranberries, or apricots
1 cup unsalted pistachio nuts, or slivered almonds, or cracked hazelnuts

To turn this into a level three, you can buy the nuts in their shells, crack them and slice each one by hand. Or for a level two, just buy them already shelled and slivered. Preheat oven to 300 degrees. In a pretty large bowl, mix oil, and sugar first. Blend well. Beat in extracts and eggs. Take a moment to breathe in the fragrant aroma, and let your body relax. In a small bowl, combine the flour, salt, and baking powder. Slowly add this to the wet ingredients, careful to scrape up everything from the side of the bowl. When this is thoroughly mixed, add the dried fruit and nuts with a wooden spoon lingering over the bowl to take in the sweet smells and how delicious the batter looks.

Wet hands with cold water and divide dough into two portions, making a log out of each one. Logs should be 2 inches wide and about a foot long. Take your time making the logs as perfectly as you can. Get into it. The process will focus you. Place the logs on a parchment lined cookie sheet. Pat each one down just a bit and bake for 35 to 40 minutes. Logs should be lightly browned and the smell in your kitchen should put you in a candy-sweet mood.

Remember to enjoy the moment.

Remove the logs from the oven, cover with a lovely dishtowel and allow them to cool for ten minutes. Meanwhile, reduce oven heat to 275 degrees.

Carefully move logs to a cutting board, and allow them to rest for another five to ten minutes. Using an electric knife, or a very sharp blade, cut logs into 1 inch thick slices. Lay on their sides on a parchment lined cookie sheet. Bake about 8 to ten minutes more, or until dry. Can drizzle one side with white or dark melted chocolate.

Cool on rack and enjoy dunked in coffee or tea anytime you need a treat.

FIFTEEN

Sex, Lies and a Double-Cross

"Wait a minute," Lisa ordered, standing next to the island between us, arms stretched wide. "Somebody's going to get hurt."

We stopped just long enough for me to come to my senses. I was participating in the madness. This had to stop, although the fact that Babe had the ring while the killer was busy planning his next attack on Lisa and me made me want to hurl more than cakes.

"That's the point," Hetty quipped and flung a glop of red preserves, using a huge spoon like a catapult, right at Lisa. She ducked and it landed on the six burner stove behind her.

Hetty reloaded and flung the glop at Babe. Hetty made contact and grinned her success.

"She's full of bunk," Babe yelled after the red preserves splashed on her now pink hair. "She's the one who snuffed out Dickey and now she's trying to pin it on me just because I have that damn ring."

She threw a plate of almond biscotti at Hetty. Fortunately, the plate was of the thin plastic variety, so when it crashed into my nose spilling the biscotti all around me, it didn't hurt . . . much.

Lisa was up and grabbed at Hetty's arms. "You ladies have to stop. What about, you can poke an eye out?"

"Two eyes would be better!" Babe retorted.

"You're full of dog doo, Babe," Hetty yelled. "You know you did it, you little vixen. Admit it before I go for what's in the walk-in."

The walk-in contained anything they may have baked for an

event, such as a wedding. I knew for a fact they had two weddings coming up that weekend. The walk-in would be full. This had to end or we'd have the wrath of two bridezillas on our hands, not to mention two mamazillas, who, I was sure, would be much worse.

I ran for Babe just as she was about to hurl an entire perfectly frosted Snoopy sheet cake, with the words Happy Birthday Sammy emblazoned on Snoopy's belly in bright red letters.

"Put Snoopy down and step away from the table," I ordered in my most commanding voice.

She poised Snoopy for launch, his little smile looking almost sinister as he bobbed up and down next to Babe's head. "I will if she'll admit the truth."

"You did it, and that's the truth," Hetty said.

"Whore," Aunt Babe yelled.

"Liar," Aunt Hetty countered, her eyes narrowing to tight little slits.

I thought I'd go for the heartstrings. "You don't want to do this. Little Sammy will be so disappointed without his Snoopy cake. He might cry all day."

"It's Sammy Nagossi," Babe told me.

"Isn't he in his nineties?" I asked.

"Ninety-four. He's lucky if he knows it's his birthday," Hetty quipped.

"But it's Snoopy. You can't fling Snoopy. That's like a sin or something."

"She doesn't care one hoot about Snoopy or Sammy or anybody," Hetty protested. "After all these years, I finally figured out that my sister is heartless. The only thing she cared about is her personal vendetta—getting even because the bastard cheated on her with me and Carla. So she pushed that millstone on top of him, pulled off that stupid ring, and shot Dickey in the head so she could get her revenge. She's worse than the men in the family. At least they wouldn't have squashed the prick first."

"Like I have the strength for that kind of action," Aunt Babe shot back. "You're the doll who can boost a fifty-pound bag of flour over her shoulder. You did it because you still think the son of a bitch killed your precious Carla. DNA proved he didn't."

Babe got a better grip on the cake. Hetty quickly went over to the walk-in and pulled out the top of a perfectly frosted wedding cake.

That's when what Babe had just said struck me.

"Wait," I yelled turning to Hetty. "Your precious Carla? What does that mean?"

Lisa said, "It means what you think it means."

I turned to Babe. She nodded and shrugged.

I turned back to Hetty. "You're a lesbian? Not that there's anything wrong with it, but I—"

She flung batter at me. "Don't give me that Seinfeld bunk. In this family there's a lot wrong with it." She turned to Aunt Babe. "Now you've done it real good. She's going to blab it to Benny and Ray and pretty soon no one will talk to me. I may as well wear a big red L on my back."

Hetty put the wedding cake down, dropped to the floor, sat with a plop right on a smashed pound cake and began to cry.

Babe carefully placed Snoopy back on the island, pushing broken cakes and globs of cookie dough out of her way then she rushed over to Aunt Hetty, plopping down on the floor next to her.

"I won't tell anybody, honest," I said, but it was too late. Tears gushed as Hetty slid down on the floor in a heap. I'd never seen her cry before, not even at funerals, and believe me, in this family, there were a lot of funerals. I somehow thought she was incapable of any other emotion but contention.

Lisa glared at me as she walked over. "Nice move."

I shrugged. "I had no idea."

She leaned in and whispered. "Do you live on another planet

or what? I think you're the only one who hadn't figured it out years ago."

"Then why is she so upset if everybody already knows?"

"Sweetie, by definition your family has that don't ask, don't tell policy going on. It's how a borgata thinks."

"I know that," I said, crossing my arms. "But it just irks me that I know so little about my own family."

Lisa raised an eyebrow.

Aunt Babe threw me a sympathetic sigh while Aunt Hetty gazed up at me, cake-smeared cheeks stained with tears, her lipstick in big streaks across her lips and chin, cake, cookies, and batter encrusted on all parts of her squat little body. For once her hair didn't stick straight up. If it wasn't for the occasional brown glop dripping off of it, the new 'do looked rather normal. "Nobody knew back then. It was our secret. Me and Carla were moving to Amsterdam to start a new life."

"Amsterdam!" I bellowed, wondering why the heck would two middle-aged Italian women move to Amsterdam.

Hetty wiped her tears away with her gooey fingers, streaking chocolate chip cannoli filling under her eyes and across her puffy cheeks making her look like a vanilla ice cream cone with sprinkles. "She had connections. We were going to open our own marijuana bar. She even had the location all scoped out. While Dickey was busy in Italy buying that miserable antique millstone, Carla was in Amsterdam putting a down payment on our future. But we never got the chance to move, or even begin our love affair. She was murdered before anything happened."

"You mean, you two never—" I didn't quite know how to ask about the details.

She looked at me. Waiting. Then she said, "If you mean did we ever sleep together? No. We kissed a couple times, but Carla was a virgin and she wanted to wait until we had a commitment ceremony in Amsterdam before she'd sleep with me. She was like that. Wholesome. Pure. Just like our oil."

Aunt Babe made a gesture behind Hetty's back telling me that something Hetty was saying wasn't true. "You better get ready for bed, honey," Aunt Babe said to Hetty, while gently rubbing Hetty's back. "We have an early morning."

Hetty nodded and stood. "But who's going to clean all this up?"

"We will," I told her, wanting to hear what Aunt Babe had to say.

"You're just like your dad. A sweetheart," she said, getting up then carefully making her way across the kitchen. When she got to the other side, she took off her shoes and disappeared up the wooden stairway to the second floor. As soon as she was out of earshot, Aunt Babe turned to me and said, "What a crock of crap."

Two hours later, the kitchen was spotless. I wore a soft pink silk robe with matching nightgown and slippers, courtesy of Aunt Babe. My hair was still wet, but free of pastry goo once again, and pulled up in a clip on the back of my head.

Lisa wore a vintage floral cotton robe over white silk pajamas that were straight out of a forties film, and Aunt Babe was decked out in a vintage cream-colored ensemble complete with feathers and big, belled sleeves that I was sure I'd seen on Ginger Rogers in The Gay Divorcé.

We sipped herbal tea out of Italian pottery mugs. "Okay, first, did you kill Dickey?" I was hoping I could see the lie in her eyes.

She gave me a warm smile. "No, doll, I didn't kill him. I never hated him enough to do him in. I'd get stinking mad at him sometimes, but I never wanted him dead like some of the other people around here."

I believed her.

"If you didn't do it, how'd you get that ring? Especially since we were the ones who found him first. We could hear the killer in the barn."

"What you heard was me trying to get that damn ring off his finger."

"That was you grunting and groaning?"

"You know how hard it was to rip that thing off his finger? It might as well have been glued on. I had to use olive oil to slide it off."

"Why'd you take it, and why did you try to keep it a secret?" Lisa wanted to know.

"I took it because Dickey owed me, big time. I figured I could sell it and make up for some of the crap I went through after he went to prison. The bum left me with nothing, and if it wasn't for your mom cutting me in on this orchard I'd still be scratching out a living."

"But the killer thinks we have it. Probably why he tried to run us off the road today," Lisa said.

"And now Giuseppe wants it or at least he says he wants it for some other family," I added. "What's up with that ring, anyway? Dickey was keen on wearing it to the party. Any idea why?"

She shook her head and took a sip of hot tea, the steam still billowing off the surface. "I don't know."

"Okay, let's leave that for now and get back to Hetty and Carla. Want to tell us what really happened between Carla and Aunt Hetty?" I sat forward, resting my elbows on the small table in the corner of the kitchen. A bank of windows on my left displayed a coral streaked sky. Dawn was fast approaching, but no way would I allow sleep to take hold. Not before I heard what this woman had to say.

"Carla was not a lesbian," Aunt Babe said, emphatically.

"Why doesn't that surprise me?" Lisa said, moving over to the cozy looking window seat with the inviting cushions. She immediately made herself comfortable and nestled up to a particularly soft looking pillow and shut her eyes.

When Lisa was tired she could fall asleep anywhere, including in a front row seat of a Kiss concert.

"How can you be so sure?" I asked.

"Because that was Carla's shtick. She tried to get everyone to believe she was pure as morning snow, trying to make up her mind which way her libido was swinging, but we all know what happens to snow when it sits around too long. Dirty slush. That's not to say the doll deserved what she got, but that undecided virgin thing was a big crock of crap."

"But Aunt Hetty's pretty sharp. Wouldn't she have picked up on that?"

"Doll, you're not seeing the tree. You're too busy looking at the whole jungle. Hetty's on fire when it comes to business and baking, but when it comes to her own emotions, she's pure stupid. She was in love with Dickey for awhile. I think they were even doing the deed when he and I were first married."

This was news to me, but then most things were. I was thinking that all those years of booze and parties put me in some sort of bubble because I had no idea any of this was going on. After all, when you start drinking when you're fourteen . . . well, it caused me to miss most of my teens, and the majority of my twenties was a complete blur. I was so hoping to catch up during my fast-approaching thirties.

"But you and Hetty are so close."

"Now. Back then we hated each other. I don't think you remember, but your aunt Hetty was a real looker when she was your age. Some believes she was prettier than me, if you can believe that." She flounced her hair, and smacked her ruby lips.

"Then how did she hook up with Carla when she had Dickey on the line?"

"Dickey dropped her for Carla. Not only were they sneaking around on me, but Carla had some other guy in her closet who thought he was her one and only. But here's the thing, Carla was a true dream weaver. It was hard to separate fact from her latest fantasy."

I figured this was the same guy Jade told me about, the missing Carlo Ponti. Things were beginning to add up.

"You know who this other guy was?" I asked.

"Carla was good at keeping secrets. A real closed door whenever anybody got too close."

"How does Hetty fit into all of this? Into Dickey's murder?"

"Don't know exactly. That's where it gets a little sketchy. I don't really think Hetty popped Dickey, not in my heart, but who's to say what's in her heart. I know losing this lifestyle and this business would be devastating to Hetty. She already lost one dream because of Dickey. I'm sure she doesn't want to lose another one."

"Do you think Carla loved Hetty?"

Babe shook her head. "Carla was a player. I don't think the woman was capable of love. I think the only reason she took up with Hetty was to keep her quiet. It's like this, doll, Carla didn't want Mr. Jealous to find out about her and Dickey, and she knew Hetty would blab it to everybody. Hetty can be viciously vindictive. So Carla comes on to Hetty, and Hetty, who told me she never dug making it in the first place, falls head over heels for Carla. She was giddy in love with the woman. Couldn't wait to move to Amsterdam. Like that was ever going to happen."

"Why didn't you believe it?"

"Because I saw Carla and Dickey doing the lip tango while standing on my front stoop."

"When was this?"

"When Dickey and me lived in Nob Hill in San Francisco. A big fancy house with a garden I loved. You remember that house, don't ya?"

I nodded even though I'd only seen it once. Aunt Babe hadn't been very social back then.

"Anyway, I'd been roosting in Chicago for a Noir film festival and caught the earlier flight home so I could fly first class. My flight only had economy seats left and a doll like me can't do economy. Ruins the image. Anyway, when I couldn't get Dickey on the phone I dialed up Federico. The man is a saint. He was busy that morning, but told me if I could wait a little while he'd send Jimmy over. Back then, Jimmy was considered an associate, not quite part of the Family, and he idolized Federico like a big brother. They were always together. Jimmy would do anything Federico asked him to do. Anyway, I told him that was cool. To take his time. What did I care? At least I was getting a ride home."

She stopped to drink tea, and to light a thin menthol cigarette, blowing the smoke over my head, getting that calm look on her face that a real smoker had whenever they lit up during a stressful moment. I inhaled the perfume, envying her discipline. She had been smoking three cigarettes a day for the past ten years. A feat I could only admire. I'd been a two-pack-a-day kind of girl, sometimes three. Anything short of that would be impossible for me.

Therefore, I didn't smoke.

"So that's when you saw Dickey and Carla. From the car window?"

"Exactly. Believe me, that woman was not a lesbian. Not the way she was making whoopee with my Dickey. They must have been out there like that for a good fifteen minutes. Long enough so I could snap some pictures. Dickey liked to play me and deny his affairs. I figured with the pics I could rake him over the coals for some solid alimony. Anyway, I saw Carla take that horseshoe ring off her index finger and slip it on Dickey's pinky. Funny thing was, I looked everywhere for that damn ring after he was hauled off to the slammer, figuring I could sell it for some cash. Money got tight, but I never saw the damn thing until the other night when he showed up for the party wearing it. He must have had it stashed somewhere."

I decided to tell her the truth about the ring.

"My mom had it in her safety deposit box at the bank."

"Your mom! Why didn't she tell me?" She took a long drag on her cigarette.

"Did you ever ask?"

She thought about this for a moment, blowing smoke up over my head again, its sweet fragrance embracing us. I inhaled memories and felt a ting of melancholy.

I so craved the taste of a cigarette, and the calm feeling one got with that first drag. It was like heaven in just three little inches.

"No. Never in a million years did I think your mom would have it. He was a smart man, that Dickey."

She took another deep drag. I watched, mesmerized by the ease of her controlled habit.

"Apparently, not as smart as everybody thought," I said. "He told me the ring was going to give somebody real heartburn."

"It gave me heartburn, that's for sure. But I didn't kill the bastard. He and I went into the barn earlier that night for some privacy, but when I left him the first time, he was still very much alive."

"What did you talk about?"

"I wanted to know his plans for the land, but all he wanted to do was fool around. I let him cop a feel or two. Why not? These are the genuine article." She pushed out her rather large chest and ran her hands over her breasts. "And most men these days don't get the opportunity to play around with a natural pair, what with all them implants these young girls get. And Dickey always had a fondness for these puppies so I figured what the hell. A little feel wouldn't make any difference. Besides, the guy was shut up for eight years. He was hungry for a little action."

"But he had a fiancée," I reminded her.

"Yeah, well, that's Dickey for ya. The consummate player."

She took a last drag then snuffed out the cigarette in a crystal ashtray. "And besides, he never said a word to me about Jade, and even if he did, I'd have known he wasn't serious. A guy like that? Married right out of prison? Never gonna happen."

She knew him better than she thought.

I grabbed for my mug and held the warm cup in my hands. The heat gave me a shiver. I was getting sleepy, but I didn't want to stop talking yet. Aunt Babe was on a roll, and no way did I want her to settle in for the night without first getting all my questions answered.

"Jade confessed the engagement was all a ruse."

She smirked, and slammed her hand on the table. "I knew it, the son of a bitch. A real game playing prick right to the end. I'm glad I took that damn ring. A ring like that shouldn't go to waste."

"But it's dangerous for you to have it while the killer is still out there. Right now he thinks I have it so you're safe, but if it ever gets out that you have it, there's no telling what he or she might do."

"I've thought about that, especially after tonight when that new Wise Guy showed up."

"I'm more worried about the killer. I think the idiot killer is the person who tried to run us off the road today. There's no telling what he or she might do next."

She thought about that for a moment. "You're right, doll." I think I must have surprised the killer while he was trying to get it off Dickey's finger. I found an open futso near the body when I walked in and some oil on Dickey's pinky finger. Thing is, I only went back in the barn to tell Dickey we were through. I was feeling a little guilty over leading him on earlier. Although, now that I know the bastard had a young sweetie, he probably didn't care one hoot about me. Anyway, whoever it was that did Dickey in was already trying to get the ring off. I just finished the process.

"And one more thing about that ring, I always felt like some royal sucker gave it to Carla thinking she would cherish it, like it would mean something to her, and then she up and gave it to Dickey just to stir up the pot. She was like that . . . one of them evil cooks."

"What happened after Carla gave him the ring?"

"Dickey admired it, slipped it on and they started kissing again so I told Jimmy to get me the hell out of there. He threw it in reverse and we bugged out. He drove me around for awhile then drove me back home right around the time my original flight would have gotten in."

I was suddenly filled with more questions. This was getting good. "Is there any way that Hetty could have known about that morning at your house?"

"Had to. She was sleeping up in the guestroom at the back of the house."

"What? But wouldn't the loving couple have known that?"

She shrugged. "That's the thing of it. Hetty phoned me the night before I came home, crying about something I couldn't understand. She lived here in Sonoma at the time and asked if she could drive up to talk to me. I told her when I'd be home, but she didn't want to wait. Dickey was supposed to be in Napa looking at some land, so I told her to drive on over and wait for me at the house. And that's just what she did. But when I went looking for her later that morning, she'd already left."

"How do you know she was actually there?"

"The bed looked slept in and the doll left her best shoes in the closet. We've never talked about it, though. I know how hard it must have been for her. Poor thing. I think that's why she's a little off, ya know what I mean?"

I somehow didn't think Hetty's quirks were a direct result of Dickey and Carla's affair. The woman was born strange, but who was I to argue with Babe?

"What if I told you that Dickey never had sex with Carla?

That it was all a hoax just like Jade and Dickey pretended to be engaged. Jade told me that Carla refused to have sex until she was married."

I could see the disbelief on Babe's face. She pushed herself away from the table, as if she was trying to step away from the truth. "What? That can't be. I saw them out on that stoop."

A strange thought hit me, one that made perfect sense, but one that Aunt Babe might never have considered. "You saw them kissing, and you assumed they'd spent the night together, but maybe they hadn't. Maybe she'd just arrived, and Hetty had actually spent the night with him. The reason he kissed Carla for so long out on the stoop was because he didn't want to invite her in with Hetty hiding under his bed."

A long couple of minutes passed before Babe leaned back in. Lisa opened her eyes. "Babe, I think you've been had."

It seemed as if Lisa had been listening the whole time pretending to nap so Babe would feel more like talking. I had to give Lisa credit. The woman knew when to keep her mouth shut and when to speak up.

With Lisa's words I remembered Hetty coming out of my mom's house the night of the party with her blouse undone, and Dickey slicking back his messy hair, and wiping his face, especially his mouth with his white handkerchief. No wonder Hetty had been so huggy. She and Dickey had been getting it on and I had disturbed them.

I was beginning to think Hetty's heart wasn't as kind as Babe would like to think it was.

"That two-timing . . . I'll be damned." And she lit up another cigarette.

"One more thing," Lisa asked. "When did all this take place? How close to Carla's murder?"

Babe sat back in her chair, took a long satisfying drag and said, "Carla's housekeeper found her lying under an overturned coffee table, shot in the head, that very afternoon."

SIXTEEN

You Look Just Like Your Papa

I awoke several hours later on my aunts' sofa, alone, covered in a pink fluffy blanket, still wearing the vintage nightgown from the previous night, with Dickey's pinky ring tucked safely into my left shoe. Aunt Babe had given it to me right before she'd slipped up to bed to grab a couple hours of sleep.

I figured if I took charge of the ring I might be able to smoke out the killer. Either this was the absolute smartest idea I'd ever had, or the absolute dumbest. Whatever happened depended an awful lot on how Lisa and I lured the fly to the ointment. I felt both scared and empowered. Lisa, on the other hand, was all about the game, whatever it turned out to be.

The house was quiet except for a ticking cuckoo clock. My aunts had their own clock from Bisnonno Luigiano. He liked to spread his cuckoos around. Even Federico had a clock.

Lisa was nowhere around. She must have gotten up earlier and was probably back in my apartment, haunting my closet, figuring out today's outfit.

As I sat up, my thoughts swung to Hetty. Did she kill Carla and make it appear that Dickey did it? If anybody had motive, she sure did, but the ring just didn't figure into it. At least not the way the clues were stacking up now.

Dickey knew enough to give that ring to my mom for safe keeping. He knew of its significance, so much so that the first thing he did when he got out was to parade it around at the party, almost begging the killer to come and get it. Regrettably, the plan backfired and Dickey ended up being just another victim, something I was hoping to avoid.

As events were beginning to gel in my head, I stood up and headed off to the bathroom.

Of course that was the reason for the freedom party. Why my mom was so insistent on having it. She knew what Dickey was up to. He never wanted the land back. It was all about Carla's killer. So why didn't she tell me? Why did she have to keep everything a secret?

Because she knew absolutely I would have never agreed to such a treacherous game. And I would've been right.

But it was too late for I told you so.

And how the hell did her charm bracelet get tangled up under Dickey's feet? I was still hoping the killer had put it there. But how did the killer get it? Did she lose it out in the yard and the killer accidentally stumbled on it? I liked that scenario. If the clasp was broken, it could have fallen off anywhere, even right in the killer's path.

Once again, I needed to talk to my mom, but today was olive picking day for almost everyone in the family, and I had no choice but to join in. Dickey's murder would have to wait. And unless I stumbled over his body in the orchard, or my mom was up in the same tree I was, I really needed to give my full attention to picking.

Ten minutes later I was on my way back to my apartment still wearing the vintage pink nightgown and robe. The ring was now hidden in the left pocket of the fuzzy robe.

The very first thing that caught my attention when I stepped on the front porch were the three turkey vultures that circled high above my head. I knew they were vultures by their unstable flight pattern. They tended to tilt from side to side while they flew, plus those unmistakable deep-red bald heads that only another vulture could love. These birds of prey had a keen sense of smell and a reputation for locating carrion even inside a building with open windows or in this case, a barn.

I didn't know where Dickey's body was hidden, but it was a good assumption that they did. And, soon, so would the entire Sonoma Sheriff's department. A clue this obvious couldn't be ignored.

Could it?

But I was on a mission this morning that even vultures couldn't keep me from.

Olives.

I knew by now everyone was out in the orchard working hard to harvest the fruit. Timing was essential with olives, and Uncle Federico had hired a small crew of twenty or so men to do most of the work. Today was the last day to pick our Koroneiki olives at their peak and most of my family would be out there helping. Even my mom would spend time out in the grove. She hated to climb up on the ladders. She'd fallen off of one once. Nothing broke, but my mom didn't like risks of any kind, and from then on she refused to climb up even one rung.

Now she used a long wooden pole with a sort of double clamp at the end to shake the olives free so they would fall in the catchnet. The pole ran off an air compressor and shook the limbs and the olives fell off. She could clear a tree in a quarter of the time it took the rest of us to pick, but Federico didn't like the mechanical rake. He said it damaged the fruit and the tree, but my mom won't be intimidated. Her harvest went into yellow bins and was pressed first along with olives that he'd purchase from other groves who harvested in the same manner. That way there was no time for the possibility of mold or rot to attack the olives. Mom had learned this technique that Federico despised while she was in the Basilicata region of Italy with my dad on our one and only trip as a family.

When I arrived in my apartment, there was a note on my front door from Lisa that she had gone home and would meet me at the ball that night. Her mom had stopped by to pick her up. Lisa probably felt a lot safer with her mom, and who wouldn't? The woman was a tiger when it came to her cub.

I could only imagine how that went down. Her mom must have been in a complete meltdown when she saw the sling. I was glad I had slept through it.

As an afterthought on her note, she wrote, oh, by the way, Dickey's finger is missing from the fridge. And might I suggest that you lock your door from now on. From the looks of things, the idiot-killer stopped by to search for the ring. Good thing we weren't home when he/she came calling.

She signed it with a smiley face.

I opened my door to find my apartment in total chaos. The mattress was off the bed, the sheets had been ripped off, the closets were open and all my clothes and shoes were scattered on the floor, all the drawers in the kitchen had been emptied out, my fridge was open and the contents dumped, and what was the worst of all was that my mom's espresso machine was in pieces on the table.

She would never forgive me or the dismantler.

Before I allowed myself to react, I immediately walked over, locked my door, not that it made a difference now, and phoned Lisa, only to get her voicemail. I didn't leave a message. She didn't like messages and rarely listened to them. My number on her missed calls list was all that was needed.

Then I sat right down on the floor and wailed, sounding very much like Zia Yolanda.

Two hours later, after I cleaned up as best I could—I was determined not to let the intruder get to me—I was out in the orchard, clad in jeans, a long sleeved sweater, a black hoodie, and hiking boots—the only shoes that weren't touched—ready to do my share with the harvest.

The sacred ring was hanging from a silver chain around my neck, safely tucked under my clothing.

Okay, I admit this was strange behavior considering my apartment had just been trashed, but my self preservation was at risk of crumbling if I allowed myself to wallow in self pity, so off I went to pick olives and show the killer my True Grit, thank you very much, John Wayne.

"Start over on that row of trees," Federico ordered when he saw me drive up in my pickup. I followed his directions, parking behind his brown Nissan pickup, along a row of countless bright red olive bins that lined the dirt road. I killed the engine and jumped out, totally psyched to pick as many olives as possible. It took a ton of milled olives to produce fifty gallons of oil. That was a lot of olives and after all, this was what Spia's Olive Press was all about.

In the past few years we've had bumper crops with no frostbite or bug infestations, thanks to Federico. He pampered the trees and the crop as if they were his own children.

It had already been a wearisome day, to say the least, and I could still see those nasty vultures circling overhead. I would have laughed if I didn't think the whole thing was ludicrous. After all, it was barely ten in the morning, plenty of time for my day to get even worse. But I refused to dwell on what else could possibly happen.

I would give my complete focus to the olives, joining Maryann and Uncle Benny as they moved from one tree to the next. I would concentrate on the task at hand.

But what about Dickey, a little voice echoed in my ear. What about the ring? And your trashed apartment?

"Over here," Maryann yelled while standing on a ladder that leaned on a branch of one of the trees that produced Coratina olives, creating an oil that had a fruity fragrance, but a slightly bitter, spicy flavor. I forced myself to think of a tasty arugula salad with goat cheese and red onions that begged for our Italian blend oils. How these trees were to Italy like our Mission olive trees were to California. How Uncle Federico had imported them less than five years ago to add the oil to our Italian blends, and how well they had grown in our rich soil.

Incredibly, I was feeling better. Feeling one with the olives. With nature. With my bucket. My olive rake.

With my very own vertical wooden ladder, always at the ready, which I always kept in the back of my truck this time of year. I slid it out and was thinking of setting it up under Maryann's tree when the vision of the endless sea of bright orange catchnets attracted my attention. The entire area was covered in a blanket of orange. They'd been put down in the last few weeks to trap the fallen olives. It had taken six men three weeks to put them down.

The refection off the nets caused the silvery trees to glow orange in the warm sunshine giving off a fun Sesame Street effect. As if Miss Piggy and Big Bird lived in our orchard and children would be hanging out of the trees playing hide and seek. At least that was the thought that always came to mind whenever I saw the catchnets.

Today was no exception. The bright orange always made me happy, and I was really trying not to let anything get in the way of that feeling.

As I walked over to Maryann, who was now waiting for me, I reflected on the hard truth that I now carried a house key in my hip pocket, something I hadn't done for the entire two years I'd lived on the property. Something I had grown accustomed to. It was like living in a safe, small town and I liked it. Liked the fact that I never had to worry about break-ins or crazed killers. Too bad it had been a big fat lie. A false sense of security. The crazed killer was living in my very own house. Well not exactly in my own house, but close enough to walk in whenever he or she felt the need.

Of course, it had taken me almost a half-hour to locate an actual key; my mom had it hanging on a hook in her kitchen cupboard, along with every other key she owned, but who squabbles over such minor inconveniences when the entire ship was sinking. And for all intents and purposes, this ship was taking on water at an alarming rate.

But I was there to pick olives, and to be happy with the sight of our orange catchnets and not to ponder un-recovered gangsters. One of whom was probably the same dude who killed Dickey, chopped off his finger, threatened me, tried to run us off the road and trashed my apartment looking for the ring.

But it was all in the family.

The family that kills together . . .

"How's it going?" I asked Maryann once I arrived under her tree.

"Great," she said. "It's going to be a good harvest."

The catchnet was littered with olives, and dozens of red bins, filled with olives, were stacked on the side of the road waiting to be picked up.

I leaned my ladder up against a sturdy looking tree limb on the next tree over, knocking the branch a couple times with my ladder to make sure I didn't hear any cracking sounds, a sure sign the limb wasn't strong enough to hold me.

"Mia?" a voice called behind me. I turned, and there jogging toward me was Adonis, or Giuseppe, if I wanted to use his formal name. I preferred Adonis. It had that ethereal quality that I so needed at the moment. Thinking he was just another Wise Guy in my sea of Wise Guys was simply too disheartening.

So yes, it was weird that he was calling me by my name and was jogging toward me—my own personal fantasy coming to life—but in this family nothing surprised me anymore.

The morning sun glistened off his shiny hair, which was loose now, and strands curled around his face and down his neck. His white T-shirt clung to that incredible chest, and his muscled arms appeared to have enough strength to pick up several of our olive bins with one of those luscious arms tied behind his back. The vision was sufficient to make me want to run right for him and tell him to take me away from all of this madness.

Oh wait, Adonis was part of the problem. He was a suspect even though he said he didn't whack Dickey. There was absolutely no evidence that I should believe this imported dude.

Pity, we could have had so much fun.

Adonis slowed as he came closer. I quickly pulled on my heavy gloves wanting it to appear as if I'd been working all morning. Why I wanted him to think this, I didn't actually know, but I decided to go with it.

"Hi," I said.

"Buon giorno. Sono Giuseppe Nardi," he said with a little bow.

"Buon giorno," I said in my best Italian. "Somehow I didn't think I'd be seeing you this morning."

"Ah, but I can no go home. Maybe I stay. Make my home, you know?" His eyes were the color of a Farga olive from Spain. A light green color when harvested early, but a sweeter oil when left on the tree to turn a dark purple which made the oil sweet and light with hints of almond. I wondered if he tasted like almonds.

Wait. Did he just say he was making this his home?

"Excuse me? But what did you just say?"

"That it is good to see you again." He smiled and the earth moved. All right, maybe the earth didn't move, but it should have. The man was a sexy menace to my otherwise unstable world.

"No. I mean about making this your home. Are you staying somewhere in Sonoma?"

"Yes. I stay in your mama's house. She got a nice house, your mamma. Many rooms."

This was not a good idea. This man, no matter how much I wanted him, was an active member of the mob and we didn't allow active members to live on our land. It was the only thing that kept us from FBI scrutiny, and we had all agreed to this when we first settled here eight years ago. No way was Adonis—regardless of his spectacular smile or his Farga eyes or those incredible arms—going to change that. My mom was like a kid who took in stray animals, only these were stray thugs.

Possibly not the best idea.

"You could have one of the apartments over the shops. Two of them are available right now, but the apartment comes with certain restrictions. Uncle Ray will have to fill you in with the details. You may not like our rules," I told him.

And there it went. My entire ship had just plummeted to the ocean floor pulling me down with it. I had asked an active mobster to give up his toughness and join the recovering "family."

Yeah, like that was going to happen.

It was as though I had no control over my words, my thoughts or even my actions. It was almost as if I was drinking again, but I was stone sober. Not a good sign for my future.

"Ah, I go see Ray. This is good. Grazie."

Deep inside, I knew how wrong this was, but I couldn't help myself. The guy had some kind of magnetism that turned me into his slave. I grinned my approval.

Now that I had his attention, I thought I might as well ask a few questions. "By the way, last night, you said you had asked Dickey for something. What was that something that he refused to give you?"

"Why you want to think of such things? It is a beautiful day, yes?"

"Yes. It's a beautiful day, but I was just wondering, that's all."

He threw me a wicked smile. "That is why I stay. I can not go back to my country without this thing. If I do—" He ran his index finger across his neck and made a slicing sound. "But maybe you know something you maybe want to tell me."

"About Dickey?"
"Yes, about the something?"
"The something?"
"Yes."
"No. Not a thing . . . about the something."
I moved and the ring tickled my cleavage. It gave me a shiver. "I have work to do," I told him.
"Ah, yes. The olives. I will help with this tree."
He pulled on the gloves that were stuck in his belt behind his back. "I go up the ladder and pick. It is better this way."
"No, thanks," I said and grabbed hold of both sides of the ladder and carefully climbed to get up into the tree. I liked to pick up high. The olives were a little riper on the top of the tree and came off the branches easier. Plus, I could smell the olives from up there.
Call me strange, but I loved picking olives. I always felt at peace up in an olive tree. Some of my best memories of my dad were in Italy during a harvest. We had spent the entire day together picking olives, him training me on what a ripe olive looked like as opposed to a rotten one, or an overripe one. How to use a rake. How to secure my ladder in the tree. How to let go and trust the limb to support me.
That one day had begun my love for olives and olive oil.
"It is a big orchard. Many trees," Adonis said.
I carefully raked the thin branch clean, the olives gently falling into my bucket then I turned slightly to get a look at Adonis, who stood off to my right.
That's when I heard it, a hint of a crack, almost a whisper, and as if in slow motion, the rung broke under my feet and I grabbed for the tree, but I couldn't quite hold onto it. My gloves were too cumbersome. I felt myself slipping out of the tree and with one more, sharp crack, I suddenly plopped right into Giuseppe's open arms. Then we both toppled to the ground. Me lying prone

on top of him.

For a moment, neither of us said anything. I was simply trying to catch my breath and understand what had just happened.

Then he spoke in Italian, "Dear God, are you all right?" And he began running his hands over my body. A pleasant sensation if I hadn't just nearly died.

I pushed him away. "I think I'm okay."

Funny how I suddenly could understand him. I guess my Italian significantly improved when death, or broken bones were imminent.

He switched to English. "Don't move. I get the help."

"Everything okay over there?" Maryann yelled from the next tree.

I sat up. "Yeah. Just lost my balance. I'm fine."

"You need my help?"

"Nope. We've got it covered."

"Okay," she said and that was that. Nothing short of a broken appendage stopped Maryann from picking. She was like a one woman machine. Every year we had a contest to see who picked the most olives and Maryann always won.

"I carry you to bed," Giuseppe said.

"What? No," I told him, but I clearly liked the vision. "I'm fine. Really. But I wouldn't be if you hadn't caught me. Thank you."

"It was my pleasure," he said with a sensual smirk.

He stood and extended a hand.

When I was back up on my feet, I went straight over to the tree to check out the branch. I couldn't understand it. I had never fallen from a tree. I was always so careful.

As soon as I walked closer I could see what had happened.

"Ah, the ladder, she was rotten," Giuseppe said.

"Impossible. I just bought it this year."

He leaned it back from the tree, tilted it on its side and there it was. We both saw it.

Someone had cleverly cut the very rung I had been standing on. Not all the way through, but just enough so that after I stood on it awhile it would break.

I was just about to collapse in a torrent of hysterics when he said, "This is not so good. You have an enema."

"Enemy," I corrected, chuckling at his bad English.

He smiled, shrugged and we laughed out loud. One of those tension releasing kinds of laughs. All I could think of was what a great laugh he had. The man was a total charmer and I was a sucker for a charmer.

He slipped his hand under my chin. "When you smile you look just like your papa."

His words felt like a slap. I backed away from his touch. "My papa? How would you know that?"

My heart raced, and there was a lump in my throat. I could feel my entire body stiffen. How could this man know my dad? That seemed totally impossible. In my blind lust for his touch, I must have misunderstood him. My dad was one of the mysteries of my life. As far as I knew, no one knew if he was alive or dead. It seemed impossible that this Young Turk could know anything about him when my own family didn't.

He held a finger over his mouth. "Shhh," he whispered, turning away from Maryann, and the rest of the pickers. I pulled off my gloves and followed right beside him, anxious to hear what he had to say.

"Your papa, how you say? He no can come out. Too many enemies in America, but he got a lot of friends in Italia."

It just seemed impossible for this Italian import to know where my dad was living when we had been looking for him since I was twelve. How could this be true? I needed more information.

"So," I said. "You never actually saw him?" I figured this Turk didn't know what he was talking about.

"Ma-sure. Your papa, how shall we say, an important man in

Calabria. He send me here, you know, to ask for the . . . ring and if he no give, then to do some work."

I decided to play along with this elaborate hoax. It had to be, right? "Do some work on Dickey?"

He shrugged and bobbed his head in complete gangster fashion letting me know I was exactly right, but not really saying it out loud. "I call him. We meet. We talk and he say no. Then before I can, you know . . . another person do my work."

"But why did my father want Dickey's ring?"

He shrugged again, grinned and looked at me as if I was the silliest person alive. "I no ask this kind of question. I am a picciotti d'onore, a soldier. I follow the orders from the capobastone."

It hit me like a ton of olives! I was convinced he was telling me the truth. My own father, the man who had disappeared like Jimmy Hoffa, was not only alive and well, but he was some kind of boss in the worst mob Italy had to offer, 'Ndrangheta, and he had put out a hit on his own cousin, Dickey.

I so needed a drink.

Fifteen minutes later, after having picked only slightly more than a bucketful of olives, I called it a day. Giuseppe packed my now broken ladder back in my truck and I left him on the side of the road with Federico giving him picking orders.

I was on a quest for a big, overflowing glass of wine. I was absolutely going to drink it this time. And not just one glass, the entire bottle seemed like the way to go. I even decided on red rather than white. It reminded me more of blood, and blood was the word of the hour. My blood, my dad's blood, and Dickey's . . . we were all related, but that didn't seem to matter in this family. Vendettas mattered more than blood, and heaven help the person who stepped in front of a personal vendetta.

I drove my truck, loaded with my viciously tampered with ladder, back to the barn and parked behind my mom's house, completely distracted by my quest for wine.

Heading straight for the case I'd shelved in the barn the night Dickey was murdered, I figured I'd grab a bottle of Leo's Pinot, and show up on his doorstep wearing my best rueful smile. We'd have great make-up sex and I'd be over this ridiculous sobriety I'd enforced on myself forever.

Whose idea was this sobriety gig anyway? Certainly not mine.

After my tryst with Leo, I'd return refreshed and renewed to help my mom and aunts prepare tonight's feast. There was always a big feast the last day of our first harvest. We had one more harvest that would take place sometime in early November when the remainder of the fruit was at its peak of ripeness. That would constitute a major party, but for now, we celebrated all the hard work and the fact that it didn't rain during the harvest. Rain during harvest is the single most destructive natural force for olives. Even a mist can hamper a successful harvest. Fortunately, neither of those scourges had taken place, so we were in for a fantastic harvest, and what looked like a profitable year.

I had phoned Lisa on my short drive back to the barn, wanting to share the news that my dad was alive and well and playing Godfather in Italy, plus I wanted to tell her the sinister details of my attempted demise, but she still wasn't answering.

Opening the barn door, I was eager to get on with my new found sobriety freedom when I ran smack into Nick Zeleski. There were several other men in dark suits who were busy snooping around. Two police officers from Santa Rosa stood watch just inside the door. I figured the whole group must have parked in the tourist lot, and had come in through the opposite door or I undoubtedly would have seen them, even if I was utterly distracted by my desperate wine need.

Before I could say anything, Nick said, "Sorry about this, Mia, but I have reason to believe something happened to Dickey Spia while he was on your property, specifically in this barn. Gloria

Spia gave us permission to have a look around."

I opened my mouth to protest just as Uncle Benny walked out from behind a row of shelves and stopped me. "Once your mom gave him permission, there's nothing we can do, Mia."

"Why? What happened?" I asked, upset that these intruders had not only destroyed my perfect wine vision, but were now causing weeks' worth of work to put everything back together again. Not to mention that they were sure to find blood evidence that Dickey was murdered about ten feet away from where we were all standing.

"Do you know a man named Peter Doyle?"

My knees almost buckled as I flashed on the notary who had signed the last page of my mom's documents, the now missing page of my mom's documents. But why would Nick know about the notary?

"I—"

Uncle Benny interrupted. "She never heard of him. And even if she did, she does not have to tell you anything."

I closed my mouth. Nick grinned. "This will go a lot easier if you cooperate, Mia."

"She has nothing to say," Uncle Benny said.

I knew enough to listen to Uncle Benny and keep my mouth shut, but at the same time I wanted to know what this was all about. I moved in front of Benny. "Never met the man."

"But do you know who he is?"

This question presented a problem. I didn't want to lie, but I didn't want to offer the truth either. Especially since I could feel Uncle Benny's eyes burning a hole in the back of my head. "What does Peter Doyle have to do with any of this?"

"Neighbor found him locked in his garage early this morning with the motor running. It might have looked like a suicide if it wasn't for the piece of paper shoved in his mouth. Funny thing about that piece of paper, it was eight years old and notarized by one Peter Doyle. Seems he'd notarized a document that gave all this land back to Dickey Spia if he was ever released from prison. Peter's mistake was he'd been blabbing that info to a few of his friends and neighbors. Do you know anything about that document, Mia?"

My mouth went dry. I wanted to spill my guts but Uncle Benny stopped me.

"She does not know anything. She has been out in the hot sun all day, picking olives. She is tired and cannot think straight." Uncle Benny gave me a look and I knew I should keep my mouth zipped, as Hetty liked to say.

As I gazed around at the people snooping and tearing at our barn, something odd struck me. Why weren't there more police, more local sheriffs buzzing around? And why was everyone dressed so, well . . . trendy? Their suits fit perfectly, and their shirts had color, not the drab white most detectives wore. And why in hell did everyone except for Nick look so Italian?

Nick interrupted my concerns. "I paid a visit to that worker your mom said cut himself while assembling the antique millstone and he didn't know what I was talking about. Not a scratch on him. Any idea why your mom would lie?"

I didn't answer. Instead I stood there, wide-eyed and trying desperately to hold it all together. Trying to piece everything together. Nothing was adding up, at least nothing that my now completely muddled brain could figure out.

"My mom doesn't lie," I told him.

Benny said, "That's all she has got to say right now."

Nick was silent for a moment then he looked at me and said, "Maybe you'd feel more comfortable talking to me at the station."

"That won't be—"

"She will talk when I see a warrant," Benny said. "Till then, I'll answer whatever you want to know."

"That's fine," Nick said. "Can you—"

But just then a woman in a designer suit called him over to the antique mill and he walked away.

When he was out of earshot Benny mumbled, "Keep away from him, Mia. He is big trouble for the family, if you know what I am saying. Go help the women with the cooking. I will take care of this," Benny ordered, cigar smoke encircling his head.

I nodded and walked away as random thoughts floated into my overworked brain. I mean, what if Benny was actually behind the murders? Maybe he felt as though he was protecting my mom or the orchard or himself from some past deed, like the murder of Carla De Carlo.

Or was this recent murder just another hit that my mobbed-up father ordered and Giuseppe snuffed out Peter Doyle right before he flirted with me out in the grove.

But which thug sliced my ladder? What motive would Benny have had, especially if he was courting my mom. And I knew Giuseppe didn't do it, he'd offered to climb my ladder.

I couldn't believe either one of these guys would try to hurt me or the orchard. Giuseppe was simply a henchman for my dad, which was weird in itself, and no mob boss would try to kill his own child. It just would never happen. Even the worst gangsters had their limits when it came to their young.

So it couldn't possibly be either one of them.

That would explain some things. I mean, why would anyone connected with this recovering family and this land do all this nasty stuff when it obviously incriminated everyone living and working on this land, not to mention that it could completely close us down with no chance reopening.

That's when the obvious answer hit me right between the eyes . . . the killer wants to close us down.

But why?

"It's all happening too fast," Mom said as she pulled the

perfectly toasted brochette bread out of the oven. She was referring to the meal she and every other woman in my family were preparing in her kitchen and not the events in the last forty-eight hours.

It was now late in the afternoon. Spia's Olive Press was already getting bad press on the local news stations and was essentially shut down until the police were finished with their investigation. It seemed the blood on the millstone was enough evidence for a warrant and those trendy detectives wanted to search more than just the barn. Now they were busy with the tasting room as we cooked. Uncle Benny was working hard on fixing all of that, but so far he wasn't having much luck. Essentially, the entire establishment was shut down. Given how slowly these detectives were working, we would probably be shut down tomorrow as well.

Nick and his team tried to get statements out of everyone, but that proved a waste of time. My extended family acted like captured soldiers repeating rank and tag numbers, only with my family they repeated the health benefits of olive oil.

"Mom, I really need to talk to you. It's important," I said, while I chopped a ripe plumb tomato for the salad. No response so I leaned in and whispered, "I need to know how your bracelet got under Dickey's feet in the barn?"

She turned to me, forehead practically wrinkled, lips tight, eyes glaring as if she was about to pounce. After a moment, she looked away, took a breath and chugged an entire glass of red wine. When she finished she carefully placed the glass down on the table and turned back to me once again, looking much calmer. "Is that where you found my bracelet? Under his feet?"

I nodded. "Plus I have other news. Can we go upstairs for a few minutes?"

"No. I don't want to." She stomped her foot, like some bratty kid. "I've got way too much cooking to do to answer your questions. I had enough questions thrown at me for one day. My head's going to explode, and my timing's all off as it is. The stuffed zucchini are gonna be done way before the pasta pomodoro, and my braciole di manzo needs another twenty minutes to simmer. The beef was a little tough. I don't know what's wrong with me today. I can't seem to get it together. We can talk later, dear. Right now, I have to cook."

She smiled at me and brushed my check with her flour-covered index finger. Mom was busy kneading a firm ball of dough for the fresh recchitedde, tiny round pasta disks that she would layer with a thick, tomato pork ragu. Fresh linguini hung from the wooden dowels of a sturdy rack that Federico had made for her several years ago when her collapsible laundry drying rack toppled over from the weight of the pasta and, "heaven forbid," she'd had to use packaged pasta for our Christmas dinner

"But—"

She held up her hand.

"Fine!" I said. "Later."

"Try to be nice, darling. It's so much more becoming."

I wanted to scream. I had so much to talk to her about, but lately it was never a good time for her. Of course, she was right, now was most certainly not the time. She was obviously experiencing a culinary meltdown at the moment and talking to her about my dad and her bracelet would only add to the cuisine challenge.

"It's all that louse's fault. May he rot in hell," Hetty said, making the sign of the cross then kissing her bunched fingers.

Maryann, who busied herself assembling the roasted red pepper and artichoke salad, had a different view. "Dickey's in purgatory, not hell and I don't care what you say about him." She slammed down the cleaver she was using to chop artichoke hearts. I was glad of that. Hurling sharp objects was not something I wanted to be involved in.

She began to weep. Zia Yolanda joined her at a much louder pitch.

Hetty went over to Maryann, careful not to actually touch her. "I'm sorry, honey. How about you play us something fun on your accordion? We could all use a little cheering up right now."

Maryann nodded, swiped at her tears then wiped her hands on the white apron she was wearing, walked over to a chair in the corner of the kitchen, picked up her ever present accordion and began to play Dean Martin's Volare.

"Volare, oh-oh, Cantate oh-oh-oh," she crooned.

Zia Yolanda smiled through her tears and began to sing. It was the first time I'd ever heard her actual voice, which was completely off key.

Aunt Hetty and Aunt Babe drowned her out and joined in. "Let's fly way up to the clouds, away from the maddening crowds."

Then Valerie and my mom chimed in. "We can sing in the glow of a star that I know of, where lovers enjoy peace of mind."

I would never admit this to anyone, but I knew every word by heart. My mom must have played it a million times while I was growing up. I sang as loud as I could. "Let us leave the confusion and all the delusion behind. Just like birds of feather, a rainbow together we'll find. Volare, oh-oh, Cantate oh-oh-oh . . ."

We sang the entire song, each of us busy with food preparation, smiling as if all was right with our little world, but we all knew better. That was the endearing feature about my utterly dysfunctional family. Each and every one of us had developed a coping mechanism that seriously distorted our perception of reality, and whether that perception was good or bad, it was what got us through the tough times.

When the song ended, Maryann continued to play while the rest of us continued to chop, pour, sauté, bake and plate the massive meal. We seemed to be in a collectively better mood, or at least everyone else was when we finally served the meal to our friends, family and the hired pickers who had helped bring in our first harvest of the season.

We spread the meal out on long sturdy tables in mom's front yard, everyone taking a seat around the yard to chow down on the fabulous Italian delicacies, enjoying not only the food, but the wine and each other. Laughter rose up from the crowd and for a brief moment, I allowed myself to simply enjoy the ambiance.

We'd be picking and pressing on and off for the next couple of months, but the first full day of harvest was the most important. It gave Federico a good idea of how good the harvest would be, and according to how heavy the trees were with fruit, we would have a bumper crop this year.

My only hope was that Spia's Olive Press would re-open long enough to reap the rewards, but from the looks of those damn turkey vultures still circling overhead, that hope didn't seem like a viable assumption.

Braciole di Manzo al Ragu – Level Two

8 thin slices of beef (top round steak, about 2 oz. each)
½ cup Italian Blend or other robust EVOO
3 large cloves of garlic crushed and minced
½ cup finely chopped Italian parsley
½ cup grated Pecorino cheese from Sardinia or Sicily
½ cup pitted and chopped Kalamata or Picholine olives
hot red pepper flakes to taste
cracked pepper to taste
salt to taste
kitchen string
A hardy blend of olive oil for frying

Grate the cheese slowly. Enjoy how easily the cheese slides over the grater and fills the room with its tender fragrance. Cut off a slice and try it with a drizzle of honey. It's divine! Set aside the grated cheese. Pit and chop the olives, tasting as you go. Have a bite of cheese and an olive. A truly great combination. Whisk the oil, garlic, parsley and cheese until thick. Add the olives and gently whisk a few more times. Place the meat on a flat surface and spread each slice with 1/8 of the mixture. Sprinkle on some hot pepper flakes, and cracked pepper to fit your taste. Tightly roll each one and fasten with kitchen string.

Add an olive oil blend (the kind you can buy in a grocery store) to a large frying pan over a medium heat. When the oil is hot, carefully add the rolls and quickly brown them on all sides. At this point, if you're secure in your resolve not to drink, you can add ½ cup of dry white wine to the pan and cook down. If you can't have wine in the house, then skip this step and remove the rolls from the pan and drain on a paper towel.

Sauce

5 or 6 chopped ripe tomatoes that have been peeled (drop the tomatoes in boiling water for no more than a half-minute. Remove with a slotted spoon and tear the skin away from the flesh)
¼ cup chopped Italian parsley
3 chopped basil leaves
2 tbs. chopped onion
1 to 2 small garlic cloves, chopped
3 tbs. tomato paste

Cook the onion and garlic in any EVOO until tender, but not brown. Add the tomato paste and let fry for about a minute. Add the chopped tomatoes and stir adding one half cup water if sauce looks too thick. Add salt and pepper to taste. Add rolls and let simmer on a back burner, turning every so often for about 1 1/2 hours. Serve over pasta or by itself with crusty Italian bread and a glass of sparkling water. Makes 4 hearty servings, so add a salad and invite some non-drinking friends over. Enjoy!

"I like to have a martini, two at the very most. After three I'm under the table, after four I'm under the host."
—Dorothy Parker

SEVENTEEN

Who's Gaming Who?

Nine o'clock that same night, after all the pickers and guests had gone home, my two aunts and I pulled into the parking lot of Cougar's Bar and Restaurant on Arnold Road where the third annual Martini Madness Ball, not to be confused with the Martini Madness competition that was held sometime in January, was in full swing. This event was a sort of prelim to the competition and a more formal affair, though the drinks were still poured in those baby plasticware martini glasses somebody designed to keep everyone fairly sober, and still able to taste an assortment of concoctions.

Personally, I never found that "fairly sober" concept even remotely possible.

Leo had phoned me earlier to let me know that he and Nick would be late. Like at this point I even wanted to see Nick ever again. The man was a problem, and if I didn't figure out who the killer was soon, Spia's Olive Press would be a fond memory. For each day we were closed down, we collectively lost approximately thirty thousand dollars between the income of the shops, our olive oil store, electricity, upkeep and countless other things. We just couldn't sustain that loss for very long. I had to figure this thing out, and fast. Too many lives depended on it.

Lisa, true to her code, was glammed up in two shades of gold, ready for a night of some serious partying. No doubt she'd found the designer dress she wore at My Roommate's Closet on Filmore Street in San Francisco, her favorite boutique, and one that I no longer could afford. Even Lisa's hospital-issued sling was adorned with gold bling, courtesy of her mom who collected jewelry like coastal kids collect sea shells. I guessed her brother, Henry, had driven her in, and was probably already inside sampling martinis, when I arrived with my mom, Aunt Hetty and Aunt Babe.

We took my mom's car, a sporty new white Mercedes C350, which she barely drove, but had to own because she thought it made her look taller when she stood next to it. Something about its "squat little body" . . . the car's body, not my mom's.

The combination of three competing perfumes was enough to force me to keep the sunroof popped open even though Babe complained that the breeze was mussing up her hair. I knew my mom liked to pour it on heavy when she went out, but I had no idea my aunts had the same bad habit. Between the three of them the car reeked, but none of them seemed to notice.

Hetty was all atwitter in the back seat, hardly able to sit still. She never missed a martini event, even though she technically didn't drink—which made sense to me now that I'd heard her declaration at the MA meeting. She went for the olives—the vodka or gin soaked olives, and by the end of the evening, after she'd pilfered olives from anyone who would give them to her, Hetty would be completely shitfaced.

The last time I attended one of these, at a location I had no memory of, I made an absolute ass out of myself with Leo, yelling at him for something I never could later remember, and ended up passed out in the ladies room while sitting on the toilet after I'd vomited up my guts. Not my best moment. My mom retrieved me after Leo called her, took me home to her house, and I've never left.

I was so hoping this wouldn't be a repeat performance.

My mom, Hetty and Babe were in a hurry to get inside and couldn't wait for me to park. "Just let us out by the front door, darling," my mom ordered, her hand resting on the back of my seat. I glanced back in the rearview mirror and caught that she was wearing the Elvis charm bracelet. But hadn't she said the clasp was broken? I never checked.

Another lie?

Mom continued, "I hate to have to walk through parking lots. They're way too dark. I might fall and break a hip or something."

I knew she was exaggerating her frailty, her last bone scan ranked her up in the bones of steel category, but I did as I was told and looked for a spot to pull over.

Mom hated to miss even a minute of the ball and we were already a half-hour late. She liked to be the first to taste some of the more exotic martinis, then chat them up with whoever would listen as if she was the expert. Afterward, as soon as she arrived home she'd write commentary about them on her blog, if she wasn't too wasted. Of course, it was the olive factor that dominated all observations. Mom believed that without the venerable olive, there would be no martini.

I pulled up in front, and stopped. The three women were out of the car before I could slide the gear into park.

"See you inside," Mom said, as she exited the car. Of course, before she took off for the party, she had to linger up next to her car, especially since bank-teller Liz Harrington, a woman my mom disliked ever since she confessed she didn't care for the taste of olive oil and only used Canola oil, was pacing the front of the restaurant.

Aunt Babe, however, clearly didn't care about anything or anyone and made a beeline for the open front door, tossing her vintage gray fox stole around her bare shoulders as she swung her hips in total siren fashion. She and Hetty hadn't exchanged two words since I picked them up. I could tell they'd been fighting, but had decided to be civil to each other for the sake of the martini.

Of course, Aunt Babe had insisted on sitting in the front seat, and this time Hetty didn't argue about taking the back, even though she usually got car sick, which didn't seem to bother her on the drive over tonight. I wondered if that was simply another of her tall tales so she would always get the passenger seat.

Funny how a good murder could clear the air in this family.

"That woman gives me a rash," Mom said, referring to Liz, and not Babe. "Why is she here, anyway?"

"I don't know. Why don't you ask her?" I said.

"Now why would I want to do that? The woman eats Canola oil. Who eats oil that isn't even a food? There's no such thing as a canola. It's just something those tricky Canadians mixed up out of rape seed 'cause they had too many plants. Did you know that pure rape seed oil will kill you? Even insects won't eat the rape weed because it's so poisonous, but them tricky Canadians found a way to make it pass poison standards and now they tout it as a wonder oil. Yeah, it's a wonder all right . . . a wonder why people eat that crap when they could be eating something good for them, like olive oil. Its name should be a clue: rape. That's what those Canadians are doing, raping everybody out of their health."

"Mom, I thought you discussed this with your shrink. Canola oil is an entire industry. You're one person. You can't do anything about it. Just try to have a good time tonight and stop obsessing over the Canadians."

"How can I when I have to stare at that damn Liz Harrington?" She leaned in and whispered. "I bet she's Canadian."

"Even if she is, that doesn't make her evil."

"No, but it makes her stupid for believing in their oil."

"Mom. Surrender. You can't save everyone."

She sighed. "Such a burden I have to carry." She slammed the door shut.

But she wasn't quite finished with me. "Be careful where you park my car. I don't want any dings in my doors, or any rocks flying up and nicking the paint. And don't, under any circumstances, park in that dirt lot next to the paved one. Benny parked there last week and ended up with a nail in his tire. He was lucky it didn't go flat before he left. The place is full of all kinds of pokey things. Try to park on the end of a row or, better still take up two spaces. That's the best."

"Will do," I said.

I found that in these types of situations it was best to simply agree with her then do whatever worked. It saved a lot of time.

Satisfied that I would heed her warnings, she finally smiled and walked off toward the open door.

Aunt Hetty hung around my window waiting to give me a last minute fashion critique, no doubt. I knew this because periodically Hetty noticed what I wore or how I looked. I didn't know why, exactly, I just knew when the onslaught was about to begin and tried to brace myself as best I could.

I sat up straight and smiled out at her completely prepared for the commentary.

"Is that hairdo some kinda new style?" she asked completely serious. I had tucked my wet hair in an oversized clip on the top of my head. Admittedly, it wasn't my best look, but who was she to criticize?

"No. I just didn't get the time to—"

"What?" She leaned in closer, trying to hear over the roar of passing cars.

"I'll fix it inside," I shouted. "My hair. I'll comb it inside."

"You don't have to get nasty about it." She unfolded herself and stood up.

"I'm not. I mean—"

"You're darn tootin' you're mean. Huh!" And she flounced off to join my mom and Aunt Babe, no doubt telling them what a nasty person I was.

Granted, Hetty was right about my hair, I'd been too distraught to think about hair after my shower, and I hadn't been able to face the mirror, so no makeup. However, the dress was fairly new, and the red heels were still somewhat trendy. That should have counted for something.

The woman clearly had a bad attitude.

I drove off thinking how I had reached an all time low in fashion and tried to figure out what that meant to my future as a diva while I circled the paved lot searching for a parking spot. After ten frustrating minutes, I entered the dreaded dirt parking lot, which also seemed full. The lighting was almost nonexistent, but despite the lack of illumination I spotted a tight open space between an old blue Chevy pickup and a suspiciously familiar-looking black Tundra, sans plates, parked at an angle.

"What are the odds?" I said aloud, as I pulled my mom's car into the space mere inches away from the blue Chevy.

I could only hope the Chevy didn't have a passenger who would ding my mom's door or there would be hell to pay in the morning.

I slithered out, and immediately streaked tan dirt on my dress from the mud encrusted Chevy. When I threw my black shawl around my shoulders thinking it would cover the stain, it snagged something on the truck's side mirror, and as I gently pulled the shawl toward me the sharp something naturally ripped a huge hole in the black mesh.

Okay, it didn't matter. It was dark in the bar. No one would notice. I wrapped the now badly torn shawl around my shoulders so the rip was hidden, kind of, and I told myself the mud smear was hardly visible.

I was doing fine as I made my way around my mom's car to check out the Tundra until I realized that my open-toed heels were sinking into the dirt and with each step I could now feel the grit between my bare toes.

Telling myself this was a naive move, that if the local Sheriffs couldn't find the Tundra after Jade gave them a detailed description, the odds of me running into it out in a parking lot were a million-to-one. The driver probably had it stashed away in some secret garage or was busy getting a new paint job down in Mexico.

I couldn't see inside without pulling myself up on the running board, which was no easy task in heels when the door was still closed, but I somehow managed, using the side mirror for support.

And there on the front seat, in the glow of possibly the worst imitation of a street light in all of Sonoma, sat the million-to-one cowboy hat and Chanel shades.

Our road warrior was hiding in plain sight, and now all I had to do was pick him out of a couple hundred people at the ball. Which shouldn't be too difficult, considering not many of my family members attended this shindig.

Headlights from another car hit the side mirror I was holding on to and startled me. I let go of the mirror, lost my footing, bounced off my mom's car right behind me, slid down into the black dust, and some poky thing bit me right in the ass.

"You look like hell, sweetie," Lisa said, as I hobbled up to the front door of Cougar's. A wide grin spread across her perfectly made-up face.

My ass was aching, my shoulder still felt tight, my dress was essentially ruined, my red shoes were now the color of mud, and a fine layer of dirt had totally covered every inch of bare skin. Olive oil was great for dry skin, but not so great if you didn't wipe off the excess. Everything clung to it, especially dirt.

Despite all of this, I was feeling somewhat optimistic that I could correct all of my cosmetic challenges with a quick stop in the ladies room.

"Yeah, but I found the black Tundra in the parking lot."
"Get out."
I nodded. "I parked right next to it."

"We should call Nick right now and tell him."

"Not yet," I said. "I want to look around a little and narrow down the pool of suspects. If we call Nick and he picks up this guy, it'll throw off our search for the killer. Let's just see who might be inside."

She gave me the once over. "But what if Mr. Tundra leaves? Maybe we should go out there right now and watch his truck. Do a little surveillance. I took a course on it a couple summers ago. I know just what to do, how to hide, where to locate your car in front of someone's house. It's fun, especially when you catch the bad guy doing something stupid."

"Trust me. Mr. Tundra won't be leaving any time soon. He wouldn't take the chance of pulling that thing out on the road without having some kind of game in mind. I think he'll stay put for awhile, at least until he does what he came to do."

"And what might that be?"

"I don't know, but whatever it is, I hope it doesn't involve body parts or hand guns."

"Okay, I won't call Nick . . . yet, but what's up with the limp?"

"I sat on something sharp."

"You need a shot."

"One won't be enough. For or five might be better."

"Not that kind of shot."

"Oh, you mean like a tetanus shot? That's no fun. I already had one of those last year when I scratched my arm on a rusty metal rake out in the orchard. I was hoping for a shot of something a bartender might pour, tequila preferably."

I opened the front door of Cougar's.

"Maybe this is a bad idea," Lisa warned. "After the raid on your apartment, and now seeing the Tundra in the parking lot, you seem a little vulnerable."

I turned to her and pasted on one of my mom's phony smiles. She didn't know the half of all that had happened today. "Moi?

I'm a rock. All I need is a little soap and water and I'm as good as new."

"Okay, but no shots."

"Nothing but sparkling water, babe. We've got a killer to catch."

I washed up in the ladies room as best I could, checked out my ass for a cut, which thankfully there wasn't one, only a red mark, and popped a pain killer to ease all my body aches. Lisa applied a bit of her makeup to my now squeaky clean face. I re-clipped my hair in a more suitable fashion, brushed off my dress with some damp paper towels, brushed off my shoes, and fifteen minutes later as we made our way to the bar in the middle of the room, I was somewhat presentable, at least in the dark.

The place was noisy, and crowded, just the way I remembered it. The music was too loud, and the room smelled like a mixture of perspiration and booze.

I loved it.

I hadn't been inside a bar of any kind in over two years, and with good reason. I could feel my resolve flowing out of me as we walked. All I needed was for one more thing to go wrong, and it was all over.

"On second thought, maybe this wasn't such a good idea. My resolve is waning," I told her.

"We can go if you want, sweetie. We don't have to stay. I'll call Nick, tell him about the Tundra and—"

That was exactly what I needed to hear. "I'm feeling much better, besides I want to see Leo. I have an apology to make."

She raised an eyebrow. "Since when do you apologize to Leo? Isn't that game played the other way around?"

"Not this time."

"I won't ask, but whatever you need to do just let me know." She led the way through the thick crowd, toward the glow emanating from the center of the room, which could only be the bar. I'd heard about it, but had never seen it before due to my two-year self-imposed bar restriction. Now, I was anxious to finally get to see it. My ass was better, so the limp was essentially gone and I was feeling a bit spunky as we walked closer to the bar.

On our way, we passed Jimmy yucking it up with Uncle Federico. I immediately thought it was odd that Jimmy would be there considering it was a Friday night and the man had his own bar to run in San Francisco. He never liked to stray too far from his "baby" on the weekends; at least he never did until tonight.

He nodded his recognition. I nodded back. Ships passing, or better still, warships passing in the night.

I wondered if the Tundra belonged to Jimmy, but immediately thought better of it. I mean, why he would he take the chance and drive the Tundra in from the city when he owned a perfectly fine BMW Roadster?

It just didn't add up.

I was busy arguing with myself when turned to take another look and spotted her standing next to him, holding his hand, whispering something in his ear. Jade, Dickey's Jade was hanging onto Jimmy, wearing a black, radically short, spandex dress, and strappy four-inch heels, your average borderline hooker attire. She sported long bangs, presumably to cover up that forehead bump. When she finally spotted me she gave me a slow finger wave, Dickey's engagement ring prominently displayed.

I felt like a deer in the headlights, unable to move. What happened to that frightened girl sneaking home on a tour bus?

Lisa stopped walking and turned to me. "Isn't that Jade?"

"None other," I answered.

"What the hell is she doing here, and with Jimmy no less?"

I had a bad feeling about this as my mind raced to come up with some sort of reasonable answer.

"Picking up her car, perhaps?"

Lisa threw me a sarcastic look. "That chick and Jimmy were

gaming us, big time."

"Looks that way, doesn't it? The girl seems to have a thing for older guys."

"What happened to that Jay-Jay guy she was rushing home to see?"

"Jay-Jay was Jimmy's childhood name. I never thought he—"

"So who the hell is this chick? And what's her story? And if she and Dickey were pretending to be engaged, was Jimmy in on it all along? And why didn't she show up at the freedom party? Was she telling you the truth about Dickey going off without her?"

I shrugged. "I don't know. She seemed genuinely concerned over Dickey's disappearance, but with this family it's all about who's gaming who, and right now I'd say Jade has the upper hand and she's flaunting it."

"Let's go over there and talk to that girl. I have a few hundred questions," Lisa said. She looked angry and I knew if we confronted Jade now while she was flanked by Jimmy and Federico we wouldn't get the truth.

I pulled Lisa back. "Let's hold off for now and I'll try to get her alone, later."

We stood there gawking at the loving couple. Jimmy intently listening to everything Federico had to say, while Jade held onto Jimmy's hand looking bored with the conversation.

"You're not getting anyone alone later. Wherever you go tonight, I'm right behind you. Especially when it comes to Jimmy. I don't trust that dude. Besides, Mr. Tundra is lurking around here somewhere. Neither one of us should be alone tonight. Maybe we should hang with my brother. He drove me in."

I'd guessed right. "Your brother's here?"

"Yeah, but he's probably already itching to leave. He gets bored at these things pretty quickly. He never was one for the bar scene."

"The exact reason why I never dated him. Maybe I ought to

reconsider now that I'm sober."

"Too late. He's engaged. Spring wedding. I'm a bridesmaid."

I had no idea. "We really need to keep in touch."

"The phone works both ways," Lisa countered.

"I'll try to remember that when you don't return my phone calls for weeks at a time."

She winced. "Guilty, but I was under a deadline and . . . that's no excuse. I'm sorry. It won't happen again, promise."

"It's because of my drinking. I know how much you hated it. But I'm sober now and I intend to stay that way." I didn't want to tell her I was tempted every other minute, especially after the day I had and more especially in this place. "Now, where's that damn bar I've heard so much about?"

Lisa giggled. "Follow me."

She took my hand and she weaved us through the crowd, the glowing colored lights getting more intense as we neared the bar itself. Soon the gyrating horde parted and there in front of us stood my nirvana, the famed square bar at Cougar's. I swear angels sang and I could hear harps playing. I stood in awe of the miracle that was all things alcohol.

She pulled me forward, saying something about empty seats, but I couldn't really hear her over the angels' sweet hymn. . . or it could have been Queen's Bohemian Rhapsody vibrating the room from the surround sound speakers, but at that moment I wasn't entirely sure.

We settled on our stools at the altar—or bar—depending on your point of view. Lucky for my sore ass, the stools were thickly padded.

The actual bar was a huge square with some kind of a clear resin top that glowed with colored lights that slowly faded into each other. The center of the square held all the booze in a tiered arrangement with coordinated lighting emanating from the center, like some gigantic mood ring that cycled between calm blue and intense red every few minutes. The ever-so-eager-to-please bartenders, about eight of them, six amazingly sexy looking men and two chic women, were dressed entirely in black, resembling disciples of a religious cult.

It felt as if I was bellied up to a liquor shrine and any moment we would begin praying to the God of all things fermented.

My mind raced. My palms were moist. My heart thrummed against my ribs. This was my nirvana, only I couldn't partake. That right there had to be some kind of sacrilege. But I was sure the God of fermentation would forgive me if I offered up a sacrifice.

I turned to Lisa. "Don't mind me. Go ahead and drink till you drop."

She crinkled her forehead. "Are you all right? You look a little pink."

"It's the lighting."

She tilted her head, narrowed her eyes and stared at me. "Maybe we should go."

"And leave all this?" I opened my arms wide, embracing the glorious moment. Queen's Mamma Mia, Mamma Mia reverberated through me.

"You're scaring me."

I took hold of my emotions, allowing the song to wash over me and sat up straight, breathing in the smells of all that was sacred. "You're simply reacting to the intense red colors. Look, we're blue now."

And we were. Calm, mellow blue.

She gave me a skeptical look, but then settled on her barstool, while I let out a long slow breath. Of course it was difficult when Queen kept reminding me of murder and mayhem.

Will not let me go . . . for me . . . for me.

I took in another deep breath, but the music just kept pounding its way into my brain.

Then the words nothing really matters ended the song and I was suddenly okay. Better now. Blue helped. Green was also a calming color. I could handle my emotions with green.

Red and gold, not so much.

Abruptly. some repetitive beat blasted its way through the building, no words, no real melody, just a pulsating sound.

But I felt much better, wondering now if Bohemian Rhapsody had merely been something I imagined. I considered asking Lisa if she'd heard it, but then thought she might think I'd gone off the deep end for sure.

Instead, I focused on the edge of the bar, closest to the bartenders. It was lined with those baby martini glasses prepped and ready to be filled with any variety of concoction. A few of them were rimmed with tiny chopped black olives, while Mary's Pizza Shack served up a bite of pizza on a stick, along with an Asiago cheese stuffed olive. Saddles Steakhouse served up an olive that was coconut battered, stuffed with Jack cheese then deep fried. I knew all this because of the info cards set out in front of the rows of glasses.

Lisa chose a simple cucumber-wrapped olive in her glass.

"Can I see the olive?" I asked.

"Knock yourself out." She handed me the glass with the speared olive.

At once I knew it was a Picholine olive from France because of the pinched, elongated ends and the brownish-green color flesh.

"This is one of our olives," I told her. "It's a mild tasting olive with a slightly nutty taste. When we press it for oil, it has a nice anis finish. A good choice."

One of the bartenders stopped in front of us. His eyes sparkled and his grin said, I like what I see. "How are you girls tonight?"

I liked that he called us "girls."

"Better now that you're here," Lisa teased.

His grin grew wider. He gazed down at Lisa's mini glass.

"Wise choice. A version of this martini, an Apertini, won the competition a couple years back. It was created by the mixoloigist from the girl & the fig restaurant."

"Perfect," Lisa said. "But I want the grandé size, please." And she slid the tiny glass back to join its companions.

He looked my way, showing off his pearly whites.

"Club soda with three olives, please," I told him.

He didn't flinch. I liked that in a bartender, non-responsive to my non-alcoholic request.

In less than five minutes he returned with our drinks, and was on to the next believer.

"So, tell me why haven't you been answering your phone today? I've been trying to get you for hours," I said, while readjusting my position on the barstool.

She set her glittery gold bag down on the bar and leaned forward. Her eye-makeup all smoky and her lips a shiny pink, hair partially up, with long curls caressing her bare shoulders. A bronze colored scarf served as a wrap. She looked positively gorgeous next to my positively like-hell.

"Apparently, iPhones don't work too well after an olive oil bath. It worked yesterday morning, but it hasn't worked all day today, only I was too tired to realize it. I guess the oil finally seeped in where no oil has gone before. I should've gotten another phone this afternoon, but I couldn't get out of bed. I really needed that sleep, but I'm charged up now, and ready for anything." She gave me the once over. "Well, almost anything. So exactly what horrible thing happened today and how can I avoid getting involved?"

"You can't. What I'm going to tell you is going to rock your world."

"That's impossible. My world hasn't stopped moving ever since I first saw those brown shoes sticking out from under that millstone."

"Well hold on tight, because my dad is alive." Just saying it out loud caused my eyes to water.

"Get out! Are you sure?"

I nodded, unable to actually say anything that would make sense.

"Oh sweetie! This is fantastic news." She leaned across our stools and gave me a hug. "And it couldn't come at a better time. Everything else stinks, but your dad is alive. Where is he? Is he coming here?"

She pulled away and I grimaced.

She said, "Wait. Why am I getting the idea this is not the good news we were hoping for?"

"Because, my dear old missing dad just happens to be some big mob boss, possibly the boss of all bosses in Italy. And, here comes the best part, according to Giuseppe, who has moved into my mom's house by the way, my dad's the one who put the hit out on Dickey. Apparently, Giuseppe was sent here to get that ring. I figure that's what he and Dickey were arguing about on Leo's porch when I saw them the other day. Dickey wouldn't give it up, so Giuseppe was supposed to whack Dickey and take it, but somebody got to Dickey before Giuseppe could do the deed."

Lisa leaned back, looking confused. "And you believe this Soprano knock-off because . . . ?"

"Because he has no reason to lie to me, and it was the way he told me. As if we were sharing a secret that could get us both in deep shit."

"Does Babe still have the ring?" she whispered.

"No. I have it hanging around my neck under my dress."

She gazed down at my chest, but the dress was loose-fitting. No way could anyone tell there was a man's ring dangling between my breasts.

"Are you nuts walking around with that thing? It's like a ticking bomb. From what you're telling me, Giuseppe still wants it, and if he was willing to whack Dickey, won't he be willing to do the same to you? Okay, so maybe he won't whack the bosses' daughter, but he can cause you a lot of pain. Then there's Dickey's killer who turned your apartment upside down last night looking for it, and took back Dickey's pinky. This person is serious, honey. Take that thing off and give it to somebody. I don't care who, but get it away from your body."

"And just who am I giving it to? Giuseppe or the killer? Either way, we're all screwed, especially my mom."

"This is getting way out of control. Just sitting here with you is dangerous."

"I don't know what else to do with it."

"Throw it in a futso."

"Oh yeah, that'll work."

She swirled the olives in her glass. "Did Giuseppe happen to mention why your dad wants that ring? Is it worth more than we think? What's the big attraction?"

I shrugged. "He couldn't answer those questions. It's not something one of the crew can ask the boss when he sends them out to do a piece of work. Besides, I was way too stunned by the whole your dad is alive thing, to think straight."

"Wow! Your dad's alive."

I watched as she took several sips of her martini. A pang of envy tore through me.

"Wait, there's more to this. Nick and his team of rather exceptionally well dressed detectives, who look way too Italian, closed down our business this afternoon while they were busy dusting for clues. I have no idea what they found, but they took a bunch of stuff with them when they left."

I wasn't sure I wanted to tell her about Peter Doyle's demise just yet. It might put her over the edge.

Lisa chewed on her top lip. A sure sign the next thing that came out of her mouth was guilt. "Mia, you should know they already know it's Dickey's blood on the millstone."

My calm meter jumped up a notch. I shook my head. She didn't know what she was talking about. "It's too soon. They couldn't possibly know already."

"I spoke to Nick. He shouldn't have told me, but—"

"I can't get a hold of you, but Nick can? How does that work?"

"I called him, but I had to. I needed to know if he was driving into the city to pick me up, or if I should catch a ride here."

I stood, angry that my best friend wouldn't bother to call me when she learned that this evidence could potentially shut us down for good.

"And you didn't call me, because?"

"Because I just learned about this right before I left and I figured it would be better if I told you in person."

I folded my arms. "You should have called me. I would have never come to this thing. I would have stayed home and . . . and done something. Maybe I would have found Dickey. He's got to be there, the vultures are circling."

An eyebrow went up. "And then what? What would you do if you found him? Especially after today. Like you'd call Nick. That's why I didn't tell you on the phone. I think we should tell Nick what's going on when he gets here. What we know. What we saw. That the Tundra is parked in the parking lot—hopefully it's still there—and that potentially the killer is in this very room. Never hide anything suspicious from the authorities. Eventually they will find out you were involved and this will only cause more problems for you. It's best to—"

"Stop quoting yourself! Do you even know how annoying you are? Like I'm going to tell Nick anything in a bar? This isn't your game. It's mine, and so far all I have is a hunch that whoever is doing this is out to destroy my mom, me and Spia's Olive Press. It's more to the killer than just getting that ring. This person wants total destruction. And as of this afternoon that person is succeeding."

Lisa reached out for me, but I pulled back, eyeing her drink. Then in one quick move, I picked up her full glass.

"No. Don't."

But it was too late. I fished out the olive, popped the damn thing in my mouth, chewed and swallowed. At once a sense of calm came over me.

Fortunately, it was pitted.

"Thanks. I needed that." I slammed the glass down, hard, splashing the mind-altering elixir all over the bar. It took every ounce of my inner fortitude not to bend over and lap it up.

Such a waste!

"Now," I said, as the bar color changed to an intense red—which sent my blood surging through my veins—and I pulled the clip out of my hair, freeing it to fall around my shoulders, "to hell with Dickey's murder. He's ruining everything, even our friendship. So I say again, to hell with Dickey! Right now the only thing I need is a man. Where the hell is Leo? I need some heavy-duty quality mattress time, and I want it right now!"

I slapped the red bar.

EIGHTEEN

Oops, There He Is

Not two seconds later, as if I was some kind of Genie, Leo and Nick appeared.

"How'd you do that?" Lisa asked.

"The olive is a powerful force," I told her, feeling naturally high.

As soon as I saw Leo, I knew I had to get out of there or I would be sucking down martinis with abandon. I didn't want to think about murder or murders, or Jade, my dad, rings or that big black Tundra parked outside. All I wanted was a night with Leo.

"We need to go," I said to Leo, completely ignoring Nick. It was a wonder to me how Nick could simply show up and pretend as if he wasn't in the process of completely dismantling my life piece by tiny piece. I totally got why my family hated cops. I was beginning to come around to their way of thinking.

"We just got here," Nick said.

Lisa glared at me then she got it. "That's why we should go," she cooed, and Nick understood her seductive message.

"We should, um, go," he mimicked, never taking his eyes off of her, looking as if she had him hypnotized.

Was she that good?

"I'll round up my mom and aunts," I said, dragging Leo behind me.

"Why? Are they coming with us?" Leo asked.

"We're dropping then off at home and then . . ."

I turned and kissed him, one of those intense, I'm going-to-fuck-you-right-on-the-floor-if-we-don't-get-out-of-here kind of kisses.

"You're not moving fast enough," he said when I finally released his lips.

He took my hand and plowed through the crowd like a bulldozer. I was in awe of his ability to slip between people without knocking anyone down. He would be great on the crowded streets of Chinatown in San Francisco.

Uncle Federico, my mom and my aunts were all standing together in front of an olive tasting bar where a forty-something woman was handing out free samples of locally grown and cured olives. Spia's olives took up half of the bar.

"We need to go," I told them trying not to sound desperate.

"Who invited him?" Aunt Hetty said when she spotted Nick.

"He's with me," Lisa assured her.

"Huh," Hetty said, turning away from us.

"We're leaving now, Aunt Hetty."

She turned halfway around, so she wouldn't have to see Nick. "But I haven't even begun to taste all the olives," she slurred.

She reeked of gin. I took a step back. "Now I know we need to get out of here. You're way past your olive quota," I told her.

"I'm going to stay," Aunt Babe said, her arm around a dapper looking gentleman with white hair and a smile to die for. "Charlie has wheels. He'll give me a lift home."

Charlie wore a wicked little grin that told me the "lift" home would be to his home and not hers.

"Whatever you want to do is fine by me," I said.

"I'm not going either," my mom added. "Benny's here and he wants me to stay, the little darling. He'll give Hetty and me a ride."

And there it was, verbal confirmation that my mom had once again gone over to the dark side, Benny being the dark knight.

"Plus, that damn Liz Harrington's been hanging around," Mom grumbled, pulling me in closer. "I think she's got the hots for Benny. She threw him one of those "come hither" looks earlier and got Benny to smile at her, the lousy witch. I gave her the evil eye, but my evil eye's not what it used to be. You gotta use these things, or you lose the knack, but Hetty's been helping me. She never lost it. Show her Hetty."

I knew it had more to do with mom's Botox injections, but I wasn't about to tell her that.

Hetty swung around and glared at me. The look was so mean, so full of hate and contempt that it sent a shiver down my spine.

No Botox there.

"See," my mom happily chirped. "Hetty's still got it. Ain't she something?"

Hetty swayed a bit and my mom steadied her with her compact little body.

"Yeah, she's something, all right," I said with a shudder.

"Okay then, I'll see you ladies back home."

My mom nodded, but I could tell her radar was up trying to spot Liz.

"Don't worry, Mia," Federico said over the din of the room. "It's all under control."

"Thanks," I told him while giving him a quick hug, the ring poking me in the middle of my chest. "I feel better knowing you're here."

I turned to my mom. "Mama," I shouted. "Don't do anything you'll regret. Listen to Federico."

She looked at me and her face softened. "Don't be silly. I know how to handle myself, but if she makes another move on my Benny I might have to deck her."

"Mom," I whined.

She gave me a dismissive glare. "You worry too much. I can take care of myself. I'm stronger than you think. And besides, Liz has a glass jaw. The last time I socked her she went down like a sack of potatoes."

"The last time?" I asked taking a step back.

"Oh yeah. Me and her go way back. She tried to take Dickey away from your aunt Babe, but that didn't last long 'cause I gave her a good right to the jaw and she never bothered him again. Although, she did visit him every once in awhile while he was in the slammer, the little vixen."

This was news to me. "Why don't I know this?"

"You were young, or maybe it was during that time. But everybody knew about it."

That time was how my mom referred to my binge drinking days.

"My bed awaits," Leo whispered in my ear, his warm breath sending a flash of excitement over my entire body. "Let's get the hell out of here."

I had been losing my lust-enthusiasm the more my mom spoke, and the more my mom spoke the more I was thinking that perhaps Liz was Dickey's murderer. After all, Liz must have been the jilted lover, and everyone knew about the wrath of a woman scorned. I wished I had known this information earlier, I could have been dogging Liz or at the very least asking the woman some relevant questions.

"Come on, Mia," Leo urged, pulling me toward him.

Nick and Lisa had already disappeared.

"Go. Go," my mom said, shooing me along with her hands.

"We need to talk about this Liz thing some more. Tomorrow morning. Okay?"

She nodded, and Leo and I took off.

When we stepped outside, Nick and Lisa were waiting for us at the door.

"I thought you'd never get out of there," Lisa said.

"My mom had some interesting things to say," I told her.

"Yeah," Leo chimed in. "Seems Liz Harrington, the bank teller from hell, was doing the nasty with Dickey sometime before he went to prison for murder, and Mia's mom punched her lights out."

I turned to him. "What if I didn't want Lisa to know that?"

I really didn't want Nick to know, but I couldn't come out and say it in front of the man. He'd be back inside questioning my mom.

"Is there anything you keep from your BFF?"

I thought about it for a moment. "That's beside the point."

We were walking toward the dirt parking lot.

"Huh," Nick said. "When did this happen?"

I knew his cop radar would go on full alert.

"Always the cop," Lisa teased. "Don't you ever give it a rest?"

"No, unfortunately it's a twenty-four-seven kind of thing."

I was thinking that maybe it was a good time to come clean with Nick. That I should make a statement or something. That Lisa and I should bare all, so to speak. I was tired of lugging this stuff around, and besides it was getting a little scary, especially since the incident with my ladder out in the orchard, which, as of that moment, I hadn't told Lisa.

Wait! Could Liz Harrington have sliced my ladder? Would she be that vindictive? She did seem awfully bitter that day at the bank and she had access while I was eating lunch at Maya's after I retrieved those papers. Maybe Liz really was Dickey's murderer and I've been thinking it was someone in the family.

Perhaps that Tundra out in the parking lot belonged to Liz Harrington. I flashed on her cowboy boots that day in the bank.

I needed to talk to Lisa alone about this new theory, before we got to the car, before we got to the Tundra.

"I'm over there," I said, pointing the way, grabbing hold of Lisa's arm, figuring Nick and Leo would have parked in the blacktop lot and I could get her alone for a little while.

"We are, too," Leo said. "Nick drove. Did you drive your mom's new Mercedes?"

I nodded.

"I thought so. We parked two rows over."

So much for getting Lisa alone.

"Not to belabor the subject," Nick said, "but did your mom happen to mention if Dickey and Liz had any correspondence while he was in prison?"

Leo started to answer his question, but then stopped, probably weighing out his chances for sex if he kept volunteering information to Nick.

A wise man.

I decided to tell Nick what I knew. Couldn't hurt to have him on Liz's trail. "As a matter of fact, they did. But maybe you should be asking these questions to Liz. I'm sure she'd love to spill her guts."

"Unlike the Spia clan," Nick mumbled.

My mom's car was one row up.

The Tundra was still parked next to it. "Look what we have here. Could it be the same truck that tried to run us off the road?"

Nick shook his head and smirked, then he pulled out a small flashlight and checked inside. "There's plates on the back seat. I'll call it in. Looks like we're going to be here for awhile."

Lisa smiled and gave me a nod while Nick called someone and gave that person all the information. He stayed on the line and waited for a response while he leaned on my mom's car.

We all waited for the response, but I knew who that Tundra belonged to.

A few minutes later, he said, "Thanks," and snapped his phone shut.

"The plates are registered to Elizabeth Harrington."

"Damn," Leo grumbled.

"I knew it," I said, satisfied with my theory.

"Then, why didn't you tell me?" Nick asked.

"I wasn't sure."

"What else aren't you sure about?"

I avoided the question, and instead I said, "Aren't you going to go back inside and cuff her or something? My mom would be thrilled to see it."

"As much as I would like to please your mom, I'll wait for backup. No telling how that woman will react. I've heard stories about her temper. Besides, she's only a suspect at this point. All I want to do now is take her in and ask her some questions. We don't know for sure this is the vehicle that ran you ladies off the road."

"There's red paint on the bumper," Lisa said.

"And you guys didn't call me?"

"We weren't sure," Lisa said.

Totally frustrated, Nick leaned in harder on the trunk of my mom's car. Then he pulled out his flashlight again, swung around and peered at my mom's tires.

"Your mom has a flat."

"I hate it when my mom is right," I groaned.

"She tell you not to park here?" Lisa asked.

"Yeah. How'd you know that?"

She grinned.

"Don't tell me," I said. "It's in one of your books. Something about parking in a dark area or is it about parking on dirt?"

"Actually, I wrote an entire chapter about parking in dirt, sand or construction sites. Also about parking in dark lots, but I think the construction site is more applicable in this situation."

"Did I happen to mention that I'm beginning to hate your books? Is there anything you're not an expert in?"

"Yeah. I can't change a tire to save my ass."

It was reassuring to finally hear something she couldn't do.

"It's easy," Nick said. "You just need to know where to put the jack. I'll give you a crash course while we're waiting for backup."

Lisa gazed at him with doe eyes. Complete adoration drenched her face. It was almost too disturbing to watch. My best friend was falling in love with a cop. If she didn't fit into my family before, she certainly wouldn't now.

The whole thing made me uneasy.

"Maybe I should just call Triple-A. That might be easier for everybody," I suggested.

"And miss seeing ole' Nick here get his hands dirty? Not a chance," Leo chided leaning up against the rear bumper.

Nick chuckled. "Step aside please, and let a pro show these ladies how to do this right. I traveled with NASCAR for an entire summer when I was eighteen. I can change a tire faster than you can spit."

Leo spit on the ground, and stared at Nick.

"Open the trunk and I'll show this non-believer how a pro changes a tire."

I held the button down for the trunk. We waited. Mercedes' trunks open after a couple seconds of continuous pressure on the clicker.

Nick stood at the ready, muscles taught and set for action.

Finally the trunk clicked open, the light went on and a strong rusty smell engulfed us.

"What is that?" I said feeling suddenly nauseous, holding my nose, thinking that rotting pepperoni pizza was one powerful odor.

"Damn," Leo said as he gazed into the trunk. "I think we just found your cousin Dickey."

The next couple of hours went by in a flurry of organized chaos. The place was swarming with law enforcement. Local Sheriffs showed up almost before I could fully understand what was happening. Then the fire department and a team from the coroner's office arrived on scene. Plainclothes detectives from Santa Rosa pulled up about a half-hour into the fray and all hell broke lose. Yellow tape was strung like Christmas lights and people with cameras took more pictures of Dickey than he probably ever had taken while he was alive.

The Italian-looking detectives appeared, mulled around, took a few pictures, asked a few questions, but for the most part stayed clear of local law enforcement.

A crowd gathered in the dimly lit parking lot, and uniforms worked crowd control as if they were protecting some big celebrity from a horde seeking autographs.

My mom, Aunt Hetty, Aunt Babe, Benny and Liz Harrington were plucked out of the bar crowd and detectives peppered them with questions. Curiously, Federico, Jimmy and Jade were nowhere to be found.

"I told you not to park in this lot," my mom admonished as she walked toward me, her squat little body swaying under a granny skirt that lost its roll-up and was now dragging on the ground. "We wouldn't be in this situation if you had listened to your mother."

"Mom, would it have been better if you had found Dickey while you put your groceries in the trunk after a trip to Ralph's?"

"Don't be silly. I don't shop at Ralph's," she protested.

"You know what I mean. You were going to find him in your trunk sooner or later. It's better this way."

"Says who?" She leaned in closer, not wanting anyone else to hear her. "Maybe whoever killed him would have buried him in the next couple days. Maybe my trunk was just a holding area. Now that'll never happen. This is all your fault."

Nick walked up. "That's not entirely true. At least about it being Mia's fault. On closer inspection we discovered that someone slashed your tire."

My mom's eyes went wide. "Now who would do a vicious thing like that to my brand new car? Maybe it was random. Some wild kids with tattoos looking for something to do."

"I don't think that's the case, Mrs. Spia or we would have found other cars with slashed tires and we haven't. No, this was meant for your car. My guess would be it was the same person who put Dickey's body in the trunk. The good news in all of this is you're not the prime suspect."

Mom thought for a moment. Then her face lit up like she figured out the only possible answer. She sucked in a breath and quickly let it out in a rush of words. "I bet it was that damn Liz Harrington. She's just mean enough to do it. I knew I should've punched her lights out." She turned, then took a couple steps toward Liz Harrington who looked completely distressed as she leaned against an empty police car. Even in the dim light I could see that tears soaked her face.

My mom didn't know yet that Liz owned the Tundra. I couldn't imagine what would happen if somebody spilled that little tidbit of information.

Leo, who had stood by me through the entire ordeal, placed himself directly in front of my mom. "Wait a minute, Mrs. Spia. I don't think that's such a good idea."

"Leo's right. You don't need anymore trouble," Nick said.

"Who asked you?" Mom spit out the words in total anger.

"No one. I'm just giving you the facts," he said in a calm, rational voice.

My mom would have none of it. "She needs a good right to her jaw. She has a glass jaw, you know. I punched her out once before when she told everybody in town that we were hiding gangsters at our orchard. She didn't press any charges then, and she won't press them now. That woman is asking to have the shit kicked out of her, and I'm just the person to do it."

Nick stepped in closer to her. "I'm sure you are, but your family has enough going on right now. Do you really want me to have to drag you in for assaulting Liz Harrington?"

This logic seemed to work on my mom. Her hand dropped to

her side and the tension went out of her face.

"Take a deep breath, Mrs. Spia. Breathe in and out through your nose. It will help calm you," Lisa said.

"That's right! I read that chapter in your first book, Coping Under Stress," Mom said.

"Am I the only person on the planet who hasn't read your books?" I protested.

"Pretty much," Leo said while everyone else nodded. Even Nick joined in on the head bobbing.

"You too?" I asked Nick.

He flashed a smile. "I finished her latest last night. They're really very informative," he said, all serious like.

As luck would have it, Liz walked by at exactly the moment my mom was beginning to relax.

So much for keeping her calm.

Once Liz walked into my mom's airspace, Mom began pressing her for information. Liz denied everything, but then Nick stepped in and said, "This is an ongoing murder investigation and we already know your truck was possibly used to run Lisa and her friends off the road. Plus, you were corresponding with the deceased while he was incarcerated. Is there anything you'd like to tell me?"

Uh-oh!

My mom lunged for Liz. It took all my strength to hang onto her. "You tried to kill my daughter? You got a lot of nerve, you old goat," Mom hissed.

"You're the goat. Not me."

"You better come clean or I'm going to start swinging."

"You think you scare me?"

Mom broke free and grabbed for Liz, taking hold of her hair and pulling until Liz was down on one knee. Nick tried to break them apart, but my mom had a vice grip on Liz. "Tell the truth, you mean old witch, or you're going to have a bald spot for the rest of your life."

"Mom, let go of her. Mom!" I was yelling now.

Liz said, "The way your family treated me, I had to show Mia she couldn't mess with me." Nick backed off, and so did I. We simply watched as my mother got Liz to fess up. "I had to show that Jade girl, too, swooping in and spreading lies that she was engaged to Dickey. Too bad that damn smarty-pants Lisa was driving or I'd have showed all three of them. I watched. I was there in the bakery yesterday, listening. Nobody knew. I'm good at disguises. That Jade girl was spreading lies. She wasn't Dickey's honey-bear. Lies! And nobody even invited me to Dickey's party when everybody knew he loved me. Only me."

"You're a crazy woman. He never loved you," my mother roared. "You probably killed him out of spite."

Mom let go of Liz, and took a step back. Both Lisa and I grabbed onto her, just in case she wanted to lunge at Liz again. No one moved for a moment while Liz rubbed the side of her head where my mom had tried to rip out her hair.

"I ain't the one with his dead body in my trunk," Liz grumbled. "Dickey told me all about how he coulda taken back his olive grove if he wanted to, and how you wrote him threatening letters not to do it or you'd have to take drastic measures."

"That's a dirty rotten lie," Mom said as she broke free and tackled Liz to the ground, arms flaying, skirts hiking way too far up for their age group. "Get her," Hetty yelled as she came up on the girl fight. "Give her a good sock in the jaw."

Hetty was totally inebriated, a state that didn't suit her. A state that turned her otherwise somewhat tolerable personality into something the devil dredged up.

Nick tried to break my mom and Liz apart, but he wasn't successful. Other officers were rushing over. I had to stop this before it got really ugly. I leaned over and wrapped my arms around Mom's midsection, which seemed to have grown in recent months, and pulled with all my might, but my mom was a hefty force not to be messed with. She purposely pushed back with her hips and I fell right on top of her causing Liz Harrington to get totally squashed under the weight. Her breath came out in a loud whoosh.

"I can't . . . breathe," Liz gasped.

I grabbed my mom tight around her oversized waist with both arms, and rolled off Liz pulling my mom with me. She weighed much more than I expected, and kept throwing punches with her short little legs and arms flailing like some beetle turned over on its back trying desperately to right itself. I could feel my lungs tighten with each of her kicks.

"I can't . . . breathe," I echoed.

But my mom didn't stop squirming.

"I'm dying here," I pleaded to no one in particular.

Lisa charged into action and somehow managed to lift my mom off me and back up on her feet in one fell swoop. Then she swung her into the arms of a burly male officer. "Stay," Lisa ordered, and my mother obeyed.

Nick knelt between Liz and me. "Are you two okay?"

But neither one of us could speak. We were too busy trying to catch our collective breaths. My mom, on the other hand, was chomping at the bit and ready to attack again. The burley cop held on tight, but it was all he could do to control her. She kept squirming and screaming, "Let me at her. Just one more time. Let me flatten that smug face of hers. I'll get her to admit she burned Dickey."

Nick helped both Liz and me back to our feet. I was completely covered in dirt, again. Just moving stirred it around me in a billowing cloud. I felt a little like Pigpen from Peanuts.

My mother was also covered in dirt, but it didn't stop her from pounding on the cop, trying to get free. I was impressed with her fortitude, but I could tell the cop was losing patience. He suddenly swung her around and clamped on cuffs, which sent my mother into hysterical overdrive.

"These things don't belong on me, they belong on her." She stuck out her chin in Liz's direction.

Liz seemed a bit dazed and wasn't paying much attention to my mom. Instead, she was intensely interested in the dirt on her hands, dress and coat. She pulled out an individually wrapped wet wipe from her purse and began washing herself like a cat even as a Sheriff helped her into the backseat of a squad car.

My mom continued with her rage. "She's the one who tried to kill my daughter. Get these things off me. They're going to ruin my bracelet." And as soon as she said it, the silver bracelet slipped from her wrist and fell to the ground. "See what you did. You broke it, and after I spent all afternoon fixing it. You're a bully, that's what you are. You can't do this to me. It's not fair."

Then she hauled off and kicked him in the shin.

And with that, the cop carted her away as my mom yelled out my name in some ear piercing tone I'd never heard before. I turned toward her, thinking I could somehow prevent this madness from happening. The very thing I'd been trying to avoid was now about to take place and I was powerless to do anything.

Nick stepped in front of me, picked up the broken bracelet, the bracelet that had been under murdered Dickey's feet, handed it to me and said. "I think you should let her cool down for the night, and unless you want to join her, you won't try to stop this. We have a lot of questions for her, and it's best for everyone if we take her to our facility in Santa Rosa to continue this."

"And you think you're going to get information while she's in custody?"

I slipped the bracelet in my purse. It seemed as though the damn thing kept popping up whenever Dickey was around. At least my mom wasn't lying about the broken clasp.

"That's the plan," he said.

"Good luck with that."

"You can probably pick her up in the morning, unless we find sufficient evidence that links your mom to the body. Your mom sure seemed to get mad over that bracelet. It mean something special to her?"

I didn't want to make up something I could get caught up in later so I took the big stroke route, instead of the minor detail that it's the bracelet that Dickey gave her, Oh, and by the way, did I happen to mention that I found it under his dead body in our barn? "She's just had it for awhile, that's all."

He raised his eyebrows in disbelief, but he let it slide, thank you very much.

He said, "I think we've all had enough excitement for one night. Everyone is free to go. But I have a lot more questions, especially now that we found Dickey's remains. Obviously, the man has been dead for awhile. So don't anybody leave town. All right?" He was looking directly at me.

I tried to act as if he was totally off base, but I knew better. The fact of the matter was Nick seemed to already know my family pretty well. Which begged the question, would I actually get on that plane Sunday night even though Nick the Cop had told me not to?

The way I was feeling, anything was possible.

Once we were released from the crime scene, I went back inside Cougars and scrounged up every pitted olive I could buy from a friendly night manager who didn't ask questions. He simply boxed them up and handed them to me, probably happy to see me finally leave the area.

Baked Reggiano Olives – Level Three or Four (recipe can be doubled or tripled depending on the need factor)

1 cup grated Parmesan-Reggiano cheese
2 tbs. softened butter
½ cup unbleached flour
1/8 tsp. cayenne
3 oz pitted or stuffed olives of choice (can be a mixture of favorites)

This recipe got me through countless nights when I absolutely needed to have a drink or six drinks, one olive at a time . . .

Mix cheese and butter. Add flour and cayenne and blend until the mixture is well combined and thick. Line up your olives in a row. (Not that you have to, but this gives you more stuff to do) To turn this recipe into a level four, stuff the olives yourself with a sliver of red pepper that's been roasted, skinned and drenched in olive oil, or stuff with a sliver of garlic, or a sliver of roasted jalapeño pepper, or cream cheese, or whatever you think might make a tasty olive. This process can take several hours and is proven (by me) to get you through those pity-party moments, or those self-aggrandizing fantasies when you think you deserve to party all night long.

Drop batter by tablespoons onto a sheet of wax paper and carefully mold around each olive, then place the olives on a baking sheet that has been rubbed with olive oil. *Note: Make sure you use a sheet with sides, or these little puppies will roll right off. Bake at 400 degrees for about 15 minutes or until golden brown. Serve warm.

NINETEEN

The Devil's in the Details

I went home with Leo, utterly scared to go anywhere near my apartment. Despite Leo's corporal allure, I slept in his guest bedroom, alone. Although I was incredibly tempted, I wasn't feeling as though sex was the answer to my problems. Basically, I was thinking sex would simply serve as another complication to my already overly complicated life. Therefore, I did the grown up thing and gave him a blow job and sent him on his way.

In my dreams.

In reality, he drove us to his house, and I was out of his car and in his guest room faster than a speeding bullet, or so it seemed. The only sex we had . . . hot and heavy with a lot of clutching and grabbing, and copious amounts of loud moans . . . was during an exceptionally long dream I had sometime in the early morning hours, while I dozed at his kitchen table. I had stayed up for most of the night baking olives, alone, in Leo's kitchen.

I awoke a few hours later in bed, in the guest bedroom (I didn't remember how I got there) satisfied that dream sex had been better than the real thing. Real sex would have led to mental anguish that I already had an abundance of, and any more would certainly cause my head to explode.

I showered, dressed in old ripped jeans I had left at his house before our second breakup, a borrowed flannel shirt and a pair of Uggs I had totally forgotten about. I slapped on minimal makeup, thought about food, but decided tea and a slice of white toast with butter was about all I could handle, and maybe a baked olive or two. Someone, most likely Leo's housekeeper, had cleaned up the kitchen, leaving the platter of about a hundred baked olives sitting on the counter.

I barely remembered making them.

It had been a very long night.

Leo drove me home around nine, after we decided to take this thing slow, whatever this "thing" was. I apologized for thinking he'd lied about talking to Dickey on his porch, and he apologized for the last five years.

He dropped me off in my mom's private parking lot—the chain still ran across the public driveway—and I gave him a long slow kiss then told him I'd call him when I landed in Maui. I was determined to be on that plane Sunday night despite the events of the previous evening.

I sprinted up my mom's back stairs, eager to return her bracelet. I didn't want it hanging around in my apartment. There was no telling who would show up to steal it so they could further incriminate her, if that was possible. Nick finding Dickey in her trunk seemed to lock up her guilt perspective rather easily, at least it seemed that way last night.

At any rate, I was hopeful that the slashed tire didn't quite fit into the case-closed theory. I mean, why would my mom slash her own tire? Obviously, the killer was still trying to set her up, but by some stroke of cosmic fate, Nick was there to see it this time.

Still, I wasn't taking any chances with anything else going wrong.

My sudden clear head was probably due to the great dream sex, or, I was obsessed with solving this whole murder thing because for one thing, my mother was not going to do time for something I knew she did not do, no matter what the evidence against her proved. Secondly, I had every intention of being on that flight to Maui Sunday night. Either way, I had a mission and heaven help the person who got in my way. This time I was determined to come up with the right Wise Guy or Wise Girl.

I'd read somewhere that mob wives and grandmothers were taking up the sword in Naples and Calabria when the men were either shot down or carted off to prison. Some of these gun toting grandmas were even more vicious than the men, and would shoot at each other in drive-by wars. Not that I had any intention of taking my vendetta against Dickey's murderer to a firearm level, but I certainly intended to ferret out the creep by any and all other means I had available to me. If that meant I had to get down and dirty, then so be it.

Of course, I didn't exactly know what "down and dirty" consisted of, but I figured when the time came my unique upbringing would kick in and I'd somehow know exactly what to do.

At least that was the plan of the moment.

Wow! Dream sex was powerful stuff.

When I walked into mom's kitchen, there were no signs that anyone was around. Of course, that didn't mean much, her back door was unlocked and an imported gangster had possibly taken up residency on the second floor.

Still, there were no signs that Benny had spent the night, no stogies in the ashtray on the counter, and his pink mug dangled from a hook under a cabinet. Hopefully, Giuseppe had already moved into his own apartment above one of the shops on the property.

What was I thinking?

As I walked to my mom's room I remembered Dickey's open suitcase in one of the upstairs bedrooms and wondered if it was still there, the one with all the price tags still on the clothes. Experience told me, from some of the other ex-cons around here, that price tags meant he or she had just been released. My gut told me there was something in that case I needed to see. What that could be, I had no idea, but I wanted to check it out.

Once I put the bracelet in my mom's jewelry armoire I intended to do just that.

No stone left unturned, kind of thing.

First, though, I couldn't stand how quiet the house was so I pulled the chains on the cuckoo clock to rewind it. Then I set the time, and once I heard that familiar tic tock I felt much calmer.

I slipped into mom's bedroom and turned on the light. The curtains were drawn, keeping the room dark and free from any family snoopers. Mom owned a fancy antique-white, hand painted jewelry armoire with eight drawers, a flip up mirror, doors on either side that held several necklaces, and tiered drawers to hold rings, pins and her various bracelets and bangles. The top drawer also served as a music box. Whenever I heard Torno a Surriento it reminded me of those lazy rainy days spent with my mom playing with her jewelry.

Mom's jewelry armoire had been magical to me, filled with fairytales and pixy dust. My mom and I would spend countless hours together trying on all her sparkly jewelry. I'd pretend to be a beautiful princess and Mom the beautiful queen waiting for her handsome king to return from battle.

All those years, waiting, wondering if my dad was still alive, and now . . .

Now I knew why the king never returned. Why be a mere king when you can be the ruler of all the kings?

Much more fun.

But I didn't have time to waste getting lost in childhood fantasies, or kings and mob bosses, not when my mom was locked up behind a fortress with no one to rescue her but me.

Where the hell was Sir Galahad when you needed him?

As soon as I opened the top drawer, the song immediately began playing, reminding me of the last time I'd heard it . . . while I was standing up on the second floor talking to Dickey.

My stomach twisted in an immediate knot. I wanted to

rubberstamp my forehead with a big red "STUPID."

Of course! That music, and all those noises downstairs made sense now. Why hadn't I thought of it before? Someone had opened this armoire and stolen the codicil almost as soon as I'd put it away. So that meant that person had to know I'd left it there, which meant they had to be in the house in order to hear the music to figure out exactly where I'd stashed the papers.

But that would mean the murder was completely premeditated, not a far stretch for this family, but I was so hoping for a crime of passion, a crime of the heart or something equally as spur of the moment. After all, we were a recovering family! Didn't that mean anything to these people?

I slammed the drawer shut, locked it and shoved the key into my pocket, angry that I hadn't thought to lock it that first night. This time, if the killer wanted anything she would have to break the lock.

Besides my mom, there was only one other person who knew I had the papers that night, and only one person who could have heard that music.

On my way out, I took all the keys to the house then locked mom's house up tight. No one was getting in this time unless they broke in, and that would leave glorious evidence. But at the moment, I was focused on one person. The person who lied, cheated, and had direct access to my mom's house.

"You killed him," I said to Hetty as I opened the back door to Dolci Piccoli. She was busy pulling a tray of four perfectly golden Italian breads out of the large oven. Without customers, she only baked enough for family and the pickers.

Aunt Babe was nowhere around.

"After last night, I didn't expect to see you all day," Hetty alleged in a calm voice.

I placed my hands on my hips. "You killed Dickey. You were

in the kitchen when I stuck my mom's paperwork in her jewelry box, heard Turno a Surriento and snuck into her bedroom while I was upstairs talking to Dickey. You snatched the documents, read the codicil and decided no way were you going to let Dickey take over the orchard. You pushed him under the millstone then shot him and planted my mom's bracelet as evidence. Then as an added bonus you stashed grandma's handgun in a futso. And,"—I was on a clue solving roll now—"you killed Peter Doyle, although for the life of me I can't understand why. He was probably a very nice man."

"He was a thief and a wife beater, but I didn't whack him."

She stared at me for a moment. Her hair arranged in its usual clown style, red lipstick radiant from the sunlight that streamed through the bank of windows behind me.

She said, "I just pulled some Amaretto cookies out of the oven about five minutes ago. They're still warm. How about I fix you a nice plate with a glass of cold milk? You seem a little stressed this morning."

I stamped my foot. "Didn't you hear what I just said?"

She slid the hot bread off of the pan and onto a cooling rack. The entire room smelled delicious and any other time I would have sat right down and took her up on her cookie offer, but at the moment I was busy solving a crime.

"How could I not hear you? Everyone on the property probably heard you. Why don't you sit down? You're making me nervous." She pulled out a wooden bar stool.

"I'm going to call Nick Zeleski in two minutes if you don't talk to me." I straddled the stool and pulled out my cell phone ready to dial up Nick, or at least Lisa. I didn't actually know Nick's number.

"Let me put the anise cookies in the oven, and then we can talk."

I agreed but it was a tentative agreement. I still held onto my phone.

After she slid two trays of cookies into the large oven, she poured a couple tall glasses of milk, and assembled a plate of various cookies, amaretto being one of them, and sat down next to me. Her flour covered arms pressed flat on the high table.

I reluctantly snitched a cookie off the dish, not wanting them to go to waste.

"You're right about the codicil," she said. "I'd heard about it, but never knew exactly what it said, so yeah, I pinched it. My future was at stake, and your mom never liked to tell me nothing. I had a right to know the truth. It was no secret that you went and fetched her paperwork that morning, and as soon as I saw you clutching that folder, I knew exactly what you were carrying. Only problem was, you wouldn't just hand it over no matter how much I might of asked."

She had a point.

"You left me no choice but to swipe it. And you made it so damn easy. Who puts something that important in a place with a loudspeaker? We all know the song your mom's jewelry box plays."

I ate two more cookies amazed that getting a confession out of Hetty could be so easy.

"So Aunt Babe was right all along."

"Don't be ridiculous. Just because I snitched the codicil doesn't mean I killed the prick."

I put the yummy cookie I was about to triumphantly devour back on the plate, and spoke with loud bravado, not wanting to repeat myself. "Why not? You love this place, and love this bakery. You had motive. After all the years of lies you'd told Aunt Babe you sure as hell didn't want Dickey spilling the truth that you were simply jealous that he was two-timing even you. Although, moving that millstone must have been quite the challenge."

I waited for a full confession, just like crime shows on TV

where the villain comes clean in the end. I especially wanted to hear how she moved the millstone.

"Are you not listening to me? I had nothing to do with that murder." She leaned in closer to me. "Here's how it went down, and this is God's honest truth. I swear."

"On what?"

"Come again."

"What do you swear on?"

"I don't swear. Your Aunt Babe has the potty mouth, not me."

I didn't want this to happen again. I took a deep breath and spoke as succinctly as I could. "If you're going to swear that you're telling me the truth, I need you to swear on something that matters to you."

"Humph," she scoffed. "You always want more than anybody wants to give."

"Then I won't believe anything you say." I began dialing Lisa's number.

She reached over and grabbed the phone. "Okay, okay. Don't go calling any cops. I swear on this bakery that I didn't kill the bastard. I'd thought about it plenty of times. Even thought about how I'd do it, while the bastard was sleeping. I hate confrontations. But when I left him in the barn, he was still upright."

"You met him in the barn?"

"Didn't everybody?"

"I didn't."

"Then you didn't know what a big stink that codicil caused with the family."

She noticed the flour on her arms and proceeded to brush it away. It billowed around her then fell to the table in a fine white layer.

"It shouldn't have. Dickey told me he didn't care about this orchard. That he just wanted to marry Jade and start a new life."

"And you believed him?" Her eyes sparkled with amusement.

"Had no reason not to."

She leaned in closer to me. "How about because he's gangster?"

"Okay, so that was all a lie, but still—"

"Look, all I did was barrow the codicil. Nothing else."

"Did somebody steal it from you?"

"No."

"Then how did it end up in Peter Doyle's mouth?"

"I don't know. I gave it to Jimmy."

Her words sent a rush of heat through me and I sat up stick straight. "You gave it to Jimmy? Why?"

"Because he wanted it."

"But how did he know you had it?"

"I showed it to him almost as soon as I took it. I wanted to make sure I understood what I'd read."

"And how did Jimmy react to it?"

"He didn't."

"Could you be more specific?"

A bell rang. Hetty stood. Something needed to come out of the oven. "I don't see what this has . . . "

I threw her my-daughter-of-a-mobster look, not quite as bad as her evil eye, but I'd been told that it could be intimidating under the right circumstances. I was hoping this was one of those circumstances.

". . . okay. Don't be giving me no evil eye. You know I haveta be careful what I say out loud if I don't want to end up like Dickey. No place is safe until the killer either disappears or we forget about all of this."

"Neither of which is going to happen so you may as well spill it."

She walked over to the large oven, grabbed two industrial sized oven mitts, opened the oven and proceeded to pull out several trays of golden rolls, then slid them onto a tall cooling rack. The smell of the warm bread was intoxicating and if it wasn't for the fact that I'd just heard that sweet cousin Jimmy was looking more and more like a murderer I would have sat right down and eaten an entire tray of rolls, along with a stick of real butter. I was in desperate need of warm comfort.

She pulled the mitts off, let out a loud sigh and said, "He folded it up, slipped it into his pocket and told me that I never saw it."

Red Mob flag.

My stomach clenched tight. Suddenly the smell of warm bread was nauseating. When one of these Wise Guys told someone they "never saw it" that meant the problem would be taken care of, no matter what the cost.

Rounding up Hetty as the killer was one thing, but rounding up and proving that Jimmy was the killer was in a totally different category. He would not go down easy, plus, I would need much more evidence if I was going to present this to the family. They would have to be convinced before they turned one of their very own over to the police, no matter how slack the "family" strings were.

Case in point, Uncle Sal:

It had been easy to kick Uncle Sal off the property three years ago for that little episode of pimping when suddenly three different women started hanging around the tasting room and leaving with some of our regular male customers. Besides, Sal wasn't technically an uncle, more of an uncle of a cousin of an aunt who wasn't a true aunt, but just a friend of Uncle Ray's sister's husband.

We had a family meeting and decided not to turn him into the Feds. He was having a problem getting the business off the ground anyway. The women were full-figured ladies, which wasn't going over as well as he had expected, so instead we bought him and his girls plane tickets to New York City.

Sal became a high profile talent agent for full-figured models. I didn't want to know if it was legit or not. Once they were off the property, they were no longer my concern.

But Jimmy was direct family, and if he had killed both Dickey and Peter Doyle, and probably Carla, he would have to be turned in, something the entire family had agreed upon when we first moved onto the land.

My only problem was getting hard evidence and only one person could help with that, and she was waiting for me to spring her from the Santa Rosa jail.

I wondered if normal people ever had these problems.

An hour later, after two tablespoons of our Italian blend olive oil—my sensitive tummy really needed it—and a handful of cured Lucques olives from France, crunchy but delicate with a hint of almonds and avocados, I headed up the freeway to pick up my mom. Those overworked prison guards had to be as tired of her by now as she was tired of them.

Santa Rosa was a forty-minute drive, give or take five or ten minutes depending on traffic. Of course, that didn't take Benny's phone call into consideration. Luckily, I had already strapped my Bluetooth earpiece around my ear before I stepped in the truck so I didn't have to go digging for it in my purse when my phone did its doorbell ring.

It was Uncle Benny.

"Your mom's been booked for Dickey's murder," he calmly said into my ear.

My speed picked up along with my heart rate, and my trusty little GPS that I'd activated through a connection in my now basically redundant cigarette lighter, estimated my time of arrival to be in exactly twenty-four minutes.

"On what grounds?" I asked, hoping against all that was even remotely good in the world this booking had no real basis and Benny could work his magic to spring her.

"The bullet in Dickey's head came from your mom's revolver."

Of course it did. Lisa already said it would. I tried to breathe through my nose, slowly, but my chest was locked down at the moment. The most I could do was take in a short burst of air and try not to drive into the nearest ditch.

"Are you still there?" Benny asked after what seemed like forever.

"I'm here," I said in some deep voice I didn't recognize. "Go on."

"I cannot seem to get a straight answer out of anyone about how them cops came across her gun. Your mom never pulls that thing out. Where did the police find it? Do you know? As I recall, they did not have a warrant to search the house."

"Umm," I hesitated, so not wanting to tell him what happened.

"Are you there? Damn cell phones. I hate these things."

I had no choice but to tell the truth. "I'm here. They didn't need to search the house. It's a long story, but long story-short, it fell out of a futso."

I could hear him suck in a breath. "How did . . . in the barn?"

"Well, no, actually. Out in Mom's parking lot."

A moment of silence.

"You want to tell me how that happened?"

"Are you sure you want to know?"

"Is your mother's life important to you?"

"Do fish need water?" I didn't know why that phrase came to mind, but I guessed because he was being ridiculous.

"Just tell me how this happened."

I told him the sordid details and all the while I could hear him sucking on his cigar. When I finished he said, "Just tell your mom I'll do everything I can to have her out in time for her weekly Sunday afternoon card game."

As if that was somehow important. "I wouldn't want her to miss that," I shot back, knowing I sounded like a total bitch.

"Mia, it is the routines of life that keeps your mom happy. You of all people should know that by now."

"You're right." But this changed everything. My mom's life was truly at stake.

"You need to reassure her that everything is going to be fine."

Like anyone had that kind of power over my mom. "Me? Why me? Can't you do the reassuring? Seems as if you've been doing a lot of that lately."

That didn't come out the way I'd hoped.

"Yeah, so what? Your mother needed comforting when she found out Dickey got it, so I spent a little time with her in the house right after we found him while you and Lisa were busy entertaining Leonardo and his cop friend. One thing led to another and now me and your mother are, shall we say, officially an item. But right now I have to concentrate on the paperwork to get her out of there, and you have to be a good daughter and convince her that this rap will never stick."

That explained his absence from the porch the night Dickey was killed. At least I knew he wasn't in the barn moving the body. He was in the house moving my mom.

"Do you know who did it?" I asked him.

"I am working on it, but I have to admit, going legit has its limitations."

This was not the news I wanted to hear. I was probably closer to tracking down the killer than he was.

How did this happen?

"But why did my mom take Leo and Nick out to the barn that night if she knew Dickey was in there?" Something that had always bugged me.

"What, you think I am crazy? I did not divulge the details of Dickey's whack to your mom. She was in no state to hear it. I merely told her that he had met with an unfortunate end. It was all she needed to know at the time."

This was good news. "But she lied about the worker cutting

his hand on the millstone. Why would she do that?"

"Sweetheart, your mom has been around the block. Give her some adlib credit, will you?"

"So my mom didn't lie, she improvised?"

"Yeah, that is what she does. She improvises."

And to finally understand the way my mother's mind works? Priceless.

"Okay. I'll talk to her, but can I see her so soon after she's been booked?"

"Yes. I got a special circumstance approval from the shift supervisor for you just a little while ago."

"How did you know I'd agree to this? Wouldn't it be easier if you just bailed her out?"

"It's going to take a few hours for the family to raise bail. Besides, you know how to handle your mom better than I do."

"You owe me," I told him. "Big time."

"Sure, hon. Whatever you want."

"A different family."

"That I cannot do."

"Then, don't make offers you can't keep."

"I will try to remember that next time."

He chuckled and hung up.

I hit number two on my phone and Lisa picked up on the first ring. "My mom's been booked. She's in jail for Dickey's murder. The bullet in his head was from her gun just like you said, but please don't tell me Nick already told you 'cause I won't be able to handle that you didn't tell me as soon as you found out. I mean, my nerves are pretty much shot right now and knowing that my best friend—"

She interrupted me. "Mia, of course I didn't know. He wouldn't tell me something like that, and if he did, I'd have called you the minute I knew. So stop fretting and slow down."

I backed my lead foot off the gas. I had been doing almost

ninety. "But how did you know I was driving?" "I didn't. I was talking about slowing down your emotions."

"Oh," I said now that the speedometer read sixty-five. "That too." I eased my death grip on the steering wheel.

"I haven't heard from Nick since last night. When did this happen?" She sounded sleepy.

"I don't know. Benny just told me. I was on my way to Santa Rosa to pick up my mom, and now it's just for a visit. This could get ugly."

"Look at it this way. You'll finally be able to talk to her alone."

She made my mom's incarceration seem like an advantage.

"Do you always look at the bright side of things?"

"Only when my best friend is running on empty. You probably hardly slept last night, and I know you're not eating, which describes the life of a teenager, but not a thirty-year-old woman. You're going to self-destruct if you don't slow down."

"I'll slow down when I'm on that plane to Maui."

"We're still going? I thought now that your mom—"

"Nothing, short of my own death, can keep me from going."

"You made my skin prickle. Don't say that kind of shit out loud. Not while there's a killer running around in the family nest."

I let out a heavy sigh. She was so right.

"One more thing to add to the family tree, whoever killed Dickey had it all planned."

"How do you know?"

"I'll tell you all about it when I see you. After catching Liz last night this sleuthing thing is getting easier. Thugs always seem to screw-up. We just have to find the screw-ups. Wait. I just realized your phone is working. Since when?"

"Since my mom picked up a new one this morning. There's a real saint under all that bluster. They were able to save my SIM card so everything's cool."

When she said "cool," I thought of Jimmy and an idea saturated my thoughts. "Hey, what are you doing later this afternoon? I'm thinking we should pay Jimmy a visit. Clues are adding up in his favor, especially since my conversation with Hetty."

"Don't jump to any conclusions until you talk to your mom. There's no telling what she might say now that she's facing a life sentence. Maybe Benny did it, or Ray. Did you ever think of that?"

"Benny was still in witness protection when Carla was murdered, and Ray was living in New Jersey running his fake plumbing business. As for killing Dickey we would have never found the body if either one of them did it. Those guys traveled in higher circles. No, either Jimmy did it himself or he's connected to the person who did. I really need you to come with me when I talk to him."

"Can't," Lisa said. "I have a signing in an hour, but it shouldn't last more than a few hours. I can meet you afterwards."

"Your signing's go that long? What do you talk about?"

"I don't. It takes that long for me to sign all the books."

"Who are you and what did you do with my best friend who once refused to read anything other than comic books?"

"I shut her down and replaced her with a clone of an English major."

"Oh, that's right. I seem to remember a dorm room, and a campus of some sort, but everything else is just a blur. Too bad. I might have a different life right now if I'd paid attention. One that doesn't include trying to finger my cousin's murderer or talking to yet another family member behind bullet proof glass."

"I've never done that. Take me with you next time?"

"I'm hoping there won't be a next time."

"Sorry, sweetie, that's my life, not yours."

"Rub it in why don't ya?"

She giggled. "Gotta run. Call me later. I'll meet you at Jimmy's bar. Wait. I don't think you should be hanging around there alone.

Might not be safe. I have a bad feeling about this. On second thought, maybe you should wait for me. Safety in numbers and all of that."

She had a point. Jimmy was now suspect number one, and he might not react well to my snooping. "I'll call Federico and have him meet me there. He'll act as my body guard."

"Good idea. Where's the ring?"

"Around my neck. Still seems like the safest place."

"Seems like it makes you a huge target."

"Only if the wrong person finds out about it."

"I'm worried about you."

"Don't be. Federico won't let anything happen to me."

"Okay, but be careful. Damn, I wish you'd read my books."

"Believe me, so do I."

We clicked off and I immediately phoned Federico who was more than happy to meet me at Jimmy's bar.

TWENTY

It's All about the Ambiance

My mom was already seated on the other side of the Plexiglas when I walked into one of several tiny, cream-colored, private visiting rooms of the jail. The rectangular space was brightly lit, with a half-glass door behind me and the same behind her. The walls were constructed out of sturdy cinderblock, and thickly painted in that yellowish white that institutions seem to favor. All in all, it gave off that clean secure effect one comes to grow accustomed to when your last name happens to be Spia.

It was the first time I'd been in this particular institution, and it was far cheerier than say, Folsom, where Uncle Ray had spent a good portion of his life. There was nothing cheery about gray, overcrowded Folsom where Ray hobnobbed with the likes of Charles Manson and other more noteworthy villains.

Mom seemed almost jolly despite her incarceration. It wasn't the first time she'd been booked and printed. According to what little I remembered this would be number three. Of course, the other two turned out to be misdemeanors, and let's not forget she was taken in for questioning when my dad disappeared, but getting booked for an actual murder had to be an entirely different experience.

Still, she seemed in good spirits.

She made herself comfortable on the stool, but could barely see over the solid speaker at the bottom of the glass and had to lean forward on her elbows to talk to me. The speaker was controlled somewhere outside of the room.

Mom looked far better than most of my female relatives when

I'd seen them behind glass. At least she wasn't wearing one of those orange jumpsuits. Not in her color pallet. Orange made her ruddy skin glow. The standard issue gray oversized T-shirt with SO CAL JAIL emblazoned on the back in large black letters, and black pants were definitely an improvement over day-glow orange jumpsuits.

"Somebody should do something about the food in this place. It stinks," she grumbled. "And the coffee tastes burnt. Horrible stuff. But my guard is sweet. I told her if she wore her belt lower on her hips it would make her appear taller, and if she rubbed olive oil into her scalp once a week it would get rid of her dandruff. I don't think anyone's ever told her these things because she looked genuinely shocked. It was a life-changing moment for her, I'm sure. She'll be coming into our tasting room as soon as we're open again. I offered her a free bottle of oil, but she said she couldn't take bribes. Not that I had offered a bribe, it was simply a free bottle of oil. Geez, they're so touchy."

I didn't know how to react to this. I thought she would be terrified over her potential fate, but instead she was busy pitching.

When was I ever going to learn that my mom always made the best out of whatever situation she landed in?

"Benny says he'll get you out of here in time for the card game."

"Good to know because that bed is a bitch and gave me a backache. I wouldn't want to sleep on it for too many nights. No wonder some of these people in here are so cranky, everybody's suffering from lower back pain."

I didn't think this was exactly the reason, but who was I to argue with my mom about such things. So far, I was probably the only one in my family who hadn't slept on a prison bunk, and I intended to keep it that way.

"Mom, I have a couple questions for you."

She leaned in closer. "I think they monitor these things. Maybe we should wait until I'm sprung."

"This can't wait, Mom. I need to know now."

"Okay, but let's whisper. It'll be tougher for anyone to pick up what we're saying."

Anything to get her to open up.

I leaned in as close to the window speaker as I could. "Do you know anything about Dickey's ring?"

"It belongs to your dad."

I was confused. How did she know this and why was she talking about him as if she knew he was alive?

"Is that true?" I asked.

"Why would I say it if it wasn't?"

"You're using present tense when you're referring to dad. You never did that before."

"I am? Huh, the things you pick up on."

"Mom, what does it mean?"

"What does what mean? Mia, we only have a short time. You should at least try to ask questions I can understand."

I sighed.

"Mom, yesterday I learned that Dad is alive. Did you already know this?"

She leaned in closer, her head bobbing up to see me. "Yes. Isn't it fabulous? Giuseppe told me after the meeting."

"Why didn't you tell me?" I said in a normal voice.

"I would have, but you're always so busy. I can never get a moment alone with you."

I narrowed my eyes. If I wasn't inside a jail I would have screamed. "Mom, we're alone now, sort of. Tell me everything you know about that ring."

She let out a frustrated heavy sigh. "Now pay attention, sweetheart, so I don't have to repeat myself. That ring once belonged to your great-grandfather, who gave it to your grandfather, who then passed it down to your dad. My great-grandfather passed down cuckoo clocks, but your dad's great-grandfather passed down his ring."

"There has to be more to it than just a ring that gets passed down through generations."

"Of course there is, dear. Don't be so impatient." She took in a deep breath and continued. "Apparently, your grandfather, Dino, pulled the ring off his finger right before he died on the street in Cosenza from a bullet during a feud with another family. Anyway, both Federico and your dad were there. Federico was just a little boy then, so I don't think he even understood what was going on. According to your dad, Dino ripped the ring off his finger, handed it to your dad, and made him promise to guard it with his life. Then the old man croaks right there in your dad's arms, but he has the ring as a keepsake. About fifteen years later, the damn thing gets stolen. Don't you remember it?"

I tried to think back, and once again I kind of remembered the ring, but not on Dad's finger. It was on somebody else's finger, and no matter how I tried, I couldn't remember who that could have been.

"No," I told her.

"Well, he didn't wear it very often. He thought it was bad luck. Both your grandfather and your great-grandfather were killed while they wore that ring. Granted, your great-grandfather was killed in a freak olive picking accident, but he died wearing the ring and your dad couldn't get past that fact.

"Anyway, like I said, somebody stole it while your dad lived with us, then years later it turned up on Carla's finger, at least according to Babe, and then on Dickey's finger. It has a long history. Kind of creepy, if you ask me, especially now that Dickey's been murdered. Why your dad would want that damn bad luck bauble is beyond me, but he does. That's why Giuseppe's here, that, and to kill Dickey if he was reluctant to give it back. There was probably more to it than just the ring. Maybe a vendetta because your dad really thought Dickey killed Carla, but I think

Dickey convinced Giuseppe that he didn't do it."

"What do you believe?"

"Dickey didn't kill her. Had no reason to. Somebody set him up, just like the evidence proved."

"No, I mean about Giuseppe."

"I know that nice boy didn't whack Dickey, because if he did, he'd be on a plane back to Italy with the ring instead of hanging around our land. Although, he does make a mean tapenade. Better than Federico's, but don't tell Federico I said that. He'd never forgive me."

Facts were finally taking shape. I was able to understand a few more things about the past. But why would my dad want to kill Dickey for Carla's murder? What was the connection?

I'd have to come back to that.

"Let's put that aside for the moment. Were you ever in the barn with Dickey?"

She nodded. "Of course I was," she whispered so softly I could barely hear her. "We planned it that way."

"Explain please."

"He wanted to nab the person who framed him for Carla's murder. The ring was the bait. He figured that person wouldn't try anything funny out in the yard, so he put himself in the barn where he could have some privacy."

"Did he tell you who he was waiting for?"

"Carla's killer. Try to keep up, dear."

I sighed. "I mean specifically. I have a hunch who did it and I want to see if Dickey suspected the same person."

"He told me he had a lot of time to think about the frame-up in prison, and he had crossed everyone off his list except four people. Personally, I think it was that damn Liz Harrington, but she was in a straight jacket in some mental institution when Carla was killed. I know, I checked."

"Who are the four people?"

"Babe, because he knew she saw them together the morning of Carla's murder."

"Babe thinks he never saw her."

"Yeah, but Jimmy was in the car, too."

"So, he told Dickey?"

"You betcha."

"Anybody else?"

"Jimmy."

"Why him?"

"Because Jimmy can't be trusted. Plus, Dickey always thought Jimmy was Carla's secret lover and when he saw her kissing Dickey he went ballistic."

"Wasn't she a little old for him?"

"Cougars have been around for awhile, sweetheart."

Still, I couldn't picture Jimmy and Carla. Something didn't quite fit there.

"Who else?"

"Federico, but I think his name came up because the two of them were at odds when they first bought this land and hired Federico to help him. Dickey wanted to grow grapes and Federico wanted olives. They fought long and hard, and some people even speculated that Dickey torched Federico's restaurant to make his point."

Federico owned and operated a successful Italian restaurant on Columbus Street in North Beach. It burnt to the ground about two years before Dickey went to prison. If this was true, Federico had motive.

"I thought there was a fire in the kitchen. Hot oil or something. Why didn't I know about the suspected arson?"

"You were too under the weather to focus, darling." Another of her terms for my binges. "But Federico was in Texas buying olive trees the night Carla was murdered. I think the cops questioned him. Hell, they questioned everybody who knew her, but he was released. I guess his alibi stuck, at least for the cops. Dickey, not so much."

"Who else?"

"Me," she giggled. "Can you imagine?"

I somehow could imagine, even though I knew she didn't do it. "Why would Dickey think you killed Carla and set him up?"

"Well, Carla was an odd duck, and went around telling everyone that I killed your dad because he had been cheating on me with her, and I buried him in Babe's garden in San Francisco. Do you remember her garden? It was quite spectacular."

"Had he been cheating on you with Carla?"

She sighed. "Sorry to say, yes. He did."

I had to hand it to Carla, the woman really got around.

I knew how vindictive my mom could be, but looking at her now, behind the glass, I seriously doubted she could ever murder someone. Punch out their lights a few times, yes, but murder?

Not likely.

She adjusted herself on the stool and continued. "I could see where Carla might get the idea that the lovely flowers were feeding off a corpse, but at the time I was sure she was lying about their affair, so I didn't take her accusations seriously. I now know better, but I can't talk about that here."

"Why not? It might be information that I can use to clear you."

"Don't be silly, sweetie, that's Benny's job."

I didn't have the heart to tell her that Benny knew less than I did. I still had one more question.

"What about your bracelet under Dickey's feet?"

She sighed.

"Well, after I gave him my gun, I—"

I had to stop her right there. "You want to tell me why you gave an ex-con mob boss your grandmother's pearl-handled girly gun?"

"I had to. He couldn't be messing around with a murderer

unarmed. It wasn't fair. The man just got out of prison and getting access to a weapon can be a real challenge. You lose all your contacts while you're doing time. I thought I'd be a good cousin and lend him mine. He didn't want it at first, and we argued, but he finally came 'round and took it. In hindsight that may not have been a good idea. Dickey must have been woefully out of practice and the killer somehow took it away from him. I imagine there was one hell of a struggle. Dickey was always a scrapper. I mean, how else could that millstone have fallen on top of him? It's too heavy for anyone to push, don't you think?"

I nodded at her point, although I wasn't sure it happened that way.

"Whatever. Okay, so you gave him your gun."

"Shhhh, you're much too loud, Mia."

I leaned in even closer. "So he has your gun, and . . . ?"

"He slips it in his jacket pocket. I give him a kiss on both cheeks and a big hug, careful of the gun, and that's when I notice my bracelet is missing. We looked around for it, but couldn't find it. I figured I must have lost it before I came in." Then, as if a light turned on in her head, she sucked in air and leaned closer. Her face twisted with anger. "Do you think somebody found it out in the yard and planted it under Dickey's feet? The dirty louse. Trying to set me up? That must be it." She smacked the glass between us. "Some low down dirty bastard, pond scum of an ungrateful prick, in my own family, tried to set me up. Of all the shit things to do, and after all I've done for him."

"Him? Who's him?"

"That rotten . . . but he's the only person who could have done this, dear. He had motive. I should have known better than to ever trust him." She was talking more to herself than to me. "That two-faced, lying . . . your father always said to be careful of him." Her face went serious. "Look, this is what you have to do sweetheart, Jimmy's . . ."

But I couldn't hear her anymore. I slapped the window, but no sound came out. The door opened on her side, and a female guard with a low-slung belt helped my mom off the stool.

"Wait. Can we have a couple more minutes? Mom, was it Jimmy? Mom!"

She tried to mouth something, but I couldn't read her lips very well because she was both talking to me, and saying something to the guard. I made out two names, Jimmy and Federico, but that was all I could catch.

And just like that she was gone.

TWENTY-ONE

That's What Friends are For

I left the jail and headed straight to San Francisco feeling somewhat confidant now that Jimmy was the killer, and my mom was trying to tell me to get Federico's help. In order to prove it, though, I needed to bait him with the ring, and trap the little psychopath at his own game. This time I felt certain I was on the right track. My mom practically told me it was Jimmy. Besides, there was no one else left with opportunity and motive.

I wished we could have talked for five more minutes. Damn prison rules. Just when I started getting some real information out of my mom, they shut off the audio and took her away.

I was thinking like some sort of prison babe, those women who visit the inmates all glammed up and complain they don't get enough time with their lover who just happens to be in there for some horrendous crime.

Like murder.

I took a deep breath and tried to relax the tension that was building in my neck.

All paths led to Jimmy, and he was just scummy enough to do it all. I had to find a way to trap the little shit and perhaps with Federico's help, I could do just that. I didn't exactly know how I would accomplish this act of daring, but I had one thing in my favor: Jimmy liked to brag, especially in front of women. Maybe I could get him to spill something if good ole, double-crossing Jade was there. Especially if I showed off Dickey's ring. I'd pick the right time, maybe when Lisa arrived, and pull the damn thing out. His reaction alone would probably be all I'd need to bring in

Nick, who I intended to call as soon as I was sure. No family meeting needed for this one. The man was pond scum.

It was almost five o'clock now and my stomach begged for food. I stopped at a Starbuck's and picked up a large hot tea with plenty of milk and honey, bought the most decadent pastry they had, a cranberry scone with icing, had them warm it and applied three squares of butter. I figured I would need all the fat I could get to settle my chronically aching stomach. Having to deal with Jimmy would only make it worse.

I ended up eating two entire scones and topped them off with another hot tea for good measure.

I was loaded for bear and ready to take on anything Jimmy could throw at me when I parked around back of his bar, La Bella, in a private tight parking area that I only knew about because Lisa and I had used it as a shortcut to get to school when we were kids. It had recently rained giving the cement street, walls and buildings a brown glow. The rain would curb our picking abilities, which meant the olives would hang on the trees longer. But at the moment, that was Federico's headache, not mine.

A damp chill sent a shiver deep into my bones, and I was wishing I'd worn a coat when I spotted Jimmy's BMW parked in tight between a foul smelling open Dumpster and the back of the building that housed both Jimmy's bar and his upstairs apartment.

My stomach did a couple swirls as I stepped out of my pickup and headed to the back door of the building. The musky scent of damp city filled the air as I crept around his car and headed for the back door.

I phoned Lisa.

The call went directly to voicemail. I hoped she would actually listen to the message this time. "I'm at Jimmy's bar. I know I'm on the right track. My mom pointed me in his direction and told me to get Federico's help, which I did. Jimmy's here. His car is parked out back. Get here quick. Federico should already be here, although I don't see any sign of his Nissan, but I have a feeling we'll be needing your kind of backup support. Okay, girlfriend, I'm going in."

I snapped my phone shut, slipped it into my pants pocket along with my keys and walked up to the back door, leaving my purse behind in my locked truck. I didn't need any extra baggage. This could get ugly.

The door was unlocked and I slipped in hoping no one would be around so I could check out Jimmy's office before I went up to his apartment. I was hoping to find some hard evidence that might link him to Dickey's murder, like perhaps Dickey's pinky finger hidden in a desk drawer or a filing cabinet, but I knew I was being too optimistic.

His office was a large room a few steps from the back door, and handy for me, there was no one around. I could hear voices coming from the kitchen area, so I figured I had to snoop fast.

The office contained a bank of filing cabinets, a large wooden desk, a round table with two chairs, and a brown leather sofa, complete with a decorative pillow and a blanket. I could only imagine what happened on that piece of furniture.

I opened drawers, fished through files, even searched a junk drawer on his desk. As it turned out, Jimmy was a neat freak, and everything was in perfect order, including his junk drawer which contained three Bic lighters of various colors, several packs of gum, Orbit, various sizes of Post-Its, an unopened pack of cigarettes, Winstons, three pens, two pencils, an open box of condoms, and a copy of Girly Girls' Guide to Bad Boy Survival, Lisa's latest book.

The woman was a great equalizer when even ex-Mafiosi were interested in what she had to say about dating bad boys. I opened the book, curious to see if he had marked a passage or dog-eared a page, wondering what this sleaze thought was important. I fanned the book. Nothing. No marks of any kind. It appeared as though the book had never been read. I stopped on the title page and there was Lisa's flowery autograph written under the title in bold black ink. The date under her name was for this last Wednesday, the day she'd signed at Readers Books in the village. But the book wasn't addressed to Jimmy.

It was addressed to Federico.

"What?"

"I said hello," a voice said behind me. I jumped, slammed the book shut, closed the drawer and turned to face Federico.

"You scared me," I told him.

"I should have. What are you doing poking around in Jimmy's stuff?"

"I, umm, was looking for a pen."

He took a few steps closer, reached around me and I swear my heart stopped, and came up with a cup filled with pens.

"Take your pick," he said, grinning.

"Thanks," I said, my mouth suddenly dry.

"There's a pad of paper to your left."

"Great." I turned and scribbled down my social security number for lack of anything better, tore off the paper and shoved it into my pocket.

I turned back to face Federico and tried to understand what his name was doing on that book in Jimmy's drawer.

"Wasn't that Lisa's latest?"

"Sure was," I told him.

"Did you get to her signing at Readers the other day?"

"No. Something came up."

He nodded. "Yeah, I couldn't make it either. Jimmy picked up a copy for me on his way over to the party. That must be my copy."

Total relief saturated my very pores. "Yeah, it's made out to you."

If Federico had been in the village getting a book signed then he had lied about his not leaving the property for three days, and if he had lied about that, what else had he lied about?

I believed him, but for some reason I wanted to double check it with Lisa.

Where was she, anyway?

"I'm sure he'll give it to me later. We don't want him to know you were snooping. We'll keep that our little secret. So, why did you want me to meet you here? You sounded a little stressed on the phone."

If I was going to use him to help me trap Jimmy, I had no choice but to tell him the truth. "I think Jimmy killed Dickey and possibly Carla DeCarlo."

He smirked, walked over and sat down on the sofa. "What gives you that idea?"

"A lot of things, mostly a strong hunch. I think he was in love with Carla and killed her when he saw her kissing Dickey."

Another smile. "When did this happen?"

"The morning she was killed. The morning Babe called you asking for a ride from the airport. You were in Texas so you sent Jimmy."

"Huh, I don't remember that. But at any rate, what proof do you have that Jimmy is our killer? What I mean is, do you think he killed Dickey as well as Carla?" He slipped a small leather pouch from his pants pocket, unsnapped it and pulled out a brown pipe.

"Yes. I think he stole the ring from my dad, for whatever reason, then gave it to Carla and when he saw Carla giving it to Dickey he freaked, and . . ."

A chill went through me and I stopped talking. As I stared at Federico, my father's younger brother, I thought of how he must have felt when his dying father gave his big brother a ring, and didn't give him anything.

"And what?" Federico asked.

"Excuse me?"

"You were saying something about Jimmy freaking when he saw Carla giving Dickey the ring."

"I was?"

My head was suddenly bogged down with conflicting emotions.

"Yes. You were. What ring are you talking about?"

He coughed and I was able to focus again. "The one Dickey wore the night he was killed."

"The one you're wearing around your neck?"

"But how . . . ?" I instantly looked down to see if it had popped out over my shirt, but it hadn't.

"I felt it poke me last night when we hugged at Cougar's, and I took a chance that you were still wearing it today."

He pulled out another leather pouch, and dug his pipe inside, packing it with tobacco.

"But what made you think it was Dickey's ring? It could have been anything."

"Not likely. A woman likes to display her jewelry, not hide it under her dress."

This was getting weird. My neck was beginning to tighten, and my gut was telling me something wasn't right here, but I pushed my apprehensions aside and kept on talking.

I decided to play him a bit. "That ring has some kind of history that I can't figure out yet. My mom told me grandpa Spia gave it to my dad. Do you remember that?"

He shrugged. "Not really . . . ya know, now that you mention it, I do remember something about a ring going missing. He was pretty upset about it. Do you think Jimmy took it?"

I nodded, but for some reason my theory wasn't feeling right. Wasn't holding up. Something was clearly wrong.

He smiled while he patted his tobacco down in his pipe.

"That's a pretty big theory. One that can get Jimmy put away for life, or were you thinking of not turning him over to the cops, and sending him off to Italy instead? Like some of our other relatives that couldn't go clean."

I shook my head. "You must be kidding. The guy is a cold blooded killer. He needs to be behind bars, and soon. Problem is I don't have any evidence against him other than theory. I can't seem to find that one thing that he screwed up on. So what we need is a confession. I've got my phone in my pocket. It records. Maybe if we work together we can get him to brag about what he's done. I figure at some point, I'll pull out the ring and bait him with it. You think Jimmy will go for it?"

"Go for what?" Jimmy appeared in the open doorway. "Did somebody mention my name?"

I instantly stood. "Yes. No. What I mean is. . ."

". . . we were just talking about you," Federico said.

"Hope it was good."

"Nothing but," I squeaked out.

Jimmy gave me a quizzical look. "What's wrong with you? You're as jumpy as a rabbit. And what are you doing here, anyway? You haven't stepped foot in my bar since you stopped drinking." He stared at me for a moment. "Oh, I get it now. You're drinking again, ain't ya? And you came here to get away from the rest of the family, right?" He walked in closer. "Well, little cuz, whatever happens in my bar, stays in my bar. Got it?"

He put an arm around my shoulder, and pulled me in closer.

"Perfect," I mumbled.

Federico was busy working on lighting his pipe while I was in the arms of a killer. Wasn't he supposed to be helping me?

"What can I do ya for? Bourbon? Scotch? Vodka?"

"I think she's more of a tequila drinker. Am I right, Mia?" Federico told him.

I so needed Lisa to pop in and break this thing up. I felt as if

I was being forced to drink by my own stupidity. And what was Federico doing promoting it? I thought he was on my side. "Yes, but—"

"Well, let's get to it. The day's young. You got a lot of catchin' up to do," Jimmy said taking my hand and escorting me out to the bar area.

I had no choice but to follow him out.

In the meantime, Federico walked close behind, and I could hear him puffing on his pipe.

As we walked toward the bar, the strong scent of sweet berries permeated the air. The same exact scent I had smelled on Dickey when I was lying on top of him on the barn floor. At first I thought it was coming from something in the bar, until I realized the scent was coming from Federico's tobacco.

My heart raced up to my throat. Everything finally made sense. My mom had tried to warn me, but I couldn't or wouldn't hear her. Jimmy wasn't the killer, it was Federico. The man who practically raised me. The man who had taken care of my mom and me when we needed him most. The man who had taught me how to shoot a gun was a cold blooded killer, and I was walking right into his trap.

Where the hell was Lisa when I needed her?

TWENTY-TWO

A Hell of a Place to Spend the Night

The fall woke me from my head fog, not to mention the hard thud of contact. Thankfully, I was able to land sideways on, of all things, a mattress. After all, if you're going to get pushed out of a window—Jimmy's second-story apartment window—isn't it everyone's dream to land on something soft or, as in this case, at least relatively soft? The mattress had seen better days thus the reason for it being in a Dumpster. Plus it was a little on the thin side, but at least I didn't hit pavement. I was thankful to the person who tossed it.

My immediate thought upon landing was that Lisa would be proud of me, that is if I lived long enough to tell her.

Living seemed to be the problem at the moment. As it stood now, I was either extremely drunk or someone had drugged me, either way my consciousness was teetering on the edge of darkness. I knew the feeling quite well, but this time I wanted no part of its drowsy effect.

I kind of remembered the conversation with Lisa's Emergency Room doctor and survival mode kicked in. I desperately tried to concentrate . . . something about flip-flops and Dumpsters and cut toes and stinky fish made you vomit.

That was it! I needed to vomit.

No easy task considering my hands had somehow been loosely tied behind my back so the old finger down the throat routine was out of the question. Willing myself to vomit had never been part of my repertoire. That was more in the bulimic realm and I was never one for chucking perfectly good food. No, the only thing I could think to do, considering I was surrounded by foul smelling garbage was to inhale something really disgusting.

I thought about my chances of finding a jar of pickled herring, like the good doctor's mother-in-law had used on the doctor's nephew, but the chances of finding anything pickled, much less fish, in North Beach was doubtful.

Of course, I had to remove whatever was covering my mouth first.

Minor details when you're talking about your very survival.

I squirmed off the mattress and wedged myself in between the metal wall of the Dumpster and a particularly putrid smelling ripped bag of rotting food, pasta mostly, with anchovies if I had my stench right. But when I spotted the torn bag of soiled disposable diapers, I knew I'd hit pay dirt. The combination was horrifying, not to mention incredibly rank. Instantly, my stomach began to pitch as I shouldered off what had to be some kind of tape covering my mouth.

Lisa would be pleased with my survival efforts.

My only problem at the moment was I seemed to be functioning on slow speed and my stomach was now on a fast track of disgust. Lucky for me, the corner of the tape hadn't exactly stuck, and I began to peel it off with the help of something poking out of another bag. It was dark due to a lack of any real street lights in what had to be an alley so I couldn't make out what I was wiping my face against, nor did I want to, thank you very much.

When the tape was nearly off I took in a big dose of putrefied stink and in a great gush of tummy eruption, my grateful body heaved up the contents of my queasy stomach ripping the rest of the sticky blue tape from my mouth in the process.

After waives of nausea departed and the dry heaves stopped, I was feeling a bit more sober. That's when my phone chirped in my pocket. I would have given almost anything to be able to answer it, but at the moment I was tied up . . . literally.

It was with those thoughts that I slowly lost all consciousness.

I woke up to the sound of a garbage truck in dreadfully close proximity. At first I couldn't quite figure out where I was. Then the smells along with the dampness of morning provided a clear picture of a totally gross—stained with God knows what—Dumpster. In all my binge days, and all the strange places I'd awakened, never had I awakened in a more revolting place. It was enough to reaffirm my commitment to sobriety.

My mouth and throat felt thick. I was desperate for water, but no way would I go digging through the firmament to find a drink. I'd die first . . . at least that was my conviction of the moment. If another hour went by without rescue I'd probably have to reconsider.

It was at that moment of dehydration when a thought hit me: I had just spent the entire night inside a Dumpster. I supposed there were worse places to sleep, but at the moment nothing could top this one.

First order of business was to untie my hands before the truck arrived and carried me off to the closest city dump. With my throat dry and sandy, I didn't think I could scream loud enough to alert the driver he was hauling away a human being.

I was feeling better—as good as anyone could feel who had been drugged, pushed out of a second story window, and spent the night communing with garbage. Now I needed something sharp, the lid from a can would be perfect. Except of course, if this neighborhood recycled I would be shit out of luck. I could only hope there were eco-criminals amongst the folk.

In situations like I was in, there was something to be said for those valiant people who weren't eco-friendly!

Luckily, my feet weren't tied and I was able to slip off my Uggs to free up my toes to go searching for the appropriate sharp instrument, hopefully not slicing my own feet in the process. After much searching there were no can lids to be found, but a crafty person has to make do. My trusty toes discovered a lifesaving bag of discarded S&M toys, appropriate for the neighborhood, and I was able to wedge some kind of a black strap dotted with metal spikes under a broken tricycle and poke holes in the tape around my hands enough times to then force a tear.

As I worked, I developed a new fondness for the kinky set.

All the while I poked, that damn garbage truck kept getting closer and closer.

Finally, just when the truck's brakes squealed to a stop in front of my very Dumpster, the tape loosened and I was able to unbind my hands, push up through the bags of garbage that had been thrown in on top of me overnight and stand up to glorious freedom.

I smiled and waved to the driver while still standing inside the Dumpster.

"What the fuck?" he said, obviously startled by my presence. "You okay?" he yelled over the roar of the engine, leaning out the window.

"I am now," I croaked, grinning while I climbed out of my entrapment. When I got closer I said, "You wouldn't happen to have an extra bottle of water in there, would you?"

He looked me over and made a couple throaty sounds, shook his head, smiled and held up a lovely six pack of water. "How many you want?"

"Just one. Thanks."

He pulled one off the pack and flung it to me. I caught it, opened it and guzzled the entire bottle, letting the glorious overflow spill down my chin.

"You must'a really tied one on last night, sugar. You sure you're okay? You don't look okay, and you certainly don't look like no bottle collector or free food collector. You look like you're in the wrong place, sugar."

I began to tell him what happened, but he didn't have the patience to listen to my crazy talk.

"All I know is, that's one hell of a place to spend the night," he quipped.

"Tell me about it," I said, tossing the empty bottle into the Dumpster then slipping on my Uggs.

"Look here, you seem like a smart girl, let me give you some advice. That kinda partying don't get you nothin' but sorrow. A drink now and then keeps the blood flowing, any more than that and your life ain't worth shit. You know what I mean?"

"More than you know," I told him as I leaned against the side of the smelly can.

"You need a lift anywhere or you want me to call somebody?"

"No, thanks. I'm good," I said, and took a few steps, my legs almost collapsing under me. I figured I was still a little unsteady from whatever I'd consumed.

He gave me a little nod. "Okay, Missy, but you think about what I said, all right?"

"Will do," I told him and made my way out of the alley to the familiar street in front of me. The piercing high-pitched warning beeps coming from his truck as he backed up did a number on my already aching head and I suddenly felt as if I was going to upchuck again. I told myself to breathe slowly and to put distance between me and the Dumpster, both of which seemed to help.

My keys were gone and so was Dickey's ring, but miraculously I still had my phone. A few blocks away, I stopped and called Lisa.

"I've been calling you all night long," she scolded as soon as she picked up. "You had me worried sick, and you know I gave up worrying about you years ago, but when Jimmy said you'd been drinking I—"

I didn't have the strength to get into it. "Can you come and pick me up? I'll be standing in front of The Steps of Rome."

It was way too early for the restaurant to be open, but at least she knew exactly where it was. We'd eaten many great meals inside that place.

"On Columbus Street? But Jimmy said you—"

"Just come get me, okay?" And I clicked off. I was feeling a bit sorry for myself and tears weren't far from the surface.

As I sat on the sidewalk, leaning up against the building, waiting for Lisa, several people tossed dollar bills into my lap. I tried to give back their money, but no one would let me. I actually scared an older woman when I approached her with the dollar. She yelled that she would call the cops if I came any closer. The final blow came when an obvious homeless man with a missing front tooth dropped fifty cents into my lap and told me I needed it more than he did.

I figured I had reached an all time low because I took all the money and bought a large bottle of water along with a box of powdered-sugar donuts from a nearby convenience store, sat back down on the sidewalk and ate every crumb. When I finished, I was covered in white powder and proceeded to collect even more money.

Never underestimate the generosity of the American public.

Twenty minutes later I was opening the passenger door on Lisa's brand new red BMW, an exact duplicate of the last one. The girl certainly knew how to work the system to get a replacement car that quickly.

"We have to go straight to the orchard before he gets away," I ordered Lisa as soon as I slid into the passenger seat.

"Who?"

"The killer."

"Jimmy?"

I shook my head. "Federico."

She looked genuinely stunned and pushed back in her seat. "Get out! No way," she squeaked.

"Totally way, that's why we have to hurry, before he disappears like my dad."

I reached for the seatbelt and strapped it around me. Lisa made a face. "Good God girlfriend, do you even know how bad you smell? You need a shower, like right now. Shouldn't I take you to my condo first so you can delouse? You look like hell." She crinkled her forehead as she pressed a button. All the windows rolled down at once.

"No. There's no time." A sense of urgency swept through me, especially since I named him out loud. It was as if he heard me and was now busy packing his hidden guns for a long trip.

"If you weren't my best friend I wouldn't even let you come near my expensive new car, let alone sit in it. We're going to my place, or I'm putting you in a cab."

"I can't imagine how much that would cost."

"Ask me if I care."

She held her nose.

"You can't be serious."

She raised an eyebrow and I knew she was dead serious. No way was she budging. "Okay, let's go to your condo." She had both hands on the steering wheel. "What happened to the sling?"

"Thumb's better, especially since I had it re-wrapped." She held up a thickly gauzed thumb. "And I can even type with this thing, and drive. Be grateful I didn't have my mom drive me over or there would be no end to her hysteria once she saw you."

"That bad, huh?"

"I wouldn't look in a mirror if I were you. It could do irreparable psychic damage."

She turned over the engine, pulled away from the curb and fifteen minutes later I was standing in Lisa's ultra modern—with Asian accents—living room staring up at a scowling Nick Zeleski.

"Holy shit," Nick said, as he backed away, his index finger under his nose, trying not to look at me.

"Yeah, I stink. Get over it." I wasn't in the mood to be pleasant, especially since Lisa set me up with Nick. I turned to her. "This isn't fair. You should've told me he was here."

"You wouldn't have come."

"Like I had a choice."

"There are always options."

She was right. I probably could have phoned Babe or Hetty, well, maybe not Hetty. Neither one of those women had been behind the wheel of a car in over five years. Lisa was basically my only option, except for maybe Leo.

I caught a glimpse of myself in one of her many wall mirrors and decided that calling Leo was totally out of the equation. One look and he would need therapy to even consider having sex with me ever again. I looked worse than most homeless people, I looked diseased. And what was that brown stuff stuck to the side of my head?

"Step away from the mirror," Lisa said.

I had no choice but to follow orders because if I didn't I would certainly toss my donuts all over her professionally decorated condo.

"Tell me the truth," Lisa said. "No bullshit. What the hell happened to you last night? Did you tie one on like Jimmy said, 'cause if you did, I can understand it. Not that I'm condoning it, but I can understand it."

I didn't have the energy to explain. "Do you think I could take that shower first? The smell is making me sick."

"Me too," Nick said.

Lisa escorted me to the bathroom, walking far enough in front of me so the stench didn't reach her.

"Tell me something," I said as we walked. "Did Federico come to your book signing?"

"He sure did, but he told me not to tell anyone. That it was our little secret. I didn't think anything of it because a lot of my male fans tell me the same thing. They don't want their macho image ruined, I guess."

"Thanks, that was the last piece of the puzzle. I had to be sure. I think he cut the rung on my ladder."

"What ladder?"

I'd never told her about what happened out in the grove.

"Remind me to tell you later. Right now I really need a hot shower."

When we arrived at the red bathroom door Lisa turned and said, "This has to be hard for you, sweetie. Federico is closer to you than your own dad ever was." She walked in closer and patted down my mucked up hair, on the cleaner side of my head, and the instant she touched me my eyes welled with tears.

"Yeah," I said. "At first I was devastated, but I find it interesting how spending a night in a Dumpster with my hands tied while soaking in my own vomit can change years of adoration into complete loathing. Let's get the son of a bitch."

An hour later, after copious amounts of hot tears, and gulping down three more bottles of water, I emerged from the shower with a new sense of resolve and decided to spill everything to Nick.

Wrapped in an ultra-soft white terry robe, I sat on Lisa's cherry red sofa, legs tucked under me, drinking honey-sweetened hot tea, going over everything that had happened leading up to last night. Needless to say Nick was grateful for my honesty. He took notes while Lisa recorded the entire miserable story on a tiny digital recorder.

"So what happened when you got to Jimmy's bar?" Nick asked.

"Not much, but once I took a whiff of Federico's tobacco, I knew I'd been going after the wrong goomba. I'd walked right into a lion's den and I wanted to run, but it was too late, so I played the game. Only thing was, Federico knew I was on to him so the bastard must have spiked my Coke."

"Can you prove that? I mean you have a reputation and—"

"Believe me, I know all about that reputation. No, I can't prove it, but I know I didn't drink any hard liquor, and I didn't take any drugs, at least not willingly. Whatever's floating around my veins wasn't something I agreed to."

"I went looking for you at the bar right after my signing, around eight-thirty, and Jimmy told me you had left with Federico. He said you were pretty well lit." Lisa said. "I believed him. Sorry. Could he have been in on the whole thing?"

I shrugged. "Maybe, but I think this was a one-man operation."

"Was Jade anywhere around?"

I thought about it for a long time. "No. Not that I can remember."

"You'd think he'd have found someplace other than his own turf," Lisa said. "Seems dangerous to play it so close to the chest."

"Not if he was aiming to pin your murder on Jimmy," Nick said.

"Never thought of that one," Lisa said.

"Wow, he had it all figured out, didn't he?" I told them as I rested my now empty cup on the glass coffee table.

"We still don't have motive," Lisa said.

"I think Federico was Carla's jealous lover," I told her.

"But wasn't Federico in Texas the night of Carla's murder?" Lisa asked.

"He said he was, and he probably had good documentation and a witness to back him up," I said. "But we're talking mob. Those guys could prove or disprove anything they want. I have a strong feeling he was right there in San Francisco watching Carla."

Nick stood and walked over to the black granite fireplace, which had a lovely gas fire snapping around fake logs. "Right now, it's still looking as if your mom killed Dickey. All the evidence leads to her. She had motive. It was her gun, and we found the body in her trunk. It'll be hard to beat all that. And let's face it, a lawyer would rip your story apart in court, not to mention dig up your past."

"I know," I said. "That's why I need to show up at their weekly poker game this afternoon to force Federico out in the open. At this point, he thinks I'm dead or at least trapped at the city dump, but thanks to Lisa who continually quotes from her own books and her many fans, namely the Emergency Room doctor, I'm alive. Although, whatever Federico slipped into my drink is still making me a little woozy."

I leaned back on the sofa.

"What you're proposing is extremely dangerous," Nick said. "We'd have to come up with something that would keep you safe, but also get him to talk. He tried to kill you once, next time he'll use deadly force. He won't take the chance of messing up again."

"Deadly force?" I asked.

"Yeah, a gun or a knife or anything that will cause certain death," Lisa said.

How the woman knew all these things was beyond me.

A sudden waive of nausea swept over me. Funny how that happened when someone told you that the man you thought loved you like a daughter would just as soon slice your throat than see you live another day.

I shivered. "Just tell me what I have to do."

TWENTY-THREE

Who's Your Daddy?

I spent the morning going over a plan with Nick and his team. I didn't ask too many questions about who these guys were, and no one offered to tell me, so we kept the conversation limited to the sting. At certain points during our rehearsal I felt certain that a camera crew would show up from behind a sliding wall and someone would tell me I needed to go over my lines one more time.

That didn't happen and right around two o'clock that afternoon Lisa dropped me off in back of my mom's house while Nick and his team were hidden somewhere out on the road. I didn't exactly know where, but Nick assured me that as long as I stuck to the plan, everything would be fine.

That right there was enough to make me queasy.

I had one last thing I needed to check in my mom's house before I walked over to Federico's house and I was hoping it would still be there.

The back door was once again unlocked. I was happy about that considering all my keys were in my purse locked inside my pickup behind Jimmy's bar.

According to Nick, Uncle Benny had bonded Mom out of jail only a couple hours ago. Nick had warned her to keep her theories to herself and to play along with me. Over the last few days I'd learned that Mom was exceptionally good at game playing, so I wasn't too worried about any slip-ups.

Afternoon sun poured in through the front windows of my mom's living room as I made my way up the stairs and into what would have been Dickey's bedroom.

As soon as I walked into his room, I knew my hope of finding his suitcase was unrealistic. The bed was neatly made, the windows and French doors were locked up tight, and the suitcase had disappeared. A good gangster cleans up his mess.

Still, I had to check the closet, which was empty except for a few plastic hangers. I did a quick check under the bed, but it had recently been swept clean of all dust bunnies. But there was something nagging at me. Something I'd seen before that I was certain I would find if I just looked harder.

I swept through the closet one more time. Nothing. I opened drawers. Empty. I ripped the bedding off the bed. Again, I came up empty handed. On my second, more extensive look under the bed I spotted a piece of white paper stuck up against the white woodwork. I hunkered down on all fours, dropped to my belly, and stretched out under the bed, grabbing the paper. When I stood up again and took a closer look someone had written Jade's name on one side and when I flipped it over, those tiny hairs on the back of my neck stood up again.

It was the same little girl in the picture in my mom's safety deposit box, only this time she was sitting on somebody's lap. A woman's lap, a woman who looked a lot like Carla DeCarlo. They were both smiling those great big happy smiles, like they'd just eaten an entire double-dip ice cream cone and were thinking about seconds. What was even more remarkable was how much those smiles were identical.

That's when I knew I was staring down at a picture of Jade Batista and her mother, Carla DeCarlo.

The motive flashed before me the instant I remembered what Federico had said the night of the party, that "olives never lie. They're always pure."

Carla DeCarlo had lied about her virginity.

Fifteen minutes later, I was standing on Federico's front stoop wearing a borrowed Betsy Johnson outfit complete with skinny chocolate jeans, a bright pink ruffled mini skirt, a tight long-sleeved knit shirt complete with decorative roses, and two different jacket type things over the whole ensemble. My legs and feet were covered in over-the-knee suede boots, and I carried an Italian Capisa bag, which was fitted with a small transmitter, so Nick could keep track of me. I also wore some kind of tiny microphone wire thing inside my bra, which allowed him to hear everything.

I wasn't so sure the microphone was a good idea considering there was no telling what my family might say at any given moment that could land one of them back in the slammer for a past dastardly deed. Nevertheless, I was trying to trap Federico and I was hoping I could get him to do most of the talking.

Lisa had dressed me for action. She said the boots had a heel that could go through bone if I stepped hard enough, plus she dropped pepper spray in my purse and slid a pocket knife down my left boot, just in case. It lodged next to my heel and with each step it reminded me that I was about to turn on a man I'd loved and admired for most of my life.

It just confirmed what Federico had taught me since I was a little girl: never trust anyone, no matter who they are.

I swung open the door on Federico's bungalow, slapped on a happy face and said, "Room for one more?"

My mom, Benny, Aunt Hetty, Aunt Babe, Giuseppe, and Federico sat around a large oval table cluttered with cards, change, small bowls of green olives, and short glasses of red wine. Cousin Maryann sat on the sofa in the adjoining room fiddling with her accordion, while Zia Yolanda dozed next to her. The kitchen and living area was all one great big room, with a bedroom and bathroom off the kitchen.

As soon as I entered, everyone welcomed me, except for

Federico who seemed to be momentarily put off. There was a subtle change in his eyes, one most people in the room wouldn't have caught, but I did.

"Well, it's about time," my mom said as she got up from her chair at the table. "Everyone was getting worried. Where were you?"

I gave her a tight hug.

"Sorry about that," I said. "I hadn't planned on staying out all night. It sort of . . . just happened." I did my best to color my voice with regret, but I knew Federico could detect the touch of sarcasm.

"It's okay. We all fall off the wagon every now and then," Mom said when we pulled apart. She couldn't have played her part better if I had scripted it.

"Yeah," I said while staring at Federico who stared back at me, deadpan. "A girl can only go so long without a drink, right Federico?" I turned to the others. "He helped me fall. Good thing he was there or I might have fallen right under that damn wagon, hey Uncle Federico?"

No reaction.

There was a knock at the door. Hetty answered and Uncle Ray and Val came in along with Jimmy, who was looking rather glum.

"Mia, you're here," Val squealed. "When your mom phoned saying you were missing, we hurried right over like she asked."

Apparently, my mom had her own plan of how this was going down.

"I thought Federico brought you home. At least that's what he told me when the two of you took off last night," Jimmy said, then he went over and sat next to his sister on the arm of the sofa.

"Nah, we were having way too much fun for either one of us to go home. Right, Uncle Federico?" I kept staring at him and he kept staring right back at me, now with a somewhat startled look on his face, as if he was trying to figure out what could be coming at him next.

"You had us all worried, doll. Federico was going to call the cops if we didn't hear from you in the next few hours," Aunt Babe said, right before she hugged me. "He told us you deserted him at one of the bars last night. That you left him some kind of note, but he was still worried. We all were."

That got me reeling. I decided to change up the plan. I wasn't much into playing passive, waiting for the cavalry to save the day. This was my family, and we had rules, and one of them was we had a zero tolerance for guys like Federico and I intended to keep it that way.

"I'm sorry. I was busy nursing one mother of a hangover." I laughed. "Woke up in a Dumpster behind Jimmy's bar. Can you believe it? Wahoo! That must have been one hell of a party, right?" I stared at Federico who was beginning to lose his cool.

"You slept in a Dumpster?" Maryann wanted to know.

"Sure did. And if it wasn't for an old mattress breaking my fall I might be dead right now."

Zia Yolanda groaned and opened her eyes.

"What are you talking about, dear?" Mom asked, eyes squinting in some desperate attempt to furrow her forehead.

There was another knock on the door. "Let me get this," I said.

Lisa and Jade stood in the doorway. "Is this where the party is?" Jade asked, all full of sunshine. I gave Lisa a quick nod to reassure her that everything was going well.

I hadn't expected Jade to show up at this little gala, but I had a feeling Lisa had something to do with her appearance.

"Come right in ladies. We're all one big happy family," I told them.

The tiny bungalow was suddenly very crowded with everyone picking out their own turf.

Federico walked over to me carrying a glass of red wine. He offered it to me. "No thanks," I told him.

"Hair of the dog," he said, and held it right under my nose. One quick whiff told me it was Leo's Pinot.

"Well, let's see, hair of the dog would have to be whatever drug you slipped in my drink last night," I said in a clear, loud voice so everyone could hear me. "And I'm not in the mood for that right now, but thanks for the offer."

The house suddenly went quiet. Only the sound of Bisnonno Luigiano's cuckoo clock marked off the time in seconds. Even Federico owned one of the many clocks, although by the sound of the jittered ticking the clock needed a few repairs.

Federico's forehead creased. "Don't get cute. You know it was all those shots of tequila you put down."

"Nope. I don't remember any tequila. Do you remember any tequila, Jimmy?"

He shook his head. "You only drank Coke while you were in my bar."

I stared at Federico. "Like I said, I didn't drink any tequila last night."

"Maybe not while you were at La Bella, but you sure threw them back after we left."

"Oh, you mean when you took me upstairs to Jimmy's apartment looking for clues, trying to help me prove that Jimmy killed Dickey? Funny, I don't remember drinking anything up there, just a lot of kicking and scratching, but no drinking. You'd already slipped the drug into my Coke. No need for more."

Jimmy said, "What? Me? I didn't kill Dickey. Why the hell would I? I got no grudge with Dickey. The man saved my sister's life. She loved him like a father. Why would I want to knock him off? She'd never forgive me if she ever found out. Besides, I'm clean, and I intend to stay that way."

Federico put the wine down on the table, ignored what Jimmy just said and walked in closer to me. "You don't know what you're talking about. I never took you up to his apartment."

I took a step closer to him, feeling bold with my other, more non-murdering family present. "Yeah you did, and you tied me up, taped my mouth shut, and shoved me out of his second-story window, you miserable lying bastard."

Zia Yolanda wailed. My mother gasped.

Benny swore. Ray punched the table.

Giuseppe stood up.

Federico pulled out a handgun and pointed it at me.

The rest of the men in my family, including Giuseppe, pulled out their own handguns and pointed them at Federico.

Who knew?

"It's over," Uncle Ray said. "Put your weapon down, and your hands over your head."

"We are all itching to shoot something, and it might as well be you, you piece of excrement," Uncle Benny said.

That's when Jade charged in front of everybody and shot Federico in the foot.

He let out a mournful yell, fell to the floor and dropped his weapon. "You shot me," he said, looking up at her, tears filling his eyes.

"Yeah, and I'll do it again if you don't confess to killing my mother, you murdering rat," Jade demanded, pointing her automatic at his head.

There was a collective intake of air.

"Are you serious?" Benny asked. "Your mother was Carla DeCarlo?" He stared at her for a moment.

"Yes, dear," my mother offered.

"You know, now that you mention it, you look just like her. Especially around the eyes. I should have seen it," Benny said.

"Talk," Jade warned, now aiming the gun at Federico's left knee.

Somehow I got the idea this wasn't the first time Jade held a weapon. She had the look of a woman who'd spent many hours at a shooting range.

"Okay, yes, I killed Carla. She told me she was a virgin. That she was pure." He laughed. "What a crock . . . lies. They were all lies."

There was another gunshot, but this one seemed to only graze his upper left arm as blood streaked across the sleeve of his tan sweater. "And that's for Dickey, you miserable dog," Maryann grumbled as she walked closer to Federico, holding her own weapon, looking as if she would have no problem pulling the trigger again. Only this time it would be fatal.

"Okay, okay. All of you, back off. I'll come clean. Don't shoot me anymore," Federico whined. "I had no choice. Dickey figured it out. He figured out that I'd killed Carla. Besides, he had my ring. That bitch gave him my ring after I told her how much it meant to me, just because I slapped her. But I didn't do anything that she didn't deserve."

Jade shot the floor right next to his other foot, grazing his shoe.

"Okay. Stop." Federico held his hands up, as if his hands could stop a bullet. "I shouldn't have slapped her. But she had that mouth. Always talking back. No respect. And the lies. She told me she was a virgin. That she was pure like our olives, and then I find out she has a kid. Lies on top of more lies."

"How did you know she gave your ring to Dickey?" I asked.

He hesitated, and Jade pointed the gun at his knee again. He said, "I was there. I saw her kissing Dickey, and then giving him my ring. My dad meant that ring for me, not my cheating brother who never cared one lick about the old man. And not Dickey. It was mine. I gave it to Carla to show my love for her, but she didn't care. She didn't care about anyone. That day in the street, in Italy, when the old man was dying he was going to hand that ring to me, but my brother got in the way. He was always getting in the way. It was my ring. Mine."

Giuseppe stepped forward, his weapon locked on Federico's head. He spoke in Italian. "I want that ring even if I have to kill you to get it. Your brother wants what's rightfully his."

Federico, hand shaking, pulled the ring out from under his sweater, hanging from a chain, my chain. Giuseppe reached down and ripped it off his neck. Federico winced.

"Wait," Jade protested. "My father's alive?"

"Your father?" I asked.

"Yes, dear," my mother said. "Jade's father. She's your half-sister, sweetheart."

Aunt Val, who was standing behind my mom, smiled and nodded And just as Nick and his team burst through the front door, the cuckoo chirped a shaky hour as Dickey's pinky finger plopped out and landed right next to Federico's bleeding foot.

It took several hours for the dust to settle once Nick and his team arrived. Curious thing, I thought for sure my entire family would be carted off to jail on gun charges, but it seemed that Nick wasn't interested in their guns. He was barely interested in Federico, but he did do enough snooping to find a cell phone, probably Dickey's, hidden in the back of the cuckoo clock, which explained Jade's mysterious phone call from honey-bear after he was already dead.

The usual allotment of law enforcement arrived to take care of arresting Federico, ask all the questions and close off Federico's house. By the time they appeared on the scene, all weaponry, along with one recently imported mobster had miraculously vanished.

Within a couple hours of the arrest, Spia's Olive Press was up and running at full tilt. There were so many people milling around the shops and bakery that my relatives couldn't ring up the sales fast enough. There's nothing like a good murder to bring in business. It was all anybody could talk about, and my family seemed to be lapping up the sudden notoriety. We were the talk of the valley, and the Spia clan was loving it. Nothing brightens an ex-mobster's day better than cold hard cash.

As far as the orchard went, Maryann offered to take over the role as groundskeeper. She'd been taking classes at UC Berkley and working with Federico for the past two years. Everyone seemed to already know this, but me, of course.

Leo came by my mess of an apartment as soon as we were open again, and made an offer any girl in her right mind would have taken, but sanity didn't run in my family. "Let's get out of here. Just you and me. Right now, before family obligations make us do the right thing. We could go to New York, stay at a great hotel, catch some plays, eat at all those great little restaurants in the Village . . . or not." He smiled and a rush of heat swept through me. I knew if I went, we'd see very little of New York and a whole lot of each other. The mental visual of Leo lying naked in bed was difficult for me to resist, however . . .

"As tempting as that is, I'm going to have to take a rain check. I'm just not ready, and besides, I have somewhere else I need to be."

"Lisa told me, but you two can go to Maui anytime. This is our chance to see if . . ."

I cut him off with a kiss, slowly pulled away, grabbed my small carry-on bag and headed for the door. "I'm sorry, but I have to go."

"Call me?" he said.

"Every day," I told him and walked out my front door, down the steps and hopped in Lisa's BMW.

What I probably needed more than anything else at the moment was admission to the nearest psychiatric ward for massive amounts of therapy. Considering that my own uncle had tried to kill me I was a prime candidate for years of antidepressants. The thought of all those fine drugs was enough to make me want to bake and fry an entire seven course feast.

"You sure you want to do this?" Lisa asked as I slipped into the passenger seat.

"Absolutely." I turned and to Jade who sat in the back seat. "Are you sure you want to do this?"

"Like, I've been waiting my entire life, ya know?"

"Then let's do it," Lisa said as she headed out of the parking lot.

Here's the thing: What the three of us really wanted to do was fly to Maui, just like Leo thought, and laze on the warm sand, chilling for about a month. Unfortunately, Adonis-Giuseppe had ruined that fantasy.

The man was on his way to Italy to return my dad's ring, and there was no way he was going to do that without us.

Mary Leo

Coming in March 2013

The Spia Family Branches Out

    Mia's much anticipated arrival in Italy is met with yet another murder. A woman's body is found in her room, and it's quickly apparent this botched hit was meant for Mia. Discovering why she has a target on her back leads Mia to more dead bodies and soon she and her best friend Lisa Lin find themselves enmeshed in a feud between three mob families all vying for an ancient olive grove. And to make matters worse, her once missing father has plans to marry her off to the oldest son of a mob boss.

    Now there's an arranged wedding in her future, several dead bodies in her past, and an ancient olive grove with disappearing trees. If Mia thought the murder in Sonoma was complicated by family, it's nothing compared to the quagmire she finds herself trapped in while visiting with Papa in Italy.